Altered

Altered

A BEYOND THE BROTHEL WALLS NOVEL

RAE Z RYANS

Published 2014 By Fictitious Publishing
www.fictitiouspublishing.com

ISBN 978-0-9916654-7-1 Electronic
ISBN 978-0-9916654-8-8 Paperback
www.raezryans.com

Cover and interior design: Raven Tree Design
www.raventreedesign.com

Contents

Prologue

Metatron

In the realm of Heaven, Metatron grasped his glass cube and flicked his wrist, dispersing the clouds floating inside of his artifact. Sharp corners dug into his skin. His eyes closed, seeking the disturbance rumbling through his bones. A child's image flickered into his mind, but as he studied the petite, dark-haired girl standing on the cliff's edge, he sensed the wisdom and spark hiding behind her amber eyes.

"Lucifer runs through you." He stroked his white, wiry beard and peered at the open wall in his observation room. He lifted the cube and waved it. Her image transferred to the space before him, and the clouds reformed his connection to her mind. "Show me what troubles you, Lightbringer."

Though slight of frame and stature, the one causing distress was a young woman. She grasped her black hood and drew it over her head. Lifting her skirts, she strolled away, steps light.

Smoke rose from crushed and torn metal haphazardly strewn over the whitewash. Antique train cars rested on their sides. Blood tainted the cargo littered snow a salmon hue.

Two men wandered from the trees and flanked her: one blond gentleman wearing orange-tinted goggles and another, a rough-cut ginger wearing a red scarf around his face. A third man lingered in the lofty pines, bound by strong magic.

Metatron clenched his fist and slammed it on the glass box. "Who let you out, Azazel?"

Pressure inside of his head pushed Metatron from the vision: thwarted.

"How can we win this war if our heroine consorts with the enemy?" He released a sigh and shook his baldhead. Footsteps echoed behind him, metal armor clinking and clanging into the observation room. He didn't turn and said, "Michael, I didn't summon you."

"Father called me," the Archangel stated, and approached. "Another Lightbringer requires our assistance. That makes two—now."

"All Lucifer's children cause is a throbbing headache." One in particular concerned him over the rest, but Metatron would need to leave Heaven in order to take down Azazel—And Father wouldn't allow it. "Do you wonder if they're more trouble than they're worth? The destruction—"

"Where one sees destruction, another sees beauty, but it takes the wisest of all to see perfection." Michael motioned to the glass cube.

Metatron handed over his artifact.

Michael shut his eyes. The screen dissipated the image, and a young man, striding through Halifax, Arcadia, replaced it. He glanced over his shoulder and peeked at the sky. What did he fear?

"This boy…" Metatron stared, waiting for the recollection to register.

"He hasn't been a boy for over three hundred years." Michael laughed.

Metatron crossed his arms over his robed chest. As the Holy Scribe, he held an intimate knowledge of all births, deaths, and events. But time had passed since he last saw the child who had become a man. "He is my Keeper of the Seven Keys."

"Cain Westcott."

Metatron thought about the young woman. She, too, was special. His muddled mind opened. "I chose the family… Yes, they're both mine."

"We're not to interfere, though, only watch. Father doesn't want a repeat of Gabriel." Michael's tone held steady, but he spoke the rule known to all in Heaven. A rule that many broke, despite its consequences.

"Such a waste." Metatron snorted at the loss of God's Messenger, flitting around on Earth and wreaking havoc. Better on the Sundered Earth than there in Heaven.

"What do those keys un—"

"End times are upon us," Father said, voice booming. "And you two are nosing about instead of winning my war against Asmodeus." A mist-like cloud crept along the glass floor.

Michael and Metatron knelt and lowered their heads. Demons, Angels, Eliouds, or any of the remaining races didn't know what to expect from God—Father—including his Archangels. But Metatron watched Earth from Heaven. The end lay farther than they could've imagined because the prophecy, the word of Father, was law.

Metatron's stomach churned, and though he hadn't proof, he trusted his gut. He glanced to Michael. Would he rise once again and battle his former brothers and sisters on the Sundered Earth to protect Lucifer's lineage? Maybe questioning his loyalty felt odd, but he had fought, defeated, and imprisoned the famed Archangel eons ago, followed by a tiff with Father.

"Michael, wait for me in the throne room," Father commanded.

With a nod, Michael rose and his armor clamored with every step.

"He troubles you still," Father said. "Let it go, Enoch."

Father seldom used his human name.

"Michael is loyal, he is my son, and you'd do better putting your resources to work, to protect my flock from Asmodeus. You are my second in command, are you not?" His essence glimmered and retreated, but halted. "I'd like to know who released him from Hell. Nothing on Earth should be powerful enough to shield my sight."

Such a device, if it existed, would prove disastrous. But what if it wasn't an object, but a person or place? So many questions and even fewer answers.

Metatron stared into the glass cube once more, concentrating on the Keeper of Keys. He tapped his teeth. Who could he trust to protect Cain while he investigated? His fingers snapped

"War, Pestilence," Metatron harked the Archangels, and summoned them to the realm of Heaven. "Death, Virtue."

Red, green, and white radiance flooded the room. As it dissipated, the Archangels stood before him.

"Where is Abaddon?" he asked the three out of four Horsemen of the Apocalypse.

"He is meeting a client for the ABDA." War dipped his head. The Arcadian Bureau of Demonic Affairs policed Arcadia and played liaison to the government. "He sends his regards."

"Doubtful." Metatron frowned at Pestilence's lack of clothing.

Virtue stepped forward, chin in the air. "Clients are a top priority for our brother. You'd know this if you ever bothered to slum it with the rest of us."

How did Abaddon put up with them?

"I have a favor to ask—"

"No," Virtue snapped. "We don't work for you."

Ignoring the outburst, Metatron said, "His name is Cain Westcott."

They exchanged a glance.

"You know this name?"

"Dorian is meeting with Cain." War scratched his chin, using Abaddon's human name.

"Perfect." Metatron grinned and clapped his hands. "It is a sign. I'm on the right track."

Chapter One

Cain Westcott

Slavery survived the Sundering. I would've shouted the mantra years ago, but what difference would it have made? Back when humans reigned on Earth, they'd swept the truth under the rug and ignored the thousands sold into slavery each year. Arcadia wasn't any different with its ignorance, flaming hoops, and countless red tape.

Electricity hummed over my skin, and I glanced over my shoulder. *Nothing.* My gaze rolled along the depreciated streets of Halifax, my steps hastening and bringing me closer to the bar.

"Try or die." Would I have time to fulfill my mother's last wishes before God destroyed those he'd left behind? I shrugged. Promises hung over my head and followed me, like the never-ending gray skies. Failure greeted me around every bend and whispered in my ear, as if a specter stalked my movements.

I scratched my smooth cheek and searched the sky for Garland's airships, skirting the unlined borders of the broken world. Boric Garland put a bounty on my head, but the men he sent, I turned to dust. Only a fool wouldn't prepare himself against his enemy, and most warlocks weren't stupid enough to let down their guards.

History wouldn't repeat again.

Iced over, vehicle empty streets were nothing new in the frozen tundra of former Canada, but despite the treacherous conditions, my steps lightened. Empty hands swung at my sides. Vacant pockets lined my thrift store jeans, and patches mended the moth holes of my pea coat. But a glimmer of hope filled my heart. Centuries of imprisonment under the watchful eyes of the Garland King had changed me from a carefree youth into a cynical man. I didn't take hope lightly.

The six o'clock train whistled in the distance, releasing a hiss of fresh steam into the subzero air. I halted on the street and peeked over my shoulder, searching the sky for the capital G that haunted my dreams. I ran my hand through my hair and tugged. Still nothing there.

"What's it like to be a slave?" a passerby wondered. Supernatural creatures, not humans, tended to be assholes. It didn't matter if they'd meant a streetwalker or me.

Allowing a small family to scurry by, I stopped and stepped aside. "It sucks. Mind your thoughts if you know what's good for you."

"Damn bloody warlocks," the man muttered, but refused to look me in the eye.

Warlocks and witches read minds, among other deviants and saviors. Part warlock, technically, but as strong as the others because of my bloodline. Too bad. If I removed the illusion spell, he would have seen the scars from three hundred years of captivity, but never would he understand the wounds inside of me, the ones magic couldn't hide.

History and all I had overcome were just that. Only the future concerned me. Mine didn't trouble me, but my sisters' futures were another story, for they were still Boric Garland's slaves.

Soon that would change.

A bitter smile drew down my mouth. Shaking, my hands trembled from the frigid flakes falling endlessly from the sky. Thin lips pressed together; I forcefully whistled an old tune, its name long forgotten. I traipsed through the ruined city sectors and steadied my jagged stride over icy sidewalks, brushing away my thoughts and the man's question.

"Ashes to ashes and dust to dust, the world belonged to us. What's left of it." I blinked at the silence of the street and in my mind. Hastily, I scanned up and down the road and searched for the source of the momentary serenity. The gray clouds parted. Light peered through, and the scattering snowflakes gleamed. A peculiar sensation tingled against my half-frozen skin, but still no signs of Garland's men or his airships.

In front of a distressed church, my steps ceased. An old iron bell hung in the steeple and clanged in the strong wind. Stained glass painted vivid biblical scenes and reflected the bold colors humanity would no longer create. Pieces lay broken in their frame, like me, showing the scenes of Revelation. I ignored the draw of muffled music from the corner pub.

The ABDA would wait.

In the final days, the humans had ascended, and the rest of us remained—demons, angels, Elioud, and so on. I laughed and shook my head. We were not all evil, but like humans, we were capable of both goodness and wickedness. The shrouded gray sky enveloped the light, and I recalled the exact color on the day of my escape years ago. Snow had blanketed the northern world, when my savior had brought me into then Philadelphia, and I, alone, had journeyed farther to Nova Scotia in search of my cousin Tomas.

"Years later the world sundered." My finger traced the line of the glass picture through the air, ignoring the fake and distorted reflection of myself. The young innocent boy had died the day my father lost his bet, and all that remained of me hid beneath a plain façade. Every scar blended into pale skin, mixing until I resembled everyone else. The same spell altered my eyes, making them change from the softest caramel to chestnut brown, opposed to the amber I had been born with.

"Reverto," I said, speaking Latin, and waved my hand over the image. The white scars marred my true-bronzed skin tone, and my reddish-brown eyes glowed, only in the replication my outer disguise held.

God gave me this broken life, yet I couldn't stomach the sight of it or me.

"Abdo." My façade smeared over the glass before returning to normal. "Better."

An urge to enter the church ruins rushed through my veins. With my palms held to the skies, its vibration reached through me to my booted toes. I shook my head and wiped the melted snow from my face.

No prayer today.

I jumped from the steps, sliding a foot along the ice. The draw wrenched at my heart, and my feet halted again, twisting me toward the battered entrance. I aimed quick glances over my shoulders. Although, I wasn't certain as to why.

Prayer and churches didn't insinuate weakness, even for the eternally damned like me. As I pressed on the worn surface, the door squeaked and I slipped through the gap. A sneeze tickled my nose from twelve years of dust and moldy decay. My eyes adjusted to the darkness.

Birds cooed, bunkered down in the rafters. God hadn't ascended the animals; we required food. Pews and papers lay on their sides, as if everyone had disappeared.

Oh right, they had departed the cruel world for a better place.

My lips pursed. Soggy carpet squished beneath my feet as I found the sturdiest pew and sat, bowing my head and clearing my thoughts. I couldn't have told anyone the denomination of the church, but it wasn't Catholic. Depicted scenes bathed Jesus in a positive light, opposed to his crucifixion. No pictures of saints or the Mother Mary either. Protestant perhaps, but that hadn't mattered in God's eyes.

"All that mattered rested in your heart and soul," Mother used to say to the three of us, and I believed her, even after all I had survived.

However, with my head bent, my lips repeated the same words I had said many times since departing Garland:

"God, please protect my sisters. You and I both know firsthand what they do and the horrors they face. Please let your love fill them, so they never know hunger, and allow your light to protect their souls in their darkest hours. I have to believe they can heal where I haven't."

Where I couldn't. The wounds inflicted by my captors had never healed. Did they heal for anyone?

I stared at the cross, focusing on the tiny splinters and rivets that the elemental exposure had wrought. A tear rolled down my cheek as I bloodied my lip between my teeth. After years of freedom, the nightmares had spilled into my waking hours, and no man alive would ever love the real me. They saw either my birth name or the various scars before sprinting away.

Bright light flooded the quaint church, and I shielded my eyes, but neither fully covered or averted them. A white clad woman floated to my side. Long, blonde hair flowed and billowed. A gold circlet adorned her head.

"Warlocks don't usually pray," she said, and my head dipped until her light had dimmed. "I am Hallowed, the Archangel of Conquest and Virtue."

Her warm hand smoothed over my forehead, and heat spread throughout my body, defrosting my shivering limbs. The darkness of the master's deeds skittered into the recesses of my soul, and my heart swelled from her gentle, motherly touch.

"Great change comes for you, Cain Westcott. Will you be ready to accept it?" She smiled, flashing perfect, white teeth.

"You know my name," I whispered. My watering gaze met her sapphire eyes, and they glowed, sparkling like jewels in the dim lit church.

Hallowed replied, "God heard your pleas and sent me."

My brow twisted, mirroring my gut. He still listened? Where was God when they'd beat me? When they... I swallowed unable to utter the words.

"Go Keeper. Your future waits," she said.

My lips parted to speak, but Hallowed had vanished. *Keeper?* My frozen hands rubbed sleep deprived eyelids, and my neck craned forward. Had I imagined her?

My watch ticked, and I removed the timepiece from my jeans pocket. I ran later for my meeting than I'd realized. A curse tickled my lips, but I dared not cuss in a sacred place. I stood from the pew and stepped toward the door, but I paused at the entry, turning, and stared at the barren cross again. He still listened.

"Please, save Lilith and Angelica. Forget about me. I deserve nothing for the sins I have committed." My eyes closed, picturing their smiling faces. Twenty years had passed since I last saw Lily. Twelve years ago, I saw Angel as Veric had handed her over to Julian Garland for safekeeping.

But my brother-in-law Veric died, and the fault had fallen to me. When I tried to sleep, I still saw the blood and heard his screams. Gunshots rattled in my head. He'd struggled with my ex-lover, Boric, and I had shot twice before fleeing. My stomach heaved at the memory, and my eyes reopened. Even in the safety of the abandoned church, gunpowder still burned my nose from the antique Colt .45 revolver.

I yanked on the corroded-iron handles. The door groaned. Fresh air filled my lungs and chased away all warmth. Change waits, future waits, but I cared little for myself. The odd draw to the church altered its path toward the bar. Had to be a sign, but try as I might, my feet refused a faster pace.

"He listened," I whispered. "My sisters will be freed."

CHAPTER TWO

Archangel Abaddon—Death

Special Agent Dorian Fox

Demons ruled the world, and everyone blamed me.
My green eyes glowed beneath the brim of a black fedora and reflected in the nicotine-coated mirror lining the bar. I drew my hat down, hiding that which pegged me as different, and averted my gaze to the corner television. The show airing leaped from the more recent fiery brimstone and earthquakes to an old infomercial revolving around self-help books promising readers change.

I rapped my knuckles on the bar.

"What brings you in Agent Fox?" the barkeep asked, and placed a rocks glass on the counter before filling it with amber liquid. "Haven't seen you in months."

Seven, but who was counting? "Meeting a client." Music blared in the background, overpowering the television's volume, but I scanned the rolling text at the bottom of the screen and disagreed with the program.

Altering one's self on the inside: A fool's game.

The barkeep strolled away and waited on another patron. I tipped my hat and slid the long coat from my shoulders. Punctuality points always fell in my courts; Belle was always late. Coughing on the rising smoke from my cigarette, I snuffed it out and swirled the amber liquid in my opposite hand before taking a lengthy sip. Its bitter burn erased neither my past nor shaped the future, but I was a glutton for punishment.

Nobody changed overnight—not me, the guy two stools down, or even the bartender clanking glasses in the sink. I didn't want to amend my ways, and doing so put the world at risk.

Experience had taught me better than that. I tilted my head, following the scrolling words on the television: "Read this book and have a better tomorrow for only nineteen ninety-five."

"What a load of bullshit."

The bar door jingled, and I peeked over my shoulder. Junior Agent Belletrist Artois waltzed in, late as usual. Misfits parted faster than the Red Sea, her hips and bleached-blonde dreads swaying. I nodded to her, and her red eyes crinkled at the corners.

A man grabbed her bicep, and Belle punched him in the gut without blinking. He toppled over, muttering to himself.

She said, "Don't you ever lay a hand on a woman without her permission. Boy, didn't your mother teach you anything?"

He dropped to his knees, shaking his head. I waited, though, to see how she handled the situation, since she was my responsibility to train. She leaned over him, her badge dangling around her neck, and the idiot tossed his hands up.

"Sorry, ma'am, must've had too much to drink."

"That's Officer Artois." She shoved her badge in his face.

Most didn't like the law, and the Arcadian Bureau of Demonic Affairs made up the police, judge, and jury of New Halifax, Nova Scotia of the greater Arcadian stronghold. Didn't matter what they were: witch, warlock, vampire, angel, demon, or a mix.

Belle kept her eye on him while he backed away. After the man had taken a seat, she strolled to the bar. Flipping her bleached dreads, Belle asked, "Mr. Westcott isn't here yet?"

"Hell's Belles, you took the call." Westcott… where had I heard that name before? I scratched my beard.

Belle fidgeted with her ABDA issued trench coat, hiding something as usual.

"What's he look like anyhow?" He could be anyone, but she hadn't given me much information. She *had* taken the call, so it wasn't abnormal. Meeting here and not in the office baffled me, though. "And why are we here?"

Belle shrugged from her trench coat and ignored my second question. "He sounded cute over the phone. A little twang."

I waved at her comment, paying attention to the self-help infomercial since she evaded my questions. Did anyone believe this crap? No one flip-flopped their life in a matter of moments. Had we learned nothing from the past?

"He said someone kidnapped his sister."

I nodded, my gaze glued to the ridiculous program, but she had my attention at kidnapped. After all, I assessed and retrieved those abducted or lured into slave trafficking. "But you don't know what he looks like?"

Belle laughed, shaking her Medusa-like dreads. "Spoken like a man. You just want to know if you can screw him."

I cracked my neck and burped before shrugging. My mind rarely ventured far from sex. We lived in the moment. Sometimes a moment was all I had.

"You're such a pig, Dorian." She shoved my shoulder. "Somethings never change."

I grinned, but it fell. Change mandated time and commitments, and I had no time for altering my ways. I lit another cigarette, and the acid burn of rotten leaves and whatever else the company shoved inside smoldered in my throat. I stared at Belle until she spoke.

"Sorry to burst your fantasy, but I didn't think to ask." She turned, half-facing me. "Does it matter?"

"Of course not." I blew out a puff of smoke, and she raised a brow, calling me on a bluff. "Don't get your knickers in a bunch."

"Death's having a dry spell," she teased.

I had his first name: Cain. But our departure had been for the best. I would've hurt him. Toxic, Death didn't linger. Father shaped me as iniquitous as imaginable, and he fashioned me for a sole reason. To kill, not to love or care. The Archangel of Death and a Horseman of the Apocalypse. Nothing short of my father would ever change the simple reality and truth. Men like me deserved to be miserable and alone, hopping from man to man to satisfy our lustful cravings.

My scarred knuckles rapped on the bar again for a refill. He nodded and reached for the whisky. The bartender refilled my glass, stretching his arm as far away from me as demonically possible.

"Thanks." I raised the rocks glass to my lips, grimacing at the brown sludge burning my throat, but he ignored me again. Since the world had erupted and Scotland had sunk into the ocean, Scotch whisky was impossible to find. Anyone who knew anything about Scotch would've known the others resembled melting plastic. Besides, whiskey with an 'e' wasn't real Scottish or Irish whisky, but most of America hadn't survived the Sundering either, leaving me with either moonshine or Canadian whiskey to tempt my palate.

"Agent Artois, how nice to see you."

"He should've been here by now." Belle tapped her nails on the bar. "I'll take a Canadian Club." She rose, smoothed over her leggings, and yanked at her holster shorts. The bartender drooled; she leaned over the bar and swiped her half-made drink. A long gulp later and she made a face, as if sucking on a slice of lemon. From her corset, she withdrew a wad of Arcadian dollars and counted out enough to cover the drink.

I contained my humor, covering my mouth with my hand, and the bartender said, "No charge."

She slipped the bills into her corset. "You look like hell warmed over and tossed to the bit, boss." Belle aimed her scarlet gaze at me, and I met it in the mirror, while drawing my hat lower to hide my eyes in the dim bar lighting. Her high-heeled foot kicked my stool.

I tilted my head toward her and glowered, leaning over my drink, but she was right. Months had passed since I last cared for my appearance. Seven months, but who counted the time between lovers or ass-kicking sessions? Belletrist had insisted I trim my beard and shower. What more did she want from me? "Hell's Belles, woman, this isn't a social call."

Belle is up to something.

Ice rattled in my drink, clinking around on its own as a train approached, but the music blocked the whistle. My arm rested on the bar, cradling my chin. In the ten years she had worked for me, Belle could not tell a lie. Her gaze lingered over the bar and avoided me. Everyone had a tell, and her avoidance of eye contact reflected hers.

"I told you to shave. You couldn't even do that right." Belle shook her head.

I ducked to avoid her dreads slapping me in the face. Those suckers hurt, but she loved the style, and they made her look badass. The thought alone created a snicker and drew a glare from my Elioud partner.

"I shaved." I ran my hand over the dark stubble. "At least I don't have weapons hanging off my head."

"Shaving implies you remove that crap you're calling a beard from your face, and I so don't have weapons hanging from my head. *Mark* loves my dreads."

Mouth gaping, I stared at her. How dare she bring my brother into the conversation? "If I find out you two are..."

"What? Fucking?"

My cheeks warmed, despite loving to cuss. "Yes, fucking, buggering, banging, shagging, or a little bit of how's your father."

Belle tossed her hands into the air in a mock surrender, while trying to maintain a straight face, but she slipped and hunched over laughing. I flashed a small smile and savored another sip of battery acid parading as scotch. She didn't like my brother, but I always had a laugh. He liked her. The only notion funnier than bringing the Archangel of War to his knees was someone doing the same to me.

"Take that stupid hat off." She smacked the fedora from my head, revealing disheveled locks. "Now the world can see your eyes." Belle cringed. Her scrutinizing stare reached the top of my head, and combed her fingers through the tattered mass. She grabbed a fistful and yanked. "You need a haircut. This ain't the sixties, and you're too cute to be growing a mullet."

"You need to get laid." Maybe then, she would leave my so-not-a-mullet-hairstyle and me alone. I added, "But please, Belles, not my brother."

She winced and paled before composing herself. "At least you left your scythe at home this time."

Yes, I owned both a scythe and a putrid green horse. At least the biblical translators had those parts right. "Hey, you're not my sister, so stop acting like it. I already have two of them I can't stand. We're here for a job, not my love life."

She crossed her legs and muttered, "Lack thereof." Belle waved the bartender down and ordered us a refill. "Look, it's not like we're swimming in cases. I just thought you might like him enough—"

"You don't even know if he's gay, and I don't need your help finding a man." I peeked at my pocket watch, and nudged Belle's arm.

She glanced down but only grunted. Mr. Westcott had five minutes before I stormed out the door. The Arcadian Bureau of Demonic Affairs didn't pay me to sit around and drink. Restless, my legs tapped as I awaited our new mysterious client.

"Knock that off." She clamped her hand on my knee.

I pushed my cigarette pack toward her.

"I quit."

"I don't like tardiness." I scratched under my chin and glanced at the door, but a woman entered, rushing toward a table of giggling Eliouds. It took time, but I could usually tell their abilities at a glance. A few baffled me. Being Death presented a unique insight on the soul, but as it turned out, I happened to be a damn good detective. Belle—one day she'd make an even finer agent.

"Thank you, Captain Obvious, and no one says tardiness. Let's give him a little more time. He was coming from the other side of town, something about getting off work."

"Fine. He has fifteen minutes, and then I'm gone, Belles. You can stay and waste our time."

She didn't argue and nodded. I raised a dark brow, but she said nothing. Despite being her superior, Belles always argued. Sometimes, I swore she did so to crawl beneath my skin, but a spine and thick skin were required to do our job—nobody in the agency wanted to deal with slaves and brothels.

A heavy ballad whined from the jukebox, and smoke clouded the bar air from the patrons puffing on cigarettes and various herbs. The music carried me away, and if I were to close my eyes, the words would make me forget the hell we called home. But my eyes were open, watching and studying those who stared and whispered behind my back. My glowing jade eyes cast an eerie radiance over the hazy bar. All the Horsemen had reflective, jewel-toned eyes, and I had spent years hiding them under the wide brim of my hat. My stiff fingers tapped along the bar surface to the bass in the song, and I swayed on the stool to the screeching rhythm of the electric guitar, trying to block out everyone's silent attentions.

"So this is what Death looks like?" Behind me, a feminine voice purred.

Frowning, I spun around on my barstool at the husky voice. A redheaded succubus, wearing a black brocade corset and matching hot pants, ran her hand down my chest, and her tail stroked my face. They were the easiest to peg, but I wasn't one to catalog demons by type. All of them were the same to me until they became Garland's victims.

I leaned my back against the bar and puffed out my chest. Women and men liked when I unfolded and stretched my broad shoulders. Guess I seemed more approachable and less Grim Reaper.

"Move it tramp, you're not his type," Belle grumbled.

"I've turned a few in my time." She slid her pointed tail down my chest.

On me, her charms were lost. "Afraid so, ma'am." Anything with boobs and a vagina held no ability to tighten my sack. The door jingled. Stealing a look over the redhead's shoulder, I smiled. Every hair on my body grew attentive of the newcomer's sweeping glare.

My thoughts halted a moment—a millisecond—my gaze locked onto him. The bar door closed, a draft rushed through the heated bar and I shivered. Starting at the bottom, his heavy boots stomped snow onto the mat. Tight jeans hugged his long, lean legs, flexing beneath the denim. A wool pea coat covered his average upper body.

My sweaty palms tingled, and I wiped them over my trousers. "Cain," I whispered, and almost pinched myself. Those coppery eyes seared me from the inside out, sending their heated prickle over my skin and leaving perspiration in its wake.

Death didn't sweat.

Before his smooth, angular jaw tilted to the right, I recognized Cain. My heart rate increased, and like lightning had struck, the air departed my lungs. The snake tattoo on his neck uncoiled as he gulped, appearing alive. If my memory served me right, the black serpent slithered along his hard chest and ended somewhere below his belt. How far south did it trail? I licked my lips.

Everyone had someone they'd loved who had gotten away. Me? I didn't stick around, not anymore. For me, love and relationships posed a greater risk to those inhabiting the Sundered world. I had yet to meet anyone whom I would break my rules for again.

No man should possess eyes like Cain with their ability to warm my belly. Light peaked where black should emerge in the center, and it flashed, calling to me. We didn't have a fling per say, but we had history. My lips quirked at the memory his heated golden eyes. As his lips parted, sucking in breath, his stare traveled over me.

What did he want? This meeting couldn't have been a coincidence, even though his wide, attentive eyes said otherwise.

"Who you staring at?" the redhead asked.

I shoved her aside, leaning forward but not standing. "Shite," I said. "Belles, I should go..." Emotional involvement was against my rules.

Cain winked, and regret stabbed through my chest.

"He's yummy," Belle said, "quite the boy next door, eh? Oh, I do think that's our client, Mr. Westcott."

I couldn't find the words to surmise an answer, but agreed with my partner's assessments. After seven months of digging, all evidence pointed toward Cain being a dream. Despite the blood and bruises he'd gifted me, I'd searched for him. But what did he need with us? Did he want me? My brow twisted. The succubus stepped away. At least she'd finally taken the hint.

He nodded, as if answering my thoughts, and my heart raced even faster.

Sure, I wanted him too. The problem lay in the rules, my rules, but ones that existed to protect the Sundered world. Besides Father, I held the ability to end this broken hunk of rock, and I'd come close once before thanks in part to a broken heart.

I grabbed for Belle, but missed my chance to cut our losses and flee. She skirted toward him, leaving me to brood on my perch. Business and pleasure never mixed. One irresistible man my life hadn't needed, but craved in a way that made no more sense than the world.

He shook Belle's hand. "How do you know Dorian?" Cain trained his attention on me.

Wheels seized in my brain and all of my usual flirt tactics stalled. I sat there, powerless to move from my barstool. Music filtered out, and sweat broke on my brow.

"Dorian's harmless." She waved in my direction, but I wasn't budging. "He's the one you need to convince."

One of the patrons' turned the jukebox on again, and I strained to make out their words over the rap song.

"Can I see your SAT phone?"

Cain reached behind him and withdrew a large device from his back pocket. He handed over his satellite phone, a small bit of technology the world still had from before the Sundering.

"Fuck this." I stubbed my cigarette out on the bar's countertop, not even bothering with the ashtray.

As Belle spoke to him, her fingers did something to his phone. Typically, we exchanged numbers with clients, but this was Cain. He stood within my grasp, but I still couldn't move. His curious stare sliced me in two, pinning me down. She ushered him closer to my position at the bar.

Three options presented themselves to me. I could sit on the bar stool and wait for pretty boy, storm up to him and shove my tongue down his throat, or run away with my proverbial tail covering my balls.

My glass slid from my shaking hand, shattering on the hardwood floor. Patrons stared at me. I slammed my palm on the counter behind me until my hat brushed my fingertips. Gripping my fedora, I crushed the rim in my fist.

Run it was.

Cain's brow rose, and lines etched into his forehead. His eyes half-pleaded with me to stay. The other half, I couldn't read, and I could decipher everyone and their motives. My boots clobbered over the barroom floor, my wide shoulders shoving past the whispering drones, and I stomped out the side door.

Crisp air greeted me, but I didn't shiver. The icy breeze did nothing to compose the surge he'd created with his gaze alone. Snow drifted from the sky, and flakes gusted into my eyes. I loved only the thrill of bloodshed and tortured human souls, as Father created me. Far from weak.

No, I slapped myself. "Get a grip, you shoddy bastard."

I stalked toward the street corner and rested against the brick wall, trying to summon strength and resolve that refused to come. In Cain's presence, everything in life meant nothing, and my limbs trembled at the thought. Without even touching him, he'd ruined me.

The brim of my hat blew forward, and I palmed my rough face. Belle was right about my appearance, though. If I had known, I would have groomed a little more carefully.

"What am I saying? When have I ever given a rat's ass about what others thought?" Impression hadn't exactly topped the list with anyone before, not even the last man I'd allowed myself to care about. Could I have been wrong all these centuries? Could I be capable of love and compassion beyond sexual release?

"No. There has to be another motive." A snort cut through the air, and I eyed my surroundings. The sound had come from me.

No. I sighed, peeking around the corner and toward the bar. The same purposely-disheveled hair topped his head, and the wind tousled it. I shivered again. The slight muscled build and lanky legs strolled with purpose. Dressed in skinny jeans and a fitted T-shirt below his open coat… full, pink lips framed by light fuzz and washed on a lily-white canvas. Bugger me, Cain caused a fluttering within my body that no weapon could have combated.

I had to reign in my obsession and stay away. Bad mojo followed men like him, and I had no time for games. My trembling hands pushed my hat down. This restless soul could not travel that road again. No one but Father controlled me, and I wasn't about to let some demon try.

The Horsemen were Archangels and set above the Arch demons, witches, demons, warlocks, and the Elioud living on the shards of the shattered Earth. Not all lived as the fiends of biblical lore. Hard to swallow, but some of the demons weren't all that evil, either. However, Cain wasn't human, and I would've bet four-hundred incubus souls rotting away in Sheol on the matter. No human could have caused the damage he'd inflicted that day. No humans existed, save for one cursed bastard in vampire custody. Only a Descendent, one of the Seven Princes of Hell, could have broken a Horseman's bones because they were once Archangels.

Pushing from my hiding spot, my head angled down, I wandered the whore-infested side streets. Arcadia had laws against brothels, unlike both Delphia and Garland to the south, but the whores were free to sell themselves on the open street in the lower Halifax districts. The sale of flesh brought in top dollar, but I steered clear of cheap release. The Arcadian Council wanted to outlaw the practice, but the streetwalkers revolted the first year.

No, I didn't judge them. Not my job. Steps echoed behind me, but I didn't investigate. My hand rubbed my chest, palming the golem's key hidden beneath my shirt.

"Dorian."

I stiffened my shoulders, recognizing the breathy shout, and ducked into an alleyway. The passageway served as a shortcut, and I barreled through the frosty mess, heart pounding, before cutting a hard right through two empty backyards. The snow reached my waist, and I cursed at the trail behind me. At least we weren't in Halifax proper, but I lived inside the city limits and navigated the streets well enough.

My head didn't sit straight in Cain's presence. I ducked into an alcove of an abandoned store. Piss permeated from the space and curled my nose. Footsteps echoed off the slushy streets behind me, but I couldn't see who made the sounds without giving my location away. My burning lungs recharged with deep breaths. My head leaned against the glass.

Click, brush, and click: the rhythm distorted; it slowed. Cain moseyed into view and halted, whistling a long forgotten hymn.

Shadows surrounded me, and I crawled deeper into their welcoming embrace. My breath held tight in my thundering chest. He angled his freckled nose into the air, and he inhaled, glowering as if he had lost my trail.

What could he have wanted from me? Was I overreacting? Yes, but when another man kicked my ass, I tended to give him a wide berth.

The tremble and odd body sensations terrified me. I had lived through the turmoil before, and I had vowed never to lose myself again. The pain accompanying past loss proved insufferable, and Sheol's gates had opened. If not for my brethren, the world would've been lost shortly after it had begun. Without losing myself, I couldn't offer Cain what he deserved: love.

Cain dragged his satellite phone from his pocket and extended the antenna. How he'd managed to hide it in his tight jeans baffled me. There didn't seem to be enough room for his rounded ass, let alone a phone. Inching closer, the windblown snow crunched beneath my feet.

I held my breath, waiting for him to turn around, and counted to ten. Seconds later, my ringer blasted. "Shite." How did he get my number? "Hell Belles," I cursed. This had her written all over it.

Cain spun around and charged toward me, but I had nowhere to run, except past him. I didn't want to flee, even though my brain screamed the command. His presence alone held a magnet and I was his metal.

The black snake tattoo wiggled, he shuddered, and his bangs tickled his forehead. A wind gust ruffled through the corridor, spitting flakes of snow onto his broad shoulders. His full lips twitched, and his hand skimmed over my jacket before sliding along my neck. Breathing hurt, thinking throbbed, and the heat of his hands surged through me. But I stared into his eyes reflecting the innocence of a baby doe about to meet her maker.

"If I didn't know any better, I'd say you're running from me, sweets."

His alto drawl drew me in, despite my back plastering against the old store's door. Nothing sweet about me existed.

His hand smoothed upward to my rough cheek, and his other squeezed my shoulder. Again, my mouth parched. We stood nose-to-nose, his warm breath brushing my lips in a lethal caress that curled my toes.

"Well, now that you know what I do, I'd say I've been—"I removed his hand from my face and dropped my gaze to Cain's hand, still clutching my shoulder, before brushing him away "—busy."

Whistles emitted from across the street, and a group of hookers strolled by. The urge to roll my eyes reared its head. Cain glanced over his shoulder, and I stole the moment to compose myself. My hand palmed my jacket pocket, searching for my cigarettes, and I withdrew one from my pack.

"What'd you want?" I lit a smoke and inhaled, wishing the nicotine calmed my shaky hands. Cain's attentions caressed me inside and out. He faced me again, and I swallowed loud enough the gulp ricocheted from the window glass.

"Imagine my surprise when I couldn't find you, Dorian."

My brow lifted, but the rim of my fedora hid the expression. He'd hunted for me?

"I searched everywhere after...but here you are." Strands of light brown hair fell into his eyes.

My hands itched to fix it, to touch him, but I shoved my hands deep into my pockets instead. A puff of smoke released from my mouth, and the breeze blew it into his face. He grabbed my cigarette from my lips and tossed it over his shoulder. My eyes narrowed, and I reached for another, but he smacked my hand aside.

"What. Do. You. Want. Cain?"

"Help." A wide smile flashed but quickly retreated. His shoulders rolled, rocking with his body. "I need someone located and retrieved."

I snorted, ignoring the somber tone. "And?"

"Why you're the best of the best, or so the ABDA told me." His gaze flickered down.

My cock stirred, rising to greet his stare.

"In more than one way I'm sure." Cain's lips pursed and he hooked a finger into my belt loop. "Shame I don't mix business..."He stroked my cock through my jeans.

I gasped.

"And pleasure."

"I... didn't say...yes...yet." Words choked from my lips while his assault repeated, my back arching and my hard length pressing into his palm. But I would, on both accounts. I never turned down a case.

Cain spun me around, plastering my face against the dirty, glass shop door. Blood flooded to my groin, and the spicy, acrid scent of fire flared my nostrils while he ground himself against my ass. He shucked my long duster to the ground.

"Take that off." He tugged on my shoulder holsters. "Colt .45's? Pegged you for a Glock after seeing the size of your cock." Cain reached around and grabbed my dick as my weapons joined my trench coat. "Don't forget the other two." He mumbled, "Hurry," and ran his hand over my clenched cheeks.

Hastily, my fingers worked at the straps, holstering guns to my thighs, leaving two more around my ankles. My lip throbbed as I held it between my teeth, halting the moan threatening to escape. *No use.* Cain yanked my hips toward him and snaked his arms around my chest.

"You're fucking beautiful," he whispered, nibbling on my ear-lobe. His other hand pulled my belt free, and it clattered against my weapons piled on the ground.

A horse drawn buggy rattled by as the sunlight filtered behind the trees and reflected off the glass. Anticipation warred with sanity. He drew my zipper down a tooth at a time. And I had thought Cain deserved better than this. Hot breath blew on my neck, and rough lips sizzled over my collar, leaving dimpled flesh in its wake. Why would I even care? Yet, I could not stop the words, my mind backpedaling. "Pleasure before business, then?"

He cursed and jerked down my trousers. I preferred commando, and his hands slapped my cheeks, alternating sides as I moaned. Fire ignited in my belly; my cock pulsed harder and harder with each smack, and the sparks spread their inferno over my skin. Breath strangled; all thoughts bordered on ceasing.

Cain twisted me around, and I stumbled forward, tripping over myself and shaking the weariness from my head. As his hands steadied me, his golden eyes captivated me.

"Whoa there, gorgeous."

Gorgeous I was not—not on the inside or out. Ache stabbed through my chest at his compliment. Despite my attempts to halt the emotion, a smile pulled at my lips. But across his handsome face, a retreating frown was dancing.

"Oh, the hell with it. I'm screwed either way." Cain used the faintest touch, running his velvety fingertips along my cockhead.

Change arrived and sank claws into my being. I wrapped my hand in his wavy hair and dragged his lips to mine. Cain's mouth parted, and I dove in, allowing his fiery flavor to mingle while massaging and sucking on his tongue. Stoked fire in my belly exploded into bright lights, illuminating behind my closed lids. He groaned, and his body vibrated. I held him tighter against me, and his shaking calmed. Noise and friction were almost enough to undo me. My free hand dropped to his crotch, rubbing over his not so hidden package, and popping the button to his pants. My guilt ended, and teasing time was over.

Without breaking our kiss, I eased us to the concrete floor. Kicking my guns away, my duster served as the single barrier between the frozen ground and my naked ass. Cain slid into my lap, fitting perfectly in the space. My hands slipped under his T-shirt, and my palms rubbed over the hardened ridges of his abs and played in the silky fur covering his chest.

Fuck, I loved hairy guys.

The heat of his skin sank into me and rushed through my veins, reminding me of a cozy fire completed by his smoky taste. I wanted to wrap myself around him and never let go, yet the same thought urged me to run. Another curse fought for release. No, I scolded myself.

Death ran from nothing.

Tight sexy jeans stood between my prize and me. My hands molded onto those tantalizing thighs. He grasped my hair, jerking me closer, but I wouldn't run away. Rough denim teased my nails clawing at the restrictive material. Frenzy lit within, like a beacon of pulsating light. Most men could not have pulled off wearing them, but Cain did, despite his muscular thighs.

He slightly lifted his ass, still not breaking our kiss, and the fabric of his pants rustled free. My hands teased over those legs and relished in the warmth tickling my palms. Damn he was beautiful, like a Seraph; like the most beautiful demon I had ever touched, kissed, and wanted to screw senselessly. Cain smiled against my mouth, and I sucked his tongue again, wishing it were another part of his body.

Our kiss broke; he trailed soft lips down my jaw and nipped at my neck. Cain ventured farther, kissing over my shirt as I stroked his wavy hair. Anticipation stirred and stiffened my dick more than I thought possible as it jerked against my stomach. Fluid leaked from the tip, and the greedy part of me wanted to watch him taste me. I couldn't recall ever being this hard.

By the time his tongue swirled over my cockhead, my internal war hadn't resolved. My skull slammed into the glass and a groan released from my lips. He inched downward and engulfed my tip. My hands curled tighter into his mop, and I tugged upward, instead of shoving him farther down my shaft.

I wanted, no needed him, yet this still wasn't right. People passed by, but no one spared even a peek.

He increased the pressure of his mouth. Cain showed no signs of relent, and for every noise I made, he retaliated with his mouth, as if he knew the pleasurable sounds urged my release closer.

"Babe…" Blood tainted my lips as I bit into my own flesh. "Shite."

Cain stared directly into my eyes and moaned along my length. My cods tightened in his hands, his fingertips brushing along my sensitive taint, and my release teetered on the edge.

"Please," I begged. My fingers coiled into his hair, and my hips rocked against him, but Cain pulled away.

"Not yet." A wicked glint shone in his bright eyes. Cain rose. "I'm not done with you."

His sculpted cock stood erect, bobbing. Far more superiorly equipped to me. Cain fisted my hair, guiding my salivating mouth to my prize, and I flicked my tongue over his shiny tip.

"Mmm." His fiery taste blended with salty splendor, and I moaned, savoring every drop. "More—" I demanded and inched as far down his shaft as possible, gagging. But I relaxed my esophagus and allowed the invasion.

"Fuck me," he whispered from his sweet, swollen mouth.

The tail of his snake tattoo coiled in the sparse hairs, and I swore the beast wiggled in joy. I stared into his eyes and swallowed him to the base. My tongue folded and molded to the underside of his cock, and I willed it to retract, pressing along the sensitive vein. Each curse became a musical blessing keeping in time with the trembling of his strong legs.

Nothing before had tasted sweeter in my cold world. I shifted to my knees. Cain gasped and dug his nails into my cheeks. My fingers wrapped around my cock, but he kicked my hand away.

"Enough." He stepped back, pulled his cock from my mouth, and reached a hand down in front of my face.

I stared at the long, slender digits, but he only flicked his fingers.

"What are we doing here?" The words blurted from my lips. A crack of lightning flashed in the distance, followed by a tremor in the Earth. Markos. I stood and shook the lightheadedness Cain had caused away. "A dirty fuck doesn't suit you."

"Screw you. You don't even know me." His arms crossed high over his chest. Sweeping his gaze over the ground, his voice heightened. "At least I know what I want."

I winced at his tone and rose from the ground. No sound aside from those of the herald angels had ever sliced through my heart. Inching closer, my feet shuffled, and my pants, still hindering my mobility, dragged against the concrete. Cain stepped back. I crept forward. We danced until his back touched the wall, and I pinned him against the bricks. Since he refused to glance at me, I leaned in and whispered, "Babe, I'm all kinds of wrong for you."

Wrong for anyone but me, myself, and I.

"Don't care what you think." He snorted.

Our cockheads kissed, and I grasped his shaft in my hand.

"What… what are you doing?" Cain's sweet breath sucked in, and his teeth smashed, gnawing against the plump surface of his lip. "Please…don't stop…yes…"

At his command, my hand pumped faster and I rotated my thumb over his sensitive tip. His cock throbbed and swelled in my hand.

"Yes…" He turned his head. So close, but he fought against the release. "Can't… maybe…"

I didn't understand and increased my efforts while staring deep into his soulful eyes. "Let go, babe. Just me and you here."

"I'm…" Cain shuddered against me before stilling. He lost the battle. Hot jets erupted from him and splashed against him taught stomach.

The whole scene proved hotter than any porn. A lazy grin flashed across his face, and his heavy lidded gaze met mine. I lifted my coated hand and licked the salty evidence clean. My tongue skimmed his bottom lip, and his wide eyes closed.

Slowly, I kissed along his neck, following his snake tattoo, and lifted his shirt. Cain caught his breath as I tongue bathed his body clean.

"You taste so good." Not a drop wasted; I nibbled over his stomach, following the snake and treasure trail. I ventured lower

to mop his cock and balls. No one ever complained about my at-
tentiveness, and he sure as hell wasn't about to start.

"Oh shit. Didn't know… never mind…" He whimpered.

At the sensation squeezing my heart, I paused until the flutter
subsided. More lay beneath his surface. I wanted to rip the layers
apart until the source was revealed.

Cain circled and pushed his round ass into the air. Perfection
sculpted into every curve of his body, and my hands grew minds
of their own, groping the fleshy mounds. My tongue washed from
his sack to his puckered bud, gyrating over the tender nerves. A
curse rumbled, kissing the spot, and I plied his cock with gentle
tugs. Cries, soft and sweet, filled the recess. Cain thrust his ass
toward my face. Those soft noises evolved into heavy breathing
and whispers of my name.

"Fuck me, Dorian." His fist pounded the wall. "I need you, now."

My finger rimmed his entrance, teasing Cain, and attempting
to relax his tightened stature. A brow rose at the discovery.

"Damn, you're tight." Either he wasn't a regular bottom, or
he hadn't allowed anyone the pleasure. I dipped a wet fingertip
into his snug ass.

Every muscle tensed, and he stilled. "Fuck."

"Damn it." My old war resurfaced. My finger withdrew and I
fought the sigh. When had Death become such a pussy?

"What's wrong?" Cain's voice and body shook.

"C'mere, babe."

He turned around, but refused to look at me again. I glanced
to the street. My knees cracked, shifting my weight back to the
balls of my feet, squatting instead of kneeling. Pink cheeks dimpled
into a forced smile, but his eyes widened, and his gaze landed on
me. I crooked my finger, beckoning him lower, and he crouched
down in front of me. Cain swallowed hard.

"Let's get a drink, and you can tell me about the lost soul. We
don't have to do this."

"But—"

I held up my hand. "Rain check?"

He nodded, and I reached for my holsters, guns, and coat, ignoring the throb and complaints from my groin. We righted our clothes, saying nothing more.

I pulled out another cigarette and offered him one.

"Nasty habit."

I shrugged. They wouldn't kill me.

"Thanks, Dorian."

"For?"

He blushed again and tried to hide his shy smile.

Damn it, what had he done to me? When had I ever cared about another man's comfort over my own release? The way he had squirmed and begged… "Don't mention it, babe."

Chapter Three

Dorian

As we moseyed the barren sidewalks, the thought of gripping his hand infiltrated my thoughts. We arrived on my street, after a longer than usual stroll through the dusky cover of gray darkness. Our hands swayed but didn't touch. Charged air swept through my widened fingers, and the scent of arousal lingered, like a thick perfume. If he had asked or offered, I would have held his hand. How strange that I was thinking about it. Handholding was for relationships.

My old Victorian sat on the corner, unmoved by the weather or destruction, serving as my office-slash-home. I had converted it, despite Belle's protests to preserve the historic building, but the ABDA had funded the project. Under normal circumstances, most of my business occurred here. For whatever reason, Belle had met Cain in public. I smelled a rat, and my mind wandered, connecting today's events.

"I live on the other side of town," Cain offered, breaking through my thoughts. "The houses here are a little out of my price range, but they're beautiful."

My stride slowed. My side of town had seen less damage from the quakes, and we bordered a rocky cliff, a port, and the railroad tracks. I watched the Halifax Station from my windows, and the train whistles, foghorns, and crashing waves soothed my soul.

"How long have you lived over here?" Cain asked.

"Awhile." Fear and doubt clouded my mind, except for the rawness he had awakened. Ache I had hidden eons ago when I forbade anything beyond a passing fancy. Not only lust, for that was the way of the Angels and Demons. No, the connection stirred something deeper and made me care. He'd unearthed feelings I reserved for my family and Belle. A sigh teased my lips, and I covered the sound with a forced cough. Lust, like a best friend or the back of my hand, and desire had driven me to his ex all those months ago.

Seven months, my mind whispered, *seven to the day*. Hunger stretched and hooked within me for Cain's touch, his voice, or even his gaze. But did he share the same emotions? Would any of it matter when the real me surfaced? My eyes narrowed, rolling over his face, searching for any indication, but he offered none.

I opened the metal gate and waved him through. Layers of snow covered the dead grass of a once-lush green lawn. He brushed against me and I gulped.

Like all matters of the world, the grass had died. And this was where doubt and fear came into play. Even if he could care, everything died and Angels ascended to Heaven. Demons and their ilk went to Hell or Tartarus—a part of my dominion.

Pain laced into his honey eyes. He strained his neck, eying past me to the street. The train chugged away from the station. He appeared captivated by the billowing steam rising in the dusk. At least we held something in common. We both liked trains and hid our pain as best as we could, yet he couldn't hide it in his eyes.

I worked the key into the doorknob. Would Cain run away, screaming when the time came to reveal my truth? His caramel gaze shot to me, and I was thankful they were mere thoughts and not spoken words.

I opened the front door and pushed the questions from my mind. Neither of us had said much, nor had he offered any information on the lost party. Part of me wondered if one even existed, and the other wished he had sought me out solely for myself.

"After you," I whispered, and his slanted eyes met mine. My throat swelled, and saliva flooded my mouth.

Cain brushed past me again, his contact lingering, and I froze. His electricity grounded my feet; dizziness rattled my head. My hands reached behind me and grasped the doorframe for support as his wet soles squeaked over the hardwood floor. I shook the sensation off and entered the dark foyer, closing the door behind me. The sun had set on the stroll here, and that meant busying myself with lighting the oil lamps. I meandered about and walked into my office. Behind me, Cain's teeth chattered. He required a fire. How easily I forgot the comforts of others when I didn't need them.

"Sit." I motioned to the large leather chairs.

Refusing my hospitality, Cain silently shadowed me; I lit the oil lamp on my desk and another over the hearth in silence.

"You're not hooked into a line here?" he asked.

"Solar." I removed my weapons, hanging them by my office door. Biofuel and steam power were old technologies, brought back after the collapse. Less daylight in the winter, but I liked the softer radiance of the lamps. Yeah, who would guess Death has a romantic streak. At least I had been before, but the old me, no, the old me had turned into a distant, bitter memory.

The blizzard developing on the horizon stole my attention. Snow thunder rattled the windows. Often, I swore my brother created the violent destruction and blended the beauty of pristine snow. He denied my accusations, of course.

Sulfur wafted through the air. I glanced to Cain. He knelt by the hearth and prepared the kindling. Thick thighs balanced his slender weight. His match dragged across the bricks and hissed to life before he held the flickering flame against the twisted paper.

I leaned against my desk and grinned, fingers gripping the wooden edge. He seemed at ease in my home. Cain cast a sideways glance, stretching for more paper, and returned the gesture. Genuine emotion crinkled around his golden eyes.

Business had slowed in the recent years for extractions, but out of nowhere women, men, and children had disappeared again. I had no solid leads yet. We dealt with smaller matters, mainly local missing persons who moved and decided not to tell their families and other small detective work too. Most of those cases I passed onto Belle, and I usually signed on for the dangerous, undercover missions and extraction gigs, pulling children and women from Garland's lands with the aid of my brothers-in-arms.

"What do you know about slaves?" I broke the comfortable silence.

Cain whispered, "The stolen are forced into slavery or killed. Sometimes both."

He faced the fire, but the defeat lacing through his words raised my eyebrows. Lost souls were what we called slaves. The ABDA thought dressing the word up would change the facts, but a rose by any other name was still a damned thorny, blood-sucking, stinky rose. I hated the technical terms. The victims faced a permanent death if their owner wished to snuff out their life. Arcadia and the ABDA didn't have the numbers to take over the southern countries, though, and that was where I came into play with my secret weapon: The Council of Seven compromised of the seven Archangels. Combined, we were nearly invisible.

"And the penalty?"

A tremor shook the house, and the windows rattled again. A steamer approached, but Cain's eyes widened and his nails scraped against the sooty hearth. Shocks occurred on occasion if the trains gained too much speed, but I was used to them.

Whistles blew outside, emitting high-pitched hisses, and Cain's shoulders stiffened. "Servitude to Hell and eternal damnation in the fiery lakes or Tartarus."

"Some would argue Hell is not so different from slavery." I had lived through the eras of slavery myself, but I never owned one. It wasn't right.

Cain's brows twisted. "How do you free a stolen soul?"

As if I would reveal my secrets, Rag would have my proverbial head. Ignoring his question, I motioned for Cain to approach my desk, and he eased his body into the leather chair. White knuckles gripped the sides, and his legs trembled, boots tapping the floor.

"Relax you're safe here."

Cain sucked in a deep breath, and his legs steadied. Tension remained in his body, though. A forced smile touched his lips, and he could not hide the sweaty sheen coating his forehead.

The ability to interpret situations and people was a gift I'd always had. With Cain, it seemed amplified, as if we were connected. Like a sixth sense almost, feeling his presence before he had entered the bar, when he was near. Having a connection touched me, but it twisted my stomach too. Anyone deserved more than I could offer them. What did I know about relationships or feelings? The damp brow and fidgeting, sharp movements didn't bother me as much as the fading light in his eyes. I sat behind my desk and flipped to a clean page in my notebook. Did Cain even want a relationship? I pressed the notion aside and asked, "Do you have a name?"

Brown brows rose and fell. "Lily Westcott. The demons renamed her. I don't know what, though."

Issuing new names wasn't unheard of among the demonic hordes. Flashy, sexually enticing names created an illusion. Lily sounded too sweet and innocent, which would have suited a virgin.

"Relative?"

He nodded.

"Physical description? Age?"

"Five foot-three inches, brown hair and eyes, and slight build," he reached into his back pocket and pulled out a wallet, "I have a photo."

"Recent?"

Cain said, "No."

I stared at the tintype-photo and the young girl with her arms around Cain. Just a kid, she couldn't have been older than fifteen in the photograph. A twinge of jealousy squeezed my heart, despite their status. A dunce could've made the connection, even with the different eyes. She had his wavy hair and a sprinkling of freckles across the nose. Another woman stood behind them, but her hair was darker, and she held ferocity in her eyes.

"Sisters." I didn't pose it as a question.

A tear slid down his cheek.

I fought the urge to smack myself. Such an asshole. I shook my head. Everything he had done in the alcove…all he had been willing to do…

"Fuck me." I hid my face with my hands, and hoped it muffled my voice. Slowly, I released a breath, but bile burned my throat at the truth. He'd used me and insured I had accepted the case. I cracked my neck. Any worry of a relationship ended, but not the unsettling of my gut. I lifted my head from my palms, but said nothing of my outburst; he didn't question it, though, and I wondered why.

"What are you? What is Lily?"

Dimples etched into his pink cheeks. Cain raised his hand. Sparks ignited and grew larger until a ball of purple fire formed, resting in his palm.

The show of magic told me zilch. But I squirmed in my seat. Illusions and curses were familiar, courtesy of Markos and Fauna's witches and warlocks, but I didn't understand them, or their magic. Father had created them, putting my brother and sister in charge. Fauna controlled the witches and warlocks, but Markos charged of a legion of demons. Oftentimes, they'd worked together to tempt the humans.

A sly smile deepened his dimples, and I tried not to swoon. Cain was easier to ignore when I thought him an incubus. I sighed. Whatever I was feeling inside for him was all me. No spell or trick. It'd make my job harder seeing his sweet face and knowing this was all a game to earn my services.

"I've shown you mine. Now, show me yours. You're not one of us."

The chair groaned as I adjusted myself. "You don't want to know."

Cain glared at me, and his mouth dropped.

"Trust me." My hand reached for my hat, but it wasn't on my head or the peg. Instead, I yanked on the too long locks, but they did nothing to hide my face. "How long's she been missing?"

"A month," he snapped, and looked away. Cain's bottom lip jutted out and distracted me.

I had to put him out of my mind and forced myself to look elsewhere. "Why'd it—"

"You're the fifth person."

Mouthing fifth, I nodded.

Cain rose and wandered to the large picture window behind my desk. "The first four failed. Two from the ABDA never came back."

That didn't bode well in my uneasy stomach, even if I was immortal.

"I called the ABDA, too, and a friend gave me this office's number." His lips trembled, and his voice softened into a whisper. "You're my last hope." Hurt laced his tender tone.

I couldn't say no. Not to Cain, or anyone. With a soft spot for rescuing the lost and forgotten, it wasn't so much because he asked me, but that an innocent girl's life hung in the shadows. After rescuing Belle, I had vowed never to turn down a case. Not even knowing if he was lying, or holding back from me, would have stopped me from trying.

"Trackers or Vampires?" I asked through gritted teeth. Both were actually vampires. Trackers, however, worked directly for the ABDA. Vampires, well, they worked for me.

Cain blinked, as if not understanding me.

I repeated, "Did you hire trackers or vampires?"

"Both."

Five in a month? Something didn't add up; a trip to Garland could take a month by train, and the only agents they sent into the Deep South were those on the council and me. Mainly Gabriel and I teamed up. Yet, it was the first I'd heard of his sister by name.

I jotted notes and made a mental note to contact the vampires in the area, along with the ABDA headquarters, to double check his accusations. No surprise they hadn't helped, though. A case like his they would've referred to me anyway. The extraction division itself was too young. They dealt with politics and kept survivors fed and alive in Sanctuary. I chewed on my pencil as my mind connected all the events and captures, searching for a recent connection.

"Dorian?" Cain's fingers slid across the desk and rested over my hand.

A breath sucked in, and I didn't know if it was his or mine. His fingertips danced over my skin. My heart beat faster, and I swallowed the pooling saliva. However, the thought of two dead trackers, or vampires, soured my mouth too.

"Sweets." Cain snapped his fingers.

"Right." I cleared my throat. "I've a few associates I can reach out to. They might know more about the vampires and your sisters. I need to know everything, though." I flicked out fingers. "When you last saw them. What they wore. Scars? Anything that will help me identify them." I leaned across the desk, narrowing my eyes. "You're not telling me something, and that something could make or break a case."

"Sister," he corrected, sitting down in his chair. "Just Lily."

The other was safe?

Cain rubbed his neck. "Not Angelica... just Lilith."

Death didn't frighten me, but Belle could die along with anyone else involved. All it took to unravel a plan was one lie or half-truth. Belle wouldn't last a minute in capture, and she was a tough cookie to crack.

Uninformed people always asked how brutal Boric Garland was. He sold out his own family, and there was another rumor. The thought curled and twisted my insides; he had raped and slaughtered his own sister-in-law too. I would love to hunt him down, but a man like that deserved Hell, not purgatory.

"What else is there, Cain?" A stiff drink to ease my bundled nerves and wash the rumor away that was what. Saying that Garland disgusted me was an understatement.

Cain's chair shifted. He rose and strode to the large window behind my desk. How perfect his wide shoulders fit the image, as he stood right where I usually did. My shaky hand reached into my file drawer. Without averting my eyes, my hand withdrew a bottle of whiskey, followed by two glasses. I poured two fingers in each, and offered the liquid fire to Cain.

"Thanks." He accepted, but placed the glass on the windowsill, and sighed, his warm breath fogging over the window. "Dorian, I'll find someone else."

I relished in the fire of alcohol sliding down my throat, searing thoughts of Garland away, and considered the man standing in front of me. "I'm the best."

A faint smile played at his lips, and confusion rattled my brain. I rubbed my forehead and ran my fingers over the deep lines etching into my skin. He had exposed his true intentions and all but ridiculed me in the process. He'd wanted me to say yes, but he changed his mind? Cain had brought me to my knees with continuous assaults of shy smiles, fluttering lashes, and deep dimples. My tongue itched to taste him again, and my hands burned to trace his soft skin. "Why would you find someone else after all the trouble you've gone through?"

"Thought that was obvious." Cain sipped his scotch and made a slight face before coughing. The cup tinkered as he placed the glass on my desk, eyes watery.

My brow rose at his statement. Nothing with Cain teetered on obvious. I stood and leaned against my desk, but kept a short distance.

Cain's lean legs spanned the tiny space in a matter of seconds. Too fast for my brain to react, but my heart registered it and hammered against my ribcage. Cain removed the glass from my hand and slid the tumbler across my desk. My brows furrowed, and my lips parted.

"Let me remove your doubt, sweets." Cain's hand curled into my hair, and he drew me closer. Our lips hovered, but the electricity and magnetic pull surged. "I want you."

My lips hummed, his words tickling. "You want me?"

His coppery eyes lightened as he stared at my mouth. "Yeah, sweets, you got a problem with that?"

I shook my head, which he was still holding firmly in his grip, and grimaced.

"Sorry," he said, loosening his fingers before cupping my face. "I like this look better on you." Cain slid his thumbs over my beard, which I hadn't had seven months ago. "I'd still know you anywhere, though."

Did he want to kiss me, or was he going to keep on sweet-talking all night? My hands encompassed his waist, yanking him against me, and we stood chest-to-chest, nose-to-nose. A ragged breath parted from my lungs. Connecting, I growled against his mouth until he opened for me.

Cain released my face, his hands smoothing over my back and settling on my ass. The fire that never ceased in his presence sparked, and my stomach twirled, churning with heat as his tongue danced with mine. Smoke and whiskey tainted his taste, developing into a sophisticated palate of old-world class.

The desk skidded slightly, his thighs nudging me back, but I didn't move as my gut twisted the sensations, redirecting the need he was creating and shooting it into my groin. His tongue massaged mine, and I craved more.

Blood surged to my cock, but my heart swelled too; feelings cemented and rooted me in place. But when the time came to run away, I would hurt him, and in turn, he would hurt me.

Dizziness affected my legs. I stumbled sideways, but Cain didn't miss a beat, and we crashed to the hardwood floor, narrowly missing the desk. My ass stung from the impact, but my arms circled his trim waist. In my arms, nothing had ever felt so right.

His hips ground and dipped against me. I could not let him go and pressed him closer, my legs wrapping around his waist. Hips met hips as our cloth covered bodies glided in sync. *I will wound him*; my head screamed, but my body responded by removing his belt. More clothing and boots followed, and our kiss broke long enough to drag our shirts over our heads.

We faced each other, held each other. I had never grasped onto another as if my life depended on it. Yet with Cain, the game had changed. Denial proved futile. Smitten with a mendacious warlock, the idea was almost laughable. Almost unbelievable.

Exposed, stripped, and no time to reflect, he enclosed his hand around my leaking cock and smeared the arousal over my ass. He tilted my hips and slid his member over my ready hole; I wiggled in anticipation to meet his thrust. A groan ripped through my chest as Cain entered me. Heat flushed my skin, coating me in a slippery sheen. "Oh, fuck."

The twinge in my heart grew, pulsing and throbbing with each plunge. From the inside out I about burst, each rush filled me more, and I thought if this was how Father wanted me to die, so be it. Cain and I, I and Cain, maybe change wasn't such a terrible progression as long as I had him to guide the way.

My cry died inside his mouth. My body convulsed and shuddered. Sticky, hot semen spilled between our bodies.

I pushed his shoulder and rolled Cain onto his back, mounting him. His fingers trailed through my spent seed, smearing it across my hairy chest. My hips and thighs rolled forward, grinding as he moaned. Cain leaned up, licking and nibbling his way to my mouth.

"I've dreamed of this. Dreamed of finding you again, and you fucking me senseless."

He stared into my eyes and said, "Do I measure up?"

I bit my lip as his hand wrapped around my semi-erect dick and stroked. Groans wrenched free from my mouth keeping time with his gentle tugs. My hand cupped his neck and trailed the path of the snake along his torso.

"Dorian?"

I chuckled. "Oh, I needed to answer? I thought this," I scooped cum with my fingers and brought it to his lips, "was proof enough."

Cain encircled my fingers with his hot mouth, sucking the evidence clean. A moan shivered through my parted mouth.

"You're fucking beautiful." I cupped his smooth cheek. "You feel bloody good inside of me."

"You keep saying that," he said, slowing. "It'll go to my head."

My lashes fluttered. "It's true." Because I had to remind myself, how breakable beauty was in this vast universe. Soft lips suckled my fingers, and his honey-colored gaze heated me. Strong arms held me as a lover, and he wasted the notion on my undeserving soul. Change didn't occur overnight, and I was the last person he should involve himself with on this planet. I broke and destroyed beauty, for I was its opposite. Relationships didn't exist for me. Love served as an enigma Father had created for humanity. Demons and Angels understood self-fulfillment, servitude, and pleasure. Love knew no bounds, yet hurdles littered my life. I didn't deserve a man such as Cain or his love, and certainly, not his heart.

"You have the face of an angel and the depth of an old soul." His thick lips pressed against mine, but he pulled away quickly.

"Takes one to know one," I teased, splaying my hands over his broad shoulders and smoothing over his muscular arms. Beneath clothing, he had hidden himself well, and nothing would have made me happier than to burn every stitch he owned.

Cain opened his mouth to speak, but I had decided no more words, and shoved him back to the floor.

A smile spread over my lips. I pinned him down, seating myself fully. "You're mine now."

Cain's breath hitched as I bottomed out and rotated my hips. Sweat beaded on his brow, and I wiped the perspiration away. My lips engulfed his, nipping at them to open. Fingers pinched and played with his hardened nipples.

Sensory overload became my game, my own pleasure forgotten. I wanted to hear him roar and break his resolve. He arched and met my downward thrusts; his breathy tone urged me, whispered against my mouth in between fevered kisses, as he drew closer to release.

Every muscle froze. Cain shook his head from side to side, fighting against himself.

"Let go, babe," I whispered. "Just you and me." Another thrust and I clenched myself around his cock.

"Fuck... No, I... can't." He shielded his face, turning his head away from me. A pink blush turned redder before my eyes, and he sniffled.

"It's okay, babe. Hush." I collected him in my arms. Tears rolled down his heated cheeks, and the wetness touched my chest. I said nothing about them because I had had no words of comfort, but each leaked tear twisted inside of me. Hate for whoever had caused them and another emotion I didn't understand.

"I'm sorry," he said between sobs. "It's me... sorry... can't... leave me."

The strained tone cut me deeper than tears. "I'm not leaving you, Cain."

I hefted us from the floor and cradled him against my chest, wondering if I could keep the promise. With Cain in tow, I kicked the door to the stairs with my foot and carried him sideways up the narrow spiral staircase. My back rubbed against the textured wallpaper from the tight fit.

He sniffled again. "Where we going?"

Admiring Cain, I found him nestled against my chest as we reached the top of the stairs. "Where no other man has gone before," I had wanted to say, but quieted him instead. Men don't come home with me.

Pretenses had to end; his words and flirtations contradicted his actions. Cain hadn't wanted me, but I would have helped him regardless of his insistence on sleeping with me. The southern countries had raveled out of control, and someone had to save the innocents, but I didn't know how. One or two was a cakewalk, but there were thousands of slaves spread between Garland and Delphia.

My hand flicked the light switch and illuminated the den in a soft glow. I had to work quickly and start a fire before the solar cells drained. His breath clouded the dark air, and his teeth chattered. I placed him on the couch and handed over a blanket.

No tender moments, just unadulterated lust had clouded my past and for a damned good reason. We traveled the same road twice today, but firsts had filled my day too. The first time I cared, or thought, *what if there is more. What if Cain is the one Father created for me?* But he didn't want me; he needed someone to save his sister, and the sting hurt. Not to my ego, though. No, his actions only slightly marred me.

A hand rested over my heart, tapping and willing the muscle to calm. My gaze brushed over his semi-exposed body. Brownish hair covered his chiseled chest and trailed to his groin. The snake tattoo danced with each heaved breath. Cain's beauty rivaled the statue of David, and his body mimicked those hard-sculpted lines.

He said nothing, grasping the cover in his trembling hand. His teeth were still chattering, but I doubted the cold had much to do with his reaction. He tracked me curiously; I strolled into my room to retrieve fresh, warm clothing. Each of my hairs stood at attention. They had earlier, whenever he watched me. I spied on him from the doorway. Questions I hadn't understood flooded my mind, more than what ifs and my future. For a moment, his motivations and insistence I leave the case rose in my mind. Were his feelings for me real? What war did he battle? What stopped him from release?

Whatever had happened to him I hadn't a clue, but Cain had altered from the man I'd met before. I drew a hand over my face and stared between my parted fingers. The frightened and submissive man lounging on my couch, shaken and huddled under the blanket, wasn't the same man who'd kicked my ass seven months ago.

If he had changed, why couldn't I? Was there a spot for him in my hectic life? Anyone else and my answer would have been a big fat thumbs down, served up with a side of never.

Cain had always been different. Soul mate perhaps, but the notion of Father giving his rider of Death a mate was laughable. I shook the thought from my head and gathered the clothing. We were the same size; close enough to fake it for a while until I found a reason to strip them back off. What if Cain never let me? I peeked at him again. A chuckle escaped at the idea, and I sounded more like the old Dorian. Like Death.

His footsteps padded over the hardwood floor. "What's so funny?" Cain leaned on the doorframe and the perfect image of happily ever after with the boy next door drifted away.

I was one of the Four Horsemen of the Apocalypse that had torn this world asunder. Would he even believe the truth? Even though I had witnessed Cain's magic, there were no guarantees. I had to let him go, even if I didn't want to. My hand cupped his cheek and I smoothed my thumb over his freckled skin.

"I'm going to jet—"

"No," I said. Dark hair shook into my eyes, and a pain radiated from my heart. "Why?" *Why would he want to leave me?*

Cain stepped backward, and my hand dropped to my side. Cold molded over my skin where there once stood heat. Emptiness where fullness had once rested. I hated every bit of it. The sex didn't matter. I wanted the man standing in front of me to stay. "Don't you feel it?"

His head said no, but his eyes screamed, yes. "What have you done to me?" Cain tripped over the rug and landed on his ass. "What spell is this?" He closed the blanket around himself and held the fabric taught.

I snorted and tossed on my clothes. If he bolted, I wanted to ready myself.

"Are you one of those demons?" Cain snapped his fingers and stared at the ceiling. He ducked as I tossed him clothes. "There's an old rock band named after them…"

"Incubus?" I chuckled at the thought. Those demons were ridiculously good looking, like male model gorgeous, like Cain. "Nah, and I'm no demon either. No saint, but…" I scratched my head and flashed a grin, because I had no more ideas left. What else could I have said? Cain deserved the truth, but I risked losing him after I'd found him again.

Those doe eyes softened, and he nodded. After saving his sister, I would come clean. He might still shun me, but maybe there was a better chance he would accept me and tolerate the fiend hidden beneath my facade.

"I'm not your enemy, but for the record, there's a few good demons left in this world."

Cain scoffed, and I sighed. Inch by inch, his flesh disappeared under the clothing, but the temptation of him didn't.

"Let's eat and figure out who kidnapped your sister."

Cain stared at his hands and crossed them over his chest. "Thought you wouldn't take the job," he said in a child-like voice, as if I had told him Santa Claus wasn't real.

I knelt and brushed the hair from his face. "We'll figure it out, babe." I wrapped my arms around his shoulder and hefted him from the floor. Our lips hovered, and I whispered, "I've still got a job to do, and it looks like your sister's disappearance is somehow connected. As long as you don't fear me, we're good." I didn't know for certain, but Garland seemed to always be behind the disappearances in some way or another.

Cain gazed into my eyes, and his dark lashes fluttered. "Why would I fear you? You didn't…"

He shook his head, but I swore he had wanted to say more. My thumb caught his chin, and I brushed my lips over his. "You're always safe with me, Cain. No matter what becomes of us."

Secrets and empty promises would not help me locate his sister, and I vowed to uncover what he had hidden, but sometimes secrets were unavoidable. Promises were also breakable, and I needed to stop making them to him. The pit of my stomach had already expected the worst about him. Bile churned and rose at the mere thought of anyone hurting Cain. Someone had, and involving himself with me would end in tears for them too. That promise was one I would keep.

"I'd lie if I said let's keep this professional." I glanced out the upstairs window. A full moon rose on the eerie coastal horizon, lined by railroad tracks. "I can promise this isn't a spell of my creation… there are limits to what I can do, Cain." I shifted, meeting his attentive stare, and caressed his roughening cheek before halting and dropping my hand. "Something is happening between us."

"Why won't you tell me?"

Straining a smile, my hand rubbed the back of my neck.

"You can trust me, Dorian," he pressed.

Trust remained a miniscule issue for me; like change, trust became a budding flower slowly opening over time. Trust hadn't come easy and humanity more than demons were to blame. Over the centuries, I witnessed firsthand how men and women turned on one another. Burned alive, hung, stoned, and drowned… Mankind had tried to kill me to no avail. Priests, priestesses, courts, kings, and even lovers were all guilty of trying to master or slay Death. Why would he be any different?

Cain kissed my forehead and fluttered his lashes again before leaning on my shoulder. Could he be different from the others who'd betrayed me in the past? No. Too soon to tell. "If you knew, you wouldn't tell you either." I shrugged.

He shivered, and I guided him back to the couch, wrapping the wool blanket around his body, and busied myself with building a fire in the upstairs living room. Over my shoulder, I asked, "How old are you?"

Chuckling, Cain stretched out on the sofa. "Couple of hundred decades give or take a few. I stopped counting after the war."

"Which war?" A smile played at my lips, and I glanced over my shoulder. Cain didn't age a day over thirty. Eliouds stopped ageing around there. Wish I could have said the same without this guise, but in it, I passed for thirty-five.

Cain groaned and his footsteps followed. He knelt beside me and shoved me aside. "What about you, handsome?" He balled paper, placing it under the wood, and struck a match.

I snorted at the endearment and blew out the match by accident. "Older than the mountains and seas." That had sounded better in my head.

Laughing, he lit another match. My fingers danced over the glass shield as he held the flame to the paper. A regular boy scout Cain grasped my hand, intertwining our fingers together. Had I ever held another man's hand? I could not remember.

"You're not just a warlock, are you?" I asked. Warlocks or witches often obtained eternal life by becoming vampires and losing their magic. Elioud could change, too, but they kept the magic. Few crossed over since they lived immortal lives, though.

"This I like." Cain swallowed hard and squeezed my hand. He added, "But I'm not ashamed of what I am." Dark brows smashed together.

I crossed my legs as he inched closer; our thighs touched. My head leaned on his shoulder, and I closed my eyes. The fire crackled, and the little space I called home became warm and inviting for the first time. For as long as this lasted, I vowed to enjoy the sensations he ignited around me. His scent filled my lungs, and opening my eyes, I licked my lips. Cain smirked and bent his head toward mine.

He said, "I need control, or I tend to freak out."

"I didn't mean to rush, or push you today." If we became lovers, he had to understand I wasn't like the southern demons. I would never have forced myself on him, or anyone for that matter. "I'm not… that kind of guy. Just tell me to stop—"

"Stop." Cain dragged me into his lap and hugged me.

At first, I had stiffened but brought his head to my chest. Warmth radiated from my bones at the simple contact.

"It's just me…" He inched upward, kissing along my shirt. "It's me, Dorian."

The whisper tickled my neck, but I loved how he said my name, as if I were something decadent. "Babe, I'm here if you want to talk about it." People did that in relationships, right?

Cain kissed my cheek, and I tilted my head. Kissing him reigned up there with everything else I had liked about him. The way his soft lips melded and moved, like an orchestra reaching its crescendo. Slow and sweet but building with passion and heat until fearing I would explode from the inside out. Cain drew his lips away too soon, and I frowned.

"Dorian, please, let the case go. Lily… I can't risk losing you too."

The ache resurfaced in his caramel eyes. Until I brought Lily home, he would feel her loss. All I could have compared that pain to was if I were to lose Belle. Until Cain came bombarding into my life, I hadn't given a shit about anyone for a long time.

But what made him so different from the others? I feared that one question's answer, as I feared my father's wrath.

Chapter Four

Cain

I relaxed my face against his bearded cheek. Fire danced behind the glass, enclosing my secondary source of warmth; he was my first. Dorian's errant thoughts of me never ceased. His questions, his assumptions, all had merit. But my past didn't matter; why open old wounds? I wouldn't rest or allow myself to depart the world until fulfilling the dying wishes of my mother. Not that Dorian knew my plans. Even though Hallowed had spoken of change, I shrugged her words away, accepting my desire for death. Hell, I had prayed for it.

"Why are you so adamant about me not taking this case?" he asked over the crackling fire.

Embarrassment heated my cheeks, at least Dorian hadn't said anything about the sex, or my continuous penchant for telling lies. My failure to perform embarrassed me enough without having the demon, or whatever Dorian was, rake a fine-toothed comb over the details of my life, least of all my past. Through the allure of seduction, it shadowed the harmless tales I'd told to protect my shattered heart and soul from further torment.

"I don't want you hurt." Truth. "What if you're shot? I'd never forgive it."

He scoffed.

Would he understand me? Few people met the real Cain, the one who'd survived for three hundred years as a Garland sex slave. No. Another lie. I'd been more than a slave, a teenaged boy so deeply in love with a monster that I hadn't seen the truth until the beast had tossed me to the wolves. Nobody comes back from that and trusts, let alone loves another. Would Dorian be the one to change me? I stifled my laugh and swallowed it. To save me from myself? Doubtful; but if being with him helped to rescue my sisters, I would try anything. "I should go."

"Just a little longer," he murmured. Strong shoulders rounded beneath the fabric of his T-shirt. Dorian slid from my lap, hunched to the left, and laid his head against my shoulder.

My hand raised to his hair, stroking through the tresses. "Okay."

My mouth dried, and the pounding of my heart increased. I found myself unable to say no. Flames danced with seduction as I quelled the thunderous beat, hoping to regain my senses. But my muscles refused every internal command to rise, to leave his presence. The power he held over me was god-like, and so were his Roman features, like a centurion out of the history books.

This wouldn't end well. It never did. Every relationship I'd had since Boric had blown up in my face. What made Dorian any different from the pigs who'd used me and tossed me aside, or the cheaters? I shuddered.

"Babe?" He pulled back and lifted his head.

"I'm okay." I offered no guarantees, except that my lover's needs would be satisfied. Would that be enough for Dorian?

"You don't sound okay." Dorian's vibrant-green eyes peered at me.

My hand smoothed up his back, over the ABDA emblem. I scooted closer, climbed into his lap, and angled my chin to rest in the cove of his hardened, fury chest. "It's me, Dorian." His thoughts fluttered, hovering on how I said his name with my southern drawl. But I scrunched my face and tried not to read the thoughts running a marathon through his head. "It's who I am, now..."

"Babe, you sure you don't want to talk about it?"

No, I didn't want to speak a word of my ordeals. Why did everyone think talking would change me? I sighed. Hellish nightmares and flashbacks sent others packing. My friends and distant relatives didn't know the terrors I had survived, or relived in my mind.

His rough lips brushed against mine, sweet at first. Seven long months and countless lifetimes spent without Dorian; I curled my fists into his shirt at the mere thought of losing him again and drew him closer. My teeth nipped his mouth open, the coarseness of his face caressing my cheek. I loved his new beard. Loved what he did for a living, saving the wretched slaves, like a death-defying hero.

His hot, wet tongue swayed with mine, and my stomached tugged and swirled. Precious seconds ticked by in his presence, but it wasn't love—a game for fools and stupid boys to pass the time until someone better came along.

No one better would ever cross my path; I pulled away and caught my breath. Ache speared my chest and throbbed at the thought of him. "Dorian, please you have let the case go. You, this…"

His tender hands cupped my face. "How many times do I have to say it? I'm not going anywhere, babe."

How can he be so sure? No one was invincible. Dorian kissed me and I hummed, vibrating my affection.

"That tickles."

My hands slid down his sides, each ridge of his abs like cotton-covered steel.

"Be right back." Dorian unfolded from my lap and ducked into another room.

All good things in life ended, but I promised myself to enjoy whatever time God allowed me to have. But I would be a fool to think Dorian would ever fall in love with me. That what sparks ignited between us were more than lust. Shivers rolled over my skin as I sat by the fireplace and tucked my knees into my chest. I lied to him and held pieces of myself back; no doubt, the process would continue. Men saw it as mystery and intrigue. To me, it was shame over the life I'd led, my choices, which weren't truly choices. My chin rested on my knees, eyes burning with unshed tears.

Why had I lied about Angelica? Right. Because eighteen years ago I'd watched as Boric slit her throat. Eighteen years ago, a cloaked man handed me a baby and swore the bundle was Angelica. I had promised Mother, as she lay on her deathbed, to save my sisters from Garland's sweaty grasp. My savior tucked the baby away in Delphia, but he'd turned on us by selling her to another man. I didn't know if the baby was my Angelica, but I had to save her. A tear slid free, and I sniffled; I had to free all the slaves.

Floorboards thudded and creaked; Dorian returned. He responded, "I thought about what you said."

Would he want me if he learned the truth? My brow rose, and I tossed the throught aside. "And?"

Dorian knelt, balancing on the balls of his bare feet, and ran a hand through his dark tresses. "I'm the best, and you know it, babe."

Pride led to arrogance and hubris, and I closed my eyes. The Dorian who ran away from the sight of me in the bar was gone. The man before me held no fear, and I wondered what that felt like. Most of the time my shadow sent me ducking beneath my covers.

Dorian tilted my chin, but I refused to move and buried my face against my thighs. Cool fingers stroked through my hair, and the tingle spread throughout my body. I wanted him. But Dorian needed to understand me.

"Cain?" The fire crackled. "Babe, c'mon. It's my job. This is what I do best." He nudged me. "Seriously. My team is the best at researching, locating, and extracting from brothels."

Turning toward his voice, my eyes opened, and I gasped. Firelight engulfed his golden skin with an orange radiance. Combined with his jeweled-jade eyes, Dorian appeared almost angelic in a dark and dangerous way. Full lips curved into an equally daring smile that burned my skin. Blood bubbled and coursed, shooting its magic straight into my groin. The look on his face sped my pulse, and I struggled to breathe as we gazed into each other's eyes.

Mother had said I would know. Angelica had said I would know. One glimpse, even though I had never put faith into love at first sight. I loved the idea of Dorian. The arrow he'd struck and lodged into my throat seven months ago, releasing its slow poison into my bloodstream and infiltrating my heart. It sounded corny and lame, even to me.

Like the last man I'd loved, Dorian would hurt me and toss me aside, leaving me to the others, allowing the buzzards to pick at my shattered bones. No, I couldn't go back there. So I concealed my reluctance beside my pain and shadowed them in lust.

Black hair framed his molded face, and deep dimples formed in his cheeks, as if carved by an artisan's hand. Lust worked on Dorian. His stare alone, heavy lidded and purposeful, sparked hunger inside of me as his gaze brushed over me from head to toe, leaving a burning blush in its wake. His calloused fingertips tilted my chin again, and Dorian's other palm unfolded my stiff body.

As he kissed me, my muscles responded to his gentle touch. I parted my mouth for him, letting him in the only way I knew how. The way my master had taught me. He wiggled against my tongue, exploring me. No trick, no magic, and no force was required. But my mind and heart still struggled between forced slave and lover.

Again, he slid into my lap, driving my legs to the floor. Pulling away, he blinked. Crimson dotted the apples of his scruffy cheeks. Dorian held beauty that only God could have created, and he thought he wanted me. My hand lingered on his thigh. Arguing appeared futile without revealing all my cards, and the more I pressed, the more questions Dorian asked, at least within his mind.

As he rested in my lap, I could not look away. Dorian's hands clamped on my shoulders, and I swallowed hard, ignoring the ache his touch seared into my belly. Despite my age, the sensation was new; it wasn't pure sexual lust as I'd originally thought. My palms roamed, rubbed, and explored his broad, muscled chest. His nipples stiffened, and he groaned, growling slightly as I pinched them.

He brushed against my ribcage and stroked the path of the serpent trailing down my torso. "Stay with me a while, babe. I'll make dinner."

Babe... I needed to get used to him calling me that, but I couldn't deny liking it. The tattoo reminded me where I came from, but not who I was. Most of Lucifer's relatives were worth more than his awful deeds painted them to be. Deeper, etched beneath my skin a longing blossomed and eased the darkness of my past. "I have to work in the morning."

"Call out," he said. His warm lips grazed my temple, and I twisted, leaning into his affection. Dorian clutched my hands and laced our fingers together. For a man against relationships, the signs he gave contradicted his warring thoughts. All of this was new to him, and the sweet sentiment touched my heart.

I hadn't lied about enjoying his caress and our shared embraces. With a handful of boyfriends since my servitude to Boric and his cronies, I wasn't equipped for the storm he weathered. The demons he kept hidden away rattled, and not even I could pull the secrets free from his head.

I closed my eyes for a moment. A moment was all it required. Raw ache built within, but my mind flashed away, and I forgot my surroundings. His house filtered out and my master's home filtered into my mind, as if it were real. An inferno heated my skin and my heart crept up my throat. Cinderblock walls and dark steel bars surrounded me. They'd broken me *there*. Chains hung on wall and their shackles mocked me. The scent of their bodily fluids infiltrated my nose and I gagged, but I didn't cry. Crying had only made it worse. By the grace of my brother-in-law, he had saved me from their clutches, but not before Boric's inflicted damage had rooted into my soul so deeply it had scarred my bones.

My hands still on Dorian's chest froze, wanting to shove the image away.

It's not Boric kissing you. Like a Virginia reel dance from my youth, the world do-si-doed, and once again, my senses and mind swam in Dorian's presence. His earthy scent replaced the filth. His gentle, caring warmth interchanged with the inferno of Hell. Wallpaper swapped places with the bricks, chains, and shackles.

No longer pushing him away, I tugged him toward me, curling my fingers into his T-shirt. My lips opened and parted as Dorian's tongue massaged against mine. Dorian twisted his fingers into my hair, holding me tighter.

After what they had done to me, intimacy became damned near impossible. Still I had tried. Flashes and nightmares of those days returned, while the ones I'd wanted to love ran away before allowing me to explain. Ned had sprinted to Dorian; or rather, he had shoved Dorian's cock down his throat. Envy had hazed over my eyes; I'd craved the earth-shattering connection and release, but observed as twisted relief spread over Dorian's face instead. Something within me snapped that day, but he never fought back. Anger had overtaken me, and the result had been less than appealing. Misdirected rage at the problem inside of me. Boric and the masters had created the man I had become, yet somehow, after meeting Dorian during that fateful situation, I hadn't known my life would never be the same again.

My hips rocked against his strained cock. We moaned in unison as I imagined myself sliding inside of him, his insides enveloping my cock and milking me. My hands gripped his ass and ground him against me, hard and fast. A rumble resonated from his chest; his thoughts undressed me as Dorian's mouth sucked my bottom lip. My pulse quaked and my body shuddered beneath the angelic man swallowing the moans releasing from me. Liquid seeped, jetting from my imprisoned cock. Desire remounted and tingled in my balls, but the control wasn't mine.

I had prided myself in complete power since those days. At least I told myself as much, but they were lies. Somehow, I tore myself away. My chest heaved, breath stolen.

Dorian pecked my cheek and peeled himself from my arms before sauntering into the kitchen. I stared back into the flames, catching myself in its afterglow, my body settling, and glanced at my still hard, denim-covered cock. Heat flooded my face. Sure enough, my seed had soaked through the fabric. My palm ran over my mouth, and I covered the evidence with my other hand, searching for a pillow to hide the accident.

No one wanted a man who shot early, or not at all.

A sigh tickled my throat, but I swallowed the emotion, along with extinguishing my burning eyes. Before today, I hadn't allowed anyone to touch me either, not there, not in my lap, and certainly not eating my ass in an alleyway. Dorian seemed to tear through my defenses as long as I gave up my control to him. My head shook, and I masked a chuckle, capturing the noise in my hand.

The dancing flames swayed and flickered in the hearth, fire died as well as passions. Boric taught me as much. Would Dorian teach me the same lessons? What would remain when the fervor between us cooled? Too many secrets compounded any hope for Dorian and me. No relationship lasted forever.

I didn't know what type of demon he was, aside from powerful. Cousin Tomas guarded his friends, and I held no doubts he knew the enigma of Dorian; after all, he had sent me to Cousin Belletrist.

Pots and pans clattered from the kitchen and footsteps followed. His beautiful ass bobbed before me. Dorian knelt; the fabric of his jeans drooped and revealed the tops of his rounded mounds. My cock ached, and I squeezed the hard-on hidden by my hand. Dorian shifted the fire and brought the coals to one side, where he placed the pot.

"All I have is canned soup or vintage MRE's." He opened the can and dumped the contents into the container.

A man that cooked; my lips perked at the thought, but I kept my stare glued to his curved behind. "Soup sounds good."

"Trust me when I say this tastes better."

I shrugged. When the Sundering hit, many had lost everything. Those not prepared starved within the first few months. Canada—Arcadia—survived the apocalypse and adapted, but the damage to the remaining world had been drastically different. In the blink of an eye, time seemed to reverse itself as the oil, gas, and fuel sank, or burned. The demons realized they must sink or swim. Arcadia swam in its wealth and bounty of food and technology. Garland dabbled in slaves and debauchery, while Delphia played the fence and wore a façade of neutrality and balance.

Dorian eased beside me on the floor. The soup was warming over the coals. How could he have no notion of starting a fire, yet he cooked fine over one? Did it matter? Dorian placed his hand over mine and pressed against my cock. I bit my lip and leaned my head back, arching my spine against the sofa.

"You should let me take care of you," he said, and his tender tone left me speechless.

I blinked at his grinning face and shook my head. *How do I make it clear? Only his pleasure matters.*

Dorian added, "It's an open offer, babe. Anything, you name it, and I'll take care of you."

I didn't think he meant sex. Dorian shifted toward the fire and swirled the pot. Chicken soup wafted through the cozy space, causing my mouth to water. His words rattled in my head, and I sought a reason. Why did Dorian care about me at all? I stared at the crown molding. Maybe he didn't give a shit about me, but only thought he did. His mind didn't help matters and confused me, prattling about his past. *Why would anyone try to kill him? Or maybe he is just as broken as I am, and he is trying to figure us out.*

Dorian crawled forward, ladled the heated soup into two bowls, turned around, and handed one to me. "Sorry, no spoons."

Again, I shrugged, lifting the bowl to my lips, and sipped the hot, salty broth. "Thanks." If I closed my eyes, I could have pictured my family long before the slavery. Angelica and Lily dressed in pastels, twirling their lace-covered umbrellas, Mama in her Sunday finest, sitting on the front porch sipping her limeade with Papa beside her. I would've leaned against a pecan tree, watching the men laying the railroad ties, in secret. How different my life would have been if my father hadn't gambled away everything, including his children and wife. I would have fought in the Civil War; I'd already enlisted. But Papa had said he would rather have lived penniless and alone, and he'd promised us the Garland family cared after their property. True, they'd treated Angelica well enough, and they would take care of us too. Papa had lied on both accounts.

Dorian asked, "You okay, babe?"

I nodded, and I fought to keep the nightmares at bay. Blood rushed from my face, and my insides twisted. Faster and harder, the images pounded and flashed in my mind, reminding me of trust's capabilities, reminding me of what and how I had survived over three hundred years of service. It didn't matter that, for the first one hundred years, I was Boric's lover, his pet. Papa had forced me into it.

"No, you're not."

The bowl dropped but didn't clatter. Dorian seized it and laid it by the hearth. I grasped my head and shook it, gritting my teeth. The binds, the scars hidden by magic, if he saw, he would know the slices of my soul they had stolen away from an innocent man—No, an innocent boy.

He shouted, "You're lying. Look at me, Cain. Be here with me. In this moment."

But I was looking. I stared right at him before averting my gaze to the hearth.

He tilted my chin, and my attention lifted from the burning embers. Dorian chewed on his bottom lip, and he followed the movement with his tongue. He cupped my face and smoothed his thumbs over my cheeks. When had any lover showed real attentive kindness? The softness of him I hadn't expected, but so much remained that I didn't understand about him. Gale force winds seemed to come and go as he teetered between hot and warm. If I held on tight enough maybe, I might survive for a while, but I knew better than to dream.

He thought, *What happened to him? I've seen this before... Was he a slave?*

"I should go." The tone of my voice strained, and I gulped, searching for something to ground me. "I really have to work tomorrow."

Dorian's brows creased, and he shook his head. Dark tendrils fell and framed his rough jaw. Truly, he was beautiful. "A little longer, babe. I have some more questions."

The thought of his questions caused my legs to shake, and I searched for an exit. Similar to Dorian's war, my own began between what we could be together, to each other, and the truth of our secrets we clutched closer than the possibility of love. Yet I didn't run as Hallowed's words echoed in my mind. I simply nodded, seeing the light flicker in his eyes. If he wanted to try, why couldn't I? Dorian couldn't hurt me any further than Boric had done.

He seized my hands in his, hefting me from the floor with carefree ease, and led me through the tight spiral staircase. The fleur-de-lis wallpaper reflected bronze tones under the soft lights. My palm ran over the textured surface, wondering if he chose the décor, or if it was leftover from the Victorian Era.

We relocated downstairs into his office. I shivered noting the fire had died to a few sputtering embers, and I worked on building it to its former glory. Papers shuffled as Dorian flipped through documents, erasing and scratching, his brows furrowed together. A slight sheen coated his skin in the darkened corner. His massive desk framed the slightly larger than average man to perfection. I didn't want to look away. But what was he? What type of demon needed no light other than a vampire?

"How can you see over there?"

"I can see without light," he replied. "But I like the glow of the fire, thanks."

Dorian gnawed on the end of his pencil. I settled into a leather chair across from his desk. Watching him work calmed me, as if watching a storm. The low hiss of the fire filled the air as he scribbled here and there. Nothing about his desk screamed neat or tidy, and the rest of his home reflected that.

"That can't be right," he muttered, and I followed his thoughts. More girls had disappeared in the past three years than Dorian realized. Over a hundred assumed stolen.

I chewed my lip and prayed, hoping God heard my pleas again. This had to stop. No, a hundred and fifty if he counted the men. The numbers rose higher as he counted in the missing children. My stomach lurched, as his mind worked the figures, and I toppled over, holding myself.

"Babe?" Dorian raised his eyebrow.

I shook my head. "Bathroom?" Sweat beaded on my forehead, and dizziness swept over me.

He pointed toward a small door by the staircase. Excusing myself, I scurried into the closet sized room. My head rested against the closed door, and I fought for breath.

"How could you allow them to take away the children?" he thought, and our minds echoed one another. How could God have allowed them to take anyone?

Bitterness scorched my throat. My feet stumbled toward the toilet, and I heaved into the porcelain throne. A knock rapped against the door. "In a minute," I replied.

Refusing me, the door opened, and his warm hands smoothed over my back. "Hey babe, you okay?" Soft, soothing words sprouted from his lips, reminiscent of sonnets. "It's alright. Let it out."

His tone pacified my lurching. But my teeth chattered, yet not from the cold.

Dorian wiped my forehead; his cool hand lingered. "No fever."

I tensed under his touch, his concern crinkled gaze skimming over me. "C'mon," he said, turning the water on in the sink. "Rinse your mouth and clean your face."

Unable to speak, or rather untrusting of my tone and tremor, I nodded and allowed him to guide me toward the basin. Icy water tightened my skin, and I swished it in my dry, acidic mouth. Dorian appeared unfettered by my sudden sickness and more concerned over my well-being. The thought should have comforted me, but the simple notion raced my heart.

He handed me a towel and shut off the water. Without asking, he lifted me from the ground and carried me from the bathroom. Salty aftershave tickled my nose and relaxed my senses as his scratchy neck brushed against my cheek.

Dorian chuckled, carrying me upstairs, and laid me on the sofa. He draped the blanket, I had used earlier, over my body, but the warmth offered little comfort, and I shivered and convulsed.

We were pretending—whatever we were—while children,

men, and women disappeared. Stolen away from their loved ones and forced into slavery. Hard labor, whorehouses, and so much more would become their lives. Starvation, flea and lice ridden slums would become normal life. Rape too… there was no safety except in sleep, and even the nightmares attacked us there. The slaves would never be the same, like me. Pain doesn't go away; it doesn't lessen with my freedom either.

A tear slid down my cheek, recalling the life I had escaped, the nightmares plaguing me after twelve years of freedom. No one deserved that life, least of all a child. For children, slavery was harsh, harder than it was for adults. That life wasn't one I would have wished on my worst enemy. Lily understood; I understood. We had been children when our father sold us. Three hundred years later and freedom was mine, but not because of strength—physical or mental. Maybe God punished me, never truly freeing me from the memories, because I had been weak in those darkest hours—had fallen for the enemy.

Dorian stooped to my side. His green eyes glowed brighter than the firelight. He brushed the tear away and brushed his fingers through my hair. I was lucky to escape, but until the last brothel burned, my tarnished soul would weep.

Tingles erupted inside and out, and he stroked the ache and memories into the shadowy recesses of my mind.

"Thank you," I whispered, and meant it. Maybe his ability to chase away the darkness was why I was falling for him. Though it didn't matter, I had no plans to tell him the truth. Or why I cried. Dorian the hero wouldn't understand the life of a slave.

"Anytime, Cain. Rest." He ran his thumb over my dry lips.

Fiery wood filled my nostrils and saturated my pores. Energy pulsed and emotions threatened to unleash the power I had worked hard to contain; my relaxation weakened the spell holding my façade together. I drew the covers over my head.

Sleep weighed in, as he touched me, and before it had stolen me away, I thought Dorian whispered, "No one will ever hurt you again

Chapter Five

Dorian

Downstairs, a cigarette burned in my ashtray, and I waved the smoke from my eyes, squinting at the notes. Cain slumbered on my couch upstairs while I explored the information he'd offered on Lily, comparing it against similar cases in the vicinity that Belle had been working. The facts didn't add up.

A shriek rattled through the calm night, and I jolted from my chair. "Cain." Rushing to the staircase, I tripped but caught myself from falling. As quickly as it began, the screaming halted. The softer noises he made, muttered, and words he sometimes shouted in his fitful sleep called to me. No, they sliced through my soul, reminding me I wasn't alone. And blaring a reminder. What caused the thrashing or other peculiarities surrounding Cain Westcott?

I paused for a moment—in case he called out again—before returning to my desk. But the house quieted; I resumed my work, sitting behind my desk and staring at names and missing person's forms. My eyes closed, and I breathed deeply. Nothing about Cain—or Lily—made sense from his clean dress to his shrouded past. Tintypes were last in use hundreds of years ago, but hobbyists and specialists still used the technique up until the Sundering, which had occurred twelve, nearly thirteen, years prior.

I stared at the image, waiting for a clue to jump out at me; instead, a smile tugged at my lips, my fingertip stroking the tintype. Cain's genuine smile reflected on the scratched and faded metal. Deep dimples and light-filled eyes stared back at me.

Corded muscles hid beneath white linen and a fancy paisley vest. Pressed slacks draped over his long but thicker legs. I blinked. The tin slipped from my fingers and clattered against my desk. *What the bloody hell am I doing swooning over a photograph?*

Boards creaked as the house settled. Wind groaned outside in the blustery cover of night, but echoed in the silence of my downstairs office. The tintype, the photograph, was well over three hundred years old. Worn edges and subtle scratches lined the image.

I had found his secret, or at least one of them. Where one hid, there lay more. Secrecy saturated him, as well as me; but I had my reasons, and my mystery had nothing to do with Cain specifically.

Cain's secret: long before the world sundered, around the time when the seven families warred in the southern regions, Lily had disappeared. A hunch really, one rustling in my gut, but nothing else made sense.

Westcott... the name mulled around and digested... nothing sparked, yet I had heard the surname before. My hand rubbed over my tired eyes, blinking and focusing on the clock. Almost two o'clock there; the call to Anchorage would have to wait until late tomorrow morning, as they were four hours behind.

I rose from my desk and stared outside the large window. A lazy grin deepened, reflecting from the glass, as the soft chuckle escaped through my lips. Belle would laugh at me, when she found Cain here tomorrow, and I would never live this down. I shook my head, running my fingers through my tresses. Smitten with a mysterious and broody warlock—according to my field reports he was also an Elioud—but I smiled at my innocent admittance. Belletrist had been after me for years to date or settle down, even though she was one of the few who knew my past... why I lived the way I did, hopping from one stud to the next.

"Fuck it." I grabbed the phone. My shaky hand dialed James, my liaison at the ABDA Communications Division. Vampires never slept, and I had no qualms about reporting in at the wee hours of the morning to him.

On the fifth ring, James answered, "This had better be good."

"We have one hundred taken this month." A hundred and one if we counted Lily. "That's more than a simple extract. How should I proceed?"

"Taken at once?" he asked, raising his voice over loud music. "That can't—"

"No, that's the fucking total currently presumed or reported missing." I squinted, watching the sprinkle of people spill onto my street from Halifax Station. The trains ran around the clock, burning trash for fuel.

James replied, "Let me get back to you, boss. Something's not right."

My eyes rolled at his boss comment; though, technically, I was every vampire's boss. I glanced behind me and cupped my hand over the phone. "Wait up. Can you do a surname search?"

"Of course," James agreed, allowing his scoff to enter his tone.

I whispered, "Westcott. Lilith or Cain."

"Repeat?"

I rolled my eyes, pinching the bridge of my nose. "Surname is Whiskey, Echo, Sierra, Tango, Charlie, Oscar, Tango, Tango. First name Charlie, Alpha, India, November—"

"Agent Fox, did you say Cain Westcott?"

"Affirmative. Whatcha got on him?" Sputtering sounded over the receiver and the music cut out. "C'mon, James, don't leave me hanging."

Typing sounded in the background. "Fuck, boss. The name's flagged, and I don't have the clearance." He muttered to himself; more typing echoed into the phone. "Can't be. This isn't right. I have top clearance. Let me call you back."

I sighed, plopping into my chair. "Right."

James hung up the phone, and I did the same. My palm rested on my face, and my churning stomach ached. I retrieved the last three months' reports from my desk's filing drawer. Another two hundred had gone missing, not from Halifax, but the surrounding areas. I lit another cigarette. "Fuck me."

I didn't want to see the countrywide reports, but I forced myself to calculate the numbers. From all of Arcadia, in the past two months, loved ones had reported close to five hundred people missing. While that didn't mean Garland had stolen them, it did mean we were not in control. Father's plan mandated that we—The Horsemen—maintain the power, and we'd failed. I had to call my family. The demons had taken over. We had to end us.

Cigarette smoke burned my lungs as I deeply inhaled the nicotine. I dialed another number, but the phone rang repeatedly with no answer. My fingers pressed the buttons again. With any hope, I was wrong.

"Bonsoir, Sang et Pain, comment puis-je vous être utile?" *Good evening, Blood and Bread, how may I be of service?*

"Puis-je parler avec, Duc Tomas? *May I speak with, Duc Tomas?*

The man replied, "Le duc est sorti. Puis-je prendre un message? *The Duc is out. May I take a message?*

"Appel, Dorian Fox." I hung up.

Tomas Artois and Petre von Baron proved indisposed. Neither worked for the ABDA directly, but both had connections since they were on the Arcadian council—liaisons representing the power company and transportation. Both were vampires, which made them mine to command. The hierarchy was more for show and order.

A yawn escaped my mouth. Even Death needed beauty sleep, but the thought of losing a second on his case troubled me more than dark circles underneath my eyes. The south had infiltrated Arcadia once again and alarming numbers had vanished.

Prostitution had amplified on my own streets too. No one wanted the southern ways to bleed into Arcadia, and we had lost our grasp faster than I had realized. To top it off, a sexy Elioud-warlock slept upstairs, and his file required a higher than level seven clearance? *Bollocks.* Level eight didn't exist. I reached for my phone again and dialed Belle. "Why didn't you tell me so many were missing?"

"No, I'm not busy, and hello to you too, boss." Sleep tainted her tone.

"Belles, I'm serious. For every one we save, twenty are never found."

She yawned. "Can we talk about this in the morning?" Without waiting for a reply, the phone clicked.

I stared at my receiver before pressing redial.

"Dorian, seriously, shouldn't you be sleeping?"

"They're all witches and warlocks, Belle. What does he want with them?" The one connection the victims shared. Boric never kidnapped actual demons, angels, or Archangels for that matter. Vampires seemed off limits to him too. I could only assume the reason—those three were physically fast and untainted by humanity, except for vampires. "I'm surprised he hasn't taken the lower choirs of angels, but I have none of them reported missing."

"How the fuck do I know? Just because I lived with them doesn't make me an expert. Now goodnight."

I dropped the phone on my desk and shook my head. It rang, and I snatched it up again.

"Dorian. The network finally reported in over repeated similar sightings and incidences." Banging leaked through the speaker.

"James, what do you have for me?" My forehead ached, and I had no idea what he was talking about. "What are you hitting?"

"The computer," he said, as if it was an idiotic question. "So, get this, boss. Missing witches and warlocks, right? A bunch of them are stowed away in safe houses set up by the ABDA for refugees. Those refugees originated in the southern Garland brothels and slave encampments in Delphia." James laughed. "Someone brought them up into Arcadia by train like a week ago."

"Who?" He had my attention. What moron would dream of such a raid and have the cods to pull it off? And why would they move them to Sanctuary?

"The details are sketchy but something about three men and a woman taking it upon themselves to take down brothels. They're mainly kids, boss. You know, the vics. Anyway, some explosion happened, and there were more, but they too disappeared. No one's told me if that's why the numbers are higher. I mean, boss, if one of the houses filed a report, you'd see it because it's your territory north east of the city."

He was scrambling. Why did people think they could lie over the phone? I'd go over his head if need be. "Do you have names?" I twisted and reached across my desk for my pencil, ready to write.

"Not yet, but they're supposed to send me over a list in a day or two. I'll shoot it over as soon as I have it." He paused for moment. "They're keeping the details quiet."

No shit, Sherlock. "How'd you find out about it, then?" A breath hissed through my teeth. My gut told me the names wouldn't match. Whatever happened, had happened within the current week, but my list spanned months unless the ABDA was cooking the numbers to hide them. It wasn't unusual, and it usually meant the Council of Seven didn't trust someone within the ABDA.

"My donor's on the rescue team," James said. "Even if they're not yours, Dorian, they're safe."

"Thanks. Let me know as soon as you do. Good work, James."

For the people living in the safe houses the news was excellent. The doctors would evaluate them before the government trained them for new jobs, but the process lasted months if not years. Rescue missions were the main source of Arcadia's new refugees, but a few had escaped their owners and traveled the vast distance over the broken continents on their own. It resembled a modern day Underground Railroad, but I wished the Horsemen could do more, save more. Death wasn't powerful enough to bring the south to its knees, and neither were War, Pestilence, nor Virtue. Even combined, we were nothing in the face of Boric and the Arch demons.

What were God's scoundrels and Hell's courtesans going to do with this shattered world if four powerful Archangels couldn't do shite?

A dial tone was emitting from the phone in my hand. I pressed end and tapped the thick antennae against my lips before placing it on my desk. A fleeting thought passed through my mind, one I didn't want to set into motion but saw little choice. My hand rested on my collar; the key made all the difference, but I didn't want to end the world... I stared at the plaster-covered ceiling. But I would if it meant Cain, women, men, and children would never suffer at the hands of Boric Garland.

In the distance, a train whistle blew its warning alarm. I checked my watch as I rose from my chair again, turning to study the world outside of my window. The three o'clock came into the station. I turned off the oil lamp and ran a hand over my beard. Cain stirred and the whistle blared again. My knees cracked and my muscles stretched the weariness away. Wood boards creaked overhead and windows rattled, alerting me that he had woken. The steam engine chugged into the platform.

Glancing at the ceiling, I said, "What am I going to do with you?" but I averted my gaze. What Cain would become to me had no name. Time would tell, or rather time would show me what I meant to him. Mirroring the demons in the south, he had blindsided me.

I stood in front of the large window, overlooking my snow-encrusted lawn and the train station. Snow endlessly cried from the dark sky. Its tears glistened from various surfaces as horse drawn buggies beat their hooves over the old streets.

The utopia I had once envisioned hadn't included Cain, or the likes of Boric Garland for that matter, but Boric was another thorn lacing pain through my Achilles heel.

An alien term and notion to me was love, or at least it had been until the day we met. Did I love Cain? Maybe. Yes. No. I had no clue what love was anymore. Eons ago, I thought I understood love until the man holding my heart squeezed out every bit of it, leaving behind a solid black, icy orifice. I vowed that day never to let love control me again.

Neither Cain nor I seemed keen on letting the other one in, but I refused to let him go. Yet that still wasn't love. We raised the bar and built ironclad walls around ourselves. The same resistance

I saw in myself was mirrored in Cain, but what secrets could he need to hide from me?

His footsteps pattered on the staircase, and the small door leading to the first floor creaked, followed by my office door.

My secrets were huge on the grand scale. A Horseman, Death… God's own Angel of Death and destruction followed my path. He would fear me, hate me… everyone else did.

His warm arms encircled me from behind, and I leaned against Cain. The comfort seeped deeper than my soul. The simple thought of moving from the embrace left trepidation in its wake.

He whispered in my ear, "You need to sleep."

My hands folded over Cain's, and I stared out the window. Snowflakes danced in the howling breeze and whisked across the serenity of Nova Scotia. Same as my façade. Merely a farce meant to lure the unsuspected into its frigid grasps.

Cain added, "The view is beautiful."

I spun in his arms and gazed into his caramel eyes. The earlier pain had disappeared, and in the low firelight, they twinkled. Compassion and love were not my usual emotions, and I skated on dangerous ground. Cain had distorted my view, yes, but failing the case could lose him forever. And if I ran from the job, as he'd suggested, what type of man would that make me? I wasn't a hero, but I wanted to become his champion.

"My view is breathtaking." I kissed his roughening cheek. He rolled his eyes, and I switched direction toward the case. "I need more details about your sister and what you recollect of Garland."

Cain glanced away and glowered. "I told you not to take the case." He stormed to the chair in front of my desk, his heat vanishing. He fidgeted with his clothing. "I will find another way to save her."

I lit a cigarette and drew his dagger stare. "The ABDA decides now." I sat as well and crossed my legs. "You do realize I work for them, right?"

"Hard to miss, sweets." His shoulders tensed.

Most clients didn't realize I belonged to the ABDA until they arrived, but I never hid the fact on purpose. In my pocket was the badge, and I had T-shirts, mugs, you name it. They owned my ass when it came down to the law. But the clients were not privy to my Horseman status.

"Babe, we've been over this. There's no one better than me. Even if there was..." Was what...? I wanted to end the pain in his eyes. But I had other motivations, like figuring out why the demons hunted Lily and if she could create purple fire. What made a witch or warlock-hybrid more prized than say an Elioud? Why and, for that matter, who had locked Cain's records?

The chair creaked as I unfolded from it and strode around the desk. I offered my hand to Cain, heaving his not so light frame from the chair, but I didn't let go. Instead, my arms slipped around him, and I drew him closer. Cain's arms ran over my chest, rubbing warmth into my dead heart.

"We can talk later after you've gotten more rest."

He released me and backed toward the staircase. Cain cocked his head and nodded. "I'll see you tomorrow, then?"

My fingers curled into his shirt. "You thought I'd let you out of my sight?" I yanked him back to me and kissed him, sliding shaky hands over his arms, tracing them along his shoulders until halting at his rough face. "If they stole your sister, babe, they'll come for you too." And I will be there in the shadows, waiting with a one-way ticket to Sheol. "No secrets. They end now. The bloody lies as well. I can't protect you or save Lily without all the facts this time."

"Protect me?" Amusement sparked in his expression, and his thumb slid over my lips. "I've done fine on my own, sweets."

Cain would not budge and dump all his secrets, but I had to try. But he wasn't leaving my sight until I found out why his last name... no, his actual name... why had the ABDA barred me from it. They knew my rules. My brow rose, and a sigh hissed through his kissable lips. Parted ever so slightly, a pink tongue grazed the bottom. A ploy, I gathered and crossed my arms over my chest.

Wide shoulders rounded forward. "Fine. Let me call work." The train chugged away, and the walls rattled. "Tomorrow though we... chat."

I guided him up the stairs. Cain had refolded the blanket and draped it over the couch. The fire crackled and hissed, roaring and heating the living room into an inferno. Within moments, sweat beaded on his forehead. He knelt before the hearth and closed the mesh screen. The glass door squeaked, gliding along its wheels. I watched from the doorway of my bedroom, leaning my weight against the crown molding. Cain rolled onto his heels and in one fluid motion, rose to his feet.

Inch by inch, my ABDA t-shirt lifted from his lean torso. "Talk about tempting the devil," I mumbled, as his shirt hit the floor. Without words or thoughts, my legs crossed the distance and grasped his hands. Cain jumped; my heart sped as he lifted his gaze, rolling it over my body. Dark lashes blinked, temporarily hiding the ache in his eyes.

"Do I get a goodnight kiss?" he whispered, but shied toward the couch.

Sweaty palms grew cold without his touch. "C'mon," I said, and angled my head toward the bedroom door. Even if he wanted to sleep alone, there were two spare bedrooms on this floor. Cain glanced between the door and the couch. "Just sleep... promise."

A slow nod did little to hide his audible gulp. Childlike innocence reflected in that moment and pieces of the real Cain shined through... the scared, frightened man who had lived through more than he led on, and the man who quickly stole away with my heart. This had nothing to do with his name, locked records, or his sister. No, it had everything to do with the man who'd haunted my dreams and waking moments, the man I ran from, not out of fear of physical harm, but because he altered me inside and out, tearing through the walls with only a melting smile.

Dreams arrived, and much like the cries of the tortured souls locked away in Sheol, the calls of my brethren roared through my ears. We were connected, the four of us. Serenity fell over the area. Blue skies lit by the sun greeted me, and I squinted into the sudden brightness.

An oasis in the deserted lands of Eden was the evening's choice. The babbling of a brook and fresh air surrounded me. My heavy boots traveled the distance to where my family awaited. Time didn't exist here in Eden, for it no longer stood.

The humans had eventually confused it with another lost city, spending countless lifetimes and money to find the hidden gem. The birthplace of humanity occurred within its walls. The apple tree that undid the innocence of Eve still stood, but this scene was merely a painted vision.

Fauna spoke first. "The quakes are growing worse. I fear another sundering." Her lavender eyes revealed no emotion and neither did her tone. Wild, gray hair was spun and weaved into a bohemian, aka I do not bathe often, style. Fauna's tastes bordered along not quite eclectic, but as the Mother of Poison and Magic, her natural state didn't surprise me. For the meeting, she dressed to her version of the nine's, and that meant no clothing as usual.

I smirked, removed my jacket, and handed it to her. Fauna sneered and rolled her eyes. At least she didn't fondle herself... yet.

"The storms too," Hallowed echoed in the same indifferent tone. At least her clothing tastes were sensible, but deadly and malicious when it came down to protecting our world.

My family wasn't without the capability of emotion, but we had this conversation enough to realize the implications and concerns. I sat on a fallen log, and my hand waved through the air. "I thought the storms were Markos' doing."

Dressed in his usual leather garb, my brother shook his head. Silver knives, swords, and throwing stars hid beneath a long, black duster. We were a mirrored image, except for our eyes and hairstyle. Where I preferred messy, he was tidy.

He snorted and bore his crimson gaze into mine. "Brother, I live for more than destruction."

I returned his snort, mocking him, and a grin lit his features. Markos lived for the flesh; whether it bled, or screamed his name in pleasure, hadn't mattered. According to the rumors, his chosen mates were all willing, and he never forced himself on man or woman. The picture he thrust onto others was a rouse, like my skin.

Fauna asked, "Then what is it?"

"Father," Hallo said, lifting her head toward the sky. "He grows impatient with our progress, or lack of it."

"We could end it all." Night after night, we digressed into the same banter. I realized how naive we had been in thinking everyone would police themselves. That somehow the ABDA would rise up and overthrow Garland. But we didn't have the power either, yet few knew that truth. Because of it, I allowed others to fear my presence, the same for my siblings. We had one failsafe, but that meant annihilation of all, including ourselves.

"No," the three Horsemen shouted at me.

White light flashed before me as Hallo manifested. Heaven forbid she walked the two feet. "Have you not learned anything, Dorian?"

Silence fell as I bowed my head.

"Your insistence on self-punishment will ruin us all."

"This isn't about me."

Hallo shoved me, but I didn't budge.

"Sister, love comes easy—"Her cold stare cut my words, and heat flushed my cheeks. I whispered, "He made you beautiful, all of you... you don't understand."

"He made us all flawed, Brother. You are not the only one who suffers ridicule and hatred. We all suffer." Hallo's scarred flesh flashed before my eyes.

Fauna's puss filled boils and Markos' blackened skin followed. We each had built our own walls, but they were still beautiful to me.

Hallo poked my chest. "The south threatens us all. Our livelihood is in your hands, Dorian. We must take out Garland before he obtains more keys."

"How? We can police our own, the angels, warlocks, witches, and vampires, but not the blood demons or those who crawled from Hell's arse crack."

Markos stifled a snicker, but I was right. Vampires, witches, and warlocks were under our control, but not the Elioud, Nephilim, or demons from Hell. The mythos spoke of such a person, one who would hold dominion over all, but most stories weren't 100 percent true.

Fauna whispered, "They're not just stories." She sat beside me on the log.

I rolled my eyes and stretched. My feet crossed in front of Markos.

Mark slanted his head. "There is a rumor…"

"Rumors don't interest me." I shifted my weight and crossed my arms over my chest.

Unfettered, Hallowed repeated my movements. "No, you're a man of fact… so why is it an enigma sleeps in your bed?"

Heat flooded my cheeks and my gaze eyed their feet. How did they know anyone was in my bed?

"Did you fail to notice you're sleeping with the enemy? We sure didn't," Fauna said.

"Cain isn't—"I glanced to her.

Hallowed's blonde brow rose. "One of the seven? Keeper of the Keys? A Prince of Hell? Tell me when I'm getting warm, Brother, because I know you've questioned why and how he kicked your ass before."

Despite her being correct, I scoffed and stared at her booted feet. Even though the facts slammed into my face at every turn, I'd fought the reasoning. But Keeper of Keys? It was a fairytale. "Seven keys to unlock the Gates of Hell. Supposedly, Father had given them to seven fallen families at the dawning of time, not the Arch demons, but their offspring. When combined, the story says they will unleash the Morning Star, and the world ends, nothing more than a diluted fairytale, including the King of Babylon." The facts were all wrong, another man made myth. "Doubtful he could obtain all the keys, or Boric's key, for that matter. If they exist," I countered.

Because if by some stretch of the imagination those seven keys were real, they would have meant nothing without mine. What I'd vowed never to share was what the key unlocked, or that Father had given it to me, with anyone other than my family. Regardless of what they thought, Cain didn't know about it. Who said he knew anything about the other keys? He cared about finding his sister... Hell, he hadn't wanted me to take the case. The pain in his eyes... No, they were wrong. No way was Cain a Prince of Hell.

Markos blinked, striding to my side and towering over me. His hand fell upon my shoulder. "You sound sure, Brother."

"Does it matter?" Fauna stretched. "Cain is one of ours. Surely we know the truth."

"He's a warlock and Elioud, so no, but I do believe he requires a gentler hand," his gaze flickered to Hallowed, "isn't that right, Sister?"

My dream-self smiled, rose, and patted his chest. Silence encompassed us again, but I thought of the legends surrounding Revelation. The sigils and horns had ended. We had survived as Father had foretold.

I had the final key; I was the Gatekeeper of the world until Heaven fell to the Earth. Boric Garland would have to collect all seven keys, defeat me, and enter the realms of Sheol and Purgatory to unleash the Golem. Even if he succeeded, I still held cards up my sleeves. Just because I couldn't kill him didn't mean I couldn't destroy his empire.

"Boric still needs a good knocking," Fauna said, drawing my attention. "His slavery rings are tearing the world a part on another level. One none of us was ready for, even though he was doing this long before the Sundering. How is a question no one can answer."

Markos stepped away. "Michael wouldn't let us, remember? We tried to take him out before Asmodeus gained power but those seven bloody Archangels stood in our way."

"Six, Gabriel wasn't on Earth yet," I corrected. "I have my suspicions." Though no one wanted to hear, one of our own had to have been responsible.

Hallo broke into the conversation, her fists balled at her sides. "And where are they now? Hiding in the crevices and clouds? They can stop him, but they refuse." She released a long breath. "Will your hordes obey, Markos? Lend your aid to the ABDA and protect those who remain innocent."

He laughed and tossed his head backward. "Whores and demons aren't innocents."

My brow rose at Markos' insolence, but he seemed unfettered. The amount of imaginary lovers he kept fuddled his mind. "Mark, how can you pass judgment on those who are trying to survive? And those in the south? They have no choice."

He shrugged his shoulders. "Death is always a choice. They choose otherwise."

"But... the... children... How..." I couldn't release the thought into words. "No wonder Belletrist despises you."

Mark froze and cocked his head, as if understanding me for the first time. Belle, the woman he claimed to love, even if he never spoke the words, had refused to die at the hands of her owners. They'd beat her daily... I shook my head at him.

Fauna roared, "How dare you pass sentences." She coiled her fists and green smoke poured from the clenched palms. Her wild, gray hair whipped around her face, and lavender eyes bore into our brother. "Father will rain down his fury if we cannot take control of the keys and the demons."

Markos glared at her, his skin blackened in patches covering his face. "Don't threaten me with your magic show. What are you, a child? Throwing a bit of a tantrum? I'll show you power, little Sister."

A smile played at Hallo's lips as she stepped in between the two Horsemen and lifted her palms. "Enough." Leaning down, she whispered, "Dorian, your Prince awakens. Find me soon, and do not worry about them. The lighthouse. We will fix this."

I bowed as my mind darkened, and our connection broke. Hallo and I were the peacekeepers, and I awoke, chuckling at the thought.

The sun peeked through the curtains and warmed my face, but not as much as the arm and head nuzzled against my bare chest. Cain's fingers brushed through the dense hair. Saltiness from my arousal filled my nostrils. His touch bordered along magical, each shock registering in my brain.

Hot breath blew across my hardened nipple, replaced by his soft lips and wet tongue. A hoarse moan released from my lips, and Cain chuckled. His hand slid along the ridges of my abs, following the hairy trail, but I stopped him at my belly button, twining our fingers together. My dry lips brushed his furrowed brow.

I drew the covers back, slipping out from underneath him, and retreated to the adjoined bathroom. Tension thickened my mind. Desire tainted the air. From the doorway, he eyed me; tingles attacked my body, surging to my groin. But where my body said yes, my mind shouted no.

"There's a spare razor, soap, and other stuff." I pointed them out on the vanity sink before easing into the shower stall.

I slid the door closed, but Cain's hand blocked it. Our gazes locked; his eyes pled, but I didn't know for what.

"Hurry, I don't get lots of hot water."

A shy smile played at his lips and widened, his coppery gaze drifting south. Angels were sexual beings in general, but Cain affected me like no other, leaving me in a perpetual state of need. Need for only him. He slipped past me, pressing himself against me, and I shut the door, willing my cock to behave.

I paused for a moment, collecting my sanity. Soap scented the air, and I turned. Suds dribbled over his chest as mine constricted. White bubbles ran along his tight abs and gathered on Cain's erection. My lips smacked, at his peeking tip and the retreating foreskin. I stood there, imitating a scared rabbit, waiting for the predator to pounce.

Cain inched closer; our cock heads touched. Reminiscent of the alleyway, but roles reversed; he grasped our dicks together. "Come for me," he whispered, and brushed his mouth against mine. Cain knelt, beads of water catching in his short hair. "Come in my mouth."

I wanted to say no, to draw away. His caramel eyes enthralled me in a spell, and his thick lips slipped over my engorged head.

Was it all a cruel trick? His hand pumped along my shaft, twisting over the pulsing vein. Did he make me need only him? My thighs trembled, and my fingers grasped into his wet hair. As if he meant to suck me dry, his suction increased until the pressure burned into my curling toes.

"Slow down…" My hips bucked. "Cain…"

But I couldn't hold on, my cods aching, and my cock engorged. His speed increased, slurping and humming over my sensitive organ. My nails scratched at the tile. He pulled back, my tip resting on his tongue. I reached for him, but he slapped my hand and renewed his assault.

The break in pleasure wasn't long enough. My hips ground forward, my cock thrusting between his puffy lips. Cods tingled, drawing into me. I warned, "Babe, fuck me, I'm going to cum." Every muscled tensed. Euphoria washed away my sanity. "I can't—"

He didn't back away, but guzzled my seed. Cain released me, and I leaned against the chilly tile, panting and collecting my senses. Soft kisses showered my thighs before trailing along my torso. He paused, flicking his tongue over each nipple and nibbling from my collarbone to my neck.

"You're amazing, babe." And I meant it. No man had turned me on with nothing more than the sound of his voice or the flicker of his lashes, and I didn't want it to end, ever.

Cain smirked and stepped into the spray, rinsing the remaining soap from his body. I blinked; he slipped through the shower door without a word. What the fuck just happened? Quickly I finished washing under the chilly water—the solar power had only offered me a few minutes of lukewarm water.

I dressed in record speed, taking zero time to coordinate or fix the bed. Poking my head out from my bedroom door, I found him in the kitchen, sitting at the table. Cain had redressed in the borrowed clothes from last night. His fingers drummed along the tabletop. Like the temperature of the water, he had flopped from hot to cold by the time I joined him. A shell had built around Cain, and it remained through the morning.

The first time I had had a man stay over and my first breakfast with anyone other than Belle; I didn't have a rulebook telling me how to behave. No matter how hard I pressed on Cain's walls, he erected them higher. Had he sensed my connection last night? What of the shower? I hoped to break through before Belle arrived and started with her banter. "So…" My brows twisted, I faced away from him.

Cain slurped the bitter—sorry excuse for—coffee-like sludge in silence and nibbled his toast. Few conveniences existed after the Sundering, but Arcadia suffered less land loss and found a way to bounce back. Far from perfect, but no one starved. Demons and Angels were resilient creatures if not always intelligent. Cain's chair creaked, denim leg sliding against denim leg.

I opened my mouth, but closed it and spun around. Bile rose in my stomach. Belle strode on the snow-covered sidewalk. She chatted to herself and threw glances over her shoulder, dreads swaying. Two men hung behind, but they appeared engrossed in their own conversation and not her, probably on their way to the train station. The door downstairs jingled, and the men kept walking. Not even a glance was spared toward my home.

"Dorian, why the hell aren't you answering your phone?" High-heels clicked over the hardwood floors.

I rolled my eyes. When had I ever answered my phone this early in the morning? Besides, the battery needed a recharge after using it last night and it sat downstairs on my desk.

"You better not still be in bed. Don't think I won't drag your ass out and dump you in the snow."

Cain snickered. Aside from the lust in his eyes, it was the only other emotion he'd shown all morning.

I dragged Belle's usual chair—the only reason I had owned two—to his side. "You can trust her. If you'd rather tell her whatever you're hiding." My hand slid over his and squeezed.

She stomped up the stairs, still complaining, but I left my hand resting on his and caressed the smooth skin. What had happened between last night and this morning? Why do I even care? I gulped. "Belle's a demon, but one of the good ones."

"Good… morning, gentlemen." Amusement danced the polka in her smiling eyes. "Cain, right?" Belle extended her bangled hand, and he accepted her gesture. A warm smile tilted his lips as exchanges transpired. "Well, this is unexpected seeing as you ditched me yesterday." She clattered about the kitchen and made her own cup of sludge. "By the by, you owe me for your splurge. Any news on our case?"

I ignored her and leaned on my arm. A fork twirled in my hand. "Belle is what we call—"

The tone of his voice snapped. "Elioud. I know what she is." Cain leaned back in the chair and bore his caramel gaze into me.

My lifelong ability to read situations left me clueless to his problem.

Cain pointed his finger and his thick drawled southern accent peeked through. "I don't know what you are. Something I ain't never seen before, and here I thought I'd seen it all. Secrets work both ways. Ya know?"

Belle's amber-red gaze darted between us, and I gave a slight headshake. Why did everyone have to make such a big deal, as if I didn't already have more than enough on my plate? She pressed her rosy lips together and crossed her arms over her corset.

"What does it matter?" My eyes closed, and I pinched between them. Between the case of the missing, Cain's sister, and now Garland too, I had more than I could handle.

Downstairs, the phone rang, and I jumped from my seat, toward the staircase. James was supposed to call. Anything to get away and lose myself in a distraction, but Belle proved to be faster, shooting a grin over her shoulder. She stampeded downstairs and rattled the old house.

Once she was gone, I asked what was bothering him. "Babe, I can't read your mind, so you got to spit it out."

Belle shouted, "Did you just call him babe?" Laughter broke through the silence, and it sounded like she said, "Priceless."

Cain blushed, despite his stiffened jaw. I rested against the doorway and squinted at the sunlight bleeding in through the window above the sink. The sun rarely shined anymore. My gut twisted.

He shoved the chair back, sliding it across the floor, and he crossed his leg over his thigh. His innocence reflected within the small moment, and the truth tore through me. I could not lie or avoid what I was forever. Hallo was right. Compared to the demons and other angels, we were grotesque. Our beauty radiated soul deep, but it ended at the soul.

"I can't take it back, babe. Once you know..." The heaviness of the statement died in my mouth as I strolled toward the living room. My hands dampened, and I shoved them into my pockets. A thickness rose in my throat, and I turned around.

He shifted again, waiting for me to reveal what he truly didn't want to know. The part of myself I'd hated, loathed, and feared. Others had dreaded me; others who had professed love and then ran me through on their blades, hefted me onto crosses, and left me to die. Memories: I, too, had survived their torments, but not without injury. It had been because of those men that I wouldn't allow myself to change.

My shoulders rolled forward, and I summoned the courage, bravery only Hallo could have offered. More so, I surrendered to the awaiting agony of Death rising.

My tan flesh melted into hardened bone. A gasp released from Cain, but I didn't dare turn around. Anyone else and it would not have mattered, but his scorned words or looks I could not face. Wings sprang forth and crackled through the stilled air. His feet tapped against the hardwood floors, and I closed my eyes, fighting the searing agony burning in their corners.

Father hadn't created me handsome. No beauty lived in death. Merely bare bones and tattered feathers existed beyond the facade Father granted to me. The ability to blend among the humans had been part of my position. Torn clothing lay at my feet. A silver-gray robe slid over my naked bones, pooling in a shimmery mass at my feet, and the wide hood covered where my face once was.

"Falcate," I said, my raspy voice resonated off the walls, and I lifted my arms from my sides. Summoned into my hand was my black-jeweled scythe, appearing in a blink of light from the void of Sheol, swirling and floating by the fireplace. Echoing the hollow of my body, the tenor and pitch of my voice had changed into sinister madness. The bones of my feet clacked, like hooves over the wooden floor, and twisted toward Cain. "Am I beautiful now?"

Color drained from his pretty boy face. The loud thud quaked through the whole house. He fainted, slipping from the chair. Cain's response was better than I had expected.

Belle ran up the steps, into the room, and scowled. "You couldn't have just told the poor man?" A response refused to come. "Don't just stand there, dumbass. Help me." Her face clenched and reddened, as she attempted to heft him from the floor, but Cain was twice her weight and almost double her height. "Dorian."

Her fingers snapped at me, but I wasn't sure what she expected me to do. Cain hadn't run, but he couldn't have either. I wouldn't have wanted to see me when I awoke if I was he, nor did I wish to watch him run, throw stones, or tie a noose.

My head hung low, and I stared at the floor. One slice, a stab, and the urge to scream ripped through my empty ribcage. No heart resided in the void, yet it ached. Cain was no different. The others before him... what they had done. He would do the same. No one existed on this Earth capable of loving what could not be loved, and those who had loved Death loved only the idea of eternal darkness, not me.

"Damn it, Dorian Fox."

My gaze snapped to her before falling to Cain's swaying head, lolling against her shoulder. Holding him from behind, she dragged him upright.

Cain's mouth moved in a soundless gesture, and his lids blinked open. My heart stilled, but I kept my distance. Moments passed or perhaps minutes, no clock ticked to measure the time in which he glared at me with uneasy eyes.

Belle sat him in the chair. His white knuckles grasped the sides. In the strained silence, my weight shifted, and I leaned on the scythe, sighing soundlessly. One of three events would unfold. Cain would run, or he would choose to stay. The third option rattled my bones; he would stay, but despise me and secretly plot my demise. No one had ever stayed out of love, and he couldn't love me.

His caramel gaze darted between my weapon and my hood. The broken wings grew heavy from years of unused confinement, pushing my shoulders forward. My bones creaked and throbbed, shifting them again, but the decrepit reaction was typical for a man as old as time.

Her face unreadable, Belle offered nothing. She had seen me before, though. My chest stinging with each passing breath, I waited for someone to say something, anything to ease my ill heart. Cain tilted his head, and his eyes widened, speckled with more green and amber than the usual shimmery brown. Slowly, he sat up more, with the assistance of Belle, but I didn't dare move.

Why does his opinion matter? I never stopped to ask myself why I even cared what Cain Westcott thought of me. We hadn't known each other, not beyond the sexual exploits; a man the ABDA barred me from understanding. But his opinion did matter.

I need someone to love what I can't and to show me how to love it for myself.

My shaking hand released the scythe. He rose. Metal clanked against the floor. I stumbled backward as Cain approached me; his face yielded no readable emotion. We inched—him forward and I backward—and circled the room. He scooped my scythe from the ground and it scratched along the floor. My ass landed on the sofa, feathers cracking, and I gave up the sorriest excuse for a chase I'd ever seen.

"A reaper," he whispered, but I shook my head. Wrinkles lined his forehead as he glanced from the scythe to my garb covered bones. "What are you then?"

My boney hand stretched from the bell sleeve. "Better to show you."

He rubbed his neck and glanced over my shoulder at Belle before joining me on the sofa.

I mumbled, "I'm sorry."

"For what—"

Grasping his hand in mine, I cut off his question. Time rapidly unwound and reversed. The world flashed before us, as did the trillions of people who had called this planet home from its inception to their death or ascension. Words described what I saw of the world, even though Cain saw it through my eyes too. Together, Cain and I relived the birth and death of humanity and with their demise, the rise of the Angels and Demons that had followed.

"Father created and named me Death, and I am the fourth and final Horseman of the Apocalypse. Welcome to Sheol, the Land of the Dead. Each human ever born I have met in one form, or another. My original job revolved around marking humans for the levels of purgatory. Those I thought might seek redemption, by the second coming, I saw again as they died and ushered them to Purgatory."

The world continued blinking through various wars and technological advancements. I didn't show him what had become of me and showed him only what I had done for Father. In the dark spans of Sheol, Cain stood, clutching my bones, and his enlarged eyes soaked in the story of my life and the history of the world.

Gasps sounded from the humans. I'd sliced through their souls, collecting them before ushering them into Sheol. Vampires were unleashed into the world as the populations boomed, and the humans reproduced faster than I could keep up. Their marks upon the victim's necks allowed me to track the damned souls.

Witches and Warlocks joined the ranks; there were too many souls for Markos and Fauna to tempt. Finally, Father imbued Hallowed with portaling, allowing her to move quickly through vast spaces. Eventually, he would give my siblings the same gift. I didn't show Cain Father's last gift to me, for it was the key.

"But... how?" asked Cain. "You're not a vampire."

I replied, "God is my Father." All roads and answers led back to our father. The grand end of humanity and his rewarding plan all belonged to him.

I closed my eyes, not wanting to re-witness the destruction and death of my hands. No tears could fall, but a burn ripped through my nose and eye sockets.

Cain tugged my robe. "No more, please, Dorian."

I glanced at him. With his beautiful face buried into my sleeve, I fast-forwarded to the day Revelation began. "Babe," I whispered. "We're here, and you need to understand."

Before us stood a pale horse, tinted the color green. "I, Death, rode the foul, heaven-sent beast and followed behind the others. Sword, famine, plagues, and by the wild creatures of the Earth, Father gave us reign to watch over his world."

The herald angel said, "Come and see!"

Our horses barreled through the streets of every country, and we strode in a clean line. "War is Markos, and Famine—Pestilence is Fauna. Together they tested the people's faith. Conquest is Hallowed, and she marked those who had deserved Father's love and would ascend to the heavens. I slaughtered and condemned those deemed unworthy that day. I murdered. It was my job, but the burden of spilled blood is mine to bear. We are family and a team, and Father gave us the Earth for our service until the final battle is wrought and Heaven comes to Earth."

My insides boiled and churned. Murder was the wrong word. Men and women had tossed themselves at my feet, and they had begged for my forgiveness, for my redemption instead of Father's love and forgiveness. I held no contempt for their fetid ways, but marked them with the beast. Bound and branded, I cast them from my sight, or drew blood.

In a trembling voice, Cain asked, "Where did you cast them?"

"The redeemable arrived here." I sighed. The vision froze, and I pointed to the swirling black mass behind me on the image. The same portal floated in my living room. Always, Sheol was there. Both my horse and scythe, all I had to do was summon it from the ethers. "Those who were not... I cast into Hell."

Cain stared at the floor.

"I am but God's messenger and personal assassin. They chose their paths." My scythe was aimed at the humans groveling at my feet in the image. "Look." The nature of my position hardened me, but I left that part out. Those final days weighed on me after living millennia of lifetimes among his creations. I glanced to Cain, wanting to prove myself wrong. The thought of loving him brought a light and warmth I had never known except in Father's presence.

"God didn't intervene?"

"It was his design." I shook my head. "The children, as commanded, along with the weak and feeble of mind I spared."

Buying my lie, Cain nodded and chewed on his lip. He turned and stared at me; his light-filled gaze bore into the darkness of my hood.

"Even if God had commanded it, children are innocent. I could not have harmed a child or anyone pure of heart."

"You would defy him?" he asked. Amazement painted his soft tone, but I didn't see his face.

"Yes." Like him, his heart and soul were pure, but I wasn't completely honest. Sheol held levels of purgatory; although, the name made it seem Hellish; the un-tortured, innocent souls saw and felt eternal happiness. I couldn't let them suffer. Cain squeezed my hand, and I returned his gesture, stroking my boney fingers over his warm skin.

"I am damned to this Earth until the very end. Cain, I cannot die unless the world dies." I pointed toward the Heavens. "He deemed it so and so it is."

Nervous laughter pursed his lips. "You've met God?" he whispered. "Why did he do this?"

I had met God—Father. Cain was the first to ask why he would destroy his own world. My finger stroked his cheek, and he didn't shy away. "I wish I had the answer, babe. It wasn't my place to question his decision or motives."

"Can I see you in the light again?" He glanced away and lowered his voice. "I'll try not to faint this time."

The vision brightened, but fading and leaving us standing in the middle of Times Square. The famous city of New York that Father had laid to rest at the bottom of the Atlantic Ocean. I spread my arms out and gestured.

Cain shook his head. "No, I want to see all of you."

Emotions rolled and warred through me. A lump formed in my throat, even though I didn't have one. "Babe," I whispered, unable to say no.

He reached into the dark spans of the hood and cupped my boney cheek. I cried, although tears didn't fall at his tender gesture. When was the last time I had shed a tear? His thumb caressed the bone, where those tears would have fallen. No sounds emitted, save his steady breath and the ruffle of my robes. I tugged the hood aside, exposing the skull.

Cain said, "Yes."

"Yes?" I cocked my head.

A wide smile spread across his face and wrinkled his butterscotch eyes. "You're still gorgeous, sweets."

I changed the subject. "You asked if I was a reaper."

He nodded, but his brow furrowed.

"I am the Angel of Death, or as I prefer, Dorian." Father hadn't given me the name, but I adopted it instead of Death. Imagine introducing oneself as Death, the mere thought amused me, but I had done so many times before choosing the name. "The others are Archangels created by Father, but as the oldest I became sort of a leader for the Horsemen, as Michael is leader to the rest."

"You said are." He eyed the image of my comrades.

"They're alive, and we are, as you would say, family." I waved my hand over the frozen image, and the scenes flashed again.

Cain would meet the other Horsemen soon enough, they would hunt for Lily too. Often I had called them in to right the wrongs, and all, save for Fauna, lived nearby in Halifax. Fauna preferred the wilderness of the far north, where her school in Meat Cove, Nova Scotia was located.

"So where were we? Oh yes, the souls had been marked. The children, weak, and feeble minded spared regardless of belief. Their souls would ascend. We retreated and spread our cause for the Lord Almighty. In his name, we warned the people, demons, Angels, you know those remaining on Earth. To the humans, we gave last chances for redemption, even if we felt they hadn't deserved one."

Again, Cain interrupted, "The day came when the Earth sundered and humanity ceased."

"Continents and countries destroyed, torn asunder into the angry oceans. From volcanoes, red lava spewed and scarred the remnants as quakes rocked through the ground. Mountains leveled, swallowed in cindered ash or ocean waves. The death toll on humanity rose with each passing day until only one quarter of the world had remained. Lingering humans ascended, died, or arrived in Hell, but those who bore the mark arrived in my domain.

"Humans lived their lives and thought themselves alone. You and I know the truth. Angels, demons, and much more walked and died on this Earth," he said.

"Half-breeds, vampires, witches, and warlocks… Father had decreed us to neither punish nor mark the tainted creatures. Only Arch demons and humans entered purgatory. The others arrived at Tartarus. All are within my domain—Sheol." I shook the thought from my mind, as it was where Cain would go when he died. "Our reward was life, life if we controlled the world, and fought the demon hordes. So far, we have continued to fail, and the demons grow stronger.

"Legions poured from the fiery depths. We were not strong enough. The Arch demons rose; the Watchers' kin extracted revenge—the Grigori. They lashed out the one way they could. Death, famine, and enslavement of all survivors, and we proved powerless to impede them. Not to say enslaving the Elioud was all right, but they stole our witches, warlocks." If they managed to trap Markos' legions, or obtain my key, the world would fall into chaos. I let go of Cain's hand; the loss of his warmth left chills in my bones.

We arrived at my living room. Belle's red eyes registered and my focus returned. She handed me my scythe and backed away. Concern laced her usually hardened features. Cain reassured her with another dimple-laden smile, but his gaze stayed on me.

Slowly, I reversed the change, and my disguise reappeared.

"Does it hurt?" he asked.

"No, babe."

Cain leaned over and kissed my cheek.

I grasped his chin and sucked his bottom lip, testing his words. Belle cleared her throat, and I whispered, "Thanks."

"For what?"

Understanding, believing, and accepting the monster behind the curtain, but none of those seemed proper. Instead, I winked and disappeared into my room to shower and change. The scent of decay and death permeated from my skin. Too bad he didn't join me.

Chapter Six

Cain

Dorian slipped into the shower, and I paced the length of his living room, telling myself I should walk out the door and never look back. The thought of leaving pained my heart; it squeezed and pumped harder and faster. I fell for him. My palm dragged over my rough face, and I shook my head.

No, I had fallen for Death.

Harder than ever before, I plummeted until up became down and down spiraled sideways. Swept into the churning sea, my fragile heart rested in the hands of God's deadliest assassin.

Death, I scoffed, wishing for a drink to steady my trembling hands. Last night… this morning… a mistake I couldn't take back. Dorian wasn't ready; he didn't need me complicating his life. I wasn't prepared, either, not for a man worth living for.

I plopped on the sofa; Belle's voice traveled up the stairwell. She chatted on the phone downstairs. My head fell into my hands, and I stared at the stone hearth, bathed in the odd rays of sunlight streaming in from the window. Particles danced in the yellowed streaks.

The man I loved had killed humanity. A sound caught in my throat, and my back straightened. "I love you," I whispered.

How or why were beside the point; without knowing much

about the man, I had tumbled into oblivion, clutching onto the coattails of his tattered robe. Breath sucked in, and I rubbed my heart. Our pain connected us, but our similarities didn't end there. Eyes echoed the soul.

Fighting wasn't my style and neither was violence. Dorian seemed equally passive, despite his job working for the ABDA and being Death.

I dragged a palm over my face again, cringing at the five o'clock shadow creeping over my skin. Warmth etched into his smiles, the shyness hidden beneath his rough exterior both spoke volumes of the man he was, not the monster he had become on that day.

Witches and warlocks were not submissive by any means, but we tended to err against aggression. Dorian had lived and breathed from the beginning of time. He saw everything, yet the horrors didn't reflect as bitterness. No, the empty sockets of Death's eyes echoed pain; as if he felt every tortured soul, he had taken.

I couldn't judge him. The secrets I held weighed on my shoulders, drawing them down. "I'm not any different."

We'd witnessed different horrors after being sold, and none of Dorian's memories replayed mine, teetering on the edge of madness. Grim and distorted faces must surely haunt him, as my masters' faces plagued me. My legs crossed and uncrossed, bouncing with nervous energy. Trembling fingers dug into the rough fabric covering the couch. Such simplicity for a man who had lived for so long, another common factor we shared, though he was older.

What am I thinking? No, I couldn't sit there another moment, wasting and drowning in my own reverie. Stay, go, stay, or go… my mind ran out of reasoning.

My eyes closed, I saw him, but opened, I spotted representations of him around me. The greenery at the farm—where I worked—had reminded me of Dorian's eyes. Olives reminded me of his skin. Black, charred mulch represented his hair. I sighed. Before he preoccupied my world. Within his home, it wasn't any different. Black wainscoting graced pale, lime-textured walls and offset walnut floors.

Dorian hummed in the shower; I leaned on the bedroom doorframe and contemplated entering the room we'd shared last night. His scented soap infiltrated my nose.

Last night, in his thoughts, he'd said no one else had ever entered, but that line was overused. I wasn't the type for cheesy pick-ups. No, I bled for my lovers, the kind who spent seven months of their life searching Halifax for the sexy man he'd caught blowing his boyfriend, not to harm him, but to see him again. I had questioned bar owners and patrons three cities over. But he hadn't visited the usual places. The club and bar scene had all but died with the Sundering, but there were places people, like us, gathered. I'd checked them all. After two months, I had given up the search and spiraled into a deep depression.

Belle crept up the staircase, jingling; boards creaked beneath her clicking feet.

My life had suffered without his presence. Because of the depression, I had lost everything, and my cousin Tomas had saved me again by paying my rent and bringing me food. Tomas had found me a new job at the farms too. Finally, I had my life together again and focused on my sisters, and then bam, there was Dorian.

But I couldn't focus on an already doomed relationship *and* fulfilling the promises to Mother. A sigh escaped, and I stared at my shaky hands.

Behind me, Belle shifted in the kitchen, running water. Metal rattled and a click, click, click followed. I read her mind, not truly knowing her, despite our distant relation. It was blank. Did Dorian know she was a Morning Star? I glanced over my shoulder, and her dreads swayed, head shaking.

A kettle boiled, screaming through the gentle thrum of running water. "For the same reasons you've never told him," she said, removing the kettle from the stove.

I scratched my head. Why had Dorian cooked over the hearth?

"He doesn't have to eat and never learned how to use a stove." She winked and smiled.

Without another word, she withdrew a chair and sat at the table. With magic, Belle levitated a book and held a mug in her hands.

Can I fit into this little world?

"You could," she said.

I shrugged my shoulders. "Doubtful."

"He cares for you." Belle sipped her tea and returned to her book. My brow lifted. "Does he?"

"You messed him up real good." With the flick of her finger, she turned a page.

I smirked and glanced toward his bathroom door. "How bad were his injuries?"

"Oh, couple of cracked ribs, but I wasn't talking about physical pain. Cain, I've known Dorian for over ten years, and he's never been like this before."

Dorian's room beckoned me. I held my chin higher. My feet froze in place, and my heart beat faster.

"Go on," Belle said. "He won't hurt you."

I swallowed hard and almost said, "Promise?" but didn't. *What is wrong with me?* The door was only a foot away, yet it might as well have been miles. "Here goes nothing." I forced one foot in front of another.

Darkness bathed the room; I lit the bedside lamp with a match from his nightstand. Too busy to see any of the room last night, my eyes didn't know where to begin. Paintings and photographs lined the walls and in the middle sat a massive bed without a frame or headboard. The furniture had sleek, traditional flair, and not the industrial crap they sold in shops.

I chewed my lip, expecting more, though I wasn't certain why.

Simplistic but heartfelt, his charming décor framed the walls. The ache in his gaze matched his soul, and it struck a chord within me. Who had harmed him?

Large smiles graced their faces. My brow lifted and I eyed the photos closer. The people in the photographs resembled Dorian. "The other Horsemen uncloaked," I whispered, grinning. "Big softie." I studied it more. Hallowed had draped her arm around Dorian. Long, blonde hair framed her angelic face, but the clothing, dated and bohemian, had almost thrown me off. The same-whitewashed glow she'd held in person was also missing. In the picture, her white hood blocked her face.

Messenger of God my ass. But her guidance was unimportant. How could she have known about Dorian and me? I refused the negative thoughts. Already my head was crammed with more than enough. A grin flashed at the mere revelation. Mind over matter.

I plopped on the bed and sunk into the softness of his side. The covers smelled of him, and I breathed in Dorian's earthy fragrance. Can we do this? *Play house and live, as if the world hasn't gone to shit?*

I leaned back on his pillow as the shower turned off. Dorian cracked open the bathroom door before slipping into the bedroom. He didn't see me.

"Hey," he said, spinning around and resting a hand on his chest. Nothing but a towel graced his olive, taught skin. Beads of water reflected the dim light and danced before my eyes.

An urge to touch him overtook my senses, and I rose from the bed. Glowing, his green gaze scanned the length of my body and left goose bumps in its wake. But as my lips skimmed his broad shoulders and eased toward his neck, Dorian tensed. He gulped and faced the dresser.

Despite his thoughts, Death is beautiful. The perfume and tang of soap washed over me. My lips explored each dip and curve of his back, and my shaking palms brushed Dorian's waist and the thick hair covering his love trail.

"Trying to kill me, Cain?" Dorian shuddered.

"Thought you were immortal?" Kissing my way up his neck, my chuckle grazed his ear, and he shuddered again. "Learning what makes you tick." I caught our reflection in the dresser mirror and grinned. We made a handsome couple, but even love wouldn't be enough to save us.

Dorian wanted to sweep in and save the day. His ever-searching gaze never ceased to unravel the pain hidden inside of me. His thoughts announced when he'd found it.

No man could save me, though, or erase the brutal years slavery had etched into my soul, but if ever such a man existed, I wanted him to be Dorian. Maybe that was why I gripped onto the idea of him and refused to leave. A sigh caught in my throat, choked behind burning eyes. My smile retreated and negativity warred. I was broken, and he had built iron walls around his heart. Besides, Dorian would end me, when he learned the truth, and I prayed we found my sisters first. No one loved damaged goods, especially those that could not be fixed, those others thought worthy of the punishment because of their blood.

How many times had my master told me as much? "You deserved it, Morning Star, and you loved it." Even in the safety of Dorian's home, I heard their whispers.

Dorian's thoughts shouted, drowning out the voices. His mind wandered between the job and me. "Cain makes me tick, but I fear for his safety." Love didn't cross his mind once. The sight, scent, or thought of me drove him to continuously question his rules, though. He released a groan; he turned and rested his damp head against my chest.

I asked, "What's the matter?" and wrapped my arm around him, hugging his heat to me.

Dorian shook his head, beads of water sprinkled my face, and he folded his fingers over mine. He pushed my free hand over the towel, shielding his cock and heavy, hairy balls. Was he always hard? He rumbled, and the noise vibrated my body pressing against him.

Guess that made two of us. Secrets tickled over my tongue. I pulled back and retreated to the bed.

An iron, skeleton-type key swayed in the air, hanging from his thick neck. Had he worn that before? No, I couldn't think about the keys, but how could it have magically appeared? I stroked my chin, considering the magic Death had showed me. Maybe a spell hid it from me before. *Why do I see it now?* I hadn't thought about the keys in years. The mere idea should have excited me instead of sending my sex drive retreating into the shadows.

Resting on my belly, my head on his pillow, I spied on him. Dresser draws opened and closed as he bent over and retrieved clothing. Garments in hand and a torn expression wrinkled his brows in the mirror, but his glorious mind circled. Dorian couldn't decide if he wanted to make out, or if he should get dressed.

For him, I was a distraction.

The towel released from his waist, and my cock ached at the sight of his muscular ass flexing. What I wouldn't give to run my tongue over the surface, to feel him squirm, and have Dorian beg for more. Could Death beg? Asking him to love me, to want me, was wrong if I could not please him fully, though. How could I make him happy if his happiness depended on mine? I ran a palm over my face and blew out a breath.

He spun at the sound. "I should ask you what's wrong, but you'll say nothing, right?"

Before I could answer, Dorian rolled me over, pinned my arms down at my sides, and his mouth covered mine. I froze, reminding myself and chanting: *this is Dorian*. My heart swelled into my throat, constricting, and I swallowed hard.

"I'm not going to hurt you."

"I… I know."

He leaned up on his arms before lowering himself again to brush his lips against mine. Sweet at first, the pressure of his mouth grew demanding. Dorian opened and slid his tongue along the seam of my lips. My hands tore and tugged through his wet locks, spastic thoughts ransacked his mind, and they all revolved around pleasuring me. I had to halt Dorian before either of us fell to deep. Us… we would not work, and he deserved better than the likes of me.

"Stop," I mumbled against his mouth, and he halted. Green eyes blinked down at me. I said, "We need to talk."

Beneath his beard, his lips twitched, and I resisted running my thumb over their swell.

"Please."

"Talk," he muttered.

I nodded, and he groaned glancing between us at his bobbing member. My tongue ran over my lips at the beads glistening over his swollen tip.

"Now?" Dorian shook his head and chuckled, but there was no amusement reflecting in his burning stare. "Fine, talk then. I'm all ears, Cain."

"I trust you."

Dorian scoffed. "Sure have a funny way of showing me."

Right, guess I'd been the initiating party that time. Wait, no, he had pinned me down. It didn't matter. I couldn't follow through. He'd taken my control away, and the surreal moment had encompassed my entire being. No second-guessing or thinking had occurred yesterday. He couldn't expect my release or blame himself when orgasms didn't occur. My body and mind didn't work that way.

Part of me still prayed that Hallo's insights came true and my curse would end, but love wasn't in the cards for me. He wasn't the death I'd prayed for. After seeing Dorian, I'd allowed the fantasy to become a half-shoddy reality, but one ending in tears.

"Maybe this is a sign, and he's more trouble than I'd anticipated."

I agreed with his thoughts and was becoming more trouble than I was worth. Westcott: we were worthless scum. Tears spilled over my cheeks and his face softened. The iron key around his neck reflected light, swaying. Power vibrated from its core. My fingers itched to grasp its shiny surface. The vision was over, and the time had come to reveal truth.

"I can trust you, now." Yet the other words refused to come. Satan's spawn, thief, former whore, Boric wanted me back… and the last, and the most important of them all… I was the Keeper of Keys. Only Angelica knew I had them, for she had given them to me. Even Hallowed had recognized me.

Each of us Morningstars had different powers, courtesy of our Elioud-witch mother. Angelica felt emotion from objects and controlled storms, Lilith's powers were unknown, but I held the ability to summon fire and create windows, crevices in space that enabled me to hide items. The energy required to summon one drained me, sometimes for days.

Dorian blinked unsure what to do with my tears. Twice, I had broken down on him. Three, if I counted vomiting. I turned my head away, allowing them to run onto his pillow. How many lovers had cried over its surface? Such a stupid thought to have and not an answer I wanted to know. Another notch for him… that was all I could ever become.

Dorian nudged me. "Hey, babe, c'mon."

I sniffled. "Don't call me that."

"Why do I call him that?" he thought. "Do you prefer sweetie or handsome?"

I peeked at a grinning Dorian, but could not muster a smile. "Did I move too fast?"

My head shook, untrusting of my voice. Any speed was too fast; he had to let me go. He leaned in, and I turned away again.

Dorian whispered, "I can't read your mind."

Warm hands stroked my tearstains and over the roughness of my face. Melting into his tenderness wasn't an option, but neither was leaving.

"You say you trust me, but then you shut down. Which is it, Cain? Because *you* can trust me."

Chapter Seven

Dorian

The bed groaned, springs shifting beneath me. Cain's puffy gaze met mine, and he forged a smile. I wanted to wash his pain away and hunt whoever caused it. The lies, whatever they might have been, didn't matter in that moment. There had to be a way to open him up.

My fingers stroked his brow and the tips tingled. Every touch, every kiss shocked inside of me until I craved the sensation rippling through my body; no one had made me feel that way before him. How many times had I thought myself in love, yet these struggles never appeared.

Cain turned his head more, staring intently at me with his innocent, hazel eyes. My breath caught, welling in my chest. Sweet lips parted, revealing his white, straight teeth. His tongue swirled against the surface. My shoulders rolled, tired from holding myself above him. Each inch strained them further, muscles frozen, and one in particular throbbed.

"I lied to you," he whispered, and my brow rose.

As a detective of sorts, I figured he'd withheld information, but couldn't figure out what. James searched for me, but if Cain came clean, my job would be easier. I shifted onto my side, still next to him on the bed. "Go on."

"They enslaved Lily centuries ago, not months." Cain didn't look at me and his fingers fidgeted.

I scratched my head and processed his words, pretending confusion. Guess I had nailed that one by the timeline of events.

"They bought us both actually, but I escaped, then they moved her from Garland to Delphia." His fingers twitched and drummed over his thigh. "You were honest with me, so I figured it was time to come clean."

His eyes glistened with unshed tears, but my jaw popped. The weight of his words clicked. Cain was a former slave. His behavior made sense, from his sudden timid nature in the bedroom to his seduction.

"I didn't know if I could trust you. Tomas said—"

My brow rose higher. "The Duc?"

Cain nodded.

I chuckled. "Did he send the vampires after your sister?" Laughter spilled from my mouth, and I grasped my sides. How that flamboyant vampire had ever survived the Sundering baffled me. We were friends, but still, Tomas held the best of intentions; the man trusted too many shady people. My hand fell over my mouth, and I shook my head.

"He had Lily, but Garland stole her back. They stormed his home, and then they went after his friend, Petre. That's the last anyone heard." His arms spread wide. "They had airships. I saw the massive engines and plumes of smoke."

Nodding, I smiled. "Wait, what? Garland has airships over the border?" I hopped from the bed and ran downstairs. Belle gasped at my nude state, but I waved her off, snatching the notebook from my desk. After retrieving the notes, I hurried up the stairs. "Shite."

Cain sat up. "What is it?"

"I forgot my pen."

As he rummaged through the nightstand drawer, I blushed. Bottles of lube appeared, and the color and heat deepened. A bottle of scented oil emerged next.

He lifted his eyebrow. "No pen, but I can give you a massage," he joked.

"Fucking hell." I ran down the steps again

Belle yelled, "Warn me to shield my virgin eyes."

"If you're a bloody virgin Mary, than I'm the fucking pope of Rome."

Cain's laughter roared through the upstairs. By the time I returned, my skin burned into the hue of a bruised tomato, but my cock still managed to bob hard against my stomach. I paused in the doorway and caught my breath.

He was flipping through my skin magazines. Not new by any means, but leftovers I had collected over the years. Lounging on his side and appearing more innocent than an angel, nonchalantly his hand stroked the outline of his cock, and his arousal wet my lips. Sex should have been the last thought on my mind or his.

I willed the sight to fade and my cock to, for just once, behave, but it twitched in response and released a dribble of precum. The primal aroma of his seed thickened the air, and I tasted his equal need on my tongue. My chest tightened at the image inside of my mind, and my breath grew ragged. Reopening my eyes, I said, "Let me give you a hand," and blinked at my husky tone.

Cain drew down his zipper and eased the denim from his slim hips. Slowly, his shirt flirted over rock hard abs, and he tucked the fabric behind his head. "This what you want, sweets?"

Yes, but I wanted his truth too. My mind flittered between the airships and Cain to Boric and then back to Cain. Everything arrived at Cain until I thought of nothing else. I licked my dry lips as he stroked his head and drew back his foreskin. *No.* Images spun in my head and a strange sensation washed over me, not a drug, but an un-relievable ache. With boiling desire, my cods burned

Inviting me, he lifted his heavy sack and exposed his tight bud. Cain flipped onto his belly and thrust his ass into the air. Fluid leaked from my cockhead, my dick jumping, and I almost came on the spot. His ass wiggled. I pinched myself, but the vision remained.

He is my cure.

My legs stepped forward on their own accord. Kneeling on the bed behind him, I grasped his perfectly formed cheeks. "You want this, babe?"

"Yes," he hissed. "I need you."

My mouth kissed each cheek, and Cain issued a deep, throaty moan.

"Tease." I slapped his ass and rubbed the surface, careful not to hit too hard. His white cheek turned a pretty pink, and I afforded the left the same attention.

Cain whispered, "Again."

"Move for a minute."

Cain rolled upright to his knees and ground his butt against me. My arms wrapped around his chest, and I pinched his hard nipples while humping his crack. "Suck me while I rim you?"

Cain nodded.

I trailed tender kisses along his shoulder, weaving a path along his neck and tasting his fiery flavor. "Top or bottom?"

"Top." He tossed his head back and exposed his neck to me.

I released him, reached around him, and grasped some pillows to pile onto the bed. With a groan, I plopped down, wiggling the whole bed, before rolling over.

"You sure about this?" He rubbed his hands over my hairy chest, playing in the curls.

I leaned up on my elbows and captured his bottom lip in my mouth, suckling it gently. "With you, I'm sure," I gruffed, positioning back against the pillows.

Cain shrugged, turned, and swung his legs over my chest, his thighs landing on either side of my head, and his cock spread his arousal between my pecks. A moan slipped from his lips, blowing heated breath over my crotch, and my stomach fluttered.

Reaching up, I grasped his cheeks and spread them before guiding his puckered hole toward my face. Warm lips circled my cock, and I groaned into his left cheek, biting the tender flesh. "Babe," I whispered, and ran my tongue along his hole.

His wet tongue teased me, flickering over my length. My head swam as the sensation built within my stomach.

Cain squirmed, and his cry vibrated over my cock, tightening my cods.

"Fuck." I forced my mind elsewhere, before I blew too soon, and plunged my tongue into his hole again; he swallowed me.

We built a rhythm, rocking and bucking. I slid a finger into his ass, working and stretching him.

"Dorian." He slammed his fist onto the bed. Molten seed exploded over my chest as his toes curled. "Oh shit."

But we both remained hard as a rock, and I was hornier than I had ever recalled.

He inserted a wet finger into my ass, and with a long sigh, I spread my legs. Another joined the first and my hips bucked in rhythm as Cain finger-fucked me and sucked my cock. Shutting my eyes, I imagined his cock buried into my ass as he stroked me to an oblivious orgasm. His touch emptied me and filled me. The mere thought tensed my cods, and a wave of pleasure slammed through my body, my ass muscles gripping his fingers.

"Knees. Now," Cain ordered.

I obeyed and flipped over onto my hands and knees.

"You want me?" He shoved pillows under me and pressed my shoulders down. "Stay just like that, sweets." His hand ran over my chest and collected his spent sperm. Cain rubbed his cum over my hole, heat searing me, and teased the opening with his slippery cockhead. "You want my cock in your ass?"

"Yes," I cried.

Cain slapped my cheeks, as I had done to him. Surges swept through my body while he smacked me and tugged my rigid, swollen cock. He thrust his fingers into me, manipulating my prostrate.

"Oh, fuck." As if a ledge had appeared out of nowhere, I stepped forth and was gone. Lights flared behind my closed lids. My body tensed before my orgasm poured from my tip. I fluttered my lashes. My eyes rolled into the back of my head, and my limbs crumbled under the pleasure. "Fuck," I screamed, my hands fisting the sheets, and silently prayed Belle didn't investigate.

Cain removed his fingers and pressed his fat tip at my entrance. A groan roared through him as he slid inside, stretching my walls in a slow, sensual glide. Familiar ache creeped into my stomach once more.

"C'mere." He yanked me up until my back lay flush against his sweaty chest.

Those perfect teeth nibbled my ear, twisting and reigniting my desire to new heights, and my cock rose. "Yes, right there."

"Damn it, sweets." He grasped my cock.

Shivering from his touch, I chuckled. "Angels…have insatiable…sex drives." But it was Cain. No man had ever excited me, captivated me, or muddled my mind until nothing else mattered.

"So do demons." Cain's hips rocked in a steady rhythm, filling and emptying me.

I met his thrusts, slamming my ass against him. My head leaned back on his shoulder and he stroked me harder and faster.

"Fuck," I said, clenching my teeth and my rim around his cock. "Cain…"

"Come all over my cock. Come for me, Dorian," he whispered.

And his words shoved me over the edge into another orgasm. Every nerve ending fired, as if he'd stroked me inside and out with a thousand feathers. Cain had drained me, stolen my energy and seed. He leaned back, and I rested on his lap. From behind, he held me against him and kissed me down.

He had only the one. Puzzle pieces shifted slightly. I added up the last twenty-four hours. Shite, why hadn't I figured his problem out sooner? It made sense. Cain wasn't like me.

"It's okay," he whispered. "Lay on your back—" I did as asked "—lift up." He piled two pillows beneath my ass. "I want to try this my way." He eased in and filled me with his cock, all the while maintaining a soft, tender tone. "Wrap your legs around my waist."

Emotion shone in his bronze gaze and warmed my heart, but I didn't know the name of the feeling. Cain thrust slowly and grasped my neck, pulling my face closer. His lips engulfed mine, and he slid his tongue into my mouth, exploring me, as his body trembled in time with mine.

I didn't want him to stop, for us to end. I held his face, my thumbs stroking his rough cheek, fingers grasping his short hair.

His kiss turned from sensual to ravenous, and the speed and pressure of his hips increased. Cain tore away. I stilled, as his cock rammed into me. I was there, an orifice, a bystander witnessing the fight he had with himself. His eyes were wide, glassy. He pressed his lips into a fine line. Determination perspired in a ruddy flush over his pale skin.

No, this was more than a little difference. He had a problem, and I wasn't certain I could easily cure him. But I wanted to.

"Fuck." He threw his head backward. His cock swelled, stretching my sore ass, and his orgasm tore through his body, pouring into me.

I smiled wide at his face contorting with gratification, his victory. Never before had I witnessed such a beautiful release... such a beautiful man...Cain panted and grimaced out of pleasure.

"Fuck you," he joked, and cupped my cheek. Drunk on his release, Cain wobbled, but I caught him before he tumbled over the edge of the bed. "Oh shit."

I chuckled, pulling him back. "C'mon babe, let's get cleaned up."

"I'm sorry." He sighed and shook his head. "I didn't—"

"Why are you apologizing?"

"I distracted you again," he whispered. "I..." His fingers trailed a path over my chest. "I did it on purpose." They moseyed closer to the key, but halted. "I didn't... wasn't ready."

My fingers curled over his, and I rested them over my pounding heart. "First, you're not a distraction, and even if you were, you'd be a welcome one, babe."

"And the second?"

"Fuck it." Some say to never mix business with pleasure, but Cain and I were shit out of luck on that particular notion. "You needed that. And I like that you want me on purpose." I winked.

I couldn't think and doubted he could either, unless we released our attraction and desire. A sticky and bumpy road lay ahead of us, but if Father willed us to succeed, maybe there was a future for us both.

After we had cuddled, cleaned, and kissed for a while, we stumbled downstairs. Belle tapped her foot and stared at her watch.

"What?" I said.

"ABDA's been calling you for hours. James is having a fucking meltdown." She slapped a stack of messages in my hand.

I blushed. Cain flashed a sheepish smile, but I grasped his hand and twined us together.

"Tomas is headed back and will see you when he arrives." She flipped another paper into my already full hand. "ABDA faxed over a sheet of known informants. They think one of them is leaking information."

A frown tugged my lips. Where did the information come from? "Bullshite. None of mine would cross me."

She threw her hands in the air and they fell with a plop. "That's what I told them, but James yacked on about orders until I hung up on him."

I laughed. "Good job standing up for yourself."

Cain's brow wrinkled with confusion, and he stroked his clean-shaven chin. "You're both agents?"

"I'm a junior agent," Belle said, flashing her badge hanging from her neck. "I thought Tomas told you."

Cain shrugged. "Didn't know they did juniors."

I released him, strolled into my office, dropped the messages on my desk, opened my drawer, and retrieved my badge before returning to his side. "Special Agent Dorian Fox."

Cain smirked and handed my credentials back. "I didn't know Belle was an agent."

"How'd you know Tomas again?" I slid them into my pocket. "Wanted to ask you, babe, about Tomas before..." My cheeks heated.

He crossed his arms. Dark brows rose and dropped. "He's my cousin, remember?"

"Cousin," I repeated, glancing between the bleached-blonde and him, but I didn't recall him sharing the information before. Belle's cousin...Why hadn't she told me they were cousins? And what of Tomas—once a Duc of some speck of an estate in some corner of southern France, but more mystery than fiction remained when it came to his valiant tales. For starters, he was an Elioud-warlock before becoming a vampire. Second, his connections seemed limitless, but only on the surface. "You never told me he was your cousin," I countered. "Fuck me." But what bit my ass was the Horsemen were right. "I've known him for a few centuries. He works as an ABDA informant." I didn't trust the vampire aside from the fact that he fell under my command. "He runs with another vampire. Petre von Baron." He remained an enigma of sorts because he had transformed due to a curse. A secret to those who knew him, but I had sensed the difference.

"Say something, boss..." Silence fell; the pings of ice and snow pelting the roof echoed in the foyer of the house.

Since her rescue, I'd known Belle's secret. She'd rarely voiced her blood relation to the damned fallen Angel of Light or Tomas. Her character spoke volumes of the person she was, of the woman she had become...But Cain had done nothing more than tell lie after lie, wasting my time. Pain splintered through my heart. The old memories charged toward my surface.

"Tomas is a descendant of Lucifer."

Cain rubbed my hand, and I yanked it away before shoving it into my pocket.

"Sorry," he whispered. "I'll go."

"Stay." I shared a look with Belle and sighed. *What will I do with him now?* Cain deceived us. Topping it off, she had touted off more information than she should have been privy to, more information than the ABDA had made available to me. *My eyes narrowed and my gaze flew over him. Can I trust him?*

He stared at his feet; hands sunken deep into his pockets, thumbs out, and shoulders rounded forward.

What else did he lie about?

"Nothing," Cain said, a strange glow flaring behind his eyes.

"What?" I blinked.

"I haven't lied about anything else."

"Did you just—"My rough palm ran over my rugged face.

"Read your mind? Witches and Warlocks do that...assumed you knew. Elioud do it."

Kind eyes stared at me, and I forced mine to my partner, seeking backup.

"Yeah, boss man." Belle crossed her arms over her chest and tapped her foot.

Of course they do. But I hadn't considered the mind reading since Cain hated magic; though I wasn't certain why I'd assumed that. I was off my game. That *was* magic.

Shite. My face burned to the tips of my ears, and I grasped at my shirt, dragging the collar from my throat. Every thought… I glanced at him. The pounding of my heart echoed in my skull. He did every move I had thought about. My gaze drifted upstairs. Every internal struggle…the keys…my past…

I shook my head and eased into a chair, staring at my boots, staring at anything but either of them. My head tilted, neck cracking. Belle in my mind didn't bother me. For years, we had worked side-by-side, and she was like a sister to me. But Cain? No, he had no business knowing Death's secrets and fears.

"Talk to me, Dorian," Cain said, sighing.

I tossed on my socks and boots, and my deft fingers crisscrossed the laces. *Don't look at him.*

"You kept shit from me too."

I snapped back, "That was different."

"You assumed I knew, that I'd put two and two together, but me? I spared you pain."

Belle snorted and her dreads shook. "He's right, Dorian. You keep a lot of secrets and toss up walls anytime someone tries to get close to you."

"Do not," I muttered, sitting upright.

"Pain? Hardly." Cain scoffed and stormed to the front door, blocking my path. "Who cares if you turn into a skeleton? Was that supposed to hurt me? Or are you referring to your 'rules?'"

"You got a lot of those as well."

I waved off Belle, hating she was even here, and why the hell was she taking his bloody side? Neither of them understood the ramifications. Everyone retreated, or tried to murder me. I blinked, staring at my shaking hands. Losing my heart wasn't an option I could afford to tamper with. Why I guarded myself, why I couldn't fall in love. Certainly not with a Morning Star. The last time my heart broke, the world almost ended. He had been a human, not a descendent of the greatest deceiver.

Shuffling feet creaked against the floorboards, and the heat of his body filled my personal space. In his hands, Cain seized my face, forcing me to stare into his butterscotch eyes.

"Give me a little credit, sweets. I grew up around demons with hooves, horns, and tails. I'm not a naïve human."

More than who I was stopped me. Father had given me the mission to protect the key, and I failed him. Warm, rough lips brushed against mine, and my hands stroked down his back. Sink or swim. I'd rather turn the key than to see anyone hurt because of me. Working on the case would have helped if he were not involved. Hallo's message blared through my mind. He was our enemy. Cain and his sister, neither was as important as the destiny Father paved, no matter how much I wanted him to be…my world…

With another breathy sigh, Cain stepped backward and shoved his trembling fingers into his pockets. Past or not, I could never become what he deserved.

I rose from my chair, strode into my office to the window, and stared at the snow. The sunlight disappeared, and gray clouds occupied the sky. My fingers curled against the molding, and my weight leaned, pressing my hot face against the icy glass. Cain deserved devotion and love, and they were two emotions I was incapable of feeling.

Then, there were the facts. Cain lied. Bile swirled in the pit of my stomach. He was still lying, holding himself back for who knew what reason, but my instincts flared to life. Without honesty, we were nothing more than two lovers having a good time and enjoying each other's company. But I wanted more from him, so much more, if he'd only let me in and show me what he feared.

I glanced over my shoulder to Cain, leaning against the doorway. Tight jaw and cemented scowl were aimed at the floor. No, he would not spill his secrets. He'd rather seduce me. Keep me blinded to his rattling skeletons, but I deserved better than that.

"I've got to check on a few leads. Stay with Belle." At least I could have some thinking time in privacy and not worry about Cain listening in. Heaven knew my thoughts strayed far from perfect or pure.

"I'm not always listening." He crossed his arms and legs

I scoffed and repositioned my attention to the outdoors.

Cain offered, "Maybe we should slow down, take a step back."

"We can't… I can't."

It was already too late. The whistle blew at the train station for midday break. We couldn't ignore the fate of our world any longer. Time for action had come and gone. Demons, witches, warlocks, and vampires spilled into the street. My head flew in too many directions and my heart couldn't catch up. Any one of them on the street could have belonged to Garland; anyone could be a former slave.

"I'll protect you, but we…can't. No more. I just can't."

"Why not?"

His words tore through my soul and opened my old wounds. Too late. I had already fallen for him, hadn't I? The pieces settled in my mind, though, I tried to wipe the image away.

Belle cleared her throat and eased into her chair, located behind her desk. It was unfair to do this in front of her, but my office door was wide open.

Yes, I was scared, but not for the obvious reasons. My throat constricted, burning both itchy and dry, my survival was linked into this Earth, and if the demons destroyed me, we all would die. Anyone I loved became a threat…if anyone hurt him…enslaved him…the keys…my hand touched my chest.

It would not be the first time someone had used a lover against me.

I cupped Cain's cheek and prayed no one else found out about him. In the wrong hands, he became a weapon. Those loyal to Lucifer probably knew by now; I held the final key. Maybe they knew he was the Keeper. The thought of caring, only to lose Cain, weighed on my shoulders. Like the others before him, one day I would say the last good-bye. But would the world become a factor. Could my heart go there again? Would Father allow him to ascend with me? To live in Sheol and not Tartarus?

Belle sniffled. "Don't think like that."

My attention turned toward her desk, but I could not bring myself to look at her either. I patted Cain's cheek before withdrawing my hand. Passing him in the doorway, and breathing in his fiery spice one last time, my feet pounded over the walnut boards.

"Dorian, don't go," Cain called.

But my fingers curled around metal and turned the knob. The door rattled, slamming behind me, and I inhaled the fresh, crisp air.

"Dorian."

Without another word or thought, I left my home and wandered the streets of Halifax. For the most part, my head remained down, but every now and then, I glanced up.

Empty, graffiti covered buildings of the once metropolitan city lined and scattered the whitewashed street. Most demons chose to live farther from the destruction. Although Halifax hadn't suffered massive land loss, the quakes had toppled buildings and skyscrapers. Twelve years later and the cleanup dredged on. With the exception of salvage, it wasn't on the top of anyone's list. I didn't blame them. They thought they had all the time in the world.

Somehow, the lighthouse on Sambro Island had survived, even though the keeper's houses hadn't. One demolished, one burned down, and the third crumpled into the bay long before the Sundering. The red and white stripes called to me, but the real source awaited my arrival inside.

I practiced speeches while meandering and traipsing through the snow. Hallo always had advice for me, but she couldn't guide me with Cain. Even Father no longer responded to my prayers. As usual, I had no one but myself, and I made for a lousy therapist.

Save the world, or risk it all to save the man I wanted to love?

Tied to a wooden pole was the dinghy, but the tide was out. I squinted over the ocean, covering what was once the bay. Waves broke, lapping at the rocky shore, and I questioned the stability of the bobbing small boat.

"Dorian!" A voice called for me from behind. He shouted again, "Dorian," and his words carried over the water.

Cain followed me, and I frowned. He couldn't tag along. Ignoring him was my only option. My stomach tossed and turned. He drew closer, yet the knot refused to give.

His hand closed over mine. "Know you heard me, sweets."

"I have to do this." I risked a sideways glance.

He released a long sigh before his thick bottom lip disappeared into his mouth, but his eyes glinted with shades of amber. The rope broke free, and I hopped into the boat. Its sway churned my stomach.

"You're running away, and we haven't gotten to the juicy parts yet."

"You ready to spill?" I chewed my lip. Silence and his pleading gaze met my question. "Didn't think so. You'll see. Stay."

Waves broke against his kneecaps.

I grasped the oars and rowed the dinghy into the frothy water. Aside from a few glances to insure I steered in the proper direction, I eyed Cain. "Sorry babe," I murmured. "But I have to do this for you as much as for me."

His head cocked. He'd heard me?

The dilapidated dock had seen better days. Half of it had fallen into the water. One final glance yielded an empty shore, and my heart ached at his footprints in the sand. Only the sloshing water and cry of the gulls remained.

I slowed my rowing, gritting at the strange movement of my muscles. The knots from my belly slipped up my throat. With a long breath hissing through my teeth, I reached the old dock. After tying the dinghy, I grunted and hoisted myself onto the dock.

All the while, Cain possessed my thoughts. Torn between fulfilling a duty and running after the man I would…*No*. No matter what, I could not allow myself to head down that road again.

I strolled up the steep bank; the briny wind whipped through my hair. Hallo waited for me with her arms spread open. Cain wouldn't meet her as I had once hoped. He wouldn't meet those who helped me in my darkest hours.

"Dorian." Her slender frame encompassed me into a warm embrace.

I spun the dark, where she reflected the light.

Golden blonde hair framed her cherub face and pale blue eyes shined. Pulling away, a smile brightened her expression. "You are in love."

"It's time to convene in the flesh." I chewed my lip again.

"Markos follows you. I'll summon Fauna." Hallo's small hand lifted my chin. "It is all right to love again, Dorian."

Once more, I glanced over the water and toward the shore, but I didn't seek my brother. Falling for Cain wasn't possible, but I would make sure his sister returned. But not in this world.

"Just friends," I lied. Warmth flushed over my skin as she murmured and gestured me to follow her. "Don't preach to me about love."

We hiked the spiraling stone steps to the top.

"I state nothing more than the truth." Her tight fists curled around the willowy skirt, and the fabric shuffled. She didn't like having her love brought up life, yet mine seemed to be fair game for them all. Men veered away because of her strength. Those that had tried learned how strong willed Conquest truly was.

I entered a small compartment at the top of the lighthouse. Large glass windows encircled us; buttons and levers lined a small desk. I rocked on my heels. "Just light the beacon, Sister. Markos and Fauna will come, and we will end this."

"End?" Hallo spun around, her eyes electrified and glowing blue. "That wasn't the plan, and you know it." She flipped a switch, and the lighthouse emitted an ear-piercing siren.

I fell to my knees and covered my ears. I shouted, "What else can I do? He knows about the keys."

Her palm touched my forehead and a white, heated light bathed over me. Hallo said, "Stop punishing yourself, you stupid idiot. I told you, he's the Keeper, so of course he knows about the bloomin' keys."

Tears poured from my eyes. "When did you tell me that?"

"You were drawn to him? You knew Father made a Keeper. Did it not occur to you that Cain is it?"

The temperature of her power intensified, but even as my skin splintered and melted, my cries were not from physical pain. Beneath her onslaught, I grimaced.

"I will not allow you to take the easy road and destroy us all, Dorian. You must face the reality and repercussions of your world, of your heart."

"It is too late," I pled. "We are not strong enough, even with the ABDA. Why delay the inevitable." We would fail. In the blink of her blue eyes, I saw the future. Cain wrapped in chains, Boric demanding my key, and I helpless to stop the torture.

"Garland will fall, Brother."

But so would Cain. I reached up a trembling hand, grasped her hands, and yanked. "How can you allow that to pass? He is innocent!"

Hallo's grip didn't falter, and the throbbing worsened, pounding deeper into my temples. The ground rumbled, as if a legion of demons marched over the surface. The world would end one way, or another.

"The prophecy—" Her tone bordered on hysterics.

"Prophecy?" The King of Babylon would return and unite the world after the end of days. The light would shine again. The whole notion was laughable and blasphemous. Hallo knew better than to believe false prophets, let alone Metatron—the voice of God. How could I make her see the truth and lead her back to the right path? "Is nothing more than the ramblings of a mad man. Father made no such prediction. Let me end this, now, Sister. Metatron is wrong."

"No, it is you who are wrong. I saw the Light Bringer. She is here. What you seek to free is not Lucifer, Brother."

Lucifer would never see the light of day again, but I would not reveal what my key unlocked. "She?" I whispered. "But you said I slept with the enemy."

A smile played at her lips. "Proverbial enemies, Brother, for you still live in the past and fail to embrace the future. You, my dear, are sleeping with the Keeper of Keys." Hallo winked

My mouth dropped. What the hell was she babbling about?

Clapping faintly echoed through the lighthouse. "Well done, Sister. A plus for theatrics." Markos laughed, the sound booming and vibrating through my head, and the banter didn't stop there as he smacked my back. "Now, take him home and stop this madness. Let him lick his wounds with some dignity." He removed her hands, and I toppled over.

I glanced up at him. Whose side did Markos support? What wounds was I supposed to lick?

His brow raised, a smirk painted over his face. "And you thought I was the difficult one?"

Markos dragged me to my feet. Hallo sulked in the corner. Fauna hadn't come at the call, though she tended to be the stubborn one.

Hallo said, "She left this morning from the Yukon."

"Boric isn't Elioud?" I ignored her ability to read my mind.

Hallo and Markos shook their heads.

"Why haven't we taken him out before now?" I glanced between my siblings and rose. "We're the damned Horsemen of the Apocalypse. The deed should take but one of us." But the truth, even as I screamed my frustrations, Father had designed us only to be superior to humans, and the Elioud varied in their human blood from half to more or less. Our dominion to rule and annihilate anything higher was in ending the world. We needed the ABDA to step up and release their full resources for us to command. My vampires, and my siblings' witches and warlocks were not enough. Markos' legion wasn't enough. All we had was fear... "We need the Council of Seven." I glanced to the Heavens. We needed the other Archangels. "Michael. Gabriel. Saracuel. Remiel. Raguel. Uriel. Raphael."

"No," Hallo bellowed. "No, no, no! You'd dare involve the Seraphs? Father would have your head, Brother. I will have it."

My lips quirked and I stepped back. That was exactly what I intended, and it wasn't the first time I'd called on the Archangels. How else did they think I retrieved so many lost souls?

"Fool. Dorian, I should maim you." Hallowed's hand shot out, and an ache grew in my head again. "Sorry, but I cannot allow it."

And then there was darkness.

Chapter Eight

Cain

Stay? I held myself and shivered. *Wait?* I didn't want to do either, but stepped backward until the water lapped shy of my boots. Eyes on fire, I knelt to the sand.

Dorian rowed toward the lighthouse island, strong and rippling muscles worked the oars. Resting a hand over my pained heart, I sighed into the humid, briny air whipping around my face. I brushed the ocean mist, cutting through the foggy mass, obscuring the picturesque vision of solid muscles contracting beneath the surface of Dorian's cotton shirt. Dark tresses clung to his head. His hat had disappeared, but I hadn't missed him hiding the eerie glow of his eyes illuminating his face.

I would miss Dorian. That much I didn't deny. Already, my heart was pinching.

Peering over the water, a blonde haired woman in billowing skirts held a hand above her eyes. The elusive and lying Hallowed—I assumed—waited for him by the red and white striped lighthouse, and by her thoughts, she knew about us already. A frown touched her pale lips; our gazes connected across the watery spans, and my former lover arrived alone.

Why had he refused my company? Maybe he hadn't known of my previous meeting with his sister in the church. Was he ashamed of me? I blew out a harsh breath and closed my eyes.

My dream crumbled into ashes. Was this all a game he played? My knees wobbled, and the tears threatened again, but I sliced my teeth into my lip and bit down hard. No more, no tears, nothing would stand in my way, but even I understood they were only words. My eyes reopened, wider, soaking in the remnants of destruction in our broken world. Waves crashed against the rocks. Surf stirred, and the ground rumbled beneath my knees, vibrating through my body.

The end, or the beginning, rushing toward us, maybe. But I wouldn't idle on the damp beach, waiting, while Dorian decided my fate. No. If he wanted me, I gulped and fisted the moist sand from the ground; if he loved me, he would find me.

"For nothing short of God will ever stand in true love's way," Mother had said.

"Then why does this feel like good-bye?" Tossing down the fisted sludge, I stood and wiped the grime on my jeans. I stomped through the frozen bank and left the bay behind with its picture perfect vision on the lighthouse. Emotions swirled inside, threatening to overflow, but I tampered and locked, swallowed and buried them where nobody would ever find them. My chance to walk away arose—Dorian's pleading eyes and kind lies couldn't stop me. With my hands shoved deep into my pockets, I strolled onto Main Street and never looked back.

Damned to his purgatory... I halted in the road. Everything connected. My gaze drifted over the ruined and closed down shops. Whores and vagrants littered the walkways, leeching off others to survive. No cars, busses, or trolleys. All of us trapped within Dorian's nightmare. Like Earth had become a level of purgatory itself. Death ruled Sheol; the Horsemen ruled the broken world.

Shaking my head, I stomped my boots over the layers of ice and snow before the cold sunk into my muscles. None of that bullshit mattered, because whether on Hell, Heaven, or Earth, Dorian wasn't mine. No one belonged to me, and I could have no sooner become someone else's baggage.

"Why did I bother trying?" A shiver shook me. I shuffled to the sidewalk, fighting an uphill war. Urges to turn around tingled through my limbs. Bitterness filled my mouth and joined the familiarity of threatened memories. I opened the tower door and paused. "I meant nothing to him."

"Good afternoon, Mr. Westcott," the door attendant greeted. "You've had visitors."

Who would visit me? Must be Cousin Tomas. I offered him a forced smile and willed my legs forward before entering the stairwell of my apartment building.

Lungs heaved for precious, piss-perfumed breath as my heavy feet ascended the staircase, trying and failing to remove Dorian from my mind again. No matter what I thought or saw, it was him. The last time, seven months ago, he'd infiltrated and dug his claws into my soul. Even my mouth tasted of him.

Ten floors later and sweat beaded on my forehead. My front door loomed before me, but as I reached into my pocket for my keys, I found them empty. "Shit." I had worn Dorian's clothes and had left my belongings in his office.

Frozen fingers skimmed over the denim fabric, and the urge to shed my tears ripped at my center. Jan's door squeaked open, and she whispered for me. Without thinking, my shoulders drooped forward, and my knees plummeted to the musty floor.

My neighbor, Jan, whispered, "Not safe, get in here." She yanked at my shirt, tugging me toward her apartment. A simple task for some, but she neared her final years.

No will remained inside of me, and I was more than happy to let whatever danger she feared consume me. Jan—despite her elderly stature—mustered the physical strength required to drag me from the hall and into her apartment across the way.

Kneeling on her floor, my shoulders slumped forward again, and I stared at my empty hands. A shiver chased from my wrists to my spine. Jan closed the door; the evidence lay in the click and rustle of chains. Mothballs and cat box curled my nose and churned my stomach. His taste, his touch, and tenderness retreated.

Without Dorian in my life what was the point in living, besides the promise to my mother?

"Men have come for you."

I blinked and stared up at Jan. Let them come for me. Why should I fight when there was nothing to fight for anymore in this world? They'd broken me, Boric had mauled me, and no one could've glued the blocks together.

Her eyes bulged from behind her glasses, but my walls remained in place. Grayed hair was wound into a tight bun, reminding me of the old lady from a popular cartoon show featuring a cat and bird. Jan even managed to dress the part with her high-collared shirts and long pleated skirts.

Rising from the floor, I sniffled and wiped my eyes. "What men?"

"Not Tomas's men," her eyes bulged again, "strange men in Garland clothing." She grasped my arm and guided me to her paisley-covered sofa.

We had no secrets and Jan treated me like a son. Even though I was older than she was, I hadn't aged. No judgments ever left her mouth either, but I hesitated telling her about Dorian. Did others know him as Death? I shrugged both at my thoughts and at her revelation. "I'm surprised it took Garland this long."

"Afraid they trashed the place." Her thin bottom lip disappeared into her mouth.

The thoughts ransacking her mind echoed within my own. Why would Garland risk infiltrating Arcadia? I rubbed my neck and glanced away. How had he known where to find me? Words Boric had said to my sixteen-year-old self echoed in my mind. *"You will always belong to me. Never forget that, luv."*

First, he'd loved me. Second, he'd crushed me, and then he'd tossed the pieces away. Hundreds of years later and I still amassed the fractured shards on my sleeves. My hand pressed against my aching heart. Dorian did the same, but this time the pieces disintegrated, leaving me emptied.

A teakettle whistled, and I raised my hand, offering to help. Mother had reared me with enough sense to respect my elders.

Strolling into the kitchen was second nature. I opened the cup-boards and removed her tea canister.

"Where have you been?" she asked

With the tea steeping, I filled her in about Dorian, but I left out the part of him being a Horseman.

"You love him," she said, and smiled wide. The light in her eyes twinkled brighter. "I can see the spark in your eyes when you speak of him. And your genuine smile shines through"

I hated being the bearer of bad news. Love simply wasn't enough. "It's over now." I turned away and removed the tea balls before handing her a mug.

"Why?" She frowned.

I glanced at my feet and thought the answer. Because he ran away, like a coward, he deserved better than me.

Jan shook her head and placed her teacup on the saucer. "Lord knows, Cain, what they did to you, but you deserve love too."

"Did you love someone?" I changed the subject and studied my waterlogged boots. My toes held no feeling. But the distrac-tion failed. Thoughts of love resurrected Dorian's haunting image. No, Jan had to be wrong. If I deserved love than wouldn't I have had Dorian? We settled on the sofa as her cat twined and rubbed against my legs, purring. Animals always seemed to sense when someone required a bit of comfort.

"Long ago, I fell in love with a man who hadn't deserved me." Jan rolled up her sleeves and exposed scars on her brown skin. "I'm a survivor, too, but after that man...I thought I'd never trust again, let alone love."

I stared off at the photographs littering her walls. I had seen them before, and though we had no secrets, Jan's past wasn't com-mon knowledge.

She motioned to the picture of an older man. "That's Paul. I met him after years of telling myself I hadn't deserved real love. For ages I told him no and one day he helped me. I went on one date out of guilt, telling myself as much, but that one day changed my life forever."

She continued with her story and spoke about the love they'd shared. He'd died before the Sundering, but had known about her secrets. Paul had accepted Jan and loved her, despite her shattered pieces. At least she'd found happiness, even if their love and union hadn't lasted forever, but I was different.

After the tea, I washed our cups, and she retreated to her bedroom to read. I sat on the sofa, reliving the last few days in my mind, and stared onto her balcony. Outside a thunder snow rained from the sky. Lightning flashed and illuminated the darkness blanketing the world.

I closed my eyes, and Dorian's image appeared. Each sound or movement, in the apartment and outside, raced my heart, and my hopes soared, but it wasn't him. I shifted on the sofa and hugged myself. At least I could feel my toes again.

Still, with no Dorian swooping into rescue me from myself, more proof compounded against the facts. I deserved no love, and he couldn't find it in himself to give his heart to me.

Maybe the fault was mine for all the lies. I snorted and rolled my sleep-heavy eyes. His secret remained one of many that I hadn't broken from his mind. Like me, something had happened, and Dorian refused to trust or love.

Who had broken Death?

I stayed the night on Jan's sofa. Sleep eluded me, and green eyes plagued my thoughts. My body tossed and turned on the scratchy surface. No warmth rested in the cushions and no thick arms protected me.

I awoke in a pool of sweat and shouted, "Dorian." Blinking, I glanced around. Why had I said his name? Usually it was my brother-in-law's name, Veric. Try as I might, though, the dream wouldn't resurface.

The following morning Jan handed me my spare keys and insisted I lock myself inside my apartment. She was always a little over-the-top, but my southern manners reigned, and I obliged her. I opened the door, pushing papers and belongings aside. Stale and musty odors wafted into my face, and my eyes adjusted to the darkness.

Someone had turned my furniture on its sides, and my personal belongings covered every possible surface. The scene unraveled, and clarity set in: they hadn't wanted me at all.

Why else trash my apartment…unless Boric Garland had known I was holding the keys that Angelica had stolen.

Scoffing, I righted an end table. My hands clapped, and the overhead lights hummed on, bathing the small apartment in yellow light. "Like I'd keep the keys here." They couldn't have beaten, starved, or raped the location from me before, so what made them think trashing my home would work? I caught a piece a paper floated into my hand, and I crumpled the document without looking first. "Idiots…"

I uncurled the paper. "Assholes."

Belle's phone number stared at me. My ass plopped onto the sofa, and my hand rested over my pulsating heart. Hands shaking, I leaned forward, willing my body to steady. *He was safe. Belle was safe.* Garland wouldn't have left the paper if they'd thought for a moment I had sought out the ABDA, Dorian, or Belle.

With a sigh, I unfolded myself from the sofa. Piece by piece, I corrected the pittance of my pathetic existence and tried not thinking of Dorian. Ache had pinched within my chest and tears pricked, threatening to drown me from the inside.

"For the best." I glanced out the window. If I squinted, I could've made out his house. I picked up my journal and thought about chucking the worn leather into the trash.

My finger stroked over the journal's soft leather surface. Memories of our first meeting and the time I had spent scouring Arcadia for the mysterious green-eyed man, living in the equally vivid green Victorian, had lined the pages. Proof of my abuse. Each slice, scar, and bruise I had written among the pages, along with the name of each rapist. Starting at the top with Boric Garland, a chunk, a bite at a time, I wrote the resurfacing memories.

Not for revenge, but so my story might one day help another lost soul clinging to a thread in this torturous world.

My hand ran over my rough jaw, pausing for a second, but my touch wasn't the same. My skin didn't tingle; my stomach didn't tighten. Safety and love didn't live in self-caress.

The doctor had suggested I write down the past. Happy times should have lined the pages, but few of those had existed. Son of a gambling drunkard, he'd sold us. To him, we were cattle. Only sixteen when Boric stole my virtue with syrupy promises. Lily had been fourteen. Saying no hadn't been an option. I'd quickly learned that, no, resulted in a beating and then rape, or rape while he'd beaten me. After a while, nothing else mattered, and I unwillingly lived to please him.

Part of me thought telling the inanimate object somehow changed my fate. Alone. Regardless of Jan's insistences, being alone was better for me. An inability to change, or block, the past stood between happiness and me.

I sniffled and leaned back, sighing. My eyes closed; his glowing, green eyes smiled from behind my lids. My hand reached out, to touch his beard, but the image distorted into a menacing demon—primped blond hair and a piercing blue gaze narrowed on me. His finger crooked, beckoning me, like a common dog. My eyes flew open and I gasped.

God had punished my family, persecuting my sisters and me, even though we had done nothing wrong. I would gladly take Boric's lashes and jabs, but all I had asked of God was to spare my sisters, and then for my death.

My shaky hand reflected my sputtering heart as I stared at the empty page. Drops splattered over the surface. Even without Dorian, somehow, some day, some way I would save them or die trying. The pen rested in the folds, and I snatched it. Furiously, I scribbled and poured my emotions, my fears, and emptied Dorian from my mind.

I rested on the empty road, hands on my hips, and stared into the rolling hills, covered in snow. Normality had returned for me, but my chest and eyes ached. Some wounds never healed: I had thought that during my one hundred and forty-block commute and meant Dorian, not Boric and his cronies. But I couldn't answer why.

Shards of sunlight reflected from row after row of glass buildings, their frames arching in a hothouse style, spanning hundreds of acres before me. The government had built the greenhouses, which allowed us to plant year round, far outside the city limits and deeper into the countryside of Nova Scotia. I was no farmer, though. Fertilizer and chemicals burned my nose. But due to seeds and crop sizes, we were limited on plants. Beans and rapeseed gave the greatest yields, compared to other vegetables, but I would be happier never to eat another bean again.

I strolled through the warehouse door and readied for my day, hoping to clear my mind of Dorian, the ABDA, and Boric. Employees wandered past their lockers, both coming and going.

The shift whistle released its hissing shrill. I stopped at my locker and retrieved my safety goggles and respirator. No one spoke to me, which was odd, and their minds were closed.

"Cain," my boss called from the doorway and gestured to me.

Odd as well that he used my first name. I closed my locker, grabbed my gear, and followed him across the hall into his office.

"Shut the door," he said.

With a curt nod, I kicked the door and blocked the bustling clamor from the hallway before returning to the front of his desk. I lowered my gaze, sweeping the floor. *This has to be about missing time.* My fingers danced over my thigh. I hadn't called out yesterday, or the previous day, and swallowed hard expecting his chew-out.

"I need you to go north and pick up seed from Plant G." He opened a folder on his desk, and handed me the paperwork and train tickets. "You'll be gone for a few days, so keep your receipts and be sure someone stamps your card."

"Yes, sir." I backed toward the door, but he stopped me.

"Call next time. Consider this your punishment. Clock out and go, now. All the arrangements are finalized, including lodging and meals. You'll be gone at least a week."

In the northwestern wilderness, Plant G was nestled among the deep, impenetrable forests of Nova Scotia. Unlike the farms, they didn't grow plants. No one ever wanted to go there, though, even if it meant paid time off, and no one spoke of what happened after they'd returned.

After clocking out, I gathered my belongings and headed home to pack. Upon reaching my floor, strange voices carried into the stairwell. I halted in the corridor, listening.

"Man, he's probably not coming back. Why we gotta waste our time looking for this asshat?"

"We've got orders straight from the big man." A rapping followed.

Through the small window, I spied into the hallway, careful to make no sound. Two men knocked on my front door. Their uniforms were a dead giveaway…green…the large G…Garland.

"Pfft. I still don't get it. We're out here, putting our necks on the line, and King Boric doesn't even tell us why?"

Slowly, I descended the stairs, shaking my head and ignoring the pounding heart in my chest. My feet could move quietly or quickly, yet not both, and time ground onward at the pace of a tortoise. I shoved through the large doors, gasping for air. Boric's laughter bounced in my head; it sought left and right for the source.

But he wasn't on the street. My hands grasped my thick hood, drawing it over my head, and I crept along the street, trying to fit in.

I arrived at the train station, but I didn't go in. My gaze fixated on the icy concrete. And I didn't glance at Dorian's Victorian house, or his fenced in yard. His mind slept, though, and even through the wooden siding and across the street, his energy brushed my face.

Withdrawing my cell, my fingers slid over the screen. I found Belle's text and hit reply. "Garland men in Halifax. Heading north. Don't tell him it's me."

Their investigation was important, more important than a relationship not working out between Dorian and me. He saved lives. While he was too late to save me, it wasn't too late for others. I glanced at the house. The front door swung open, and Belle looked up and down the street, rubbing her arms.

"Take care, Cousin," she said.

A man resembling Dorian stepped outside, but his eyes were red. Markos. He yanked her arm, his gaze narrowing on me. I turned, quickening my steps, and entered the train station.

The train arrived at Meat Cove Outpost on the mainland four hours later. I knew nothing about the area, other than Meat Cove was Nova Scotia's northern most-settled point and that you could reach the island by boat or bridge. Too bad the bridge hadn't survived the Sundering.

Gray water rolled and smashed into the rocky coast. I stood on the docks, arms wrapped tightly around my knapsack. My feet tapped impatiently waiting for the ferryboat. Minutes later, it chugged into the small harbor.

After handing over my ticket, I boarded the vessel. I leaned against the thick railing, gloved fingers tapping the white metal. No one else crossed with me. Twenty tedious moments of waiting passed before we set sail.

The sun had lowered in the dismal sky, painting streaks of fiery gold across the horizon. Behind them, however, inky black clouds were churning.

More and more I had grown sick of the salty seawater surrounding me, and today's journey hadn't proved any different. My eyes shut tight; the boat rocked, and the wind wobbled us back and forth.

The Captain yelled over the tremulous action, "Are you daft? Get inside, boyo, before the drink takes it fill."

With nothing left to live for, I spun around and extended my arms to the heavens, silently demanding God to strike me down, however he saw fit. Waves crashed over the deck, drowning me in purified waters. Briny liquid infiltrated my nose and mouth forcing me to cough and gag. Flying open, my eyes stung.

Utter destruction stirred within the blue-black clouds. Beauty and angst fought, slicing aqua-white bolts into one another. God didn't listen, and no Horsemen disguised as Angels intervened.

We docked. I stepped from the boat, taking one last glance at the ferry, and shook my head.

"Cain Westcott?" a man called. "This way, laddie." Without waiting for me to turn, he ushered me toward the lodge.

Clutching my soaked bag, I blinked at the lush greenness of the land surrounding me. Such an opposition to the whitewashed snow I had become accustomed to seeing every day. Though still cold, Dorian would have fit in with the environment. The mere thought of his green eyes caused a sob to choke in my chest.

"Ye all right there, laddie?" the man asked in his strange accent.

I coughed and nodded.

"Right, ye can take a wee rest."

"How will I get to Plant G?" I doubted they had running vehicles, but I also wondered where this elusive plant could be.

"Don't worry yerself over it," he said, grinning.

We strode along the path, lit only by a small lantern the man was carrying. Owls called their nightly song and insects serenaded in tune. I allowed their peaceful lullaby to settle my pulse.

Dripping wet, we entered the lodge.

My escort poked his head into an open door, marked for employees. "Found another one, Miss Fauna."

Another what? My eyes adjusted to the oil lamps flooding the open space with light. Moose heads and photographs lined the walls, and a large fire roared in a massive brick hearth half the size of my tiny living room. Its smoldering scent reminded me of campfires.

"Welcome, Cain, welcome to the Wilderness." Lavender eyes peaked from beneath an untamed mass of gray hair.

Again, I blinked, recognizing the near naked woman at once from Dorian's photographs. My feet stumbled, my knees falling to the floor. "You…"

"You know who I am? Oh, you must be special if he told you about me." She closed in on me.

I shook my head, and she frowned.

"But then, how do you know me?"

I tossed my hands up and flinched. "Pictures... I assumed... Dorian never told me about you." Nothing aside from that the Horsemen were his family.

She knelt at my side tousled my hair. "He would have told you. Handsome," she exposed rotten teeth in a gruesome grin, "Yes, I see what my brother sees. There it is. Shining like a twinkling star."

The foulness of her breath turned my stomach, and I swallowed the rising bile down.

"Pity his head is shoved too far up his ass to notice how he's hurting you."

Had she read my mind?

Fauna shook her head. "You wear it on your sleeve, Cain."

"Aye, the Captain said he's got a few screws loose." The man twirled his finger near his ear.

I scowled and crossed my arms over my chest. I wasn't crazy for wanting my life to end, for the nightmares to stop.

"He said the laddie tried jumping off the ferry."

Fauna gasped and cocked her head. "Dorian isn't worth the life of a Morning Star. Right then. Let's get you fixed up. You're sopping wet."

Her musical tone gave me pause. Fauna said the name without my skin crawling. Still, I corrected, "Westcott." From behind, someone's hands clamped on my shoulders, propelled me up, and then forward. "Watch it," I said, turning to the strange man, who'd escorted me.

"Westcott, Morning Star." Her broad shoulders shrugged. Delicate, long fingers grasped my hand, and I stared at the boil-covered arm, puss oozing from their centers. "You see me as Father made me. I can cover it, if it bothers you."

Acceptance: I extended the same to others. "No." Fauna would take getting used to with the popping sounds her boils made as they erupted.

"Don't worry, it's not contagious." By the hand, Fauna led me upstairs and into the darkness.

I found my words, but retorting her earlier claims about Dorian seemed futile. My soggy boots shuffled along the wooden floors.

Who was I but a bastard, Elioud slave, while she was a Horseman created out of love? "Is this where you live?"

"Yes, this used to be a school before the Sundering." She motioned toward the walls.

Murmuring a reply, I scanned over the dim lit hallway. Oil paintings graced them, and some of the faces were familiar family members. Others, I didn't recognize.

"A most-trusted source claimed you were missing, and now, I've found you."

Had Dorian always known where I was? My brow lifted a fraction before falling. "How did you know where I would be?"

"I have my ways of tracking those who fall under my command." Her steps slowed.

My heart leapt from my chest, I blinked and let go of her hand, feet halting. "Could you locate my sisters?"

Over her shoulder, she flashed a gruesome smile. "I have located one, but as to which witch, I am uncertain. Dorian sent out the word the day you came to him, but messages don't travel fast I'm afraid." Fauna tapped a finger to her nose.

A misconception among some, but the old satellite phones had limitations. How did she manage reception up here?

I strolled forward and lifted my hand, shielding my smile. For me, Dorian had tried to find my missing sisters—both of them. "How does your magic work?"

Fauna spun on her heels. "A woman can't reveal all her secrets. For the record, I don't like cell phones and believe they'd caused cancers."

I nodded, not at all certain her screws were in order. Or was she lying?

"Ah, here we are." She escorted me into a large bedroom. The curtains were drawn and only her soft footfalls alerted her movements. Sulfur filled the air and a soft glow illuminated her location. Fauna placed the match against a hurricane lamp, and its wick ignited, spreading its luminance over the room. "There is no electricity up here."

How do they run the plant without electricity?

"There is no Plant G."

Unable to move, I processed her words. What had the others before me come for? Learning perhaps? She did claim this place was once a school. I doubted Fauna could teach me anything. Not that I knew all there was to know about magic, but nothing mattered to me, except my sisters.

"Listen to me, Cain." Fauna lit another oil lamp and placed the glass container on a small table. "Dorian tried to erase the world for you. We had to intervene and protect you." She turned the dial and more light bathed the room in. "Dorian will try again if anything happens to you."

I mouthed the words. My arms crossed over my chest, and I shivered. Dorian would not have done that for me, would he? Lightning cracked, its thunder shaking the walls, and my heart ached. "He doesn't even like me enough to tell me about his family, but you think he'd destroy the world for me?" I snorted and stared at Fauna's bare feet. "No, if he cared that much…"

"He cares." She sat on the four-poster bed and patted the quilt-covered surface, but I didn't budge from the doorway. "Dorian carries a great weight on his shoulders. A burden that you too also hide."

My brows rose. "How did you know?"

"It's my business to learn what my people are up to." Fauna grinned.

I gulped. "Does … he know?" I couldn't finish the sentence.

"That you have the keys?" She shook her head.

"Good." No us existed, but I didn't want Dorian to think the keys were the reason for my love. Curiosity, yes, but the love blossomed long before I had seen the metal key dangling around his neck.

"He does know you're the Keeper."

"Come again?" Hallowed had said something similar inside the church.

"No one but Dorian can see the key, yet you saw it."

My back straightened. "So?"

"That makes you the Keeper, Cain, not my brother."

Why me, though? Dorian made sense as the Keeper. At least he was an Archangel. My gaze fell to the floor. The world spun before my eyes, my past vividly flashing, rising; I winced with each lash the masters whipped against my skin, cutting my flesh. Did Boric know too? Heat flooded my cheeks, and my limbs trembled. I had been weak. If that were my only skeleton, life would have gone on but…he'd…they'd raped me. I gulped again and swallowed the tears running over the scarred skin beneath my own veil of magic.

"You aren't the only one who has suffered," she whispered.

My gaze snapped to her vivid eyes. Boils erupted over her face as her flesh cracked into green ooze. I heaved and clutched the doorframe for support. Without food in me, only bile rose and I ate the bitter, burning liquid.

"He cared enough to take your pain away, but we stopped him. With you and your sisters, we have a fighting chance to overthrow Boric. Give me your hand."

"My sisters?" I hesitated, chewing my lip and clawing at the wood. "What do they have to do with this?"

Fauna's hands steadied on her hips. Her lanky legs padded over the rug. I blinked, staring up as she towered over me.

"Dorian loves you, but you are almost as mortal as the humans. Now give me your damn hand." She grabbed me and shoved a ring on my finger. "I forged this for a lover out of St. Peter's iron chains."

And why didn't her lover possess it? I slid into the room and leaned against the wall, asking, "What does it do?"

"Allows you to escape death as long as you wear it when you die. And you will." Fauna tapped my cheek.

I stared at the thick, tarnished ring, its weight drawing my hand toward the ground.

"Keeper… Go back to Halifax, to Dorian."

High-pitched laughter left me, shaky. The wallpaper scratched my skin where it broke and peeled. Like a chameleon, I wanted to disappear into the gray diamond pattern. No, he'd refused to love again. I'd heard Dorian's struggles; she was pulling my leg. No one would miss me when I passed. "Whatever." I waved her off. "I'm wet and miserable. Obviously, he didn't end the world. Thanks for the ring."

I hid my balled fists beneath my arms, rising, and lifted my chin. The one thing in life I wanted for me and she presented me with the opposite. If Dorian truly wanted me to have it then why hadn't he given me the gift? The iron chain fastened into a ring weighed me down, and I slipped it off, extended my closed hand, and choked, "I...I don't need it."

Fauna contemplated me for a moment, cocking her head to the left. She stepped closer and shoved a curled finger into my chest. "Fix this."

"No," I whispered, wincing. "He knows where he can find me. It's his turn to chase me down." My lips trembled as the words filed forth. Tears threatened again, but I had to stand my ground. "I can't spend the rest of my life running after a man who doesn't love me..." Silence drew between us, and I fiddled with the ring still tightly enclosed in my sweaty fist. "It's for the best, Fauna. Let Dorian forget about me and me him." I twirled my finger in the air. "The world will go on."

"And if your love made him a better person?"

Amusement reverberated from within my queasy stomach. "Death isn't a person, you are no person, and last I checked neither was I."

Fauna snarled, "And if your lack of love destroys us all?"

But I didn't flinch. My brow arched at her lack of love comment; I gave him all I could, but love would never be enough. I whispered, "Then, I'll see you in Hell."

"You're playing a dangerous game, Cain." She stormed to the dresser, opened the drawers, and tossed dry clothes at me.

I didn't try to catch the flung garments and let them pool at my feet. "Send me home. Forget about me."

"No, you are the Keeper."

I didn't want to live, let alone be the keeper of anything, least of all Death. Despite that, I eased the ring back onto my finger.

Chapter Nine

Dorian

Seven days passed. I rested in bedroom, curtains drawn and blankets tossed over my head. Easier to breathe without Cain, or so I told myself. With a sigh, I rolled over. Only a tad bit simpler to force the air through my lungs without his overwhelming fiery scent rebirthing the memory of us. After such a short time with each other, his affects over me were profound, as if we had spent a lifetime as one.

Hallo's light trick wasn't to blame, but I was. Somehow, I knew this. I had told him to wait, clamped down my thoughts, and rowed away, damn well knowing I hadn't planned on returning. *Such an ass and undeserving of his love.* What was I thinking?

Even now, I couldn't answer for my actions. As if the past had reared up and assumed control of me, I'd decided the outcome would be death. I tossed and turned beneath my darkened cave of loneliness.

"I am in love and frightened, like a child." Little nuances decided my heart's fate. How the hair stood up on my arm when he gazed at me, or the increased rhythm of my heart in his presence. Inside of my brain, I had plastered and embedded the taste of his skin and the warmth of his touch.

By the third day, my eyes had run dry from the cindered ache of tears countlessly shed. All because Cain hadn't returned, and I lacked the proper strength to leave my bed, eat, not that I needed nourishment, or care about anything all over again. Emptiness filled me, despite the result's benefits.

"I can't hurt him now, and he is safer without me in his life." I flopped onto my belly and buried my face in my pillow, breathing in the remnants of Cain.

"Talking to yourself again, Brother?" The curtains rattled, and Markos flung the shades open. His footsteps drew nearer, and he snatched the blanket away. "He's watched over, regardless of what that pompous vampire downstairs says."

"What vampire and who?" Who was that vampire? Why was there a vampire downstairs? I lifted my head, blinked at the sunlight pouring through the opening, and winced at the stabbing ache coursing through my head.

Markos moved quickly, his gaze darting…I flung my head to the pillows. Nothing mattered. Not anymore and least of all my brother's ramblings.

"The one you call Cain." Markos sat at the edge of my bed and crossed his legs.

I had half-expected him to make childish kissy faces for me to rouse.

"We've called in the vampires, after speaking with Belle and pouring through that sorry excuse of a desk. She's still a feisty one." He sighed and flicked his gaze to the doorway. "They arrived in the middle of the night and are patiently waiting in your office."

"How is it you both read my mind? And who the fuck is *they?*"

He laughed and ran a palm over his clean-shaven face. "Brother, how do you even live in this world and not embrace the magic?" Markos shook his fist, as if magic were the end all answer.

I had no need of magic. The answer was simple. The ability to read situations hadn't failed me until Cain, and the power failed only with him. *Why does everything revolve around him?* A sigh tickled my chest, and I prayed for Father to listen, to end this already.

In a soft voice unlike him, Markos said, "What if the answer is love? Father preached it to us as well as the humans."

"Cut the crap, Mark." I groaned, shimmied into a sitting position, and ran a hand over my face. The stench of myself almost knocked me out, even War's nose curled. His well-being wasn't my concern, though, and he could deal with my stink or leave.

"You know I care not for the ways of others." He did, though; Mark hid it better than the rest of us, but only a moron would miss the way his eyes lit whenever Belletrist entered the room. "Okay, so *she* matters. But you've already forbade me." Pain laced through his tone.

My head squeezed and ached unlike ever before. "Leave Cain and Belles alone," I pointed my finger, "that's an order."

Red eyes sparkled and bore into me. A reflection of me, but Markos was taller and more muscled. Some might have said intimidating, but his tactics didn't work on me. I saw the truth, the lies, and rumors he'd made up to keep everyone away, in his gaze. We went hand-in-hand, yet we were opposites as much as we were alike. I gave into carnal pleasure, whereas my brother had been celibate since meeting Belle. On his asking, I'd maintained his façade of whips, whores, and chains, partly assuming there had always been a little truth.

Studying him, I didn't believe a word of it. "Bastard. Why didn't you tell me, Mark?"

Markos curled his fist and shook it in the air again. "You are blind and a fool. Father should never have chosen you to lead us. You punish us. You choose them over your own brethren." His voice lowered. "I love you, Brother, but I love her too. I've loved her enough to change, to be the type of man she deserves because making her happy, seeing her smile, brightens my world. You had that and wanted to destroy it."

I rolled my eyes and groaned. "We've established that."

Voices filtered from downstairs through the old ventilation ducts. The Old Norman-French accent I recognized straight away, belonging to Tomas. I strained, waiting to hear Cain's southern draw, but the others were alien to my ears.

"Good, because you have visitors, but take a shower unless you'd rather make them enemies." Markos said nothing else, rose from my bed, and departed.

I flung myself over, back onto the bed, and winced as my head rattled and throbbed. A deep breath brought hints of Cain's scent. The slight smolder and spice had attached itself to my pillows, sheets, and blanket and refused to vacate. My bed became a prison, a warm and memory filled cell of the man I had let go. I wasn't like Markos; I couldn't simply change for another person.

Cain haunted my thoughts once again. At times, I even searched for his caramel eyes in the shadows of my room. Over the past week, I had tried to venture downstairs. When I had managed to, the walls closed in on me as soon as the remnants of Cain caught my attention. Piled neatly on my office chair were his clothes. He must've taken his boots, but Belle had moved the rest. Forgetting proved to be another story, a story that would not have a successful conclusion.

In my absence, Belle had followed standard protocol and contacted the vampires, ABDA again, and as I had requested, the Arcadian council. Daily, she had made her reports.

She knocked on the open door Markos had failed to close. "Cain's missing according to Tomas," Belle said in a somber tone. "No note."

I blinked at her. "Bloody fucking hell." I yanked the covers away. Rarely did I say bloody hell anymore. Pain surged through my brain once again from the motion. I attempted to focus and grasped my dresser for support. His disappearance was my fault. She didn't need to say the words. My hand tore through my hair, and Belle made a face, curling her nose in disgust. What had Markos said about Cain?

"Shite." What if my brother was wrong? No, I would take no chances.

Belle cleared her throat. "You need a shower, and you look like shit frozen over, boss."

No one else would ever dare speak down to Death, but Belle and my fellow Horsemen. Even the ABDA chose their words wisely, but I cared little about jabs or empty words.

Belle shoved me away from the dresser. "Get your skanky ass in the shower. Damn it, Dorian, you're being such a pussy."

I smirked as she pushed me, this time toward the bathroom. My hands flew into the air. "Alight. Damn it, I'm going."

"And wash behind your ears." She slammed the door.

My reflection loomed before me. I resembled a lumberjack more than Death. Twenty minutes later, clean and trimmed, I had redressed and stood at the top of the stairs.

"Get a grip." I smacked myself and trembled from head to toe. Every step became a rollercoaster rushing downward, and pins and needles pricked throughout my body.

Firelight bathed my large office in an orange glow. I didn't know the day or time and frankly, I didn't care.

"Dorian." Tomas leaned against his cane. His pale blue eyes studied me, squinting behind ridiculous, orange-tinted goggles. He pushed them upward and left them on top of his straw colored hair.

Out of respect, I bowed, and Duc Tomas Artois reciprocated.

A longhaired man stood at his side by the fireplace, his hair obscuring him; he was wearing an outdated pantsuit, complete with long tails.

They need to stop raiding the theater. A loud ruckus rose from outside. Two voices shouted. The male held a thick British accent as he said, "Angelica, we don't have time to waste on toffers and twits. My brother…"

A woman said, "Your brother? What about mine? And stop calling me Angelica—she is dead!"

Two Elioud crashed through my front door and stumbled into my office.

"You are Angelica…" The redheaded male trailed, his amber eyes meeting mine.

I cocked my head. On a second take, the tiny—midget seemed more fitting—dark-haired Angelica was an Elioud vampire, like Tomas. More so, though, she strongly resembled Cain's sister, the one he'd told me not to worry about, except the woman barely came to my waist. The one in the tintype had been taller. I tilted my head to the left.

Grasping her arm, the ginger-haired man could have passed for Nephilim, even an Archangel. Power radiated from his center and jumped with his heartbeat. He swallowed hard and composed himself, his energy waning.

"I am neither a toffer," my lips twitched at his whorish reference, "nor a twit."

"Right you are, Dorian," Tomas said. "On both accounts, now, let me introduce my friends, Veric, Angelica, and Nicolai."

Ginger man scoffed at his 'friends' reference, but the pixie vampire beamed as she grasped my hands. My brow rose. Tomas introduced his cousin, Korrigan, not Angelica or Angel, but he supplied no last name.

Nikolai von Baron, the former human, turned demonic horse but turned back to human, bowed to me. He said, "Sir," before turning around again.

ABDA Special Agent Veric Garland, the elusive Elioud who supposedly headed my division, although no one had met him, tweaked his lips. "Charmed," he said. "Now, let's get on it blokes and madams. We're wasting our bloody time."

I eased behind my desk, noting it thoroughly ransacked, and frowned. My siblings remained upstairs, and I cursed them out within my mind, praying the meddlesome pricks listened.

Tomas ignored my mental outburst and asked, "You accepted a case involving an Elioud witch named Lily Westcott?"

"Yes." I offered them seats.

Belle dragged in extra chairs, but the human shook his head. Tomas and Korri slipped into the leather seats, and Veric paced behind them, his hands folded behind his back. Boss or not, this was my office and my operation.

"Cain," I whispered, and the sound of his name off my own lips squeezed my heart. I coughed to disguise the twisting of my face. "Cain Westcott brought the case to me."

Belle scooted her chair across the wooden floor, pulling up beside Korrigan.

Tomas said, "Two months ago, we attacked a string of brothels in Delphia owned by the demon Jules Garland."

"We? I know of Jules."

Belle shrugged and shook her head. I hadn't known Jules was a Garland. We didn't have this intel, and I scribbled the new notes down on a piece of paper.

Veric replied, "Knew mate, my father is dead."

Tomas held up his hand, and Veric flashed me a crooked grin. Despite the red hair, he resembled his brother, Boric, the self-proclaimed King of Garland. Jules was their father? Why would he not have been the king?

"We meaning Petre and I."

Laughter rippled through me, and I shook my head, scratching the words into the precious paper.

"Surely, it's not that unbelievable." Tomas crossed his legs and pretended offense, but a small smile played on his lips.

My elbows rested on my desk, and tears pricked my eyes. The pompous Duc raided a brothel?

"Merde, Dorian, I know. Surprised me too."

"Sorry." The laughter refused to leave my body. "You had possession of Lily, then?"

Veric mumbled, "Not by choice," under his breath, and Korrigan swatted him without so much as a glance behind her.

Something more was going on here. What were they trying to hide? "What do you mean not by choice? Did you or didn't you have her?" I stared directly at Veric.

"We, meaning Angelica and I, didn't know until now that the woman we'd rescued was most likely her sister." He leaned and looked down at Korrigan. "Tomas knew but as usual, he failed to relay the information in a timely fashion."

Tomas ignored him and recounted the raids, elaborating where he thought it necessary to prove himself capable. "It's true. I kept her identity a secret."

I stretched and cracked my back. "Why?"

"Because I didn't want to hurt anyone...What happened before...It's too late now, but I'm almost 100 percent positive." Tomas lowered his head.

My hands pressed against the top of my desk. "So you and Petre

raided brothels in Delphia and freed women, men, and children."
I cracked a small smile. "I'm impressed. But how did Garland find
you?" Sounded as if Petre did most of the dirty work.

"Jules had stolen me," Korrigan whispered. "Petre bought me
from him, and Jules knew where he lived."

"We're not exactly unknown up here,"Tomas added and leaned
forward on his cane.

What I waited for Tomas to explain was how the demon horse
had become human, but it didn't arrive. My eyes locked with Veric's
amber glower. "We have a common enemy, then. Your brother
has something in his possession, and I'd like her back." For Cain.
"And if she isn't Lily, I'll keep looking and looking and looking."

Korrigan rose from the chair and cleared her throat. A light
shined in her amber colored eyes, and I had to wonder if she wasn't
Heaven sent. The quiet strength she held made me pause and listen.

Childlike in appearance, but her words flowed forth and
reached beyond her years. "I know Lily. We grew up together in
Hampshire House in Delphia. Jules had owned us both, but he
called her Roxie." Her bottom lip trembled, and her eyes glistened. "When Petre liberated them…" Her resolve faltered and
her strength crumbled. "I'm sorry."

Footsteps carried overhead and trailed into the stairwell. Those
who breathed held their breaths while the first tear leaked from
Korrigan's eye. Crying didn't make her weak, though. Elioud and
vampire combined, yet the woman before me appeared pure, and
her reactions almost human. She loved. An aura, the light of her
heart surrounded her.

Hallo eased from the staircase and strolled forward. Her head
nodded and she mouthed, "The queen." She halted in the doorway
of my office.

Another misprint in history I hadn't caught? I rubbed my
chin. My sister nodded again.

"She walks among us," Fauna had said.

Damned yet pure. The same light radiated from Cain, and
the radiance spread, glowing from Tomas, even Belle. They were

all descendants of Lucifer...puzzle pieces plopped into place. My brother may have been damned, but his kin were not.

Veric gathered Korrigan into his arms and shushed her. He continued on her behalf, as she sobbed against his chest, "Some of the victims turned on us. Stockholm syndrome, or who the bloody hell knows. Garland led an airship and ransacked some of the safe houses too. The majority of Petre's people are safe with the ABDA, but a ship captured Lily and those staying with Tomas. They may have taken Cain again. I don't know."

My attention snapped up when he said again. Part of me suspected he had spent time in the brothels. Part of me hoped he'd been a labor slave, like Belle, not that her life had been any easier than those in the brothels. Cain never elaborated. I never pressed him either. The fire popped at the same time as my jaw, and my gaze darted to the floor.

"You all right, mate?"

My fists curled, nails scraping the papers strewn over the desk. No, I was not all right. Further from all right. Red tinted the edges of my vision, and heat spread over my neck. I palmed the sweaty surface, scratching deep into my flesh. The demons would pay. I would track and kill every one of them. Hunt them until the end of time itself if that was what it required. Wrong to shove Cain aside. My head hung in shame.

Tomas clamped a cold hand on my shoulder. "You didn't know, Dorian, did you?"

I hadn't noticed his movement. I shook my head and stormed through my desk. Papers flew and my hands blindly searched for the photo. "Why the fuck did you move my shite around. Do I call you up for a chat, visit, and move your shite?"

Besides Cain's clothes and my memories, the tintype was all I had of him. If the Horsemen would not let me end the world, I would destroy those who had harmed Cain.

The two Elioud spoke in hushed tones, and the strange human said nothing to my outburst. My finger touched the cold, tin photograph. Pain seared through my aching heart. Their eyes reflected no pain, yet I had witnessed the yearning in his butterscotch gaze; the same reflected in Korri's amber eyes now. A struggle had warred within him, but not the same as mine. What ghosts had chased him when he closed his eyes? When I'd kissed or made love to him? I glanced at Korrigan, shifting toward the photograph. Her gaze lifted as I said, "This is you…you…"

"I'm not Lily," she said.

My finger flicked the older woman standing behind them. "Angelica Westcott."

"Garland," Veric corrected. "Westcott-Garland."

She balled her tiny fists at her sides. "Korri Von Baron. Why can't you get that through your thick skull?"

A sudden urge to smack my head against my desk overtook my senses. The last name didn't matter.

"We were on our way to find Lily and the others, when we ran into rather unfortunate circumstances," Tomas said. Nikolai snorted, but Tomas' attention remained on me.

My gaze fell and fixated on the photograph shaking in the air.

"We lost Petre, then I heard your summons."

"I wasn't going after her, yet. Cain had only brought me the case a week ago before we… parted." Maybe longer depending on what day it was. Well not just her, I had to find the others, retrieve the keys for my siblings, and manage a way to control the south. But without a solid lead, I hadn't known where to begin, and Cain had been trying to stop me from uncovering the truth. Why? So he had a past. So what. We all had one.

Tomas frowned and shook his head. "I gave him Belle's card seven months ago."

"Fuck," the curse ripped through my lips, and my cheeks flushed at the memory.

The Duc moved to his seat. "Cain went through a rough patch after his boyfriend cheated. He lost his job and almost his home."

I pressed on my throbbing temples. Shite was I an asshole. *Do not think about it. They will all know the truth. You broke Cain.*

Tomas's hands folded, unfolded, reflecting a man deep in thought. "I assume you care for him."

Yes… maybe love…if my battered heart can love again…oh look who is lying now, you shoddy bastard. In hell and up a creek without a paddle, fuck me, I do love Cain.

Veric's foot tapped, and Korrigan's brow rose. The pixie slid from his arms and sat beside Tomas again, wiping the puffy bags lining her porcelain face. She grasped the photograph, and my boss leaned over her. Tears sprang to his eyes.

"He's a good bloke." Veric sniffled. "Went through hell and back with me after we left Garland, but I…lost him in Delphia, after an ambush."

Veric was Cain's brother-in-law? I glanced from Veric to Korrigan, finally understanding. He was Angelica's husband. Despite appearing as a miniature version of herself, Korrigan truly was Angelica, Cain's older sister. Shite, and I thought my family had issues.

Tomas leaned on the chair's arm; his body twisted and he studied Veric. "You didn't tell him you were alive? Salaud."

Veric shook his head, face beet red.

"He escaped and traveled north," Tomas said. "I found him, barely alive, nothing but skin and bones. It took une, deux, trois years to nurse him back to health." The room fell silent. He sat there, chewing his lip, his face holding a hard scowl. His chair skidded across the floor as he drew himself closer. "You know what they do to the men like him in Garland?"

Slavery varied in the south, but it wasn't all-backbreaking labor. Homosexual and good-looking, Cain made a prime candidate as a sex slave. But was I any better than the swine for lusting after him?

Veric averted his eyes. He knew something more about my Cain. My lips parted, preparing to ask.

"The brothel changes us," Korri interrupted, dark brown brows scrunched and her dainty legs swaying, knocking into my desk.

My brows scrunched too; I wouldn't have pegged her a former whore. She was too mouthy.

"They break us, leave us to collect the pieces. Lily is strong, like me, but we each have our breaking points." Korrigan stood and handed me the photograph. "This is Lily," her finger flicked the picture, "I don't recognize Cain, but *I* wouldn't." She touched her nose.

"You knew the lad,"he whispered into her ear.Veric's boots squeaked; he stopped behind her. The overprotective nature was common.

My chair groaned, leaning back. The intimacy of his touch wasn't lost on me either. Veric loved Korri, but she didn't love him. He comforted her, but nothing sparked in her eyes when she glanced in his direction.

"If my brother has him…" He bowed his head. "Our families were…friends before the Sundering…"

Veric kept on talking, but my gaze narrowed on her. Why would she have knowingly lied? Even now, she held up the pretense.

"Morning Star lost a bet to my brother over three hundred years ago."

"Excuse me?"I yelled to the agent. My chair snapped forward.

Belle spoke the name again. "Morning Star."

"Angel, Lily, and Cain are all Morning Star Elioud. Doesn't anyone read the bloody files? We 'ave one for each of the Seven families." Veric marched to Belle.

She gulped, her eyes both wild and wide.

He thumbed to her, but Veric glanced to me. "She's one, too."

My fingers pinched the bridge of my nose. "I missed that memo. Back up to this bet…I know what they all are, don't care."

"Cain is a victim and so are his sisters." Tomas infiltrated my mind.

My teeth clenched against the fuzziness washing over my head. "Get out," I shouted, and tossed my hands into the air. "Go." My fists slammed onto the desk, and I slung the papers onto the floor.

No one listened. All eyes turned on me.

Veric said, "Not all demons are bad. Look at me, mate. I'm a Garland, and the head of the ABDA Elioud Extraction Division."

I glared into his amber eyes. My fingers ached, the skin stretching and bone rising. "Tell me about the bet or get the hell out of my office." I dropped my head into my hands, gripping and tugging my hair.

"They're a bunch of conniving demons like their ancestor." Mark glanced to Belle and grinned. "Except her."

Belle shook her dreads at him. Man, he needed to work on his execution.

"Just because Lucifer's blood runs through my veins doesn't make me him," Korrigan whispered. "We are not him. We don't want to be him." Wide, light-filled eyes released two tears. "We didn't ask for this life."

My heart pounded with each word she spoke. She reminded me of him, and the words were something he would have said. *I must find Cain.* Had to leave...had to hold him one last time.

"He's right. I am one as well." Tomas palmed his face and removed the goggles from the tops of his head. Before my eyes, his blue eyes blinked and turned amber. "I mentored them both, because they are my family."

I sensed Hallo's stare. She crept farther into the room.

"Cain wouldn't tell me how he came to be in the Garland service, and Lily was far too fragile still." He leaned forward. "I, too, would like to know more about this bet. My dear cousin died because of it."

Why didn't Cain tell me?

"Brother, look how you reacted." Hallo halted beside Veric. "Look how I've reacted in the past. We saw the Seven Princes as enemies, but we have proof not all are evil right in front of us. Lucifer they are not. You see their light."

"We're not even talking about that, Hallo. I'm fine with who Cain is, what I'm not fine with are all the lies." And whoever lost this bet. Whoever hurt him. I wished to read Hallo's mind, though. Did we share the same suspicions about Veric?

Pale light beamed from Cain and Tomas, but Korrigan's illumination blazed brighter than any Elioud I had ever met. She was right. Belles blinked at me; her heart was pure. My hand scrubbed over my face. The same light in their eyes was what attracted me to Cain. Like the sun, it became a sign of hope and renewal.

"Lucifer was Father's most beautiful Archangel," Hallowed said. "Is it any wonder that his children share his light?"

"I'm sorry," I whispered through dry lips. Judgment was once my duty, but it was no longer my place. It didn't answer my question either.

Tomas offered, "It's possible Cain's still in Arcadia, even Nova Scotia, but he's not in Halifax."

Hallelujah, if the sound of trumpets didn't go off. I was going plum crazy. He gave me a quizzical glance, and I smirked. Veric, on the other hand, wasn't ready to reveal his secret.

"Where is Petre?" I changed the subject. "What happened?"

"He turned into a human. Korrigan attempted to sire him, but she failed when Jules blew up the train," Nikolai said. "My brother is lost."

Silence enveloped the room. Looking to my sister, she nodded in agreement to the one thought floating in my mind: Petre could not be dead. Hallo mouthed the words in agreement. Nikolai spun around and met Hallo. The spearing stare caught him by surprise, and he quickly averted his gaze.

"Belle," I called, and motioned her forward.

Markos tilted his head and eyed us. We would need all the help we could get, and I trusted her like my family.

"Track down Fauna. Witches and warlocks are her domain. If anyone can trace Lily, it's her." I crossed my leg over my thigh and stared at my folded hands. "Wilderness is a good place to start." Wilderness was a school she'd run prior to the Sundering.

Tomas shot me a pointed glare, and I sighed. If there had been even a small chance Cain was in Arcadia, I didn't want to lose the opportunity to hunt down his ass. Once I knew he was safe, I would leave him be.

"She can track Cain. If I can't find him first," I said, and nodded to Belle before rising from my chair. "Fauna knows you, but don't travel alone. Tomas, go with her."

She scribbled the coordinates to the cove on a piece of paper and handed the note to Tomas. *"Don't leave him be. You were the one he sought, Dorian.*" Aloud he added, "Mon ami, il vous aime. Vous êtes flamme pour sa bougie. Sans vous, il ne survivra pas." *My friend, he loves you. You are flame to his candle. Without you, he will not survive.*

"Don't take the human," I yelled, and ran up the stairs, searching for my hat. Circumstances needed to stop changing. But I had a solid plan. As intriguing as Nikolai was, a living and breathing human would pose a problem. Fauna tempted humans, and the temptation served as a distraction we didn't need. Markos likely already ran him through the ringer the moment he saw him.

I rushed back downstairs and cursed at my missing hat. Where had I lost it? I combed fingers through my hair. I liked my fedora, but enjoyed hiding behind the covering more.

"He refuses to leave my side," Korri said, glancing toward Nicolai.

Veric's jaw stiffened, and he inched a fraction closer, wrapping his arms around her tiny waist. I smirked at the reaction, but refrained from saying I would've preferred him to Korrigan any day. But the truth…I wanted Cain.

"Belle will accompany Tomas." The faster everyone departed, the quicker I searched for Cain. My hands trembled at the thought of seeing him again. "Fine. Veric, Korrigan, and Nikolai will go with Hallo."

"Sorry, mate, but I don't take orders from you."

Hallo snapped, "You don't speak to him that way."

I lifted my hand and cracked my neck. Korri stepped in front of Veric and hissed at Hallo.

Hallo rolled her eyes and pointed her finger at Veric. "He can undo you all. Don't be such a wanker."

I chuckled at the scene, especially because Korrigan was so small. Like we were watching a Chihuahua and a Great Dane.

Markos muttered, "Calm down, he doesn't know who we are, Sister."

A wide smile spread over my lips, and I rocked on my heels. The ABDA hadn't told him? "Allow me to offer the formality Tomas neglected. This is Conquest better remembered as the First Horsemen. Markos, whom you've already met, is War, and

Fauna whom you will shortly have the pleasure of acquainting is Pestilence."

Veric stumbled backward. "Bloody hell that makes you—"

My hands folded in front of me, fingers dancing, and a smirk tilted my mouth. "Death." I leaned on the desk and collected my thoughts. "Oh, and Petre is very much alive."

"Bullocks." Veric's mouth gaped. "Pardon?"

"How do you know?" All three voices sounded together.

I eyed each one, while silently summoning my scythe and drawing from the swirling darkness no one else saw unless I wanted them to. "Because I am Death, in case you missed that tiny fact, the Fourth rider of the Apocalypse, and Petre von Baron, the former priest, bears my mark for purgatory, just like you, Nicolai." The jeweled weapon flew into my hand.

Tomas jumped from his seat, and the others inched away. Feet shuffled and chairs skidded across the floor as Mark and Hallo's laughter filled the room.

I pointed the weapon toward Nikolai. "His soul lives on, and I have not felt a call to retrieve him. Have you, Sister?"

Without another word, I left the stunned and wide-eyed guests gasping in surprise. My goal remained finding Cain and making sure he stayed safe, but I had not lied. Petre lived, and Hallo would find him. They were safe, her virtuous nature would protect them, and if I knew my brother, Markos would join them to shadow Belle. Now, there was a headache I didn't need.

I glanced around the old neighborhood, and my feet pranced lively over the packed snow. Tomas had his assistant pull Cain's files from the quaint Blood and Bread on Main Street. I made his last known address my first stop.

The high-rise was once an office building. Halifax had many buildings that'd survived and became housing for those who had lost their residences after the Sundering. Tomas eventually bought them for his workers employed at various businesses, making housing part of their salary. Those living there, I assumed, worked for one of the electric companies he co-owned with Petre.

I blinked, wondering what Cain did for a living, and stared upward at the charcoal windows lining the street. Some had balconies jutting forth. But he didn't work at Blood and Bread, or the electric company; he had come from the other side of town the day of our meeting. I shook the thought aside and opened the door.

The lobby was empty; the attendant gone, evident by his sign. An elevator dinged in the foyer, but I didn't trust the power grid and spied the emergency stairs. Heavy and metal, I hefted my shoulder against the cold door. The damp staircase reeked of mold and mildew.

Piss permeated in the stairwell. Paint chipped and peeled, but warmth radiated from the hissing floorboards. Various sounds echoed into the hallway and staircase. Graffiti painted the floor, ceilings, and walls.

The higher my legs climbed, the more the destruction lessened. A good sign, even if Cain still deserved better, but from what I understood of brothel life, a slum was high living in comparison.

I paused on the stairwell and clutched my pounding heart. The biggest mistake of my life was letting him go. After he kicked my ass, I should've shoved my tongue down his throat. Instead, like a coward, I sprinted away to lick my wounds and drowned myself in a sea of misery trying to forget him.

Cain was a Morning Star...Lucifer's ilk. My head rested against the painted-stone wall. I didn't care what blood coursed through his veins. "No, I sought any reason to let him go before snuffing out his radiance for good."

What bothered me were his lies. Plus, he'd been abused, sexually. I tried to think of something else, concentrating on our short time together, and admitted him orchestrating my mind's desire was hot. When Cain had made love to me, he'd etched himself into my soul. On some level, we'd connected in a way I had never experienced before him—a way I never wanted to experience with another.

But Cain still deserved love, and I found myself incapable of releasing the barriers of my heart. Old wounds resurfaced, bleeding, as if inflicted yesterday. I didn't know how to let them go.

A sigh tickled my tight chest; I glanced into the stairwell and checked the address again—four more floors to go.

In a matter of days, Cain had changed me, and above all odds; he had made me want to change. Not for him. No. Love didn't work that way, did it? I wanted to be a better version of myself for me.

Part of me was already halfway there, but like him, the past haunted me. Time to let it go. If I could figure that out, and he stopped lying, maybe we had a fighting chance.

My heart pounded, and sweat beaded on my forehead. I leaned my head against the bricks. On an exhale, I hissed air through my teeth. "C'mon, stop being an arse. You can do this. You can love again you sodden wanker, so pull your shite together."

My legs bounded up the stairs, taking two at a time until reaching his floor. I glanced left and right into the long, straight hallway. The pep talk wore thin on my nerves, my body heavy. I shuffled closer, reading the numbers. Smack dab in the middle sat number six—Cain's door.

I caught my breath and willed my heart to steady. No sounds or strange scents emitted, unless the slight odor of manure was odd. My hand lifted, and I stared at my trembling fingers as they curled into a tight fist. What would I say to him?

I rapped over the surface and paused, placing my ear to the door. Behind me, a door creaked, and I twisted.

"He's probably at work." A soft, feminine voice spoke.

I turned and blinked at the gray-haired woman, hunched over and gripping her door. I offered a warm and inviting smile. "When does Cain come home?"

"You're not from Garland." Her arms crossed over her chest, and she looked both ways.

I reached into my pocket and retrieved my badge before flipping it open "I'm..." Lover, boyfriend, or friend? With my other hand, I scratched my head, reaching for my hat. "I'm Special Agent

Dorian Fox with the Arcadian Bureau of Demonic Affairs."

Her face brightened, and she opened the door a little wider. Large warm eyes crinkled at the corners. "You must be Cain's Dorian. He's told me all about you."

I returned her smile and added a nod. I wanted to be his.

"Wait a moment, and I'll let you in, dearie. I have a key here somewhere."

My cheeks flushed at her pet name, and I chuckled. Who called Death dearie?

She closed the door, and keys rattled. "He'll be home any minute now. I'm Jan." She worked the locks.

My heart thudded. "You mentioned Garland. Has anyone else come by?"

Jan nodded and scowled. "Yes, but I sent those men away. They scared me. Had a big G on their uniforms." She started toward her apartment.

Did she send the anonymous tip to Belle? My brow arched. Behind me, her door shut. I stared into his dark flat, inching inside, and closed his door. A deep breath filled my lungs, and Cain's smoldering scent hit me at once. But I resisted the urge to roll myself against the walls.

Light filtered through the windows, and I glanced around, my eyes quickly adjusting. Pictures lined his white walls. Some were of his sister, Lily; some I didn't recognize, but Angel's photo hung too. Volumes of battered classics packed his bookshelves, and sheets covered the lived in furniture. The level of cleanliness didn't surprise me either.

I removed my coat and hung it on the hook by the front door. I placed a hand on my revolver, nestled on my hip. Jan said strange people came looking for him, but Markos said he was safe. Neither of those truths sat well in my stomach. More lies or Cain decided to evade everyone. I stroked my chin and studied another photograph. Despite his stated age, his caramel eyes reflected youthfulness, innocence.

Where was the logic? None of this made sense. His departure or the need for secrets didn't make for good judgment either. Snooping—not beneath me—I bee lined for his bedroom.

T-shirts and long sleeved shirts filled his closet; no signs he was planning to flee. His dresser held different bottles of cologne. Sniffing each one, I found the smoldering scent I had come to crave. My stomach tightened, the wooded fire hit my nose, and my groin stirred with life. If I closed my eyes, I would see him…see us wrapped in a warm embrace. A touch of my lips served as a remembrance of his fierce kisses. My hand ran over my heart, and the emptiness there led only to a grimace.

"Get a grip," I mumbled at my own distractions, and spun around. Bottles clattered at the sudden movement, but I ignored them, like the emotions reeling around me.

Loving again would end in pain and eternal agony. I had mislaid my heart to another before, vowing never to allow its loss again. Leading purgatory didn't exclude me from prison. Earth became my own hell; the ones I loved condemned me.

Cain's bed appeared slept in, but I resisted wrapping myself in the covers. My eyes closed, centering myself instead. If I were he, where would I hide my secrets?

The bed squeaked as I sat and reached underneath. Nothing there. Gold lettering flickered in the soft light. Two leather-bound books rested on the nightstand. Cain's journal and a Holy Bible, but Father's divine words didn't pique my curiosities.

A better man would have left the second book alone, but I was neither better nor a man. No larger than a pocket and the writing inside was etched in a tiny, neat scripted hand. It had to be a diary of sorts. Dates marked each entry, and I thumbed to the last record and flipped to seven days ago:

Well, I finally approached Dorian. The kicker was I didn't realize he was the tracker until it was too late. The past seven months came rushing back when I saw him. All the dreams and fantasies resurfaced, along with the bitter angst of our original meeting. Bit by bit, he buried me with his thoughts and secrets. I swam in his mind and memories, but found no reason for his behaviors.

Seven months wasted on a dream…time to move on with my life, find another way to save Lily, and find Angelica. We are few and almost the last of our kind.

"Kind?" The last Morning Stars. Had Boric managed to trim them down to a handful? No wonder he wanted Cain back if his goal was to control the remaining six families. Of course, it was an assumption. I slapped my face. The idiot sought their keys. My fingers rubbed over mine. At least I held the real key.

I skipped to the next page, but it seemed mundane in comparison. Curiosity gained the better of me, and I skimmed backward, reaching the day we actually met.

Broke up with Ned today and met someone new. The meeting didn't go over so well, but I'm trying to find him. So far, all I have is a first name: Dorian.

I read on, scanning through the pages over the following months. Each day, during his free time, Cain had searched for me in Halifax and the outskirts. My heart tightened at the gesture and thoughtfulness of his actions. I had headed to the Wilderness with Fauna to forget him.

"I never gave-up. Pathetic, right?" Cain said, and I slammed the journal shut. He forced a smile. "Now, you found me."

"Tomas said you were missing." The words sounded wrong, and they weren't the ones I wished to say.

"I'm not, so you can leave now." His biceps flexed before crisscrossing over his chest.

"No."

"No?" Cain raised a brow.

I placed the book on the nightstand. "You're coming with me."

"Not a chance in Hell, sweets."

"Feisty." I leaped on him, fast, offering Cain no time to react. My hands smoothed over his rough face, and his stare burned through me, but he didn't push me away either. "Please, don't fight me on this, babe."

No response. He lifted his hands in the air and refused to touch me. His reaction stung, squeezing my heart in a vice grip.

Someone pounded on the door, but as Cain opened his mouth, my own silenced him. I wiggled my tongue against his and groaned at the fiery flavor invading my senses. My hands rubbed over his chest, beneath his sweater, searching for the heat I lacked.

He bit my tongue.

"Ouch." I drew away, but pinned his shoulders to the wall. "Be nice, babe."

Cain whisper yelled, "No, you don't get to come in here and play hero. Screw you, Dorian, I can take care of myself." He puffed out his bottom lip, and I wanted to lick and nibble the tender surface. Cain sidestepped me, gaze skirting his surroundings, readying to flee.

"Like hell you can." But I followed him. The pounding continued, and I pushed past him.

Cain reached for me, but I eased from his grip. "Dorian."

Voices echoed from the hall, and the sweet, little, old Jan raised hers' the loudest. "I told you to leave."

Spying through the privacy hole, I caught the backs of two men dressed in leather jackets, green slacks below. My fingers pointed and snapped at Cain to move away. As quietly as possible, I opened the door and slipped into the hallway.

"Can I help you, gentlemen?" Both spun around at my voice, and my shoulder eased against the doorframe.

"We're looking for someone." The taller man cocked his head.

My eyes rolled, and I shifted my weight against the frame, crossing my legs and folding my arms over my chest. If they were armed, they would think twice before drawing on me—hopefully—bullets still hurt like the dickens. My thoughts remained on mundane events, but they were with Garland. Idiots might as well wave a red flag while they were at it. What moron walked into enemy territory and didn't wear a disguise?

"Is she seventy-five?"

"Nah, it's a he." The taller man smacked the shorter man. "Ow, what you do that for?" he said to his friend. "You look like him sorta, but he's got different hair and eyes. You're too tanned."

"Maybe it's a disguise, dummy." The shorter man rolled his shoulders into a stiffened shrug. "How we know you're not the man?"

I re-crossed my legs "Leave the lady alone, and we'll sort this out…like gentlemen."

They turned and apologized to Jan. "Sorry, ma'am."

I blinked. Their type didn't seem capable of manners. I scratched my neck and rechecked my surroundings. I wasn't the apologizing type, but my future included graveling at a certain someone's feet. My fingers drummed while we stared at one another. "Now, who are you looking for?"

"Cain Westcott."

Only every ounce of self-control stopped me from killing them on the spot. I asked, "Why?"

"What's it to you?" The men exchanged glances, and the taller one messed with his coat's lapel.

I blew on my fingers. "Depends."

"On?" He stepped forward but stopped.

"Your answer…Maybe I'm looking for him? Why else would I be in his apartment?" Demons were too easy to mess with, and I couldn't help myself. I inched back inside and said, "Think about it."

I spied through the peephole again. The men were arguing in hushed tones. The taller man wanted to kick down the door and kill me. I would pay to see him try.

Cain's hand touched my back. My hand wrapped around to caress his fingers. Cold metal greeted me. Where did he get the ring? Had he moved on already? *No, stop thinking like that and pay attention.*

My heart thundered, each second passing, but there was no way in Hell or Heaven those men would lay a finger on him. Unsure how his mind reading worked, my thoughts instructed him to pack a bag. He could not stay here if men were looking for him. Cain didn't budge. The feel of his skin, his warm hand touching me, I had missed all of him.

"Missed you too, sweets."

Heat warmed my cheeks, but I shook Cain from my mind and concentrated on the men outside the door. His strong arms engulfed me, squeezing me tightly from behind, and Cain's head rested on my back. Concentration was futile. Nothing had ever felt so damned right, even in the wrongest of moments.

The shorter man knocked, and I shooed Cain away.

Cain grasped my hands and tugged me from the door. "No," he mouthed.

I nodded and wrestled from his grasp. The security hole showed the men had left, and Cain slid the security chain over.

"Why did you come?" he asked, grasping my backside and squeezing.

A groan left my lips, and my ass pushed into his palms.

Cain whispered, "Did you miss my cock that much? Hmm?" His hand skirted to my dick and massaged the tented hard on. "Sure looks like you did."

"Cain," I swallowed hard, "I came to talk." Words choked in my throat as he stroked me through my jeans.

He whispered, "Talk huh? Didn't take you for the type," and spun me around.

"Watch the guns." Man had a point. Talking and sharing wasn't my game. Kumbaya and feelings suited others, but with Cain, I wanted to try and desired more than sex, even though it, too, was phenomenal.

He slipped his hands into the gap of my jeans and slid around front. "Sweets, you blow my mind sometimes with your thoughts." Cain adjusted my cock and rubbed his groin against my ass. "But I need you."

"Really? Now?" I blinked through the peephole, and a strange sensation rolled over my skin and prickled each hair. My holsters and belt unbuckled themselves; jeans unzipped themselves.

He yanked down my pants and grasped my cock. Slowly Cain pumped me with both his hands.

I glanced over my shoulder. "Oh, fuck."

Cain winked and twirled his finger in a circle; my garments plopped to the floor.

"Now turn," he ordered.

My back pressed against the cold door, the chill causing me to shiver. I glanced to the floor, sweeping my gaze everywhere but him. "So…"

Cain cupped my face, guiding my chin until I looked at him. "Why are you really here, Dorian?"

"For you."

"Me?" His watery, sleep-deprived, butterscotch eyes spilled over. "You really came for me?"

"C'mere, babe." I nodded and parted my dry lips. He was my everything. Heat radiated from him and penetrated my bones. I didn't want to be without him, ever. So much more I wanted to say to him, but the words didn't arrive.

Cain inched closer, and I grasped his t-shirt, hauling despite the threads groaning in protest. Nose to nose, we stood, embracing. I tilted to the left; he slanted to the right. Shocks registered and the air between us electrified. My parched mouth parted. His bottom lip trembled, and he swallowed hard. Our foreheads touched.

Our lips brushed, and my tongue teased along his thick bottom lip. Sparks flew behind my half-lidded eyes, and a moan ripped through me. His teasing flavor drowned me in fiery heat. *Fuck sex, you are all I need.*

Gasping, his hands seized my hair, hauling my head closer, as if I could have been any closer. Cain's tongue slipped into my mouth, stirring my groin into overdrive.

A knock vibrated through my shoulders.

"Don't," he said, breaking away. Cain kissed my neck, trailing a path down my t-shirt covered chest, his rough fingertips sliding beneath the fabric. Kneeling, he stared into my eyes, and my cockhead disappeared through his lips.

"Fuck." Hot lava ripped through me, surging into my gut, as my head slammed against the door. One full week without him in my life and I would not last long. My cods tightened, rising and aching.

His hand glided over my shaft, and he shifted his mouth between my legs. My fingers curled into his hair, nails digging into his scalp, as wet warmth encompassed me.

"Stop," I hissed, and didn't mean the word, not really. "Fucking tease."

Laughter rocked through him and each tremor squeezed my sensitive sack. Cain kissed and licked his way along my shaft to my tip. I shuddered, clinging to a sliver of sanity; my toes curled and my hips gently rocked. He stared at me with smiling, mischievous-filled eyes.

The pounding restarted. "Yo man, you in there? What the verdict?"

I grunted and bit my lip. Cain swallowed my dick, his nose rubbing my pubic bone.

"There's a bounty on his head. We'll give you a cut if you help us out."

"Uh-huh. One..." My head slammed against the door again, eyes pinching shut. "Babe, fuck, I'm going to..." Gritting my teeth, I was holding out for as long as possible, but my body quaked, my cock pulsing ropes down his sweet throat.

They banged again. "What the hell, man?"

"In... a min..." I rested, catching my breath and allowing my heart rate to settle, against the front door. "Minute."

After swallowing every drop, Cain rose and wiped his grinning mouth. The light brown fuzz covering his cheeks appeared red, his face heated. "Sweets," he mouthed. "Don't."

"You're going to get yourself hurt." I kissed him, squeezing his cheeks. "Let me get rid of them, then I'll take care of you."

I righted my clothes. Damn, he might figure out a way to get himself killed with that mouth alone. No way would I ever give that up. But I had done so once before and came here expecting to do so again. I sighed inwardly but grinned outward.

Cain disappeared around the corner. I cracked the door and glanced through the chain lock. The same men waited.

"About time man."

Metal clicked against my head, and a chuckle escaped my mouth. "Let us in."

I chewed my lip and pretended to think, staring at the ceiling. "How about I don't?"

"You's got a gun to your head, and you tellin' me no?" the short one asked. "Man, who the hell are you?"

"Let me show you." My head tilted, ducking beneath the chain, and I squeezed through the opening, my body dropping its facade. Neither man noticed my skin melting into nothing but bone, as I didn't alter my face, but it allowed me to slip through the tiny opening.

"Show me what?" Tall man stepped closer with his fist curled.

I chuckled and whispered, "Falcatae."

Both men stepped backward, exchanging a quick glance, but when nothing happened, they lunged. Metal slid and rustled behind me. I ducked and the door creaked, opening. Cain stepped out and shoved me to the right, knocking me to the ground.

Purple fireballs danced in his open palms. With a flick of his wrists, both volleyed toward the demons, hitting their chests. Igniting in violet flames, their screams faded and their fire blackened bodies eroded into piles of ash.

"Told you I could take care of myself," he mumbled, grasped my t-shirt's collar, and dragged me inside the door. "Your scythe failed?" He dropped me and slammed the door. He stormed into the living room, the locks all clicking into place with a wave of his hand. Cain swiped a bottle from the coffee table, sipped his water, and acted normal, as if he hadn't murdered two demons in the hallway, or moved the locks with his mind.

My forehead pinched. They were lower level demons, but still demons.

"You know, I didn't call it right on purpose. Wanted to see them try to kick my ass." I smirked and leaned up on my arms. "You're the only one who's ever succeeded."

He raised his eyebrow, a glint flaring in his eyes. With a shrug, he sipped his water again.

"You still can't stay here," I said.

Cain plopped on his sofa. "Watch me."

"You can't be serious, babe." I jumped to my feet. There had to be a compromise. I sat next to him and wrapped my arm around his shoulders. For a second, I thought about straddling his lap, but thought better of it. "Fine, then, but I'm staying too."

"Why do you care? I don't understand you, Dorian."

Because he'd mattered when no one else had.

Cain asked, "But—why?"

I had no answer. More so, I wasn't ready to tell him in words. As soon as he was safe, I would leave him in peace, if he wanted me to, but I could not walk away on my own again. That was love, right?

"Obsessions and promises fuel me, but what drives you?" he asked.

Thrill and justice would have been my answer, but he drove me. The job mattered, not the client, not until him. A long miserable week had passed, and I hadn't the strength to accomplish any task. I should have.

Cain reached over and curled his fingers around mine. "I want you in my life." A sweet sound sighed from his pouty lips. "Dorian, you stay, or you leave now and never look back." Cain's eyes flashed red, but they quickly reverted to golden brown.

I winced at the truth flickering before my own eyes. The Seven families all had offspring with amber eyes, not all Elioud, only them.

"What will happen when the next secret is unleashed? I'm not sticking around for you to split when shit gets tough, and it will only get tougher. I'm full of 'em, sweets."

Only one way I could think of to solve this. "Fine. Let's air the dirty laundry now and end the secrets."

"I know your secrets." He snorted and shook his head.

"The ones I've thought about, yes, but I have secrets too."

Cain gestured me to begin and drank his water.

"I slept with a woman by accident once. Your turn."

Chapter Ten

Cain

Water squirted from my mouth and burned my nose, spraying over my coffee table and myself. I coughed and wiped my face with the back of my hand. I ignored the stinging in my nose, but plastered an unmistakable grin on my face. "How exactly do you sleep with a woman by accident?"

Dorian slapped my back, and I coughed again, shaking the drowned sensation from my head without making a fool of myself.

"This I've got to hear, sweets." The story intrigued me, but what ran through my mind sang a different tune. Dorian returned for me. Maybe I had been wrong. On some level, God listened, and love could become mine. If Dorian allowed me a chance, why couldn't I afford him the same and try?

He glanced away and blushed. "Yeah, because telling you the first time worked out so well."

I wrung the water from my clothes.

"Go change."

He watched me, and the hairs rose over my arms. The sweet taste of him swam in my mouth again. My couch groaned as I hopped to my feet. My fantasy had played out, and if he left, at least the man who birthed the desire within me had fulfilled it. I walked to my bedroom, down the hall from the living room, shaking my head.

Upon entering my room, I paused by my bed and glanced over my shoulder to find Dorian framing the doorway. His emerald green gaze smoldered, and he ran it along the length of my body. But his mind wasn't patient, not like his stoic composure, and my lips pulled into another grin, that time over his internal battle.

"What?" His inky lashes fluttered.

I wiggled the wet jeans down my thighs, revealing the damp underwear clinging to my skin in all the right places. At least I hoped as much. His pink tongue slid across his bottom lip. Blood pumped harder through my body, thickening my length. From the moment I had strode in and found him on my bed, more than need surged through my veins.

But what do I call it when I need another's presence, touch, and taste more than air? Is that love?

My eyelids lowered. Denial was useless, but I had to know more than lust blossomed between us. We could be more than casual lovers, fucking whenever the mood demanded. My lashes flickered. Heat colored my skin. More than desire simmered inside of me, clutching and searing claws into my heart.

Despite his role in our hellish world and his unlockable secrets, I still love the idea of Dorian, but is this more than love for him?

What was more than love? No word existed in my world.

My finger crooked, and a smile played at his lips. Heavy steps brought him within my grasp, and I reached my palm toward his rough cheek. The contrast amazed me as much as the growth attracted me. Thick, kissable lips parted, and pressing the digit against his mouth, my finger shushed him.

Standing there, half-exposed and gazing into his endless eyes, my heart hammered, squeezing so tight it might burst. The world around me filtered out until his thoughts alone ransacked my mind. A man torn between worlds trembled. No, not a man, but an Angel worthy of both love and light, yet he believed he'd deserved neither.

"Cain?" Like a breathless whisper, my name rolled off his tongue.

I shushed him again, seeking whatever tidbit he hid from prying listeners. His mind constricted, now revealing nothing.

Hot breath bristled my ear, and he said, "You can ask me what I'm thinking, babe." Crimson colored his cheeks. Dorian had learned new tricks.

"You felt me?"

Rough palms ran over my biceps and dragged me closer to him. His nose touched mine, and he thought, "*From the day we me, I have always felt you.*" His lips feathered against mine, tickling. Dorian placed my hand over his pounding heart. "The bar…I felt you before you walked inside."

"Defluo," I said, holding his naked image in my mind. His shirt disappeared.

Dorian shivered. "I have to get used to the magic."

A moan slipped through my parted lips, and my shaky hands explored the planes of his smooth back. He gently shoved me. Drunk on one another, we stumbled and landed on the aged mattress. It groaned beneath our combined weight. He laughed and shook his dark head, and a lone tendril fell into his eyes.

I smoothed the stray lock into place and sighed. God but was he sexy when he towered over me. "You're impossible." My palm rubbed against his denim-clad hard-on, and Dorian bucked his hips against the friction. "Defluo," I repeated the spell, and an idea sparked. His belt rattled against the floor as I nibbled kisses over his bare stomach.

His thoughts bounded between release and making sure I was still okay.

"I'm fine," I murmured against his soap-scented skin.

Dorian's fingers combed through my hair. I worked on his button, freeing him from the prison. He kicked his jeans to the floor before crawling on top of me.

"You wore underwear?" I chuckled, recalling his commando thought from the other day. The boxer briefs left little to the imagination, tenting and straining to hold his member.

Dorian offered only a faint shrug while he brushed his cock against mine. I arched into his grind, pressing and rubbing my groin against him. As if lightning struck my body, pleasure emerged and spread over my skin.

"Shite," he cursed, and smirked. With each pump of his hips, Dorian's green eyes brightened until a strange haze illuminated his olive skin. He slanted forward and sucked my lip between his teeth, slowing his momentum. Sweat glistened from his body and his arms tremored. "I am such a fucking twat," he whispered. "I never should've left you, Cain."

"Water under the bridge," I lied, recalling the same words releasing from Boric's mouth before. He'd usually followed them with gifts, more kind words, or sex.

Forcing myself to stay in the moment with Dorian, my hands explored his chest. From the forest of hair caressing his nipples to the subtle outline of his pecks, my fingers roamed until he had gasped and cried out, "Cain...don't fucking stop..."

I closed my eyes and tiptoed the fine line between reality and my past.

"Look at me," Dorian said in a breathless tone. "Babe, no, stay with me." Concern laced into his words.

My eyes shot open. His wrinkled brow deepened before softening.

"That's it." Dorian grounded me with his eyes and voice. "Come with me."

"I don't work like that," I said, head shaking.

Dorian slowed his thrusts, but I stared at the dresser. His cock throbbed against mine, but he stopped and I glanced at him without moving. Sighing, he reached for me and stroked my face. Without words, his gentle caress soothed my spirit.

"What are you afraid of?" he asked, his hand trailing down my neck. "That I'll leave you if you don't organism every time we make love?" A long breath hissed through his teeth. "Or are you afraid of the pleasure itself?" He grasped my cock.

"Oh." My body trembled beneath his thrusting hand. "Dorian." The words seemed foreign and distance. His hand released me, and his cock rubbed against mine once more. I clawed into his shoulders, and my world exploded into colors. My toes curled into themselves, my being shuddering to a pattering stop.

He cried out, "I'm coming," as hot ropes pulsed from his cock, joining mine.

On top of me, he collapsed, kissing me down from the high. His eyes reflected the color of love, sparking and swimming among the green. Tender lips kissed my neck and trailed along the outline of my snake tattoo. Aftershocks vibrated through my body. I blinked and watched his descent. He paused at my belly button, and I gasped at his tongue darting across my cum-coated skin.

Dorian moaned, "I can't get enough of you."

"Plenty of you there too."

Air rushed over my groin as he removed my soiled boxers. Dorian brought them to his nose and inhaled. Green eyes dilated, and his fists tightened around the cotton.

My insides pooled and burned at the reaction. I was not the only one, and my head shook.

Dorian asked, "What?"

"You know what," I said, sitting up and laughing. My palm grasped and tugged his cock through his cum-soaked boxers. When it came to sex, the man was insatiable. Not that I minded servicing his needs, but what if this was another fluke? What happened when the flashbacks returned? The thought flittered away, and I shoved it deeper into the recesses of my mind.

Dorian was not Boric.

His mushroom tip strained and poked out of the fly. Saltiness and sex permeated the air. My mouth hovered, teasing Dorian.

"Babe, you…"

My lips slid over the tip and down his shaft. My intent vibrated, and I hummed and sucked. Our gazes connected and energetic, green eyes peered at me through heavy lids.

"Fuck, you can't get enough of me either."

He curled his large hands into my hair and tugged. Dorian bit his lip. His mind jumped from unleashing to the weather as his laboring muscles shook the bed. His attempts failed to slow me, and I increased my speed; he thickened and swelled. Sweet cream erupted, tickling the roof of my mouth, and he stilled and grunted. I swallowed every spurt, holding his cock hostage between my lips.

Dorian grasped my arms and yanked me against his chest. The hammering of his heart echoed my own and thumped against my ear. I clung to him. His mindless fingers danced over the hidden scars along my back and shoulders.

"We'll figure this out," he whispered, and brushed his mouth over my hair. "I'm not letting you go, Cain." Thick, muscular arms tightened their grasp, as he spoke, and squeezed me tighter. "Don't run."

I gulped and nodded, recalling I had dashed away from the shore after he'd asked me to wait. "I'm broken and can't be fixed."

Dorian grasped my chin and forced me to fixate on him. Green eyes lit with spark, and my breath sucked in.

He said, "I will chase you, and babe? I don't know how to fail. Nod if you understand."

"I can say yes." The same way I'd said yes to Boric all those years ago.

"As for broken? We're all broken, including me." He tapped my cheek and smiled. "You need to pack. Garland will send more men."

I grunted and allowed my gaze to take in my belongings. Not much, but the thought of leaving it all behind didn't sit well either.

"We can take it all. I meant what I said." He brushed his lips over my cheek. "Let me take care of you."

Without another word, Dorian gathered his clothes and left me alone in the bedroom. I drew a hand through my hair and down my face. He gave me what I wanted, yet why did my stomach churn, like impending doom. My palm rested above the rumbling surface. I glanced at the smooth ring and sighed. Everything spoke to me of love, yet he hadn't said the words. But if the time ever arrived, would I believe him?

Dorian waited in the living room for me to compose and redress before regaling the earlier promised tale of his accidental hetero sex. After packing a small bag, I sat with him on the sofa and rifled through a stack of work and personal papers. Anything indicating Belle, Tomas, or Dorian left behind for Garland to find, Boric would use against me. I might have been Death's weakness, but like my sisters, he was mine.

"This one goes way back into the fourteen hundreds. There was a lot of wine involved, and she'd dressed like a guy…needless to say, we'd both had a surprise that night."

I dropped the papers and turned toward him. My hand ran over his thick, denim-clad thigh. "You didn't cop a feel first?" My fingers danced up his stomach and squeezed his pecks.

Dorian swallowed hard, and my mouth turned drier than a bone

I tweaked his nipple. "What about her bosom?"

"Alcohol makes the senses fuzzy. Maybe I thought her plump. It was centuries ago, Cain." His white teeth flashed against the darkness of his beard. "Besides, I'm an ass man, to which I can recall hers being delicious. Your turn."

"Mine is a little darker. Sadly, I don't have funny tales."

He stared at my hand, and I drew myself away, willing the blood not to rush straight to my cheeks. The walls closed in around me, and I shut my eyes. You can do this he will not run. But I didn't believe my own words, or his. The test of all tests had begun, and I didn't dare look at Dorian. In a gentle caress, his hand rubbed over my back.

I exhaled in the warmth he shared without knowing my damned past. "I was born and raised in the southern states, Texas to be exact, three hundred years ago. By the start of the Civil War, I had just celebrated my sixteenth birthday. Even then, I wasn't yet a man…" My words shook and the memory of that innocent boy peeked into my mind. "Lily and I found ourselves sold into Garland's service shortly thereafter." After the war, he'd shipped us over the border into Mexico. I didn't return to Texas until ten years prior to the Sundering, escaping shortly afterward, but Jules had taken my sister, Lily, away long before then.

"How?" His hand fisted my shirt.

My body trembled, and Dorian's grip loosened. "Our father gambled," my head hung lower, "he'd lost everything…he sold us as payment. That's my older sister Angelica She was sold off in an arranged marriage to Veric Garland," I pointed to a photograph Tomas had found for me, "Or was...I don't quite know if she survived."

My restless fingers tapped over the coffee table. Dorian's gaze raked over me, as if assessing the damage. My face burned hotter with each passing moment, breath held.

"Tomas had hinted as much. And the strange pixie...Veric..." Dorian wrapped his arms around my trembling body.

His thoughts confused me, but I couldn't linger on them, or else I'd lose my nerve to explain. Words and sobs unleashed, but I continued, "Neither of us understood the ramifications. We were only kids. My father told us we belonged to the Garland family, and we were to do whatever they requested. I'd assumed that meant chores, and we would return home each night...Like servants... Lily was fourteen at the time." I sniffled and blinked my burning eyes. "I...I still hear her cries...and the...screams. We weren't the only ones. They're drowned out only by my own."

My voice lowered. "I couldn't stop...them." I stood and lifted my shirt, willing the spell to end within my mind. On my body, I hid scars, but I carried others blind to the eye. Deep lashes riveted my tender skin, a constant reminder, yet beneath me lay the wounds perpetuating my lies. Ones that bled every second of my existence and still held the knife the masters and Boric had plunged into me. "Magic hides them," I whispered, eying him over my shoulder and releasing my shirt.

Dorian chewed my lip, already plotting revenge in his mind. "How did you escape?" he asked, but his mind also asked when.

"Eighteen years ago, after Angelica died, or the first time?"

"Both..." The couch let out a groan. Dorian shifted, his leg touching mine.

"Lily traveled to Delphia. I'd overheard the chatter and planned to flee, hoping I could overthrow them. Guards caught me stealing provisions. The demons..." I shook my head and stopped. "They were always a step ahead of me, like...I don't know. Like they wanted me there for more than…" A few times, I made it farther, but either the guards or elements caught me.

"The last time?"

"I had help…My brother-in-law smuggled me out. Boric and the masters were furious, though. I'd stolen from them again." I smirked, thinking of the keys. Quickly dissipated, though, since he'd killed her because of them.

Dorian hoisted himself from the couch and engulfed me in the bulk of his arms, pressing me against the wall of his chest. Tales and horror stories had traveled; even into Arcadia, of what Boric Garland did to his personal slaves and of how he encouraged others to do the same. Dorian's thoughts wandered over three questions: did he rape me, did he beat me, and what had I stolen from him.

They had raped me. "Yes." They had beaten me. "Yes." But that was life for many stuck in Garland or Delphia. "I stole his source of power." No matter what they'd tried, though, I wouldn't reveal the location of Angelica's keys. I held on and remained strong for her sake alone, but the bastard murdered her anyway. Still, her dream of peace among the seven families had survived.

At least we had led everyone to believe her death had been real, but I still struggled with the truth. Our mother had cast a spell and put her soul into Angelica's body and Angelica's soul into a stillborn baby she had birthed from magic.

My tears wet the fabric of his shirt. Dorian rubbed circles over my back. Gentle murmurs shushed me, and he rocked us back and forth. No matter the might of my faith, God had allowed the bastards to rape and murder my sister. Forget about what they'd done to me. The purest soul the world had ever known died at their hands, and they still had my sweet, innocent Lilith. Those demons belonged locked away where they could not hurt anyone but themselves. Out of control, the demons created their own hell on Earth, and I held no power to stop them.

"I'll bloody fucking kill him," he whispered in my ear. "We're planning on taking them down, but it will take time and manpower."

I sniffled and brushed my palms upward over his chest and around his neck. Assuming we had meant his family, I asked, "How can we stop them?"

"What follows Death?"

My brow rose.

"Sheol, babe, I control purgatory."

I played with his collar and smirked. "That's hot."

"Replying with your hot seems redundant and inappropriate given the situation," he thought. All words seemed meaningless in that moment.

"The past is the past, and I'll hunt down every demon that dared hurt you, Angel, or Lily."

"Angel." Never had I called her that in his presence. My thumb caressed his soft lips, and he kissed the tip. "You know about Angel, don't you? You already knew about me..." A shiver rushed straight to my groin, and I urged my cock down. With the wrong head in charge, we would wind up at square one with his ass in the air, and my dick buried between his muscled cheeks.

Dorian smirked and patted my face. "The three of you look alike, babe, kinda hard to miss. Tomas told me some. He's back in town." We inched closer holding—being in the moment. "I have a surprise for you."

"Oh?" My nose brushed his and my hands tightened on his forearms. I didn't like surprises.

Warmth filled every gaping hole, and even those I hadn't realized existed, marking the difference between Dorian and Boric. In the hundreds of years spent serving him, not once had, his presence invoked such a sensation from my heart. No flutters or pangs of loss when he'd departed, but the lack of feeling didn't make his barbs any less painful.

"Are we good now, babe? No more secrets?"

I closed my eyes; my brows scrunched. I wanted to tell him more, yet I couldn't bring myself to spoil the good mood and bring up my relationship with Boric. Dorian would undoubtedly brand me a traitor and never speak to me again if he learned that part of me, despite the abuse, had fallen in love with a monster.

"Please, I'll beg…you can kick my ass again…I'll wash dishes and take out the trash." A chuckle shook his chest, as if he hadn't done those chores already. "We can take it slow. Whatever you need."

Blinking, I smiled at him and allowed my revelation to root. He grinned, and my heart trembled and sputtered, trying to keep up.

"Who knew Death could swoon," I said, twining my fingers into Dorian's hair. "I don't need slow, but I need honesty and understanding. Most of all, I need you."

He whispered, "You got me, babe."

Dorian's teeth nipped my mouth, and I opened for him, wanting to believe him. My lungs ached; he stole away my breath. Energy charged the air rushing between us and pricked my skin. He consumed my entire being. His hands gripped my hair, slamming my mouth harder and closer against his until we had no beginning and no end.

We were one; Dorian would kill anyone who tried to alter that and so would I. Every inch of my soul, heart, and mind rested in the palm of Death's hand. The one difference was now he knew it. The sheer sight of him had me wanting him. From the first taste, I had gained a new addiction. Dorian drew away, but didn't let go of my hand. He scented the air filling my lungs, but the much-needed breath settled my dizziness.

"Besides the dudes I burned and your overdrive libido, what else happened? You said Tomas sent men too? He's back?"

Dorian filled me in on the new comers. "They're looking for Lily. You were right about the Duc having her. Babe, why do you think they would cross the border?"

He held something back, my surprise maybe, but there was more to the story. A few theories came to mind, but I swallowed hard and shrugged.

"And not that it matters," he scratched his head, but something wasn't right, "but what are you guys?"

My eyes pinched for a moment. Dorian already knew the answer, but I whispered, "Descendants of the Morning Star. Why does it matter?"

What Dorian didn't know was *why* Garland wanted us. They wanted the keys; the keys equaled power to whoever held them all. Some whispered they unlocked a great treasure and all the power on Earth. But I had honored the promise vowed to Angelica. Bitterness rose in my throat at lying to Dorian again, though.

"Sweets? You ready?" I'd finished with my papers and motioned toward the door, but he stood there still as a statue, his broad shoulders facing away. His attention pointed out the sliding glass door, but nothing was there on the balcony.

"Why, not what, Cain. Why the Morning Stars? What makes you any different from me?"

Simple—I possessed six of the seven keys Boric Garland and the Arch demons sought. But why my family? God bestowed special powers upon us that the other families didn't possess. A gift for Lucifer's sacrifice.

Chapter Eleven

Dorian

Cain strode across the living room, chuckling, and kissed the wrinkles forming on my forehead, but I was being serious. What made Lucifer's children any different from Asmodeus' line? They all held magical, dark powers, but why did Asmodeus—Eoric Garland—risk crossing the border for them?

I had watched from Earth as the Archangels rose and warred against Father. Hell, I knew Lucifer...like a brother. The Watchers—*Grigori*—had lived on Earth.

Cain's warm hands held my cheeks, and I tilted my chin. He didn't look like him at all. I knew the answer to my own question, but all I learned had come second hand. Color me curious, I wanted the truth from the horse's mouth. My brow raised a fraction.

His scars held no importance beyond the bastards that had dared mark the man I loved. My heart beat faster. No stranger to abuse or pain myself, but I'd had my revenge. His warm fingers brushed my neck as he grasped my collar. My lips parted but the words would not release the secret battering inside my heart. The man standing before me—scars and all—was the only one that mattered to me: I loved him.

"I'm a distant relative of Lucifer. A spat in the ocean really, but we do share blood."

Cain's lips brushed against mine, and I gasped at the electricity of his touch. Again, he pressed those death-defying lips to mine, and my hands clutched his waist. Screw questions. My mind reeled, and I deepened the kiss, sliding my tongue into his warm mouth.

His bloodline didn't matter, did it? Lies...More deceit. More distraction. Would it ever end? History repeated itself before me. A thought flittered into my head, and a memory I'd long ago buried exploded. *The deceiver...* I pushed back gasping and clenching my eyes shut.

"No," I warned, and held my hand out. My body hunched over and my chest tightened. "A minute...give me..." My knees buckled and slammed against the carpet. I fought the old vision:

Stone buildings sat in the foreground, surrounded by endless desert. Men in red and gold uniforms stripped me bare and bound my bones to a wooden beam. Inside, I battled the reason for my lover's revulsion and treason. People gathered; they gawked and threw items at me. An officer held a whip made of spiked metal. The weapon crackled through the air, and their barbs sliced through my flesh.

I screamed. Tears hazed my vision, and despite my lack of flesh, metallic blood misted the air. I tasted the bitter fog and still asked him why. My lover refused to face me, refused to answer my pleas, but I had known him.

"Malum," the crowd chanted.

The officer thrashed his metal whip again, and while cackling, he whispered in my ear, "Mors certa, hora incerta." Death is certain, its hour uncertain.

"Mors vincit omnia," I shouted back. Death conquers all. The words, Father had taught me, and the key fastened around my neck weighted heavily on my soul. My putrid horse neighed in the distance, hearing and feeling my agony. More lashes prevailed until I knew nothing but pain.

Later, I awoke in the middle of the town. They'd tied my bones to a crucifix. Screaming pleas went unanswered. People ignored me and traveled about on their daily doings.

So I had baked under the blazing sun for days.

One night, fires crackled and spread along the houses and businesses. Conquest stood before me, her hands clutching her hips, her face scowling. Their cries and screams echoed. Markos and Fauna strolled forward from the thick, billowing gray smoke.

"They will burn in life and death for their sins," Fauna said, extending her hand and pulsing purple magic until it engulfed the town.

Beneath me, the ground rumbled. Markos kicked the crucifix. "They're undeserving of your love, Brother."

But the damage scored my heart forever, and I vowed never to show humanity my weaknesses. "I can't do this anymore, Markos." Grimacing, my façade washed over me. "Never will I again."

"Surely, Brother, you will love."

I leaned against my brother. "No, love will kill us all." I glanced over his shoulder to our sisters and the burning town. "Michael was right. Love is the end."

Cain's strong arms ushered me outside onto the balcony, and cold air bit at my senses.

"Breathe, sweetheart. Center yourself on my voice."

City ruins flickered into view, replacing the ancient desert of my past. The bone was poking through bits of skin. Death rose; every part of me lost to the vision.

"C'mon Dorian, you can do this. Look at me and know where your heart belongs."

Heart…Love…"I can't do this…" *Can I?* How could I have fallen for another liar, a master of deceit? I blinked, and his caramel gaze met mine.

A tight smile played on his lips, but the evidence reached higher. "You are more than what God made you, sweets. Angels can love."

I was more than a fiendish, sex driven, killer Archangel. More than my past and evil deeds done in Father's name, but was it enough to forget the evils done unto me in God's name? For years, I had teetered with the notion of destruction, and for eons, shattered myself. And for what purpose had I punished myself?

Cain cocked his head and followed my thoughts—I assumed. A tingle ran over my face, and I understood what Markos and Hallo had meant about magic. My eyes opened wide, and, for the first time, I saw the whitewashed world bathed anew in all its glory. Peace reigned, and love triumphed over evil. A darkened shroud hung above me, though, and the shadows flourished, raining its bounty over my pores.

Cain's attempts failed; the maddening struggle increased. Doubt whispered in my ear, and my past resurrected itself in full force. It whispered: I did not deserve him. Death deserved only death.

"Stay with me, Dorian."

Wings cracked into the air, despite Cain's voice, and my knees weakened once again. He gasped, and I glanced at the tattered, translucent feathers hanging from the boney wings, which protruded from my spine.

Before my eyes, the wings darkened into midnight black, and I shouted, "No." bowing at his feet. "Father? Why? Why are you forsaking me?" I begged him to take the tarnish away, but Father refused intervention.

"Bare your sorrow, and together we will carry it." Cain stroked my hair, tucking the strands behind my ear. "Let me help you abide this burden." He whispered, "Let his light in and destroy the darkness, or fall into its eternal damnation forever. The choice was always yours, Dorian."

Lucifer walks among us. I blinked and rocked back. Cain was no more Lucifer than his children were. True, he'd lied, but why was Cain still lying to me? What was he so afraid of?

Cain knelt and tilted my chin. "Long ago, before the first war, before the fall of the Archangels, my ancestor was a loyal Archangel like you." Cain released a whistled breath. "These were the words my grandfather shared with me: 'God came to me and introduced me to the great plan.'"

He shifted. I squinted, and the stray shard of sunlight blinded me.

"'My brothers and sisters had chosen me…me his most beautiful and beloved Archangel to fall from the grace of Heaven. They also chose two hundred more that I was to lead to this Earth. We became the Grigori.'"

His thumb stroked my chin, and I relished in its warmth. Cain grinned and lifted us from the balcony floor. White wings were jutting from his back.

"He played his part and led a rebellion against God, knowing the Lord would repay him someday. What my ancestor hadn't expected was the defiling of his once good name and the twisted imagery among the humans." He shuddered.

I understood. The demons appeared nothing like the depictions in paintings or books. Some had tails or horns, but they were not ugly or grotesque. Above all else, not all were evil for the sake of being evil.

Cain said, "Even then, he never ceased loving God but watched as his family fell to those who embraced the evil and malevolent ways created by him in God's name."

Despite knowing the answer, I asked, "God created evil then?"

"One could say that, since he created us all, but it was each man, woman, angel, or demon that chose to act upon evil which wreaked havoc. That's my belief at least. We all have the choice, Dorian, and that includes you."

"You're Lucifer's heir." It wasn't a question. "But you're more than him, greater."

"Hêlêl," he said Lucifer's name in Hebrew. "Lilith, Angel, and I are descendants of the Archangel, and we aren't the only ones. He had loved many before the uprising. Tomas and Belle are light bringers. That's what he supposedly called us." Cain sighed and pressed his lips together. "There you have my whole world of dark and dangerous secrets. The source of my power, and Lily's, birthed from the fallen and condemned soul of one Archangel."

I kissed his cheek and nuzzled against his rough neck. Cain's arms wrapped around me and held me hostage. The sun hid behind the clouds.

"When the Garlands brought us to their home, they thought they'd stripped us bare and bound our powers. They knew whose blood ran through our veins, and that one of us would eventually destroy his empire. So he kept a tally, kept our line culled. Father flaunted the notion from the first time our families met, but I am no more him than I am my ancestor. None of us are, but everyone treats us like we were the ones who defied God, failing to see that it, too, had been a part of his plan." He sighed. "But I can't sit by while Boric destroys my family, and yet I am powerless to stop him, Dorian. If I marched up to him, even with a weapon that was sure to kill him, I would falter."

No, he was not like Lucifer. Cain was Cain, and I loved him for who he was. My lips trailed over the serpent tattoo, and my tongue traced its head, relishing in the salty flavor of his skin. His hands tightened on my waist.

"That tickles," he said, followed by a groan slipping from his lips.

My hands ventured to his crotch. He had distracted me from my darkness and shined the light in my eyes. No longer did my mind chase the past, and the whispers of madness ceased. Cain pressed his hard outline against my hand.

"It's your turn to let go, babe." The button popped free on his jeans, and I dragged down the zipper.

Cain swallowed hard, and his gruff voice sounded his answer. "No."

I tugged the fabric down, alternating sides until he sprung free. He needed to see what I did was out of love and not a play for power. I wanted nothing more than for him to seek release, because he needed me to be the one. *Needed again*, the thought made me dizzy.

"Dorian, why does everything revolve around sex and release?"

A storm brewed in his eyes, and I leaned in to kiss those full lips. "Trust me," I thought.

I pressed my tongue against the tight seam of his lips. The heat of his cock seared through my palm. Slow strokes matched the rhythm of our tongues, dancing a line I had never meant to cross again.

Love him? Yes, I could no longer deny. But tell him? My mind remained conflicted, and Cain tensed at the war brewing within me. He backed away and glanced over the balcony, drawing his clothing into place. Hurt glistened in his eyes. I could neither admit nor ignore it was of my own making.

"There's more to life than sex. Get the fuck out of my life if you can't see past your own cock." Cain finished righting his clothes before storming into his apartment and slamming the sliding glass door.

My disheveled reflection and strange glowing eyes stared at me. Cruel cynical laughter sounded in my head, and I reminded myself whom I was. Of what I was. "Fuck."

His butterscotch gaze met mine. My wings snapped back while his remained free. Damned Elioud…I ran a hand through my hair, tugging hard on the greasy strands, but when I glanced up Cain was gone.

Forever, until the end, I would be alone. My shoulders rounded forward, and my head hung low, gazing at the concrete floor of the balcony.

Death couldn't freely plunge into love again. Last time, it had broken me. The pit of my spirit screamed, and my arms spread wide. I tilted my head toward the mighty heavens and released a bone-chilling cry…one, two, then three voices echoed the torture extending in a blanket across Arcadia.

Lies, lies, lies: they compounded against me and strangled the breath from my body. Lightning sounded and flashed. Sleet poured from the gray clouds that hadn't existed a moment prior. Air swirled at my feet, and my scythe appeared. Words were only for show.

Cain pounded on the glass, and I glanced over my shoulder. *End the pain…no more pain for either of us.* My blade glinted, and the ebony gems reflected the man who would have saved this world from the depths of Hell and banish those who broke the laws of Father to Sheol. A man who could have loved without the release and sexual fuel of desires propelling him into oblivion. Protect the weak, the innocent damned, from the likes of me.

But I could not change, even though I wanted to be the type of man who deserved love and devotion, who warranted honesty.

Instead, I grew out of the bitter seed altering into hardened bone. My heart, battered and blackened, knew nothing but sin. Nightmares had happier endings than what I'd planned for this cold, cruel world.

"Callous, cold, and cruel..." My finger slid along the sharpened blade, and my tainted blood coated the surface. "I'm tired of pretending, of hiding." The half-truth and half-whisper left my lips. I spun and stormed toward the glass barrier. With my blood, I drew a heart over the pane.

Cain mouthed words I could not hear.

"I love you," I said. "But I can't do this. I tried...I came here today to tell you, to lay my heart bare, but it's of no use. You won't budge." *Truth.* I would've lived with his lies if he only admitted telling them. How lame to accept he deceiver within him.

He backed away, tilting his head. My scythe lifted and sliced through the air.

"No," he screamed. His caramel eyes flashed red. He sprinted toward the barrier standing between us, face-hardened.

Glass shattered, cutting my skin. "Shite, you bloody fucking wanker." More curses lurched from my mouth as Cain's body knocked me against the railing. We bounced before tumbling to the balcony floor. Ribs cracked and crushed into my lungs. Breath refused to come, and stars littered my blurred vision.

Cain slapped me. "Dorian what the hell is wrong with you?" Metal tapped metal. His arm shook, holding the scythe in place.

The balcony quaked, and three whooshes followed. Mark said, "Brother."

"This is your doing," Cain accused Markos.

Upside down, I blinked at Fauna, Mark, and Hallo, weapons drawn and pointed at his throat. I cried, "Enough! Stand down."

Two swords withdrew, and I stared into Cain's eyes, and at the blade teetering at his jugular. My trembling hand stroked his fuzz-covered cheek, and I forced a bitter smile. *This is not how I pictured him meeting my family.*

Glass shards protruded from the sliding door. Hallo narrowed her blue eyes on Cain and pressed her blade against his neck again. Wind whipped her wild, sleet-covered blonde hair, and her lip lifted revealing a sneer. "Satan's spawn dares to kill a Horseman?" She spat in his face.

"Watch it," I warned, wiping her spittle.

Fauna and Markos grabbed an elbow and pulled her back.

"Ouch," Cain said, reaching toward his neck. A thin river of blood marred his skin, its mouth starting at the snake's head.

I rose and sealed my lips over the wound. Cain's jaw shuddered, and his hand slid over the handle of my scythe.

Fauna whispered, "See the truth in his soul, Sister. It is he who has saved our brother and our world."

Her wings cracked, and Hallo breathed. The golden hilt sword blinked from her grip, and her hands swiped down, grasping the scythe.

Cain melded and squirmed under my mouth. The blood had stopped, but I sensed his closeness and could not let him go. Why had I lost control again? Fear: loving the man in my arms drove me to destroy, instead of being a better man.

His breathing became ragged and rushed. The heat in him rose. My heart ripped open, and my love bled for him alone. *I love you.* Despite my strength, Cain tore himself away. Blazing eyes alight with fire pinned me down, and I forgot for a moment what I had planned, or how I'd ended up on the balcony.

"You're covered in glass because you're an idiot." Markos loomed over me. "I should leave you there, Brother."

Leaving me with Cain was not a bad idea.

"But you'd enjoy it too much."

A blush flooded my cheeks with its heat. *Markos is 100 percent correct.*

"Where *are* the others?" I asked. "Tell me you didn't leave them alone."

They exchanged worried glances, and the wind picked up at their feet.

My hands curled behind my head, and I grinned, like a lovesick fool. "It's good to be the boss."

"What was that about?" Cain blinked, still staring where my family had been moments before.

"Babe, think about who I am."

"Death." His brow rose.

"I can kill the world." And them.

"Yeah. No shit. Let's not try that again, okay sweets?" He scrubbed his hand over his face. He leaned back and stood up, extending a hand toward me. "Why would Hallowed want to kill me...her eyes." Cain shuddered again as he hefted me from the ground.

Hallo would have slaughtered him, because she had witnessed the destruction from my past. Furthermore, she had her own story, but it was hers to tell.

"Seriously, sweets. Don't pull that shit again."

Damn, his naughty mouth was sexy.

"I...I love you."

Not our end of course, but rather a new beginning. We would learn much about each other from those first weeks, but we understood the future held uncertainty, mysticism, and more than either of us could have handled alone. Our journey was far from over. Little did we realize the real trials of our companionship would face and truly be tested the moment we returned home—our home.

Never had I allowed so many people to gather inside my house. Everyone save for Veric and Petre, who was still missing, stood in my downstairs office. I sat behind my desk. All nine of them spoke at once, arguing, and I squeezed my temples, rubbing circles over the tender throbbing veins.

Korrigan wanted to search for Petre. Veric had stepped out before our return, but I pictured him torn between Korrigan's wishes and capturing his brother. My family sought to take the south by force, but Tomas objected, cursing wildly in vivid French about the innocent lives. Nikolai sided with Korrigan, and Cain had sided with Tomas, though he didn't seem to recognize Korrigan as Angelica, but I couldn't be sure. Regardless of a reunion, the case came first, and they left me as the deciding vote, or making a clear tie since Belle refused to take a side.

"Brother." Markos pounded his fist on my desk. "What will it be?"

I glanced to Cain, not for any particular reason other than admiration and distraction. During the heated debate, pride and spark had ignited his rosy cheeks. Damn it if the scene hadn't stirred my cods.

"You can't be serious!"

"Out, everyone get the hell out of my office."

Cain rose and stepped toward the door.

I jumped up and captured his hips. A rumble filled my chest, and my hands dragged his ass against me. I seized him in a reverse bear hug against my chest. "Not you."

An office debacle was the last thing either of us needed. My lips kissed over his neck, and Cain's ass squirmed over my crooked hard-on.

"Upstairs… now." I smacked his ass lightly before releasing him.

He slid from my grasp. The cold crept into my bones, but he froze; every muscle tensed. Cain's arms trembled, and I tossed my hands in the air. My mind fought to shut down. How could I have forgotten his problems with intimacy?

Damn, I am an incorrigible asshole.

I covered my eyes, daring not even a peek. Fear of fear or pain in his eyes stopped me dead in my tracks. All I had to give; I had given but still pushed, waiting for the day he opened his heart with more than words. Until Cain trusted me not to harm him, he couldn't love me. I gave him as much, despite his empty words. Maybe that day would never come, and the damage had been dug in too deep. My poignant thoughts could've made a grown man weep.

Cain spun around and snapped his fingers in front of my nose. "Dorian, come back to me."

His warm hands pried mine away from my face. Beautiful and rare, yet not quite exotic…those words described my Cain. He held traits reminiscent of a male Snow White and all the innocence of a cherub in those murky, golden eyes. Light reflected off them, and they came alive, melting into molten pools of caramel. Pale skin framed by wavy wisps of chestnut hair. Like a painting, I could have stared and studied his face for hours on end, for eternity.

At my thoughts, Cain's lips tilted, and he shook his head, trying to hide the blush coloring his cheeks. His powerful legs knocked me back into my chair. I said nothing, giving him control. He straddled my lap and yanked the hem of my shirt over my head. Deft fingers traced the lines of my abs, and he explored my body, leaving gooseflesh in his wake.

We were alone. Heat penetrated the back of my head and streamed through the window. He touched my chest, his long fingers stroking through my hair. My stomach flipped, tugging from the top to my cods. How much more of his torture could I bare? Composure held-on by the grace of God himself. His fingertips tickled up and down my stomach, and a soft chuckle left my parting lips.

Is his plan to tease me until I tear his clothes off and fuck him on my desk? I half-expected him to raise a brow or poke fun. Instead, Cain retreated from my lap, and his gaze swept over my body. *Did I go too far?* I kept forgetting his fragile state and chided myself.

"Get up." Smiling, Cain leaned his chin on his fist.

I stared at him and blinked. Had he said get up or get out? No, he wouldn't have kicked me from my own house.

Again, he commanded, "Get up."

His forceful tone threw me off guard, and I gaped at him. He yanked me to my feet, courtesy of grasping the waistband of my jeans. The button popped free as I stared at him, both dumbfounded and reminiscent of the alcove. *Aha, I lost my fedora there.* Who knew that day would have led to Death falling for a Morning Star. A palm ran over my face hiding the goofy grin. No mirror needed.

"You're cute when you're confused," he whispered in my ear, and dipped his lips to my neck. "The world is going to shit around us, and all you can think about is fucking me."

My cock jerked against its fabric prison. Sex lingered on my mind, like his fiery fragrance, but it was no longer about the next score. Nothing would've made me happier than to wake beside him, to be with Cain, always.

"But you want to coddle and protect me too." He nibbled my skin, and a shiver erupted over my flesh. "You're in way over your head, sweets."

"Keep talking." I ached for his words.

He enclosed his hand around my cock and stroked.

"Mmm, just like that." My breath gasped, and my cods grew heavy, filling with each velvety tug.

"I'm the lucky bastard, who gets to love and save your sweet ass." He kissed me, sucking my lower lip, until I had clutched his hips and twisted him around.

"You can save me right now." My hands tore his jeans to his ankles, and I widened his thighs. No accessible lube, except a bottle of hand lotion. I grasped it from my desk drawer, squeezed a generous amount into my palm, and worked the lubrication over my prick. Through this all, I waited for him to use the word and mentally reminded him of our pact. I loved him and respected him too.

With my jeans kicked away, I leaned forward, kissing and caressing his cheeks.

"Oh," Cain moaned, as my tongue crept between his ass crack and caressed his sensitive bud. His hips gently rocked and swayed. "I need you inside of me," he begged.

I slid my fingers over his inner thighs, stroking just shy of his swinging cods, noting each moan or movement he made.

"Now." Cain folded his body forward and shoved his ass toward my face. His hips still rocked and arched as he ground himself against my face while stroking himself.

I eased a glistened finger into his tight hole and moaned, plastering kisses over his skin. "Patience, babe."

Cain thrust himself against my finger in response.

"This angle won't do." I wanted to watch him and see the expression of pleasure wash over his beautiful face. The way he nibbled his bottom lip drove me wild. I withdrew and scooped him into my arms, not allowing him a moment of protest.

I carried him upstairs and into the bedroom. His ruddy cheeks enhanced the freckles sprinkled over the bridge of his nose. Amusement colored his muddy eyes.

What was he thinking? I planted us on the bed, Cain on top of me. He didn't miss a beat, his strong thighs falling to a rest over mine, and his feet crossed behind my back. I brushed my hands through his mousy, tasseled hair, pulling his face closer. His lips captured mine. Passion tore and melted away his restraint, his body steadying and his shaking ceasing.

"You can retain control, and I can still see. If it's too much, tell me to stop, babe." I wasn't sure what reaction he would give me.

Cain whispered, "I don't deserve you," and pressed his lips to mine before I had time to retort the claim.

I didn't deserve him. The monster lived inside me, no him. The warmth of his tongue slid into my mouth. I clutched his butt cheeks, lifted him, and lowered him over my cockhead, the sensation sending shivers deep into my belly. But he didn't cool the flames. Flurries ignited and seared me from the inside out. The firmness of his lips stiffened, and he gasped against my mouth, but when I tried to pull away, Cain moved with me.

His body trembled, and his fright cut. I wanted to hold him to my chest and promise him everything would be okay, but he wouldn't let me go.

My hands slid light touches over his hunched shoulders and along his spine, soothing and chasing the demons away. Inch by painfully slow inch, he descended over my shaft.

"I love you," I whispered against his mouth between kisses. "Babe, fuck me...you feel good."

He rocked his hips, adjusting to me. "Love you too, sweets. Show me...show me how good I feel."

With slow, teasing thrusts, I matched his movements pushing me closer to release. My mind backpedaled and tried grasping onto anything but him. Each plunge into his snug hole towed my cods tighter against my taint. Each motion rubbed the thick vein, heightening the quivers rushing over my skin, like a pulsating electrical current. Out of breath, Cain pulled away, and my hands rubbed over his erect nipples vying with my body for any distraction.

"Sweets," he said.

And I glanced at his face. His teeth sank into his bottom lip, and I was a goner, lifting him up and pulling out, just in time to explode over his rigid cock and chest. "Fuck," I said, slamming my head back into the headboard, and covered my burning face with my arm.

Cain laughed and slanted over me. He shoved my arm from my face and pecked my burning cheek. "Well one of us got what he wanted." His gaze drifted to his hard dick resting on my spent cock. Mischief sparked in his eyes.

I scooted until I was lying down. What exactly did I unleash?

"Lay down."

"I am lying down."

"So, stay there." He rubbed my seed over his length and slimed a glob over my hole. "Now, you can watch." Cain raised my legs onto his shoulders and tucked my knees toward my chest. He entered me in a swift stroke.

"Oh shite," I cried, clenching his cock with my ass muscles and my toes curled. "Right there, babe."

Cain smirked and repeated the action. "You like that?" He stilled before nudging and teasing me with his miniscule strokes. "Beg."

"Fuck me," I whispered, not recognizing the drunkenness of my own voice.

Cain cocked his brow. "You call that begging, sweets?"

"I need you, babe. I love the way your cock fills me. Never again do I want anyone else buried inside of me but you. You have ruined me, Cain, and I love you more than I love anyone, or anything, in this fucked up world, so you better live up to that shite."

He chuckled, rubbing his smooth hand over my neck. "Damn, you're too cute. C'mere," he said, but I didn't budge. Cain eased his member over my prostate again, rotating, and he nibbled his thick lip. Beads of sweat dampened his brow, thrusts increasing. "You feel incredible."

My hands rubbed his thighs. Twisting my torso, I reached between us and caressed his balls. As he grew closer to release, I twisted my upper body again—to improve my range—and managed to wiggle two fingers into his tight ass.

"Right there," he half-moaned. Cain's eyes rolled back into his head.

I fingered him, feeling for his sweet spot. "Babe, I love you."

His driving quickened, curses rolled in breathless waves, and his breathing turned ragged. Every muscle tensed. Screams ripped from his mouth, and Cain squirted his release, spasming between my fingers and my ass. Too much passion, as his fiery aroma filled the air. He pulled out.

"Fuck," the strained cry ripped free from my mouth. My body griped his cock and held him hostage.

He collapsed the moment my cheeks released, and his lips skimmed over my sweaty chest. My heart about pounded out of my ribs.

"I needed that more than I realized," he said

Everything I need lay in my arms.

"Love you too."

My hands stroked through his damp hair, and Cain nuzzled my chest. Clarity buzzed through my sleepy mind. Screw my family for not realizing the importance of our solitude and connection. Screw Cain too for not recognizing his importance to me.

Pressure built around my brain; he was listening.

"You okay with that?"

"Yeah, babe," I lied. Maybe one day I would be okay with him hearing my thoughts, but it would take time.

We had a larger problem. *We* meaning my family and the fiasco of a circus that had paraded into my office. I agreed with them on the magnitude of the world's issues, but my family was wrong about storming in, guns a blazing. Innocent lives mattered, not only to Cain, but to me too. Yeah, I would have to figure out a way to save us all and bring down the south.

I rubbed his neck, allowing my fingertips to knead into his flesh. But I wanted my time with Cain. Without him, the world simply wasn't worth saving. He squeezed me tighter and kissed my chest.

The problems we all faced were two-fold, though, and the primary decision was deciphering who or what needed to come first.

Petre…the odd created vampire was my second problem and his brother. Two marked souls roamed Earth. Nikolai was mine, but not Petre, not in the sense of Sheol. How important was he to the overall mission? He was one man, albeit a decent one.

Cain interrupted my thoughts, saying, "One man that managed to free a handful of brothels."

"True." My hand skirted down Cain's neck, and he sighed, clutching my ribs tighter. "But how much was Tomas with the mind reading thing?"

The mere thought of either them pulling off brothel raids still baffled me. And to what purpose had Jules left them unattended? What role had Korrigan played? She had said Jules had housed Lily and her together.

Cain said, "I do think you're both right, though. The mind reading would help sort friend from foe…pity Petre doesn't have the ability."

But why had the agent appeared torn? Did the agent's strange behavior even matter? Oh crap, I hadn't told Cain about him yet. A beautiful surprise it would be for both men to see one another after all the years spent apart. His reunion with Korrigan wasn't grand, but we had entered during a tense argument, and he hadn't recognized her.

"Another surprise? I still can't believe she's Angelica." He rested his chin in the crook of my chest.

If I lingered too long, we'd never leave the bed. My brows twisted. "Didn't think you noticed her." My thoughts strayed to Korrigan. Why had an Elioud become a vampire? They didn't age and were immune to sickness and disease. Her size baffled me too. Elioud were large, but she was more childlike in her build.

"It's not easy to fathom. The spell, I don't know. I believe in magic, obviously, but what my mother did was some heavy shit." His fingers walked over my pecs. "Her size is strange, but not really. Jules…he wasn't all that different from Boric in his tastes, except he preferred girls to boys. Maybe she was threatened or close to death? We can die you know."

Snorting, I stroked my chin. "There's more to their story, and I won't budge until I figure it out."

Cain rolled over, laughing and tossing his head. Damn if he were not a glorious distraction…I followed, holding him, and rested on my side.

"You can't be serious." His gaze glided down my body, to where my hard cock rested between our stomachs, and I flashed a sheepish smile; my body twitched as he crawled closer.

Cain sighed. "Remember the day we met?"

"Hard to forget, seeing as you kicked my ass into next week." Cain alone had made the day unforgettable. I hadn't believed in love at first sight, but that moment connected us for eternity. All it had taken was one glimpse into his eyes.

"Yeah," he rubbed his neck and eyed me, "I'm sorry about that, sweets."

Heat filled my cheeks, even though this wasn't the first time he'd called me an endearment. I liked when he did.

"I wanted you, then, but I wasn't ready." He flipped his back to me, but twisted and glanced at me over his shoulder; his nostrils flared. "I'm ready now."

Cain unwrapped himself from my arms, crawling away on all fours and peeked at me through his legs. I stared, half-stunned, my hand stroking my cock. A low growl released from his thick lips, and I fumbled, reaching into the nightstand for lube, but my eyes never left him.

"Hurry," his ass shook in the air, "I need you inside of me again."

The bottle clattered to the floor when he said those words. Words I had longed to hear. Cain needed me as much as I needed him.

He wiggled again, and I scurried between his legs. A groan released as my tip pressed against him, and Cain squirmed his ass back. My eyes rolled into my head, stars, fireworks, who the hell knew what I saw, but the lights blinded me, wrapping and caressing my cock in their flashy seduction. My body and mind fought for dear life to hold on. He withdrew and slammed himself back again. Cain rode me hard, and if he didn't slow down, I would explode.

I grasped his hair and pushed on his shoulder blades, but it was of no use. His ass continued its grinding onslaught over my cock and my insides churned, boiling to the point of no return. If you cannot beat them, join them. "You want rough?"

He breathed his reply, "Yes…"

"You want hard?" I asked, unbelieving he was my shy Cain.

Cain's hands curled in the sheets, and he spat, "I. Said. Yes."

I pulled out; my cockhead nestled between his cheeks. Cain whimpered softly at my head rubbing against his entrance. The sounds stirred a primal need much like our alcove rendezvous, and I fought to think of anything but his sweet ass, smile… No, baseball, mountainsides, snow… But his noises and begging brought me back, closer to release, and I wasn't even inside of him.

His rigid cock dangled between his thighs, and I grasped the smooth heat in my palm, squeezing, as Cain pled, "Dorian, I need you." His brown hair tossed back and forth. He fisted the bedding.

Once the urge to erupt subsided, and I had bought more time, I ran my hands over his cheeks. Spreading them wide, cupping, and slapping his flesh until the pale white surface was marred pink. My lips followed, cooling the heat. When he thought my playful torture was over, I spread his round cheeks wide and thrust my tongue over his wrinkled bud.

Cain's back arched, and his head flung upward. A throaty moan shot from his lips and he panted hard. "Oh shit." His fist slammed against my bed. "Stop torturing me," he whined.

My assault didn't end there. I repeated the motions, enjoying the slow burn, building deep in my cods, while he took over and jacked himself. Slapping skin. Heated, salty flesh and raw testosterone infiltrated my senses. I kissed and licked his crack, swirling my tongue above and below his hole, and listened to his cries.

Unintelligible words sprouted from his mumbling lips. Musty sex thickened in the air as he stiffened.

"Not yet," I echoed his words from the alcove, and knocked his hand away. He reached for his cock, but instead of smacking his hand away, I slapped his ass hard. "I said, not yet."

Before he had time to protest, I pinned his arms behind his back, yanking him upward, and entered Cain in one painfully slow movement, though careful not to injure him.

Curses flew from our mouths. Sweaty flesh joined. His ass bounced, slamming against my pelvis. From my head to my toes, the burn ignited and flared. My lips dropped to his neck, all the while I thrusted harder and built a momentum to match Cain's cries. Heart pounding, as if running a marathon, I breathed hard.

I stared down his chest, my gaze scanning past the hard, chiseled ridges of his abs, and watched his dick slap against his stomach. The head shiny, presenting drops of dew, watered my mouth. All the ways he could fuck me ran through my mind, and Cain's breathing rotated from panting to erratic.

Visuals flashed, and he murmured, "Harder, faster."

I released his arms and encircled his chest. Warmth filled my achy heart as the embrace had so many times before. Lost in his touch, his silkiness, and having his ass clench around my cock was surreal, almost unbelievable. His back arched, curving against me, and nails dug into my arms, scratching and drawing blood.

Cain slammed his head against my shoulder and erupted with a deafening scream and titan grip. His orgasm rippled over me and caressed me inside and out.

Like the first moment our eyes had met, I came hard.

"You'll be the death of death," I said, grinning and catching my breath. My weakness, my Achilles heel, and, damn it all to hell, I would fight to the end of time to protect what was mine. If loving him made me weak, so be it.

"Sweets, you're far from weak, but then again, so am I." He heaved for breath.

We toppled over sideways, legs and arms entangled. For once, I was spent and closed my eyes. "How did you manage to escape the Garland base? You said you had help?"

Again, I couldn't quiet the detective in me. Cain I trusted, but Veric Garland soured my stomach. Maybe the sheer association to Boric was to blame. Or maybe the amount of power he possessed threw me off, seeing as he wielded too much for a simple Elioud that he claimed to be.

"Veric," Cain flopped onto his stomach and flashed a grin, "he stowed away with me and a baby he'd called…oh shit."

My brow rose at his outburst. "Your eyes flash red when you're excited." I stroked his back, enjoying the energy humming between us.

"Korrigan *really* is Angelica, isn't she?" He slapped himself and left a massive red welt, ignoring my statement. "Mother did it. She pulled off the spell."

"Believe so, babe. Thought you'd figured out that one. Bloody fucking crazy shite." What was going on down there? Boric's own brother risked hightailing for the border with escapees?

"Why do you use British English?" He cocked his head, brows drawn together. "Not that I mind. Kind of sexy, even without the accent."

"Most Archangels have British accents. Those of us who were on Earth longer lost them for the most part. Some of us lived here in the beginning. When the Angels fell, many landed in England." Father had sent me to Eden.

"What about demons? Elioud?" He shook his head.

"I'm certain there's all sorts of accents and nationalities among us. Remember, Father gave everyone on Earth fair warning, so many hightailed it from across the pond and beyond, babe." I paused for a moment before switching gears back on topic. "I didn't get the whole story, didn't pretend to understand it, either, but when did this escape go down?"

Cain snorted. "Years before Armageddon fucking hit like a freight train, but it took me longer to cross into Arcadia on foot." Tomas had verified as much. Cain reached for my hand and laced our fingers together. "I might've never made it to Delphia if not for Veric."

"I met him."

"How?" He blinked, emotion washing from his face, and opened his mouth. A strange sound emitted before he said, "He's dead."

"Babe, he survived," I chuckled, "and he's kind of my boss. A prick but... yeah." I shrugged.

Cain's mouth fell open again.

"He remembers you, said he lost you in Delphia." A statement. I wasn't accusing the agent of dumping him in the hellish world. Honestly, I had tried to make sense of it all. Their whole posse intrigued me, and the more I learned, the more curious I became. Like internal avengers fighting against their captors. "Do you know why he turned on his brother?"

Cain glanced toward the bedroom door, as floorboards creaked, and the front door closed downstairs, rattling the windows. "I think you can ask him yourself."

"Shite." I shuffled and scurried to dress before Veric moseyed upstairs.

Cain laughed at me and dragged the blankets to his chin. I sighed, glancing back at the warm and inviting bed, and closed the door.

Tiptoeing down the steps, I meant to catch Veric off guard, but he waited. The redheaded demon sat in the chair by my desk, dressed in an ABDA issued, all black, tactical uniform. A sad comparison seeing as I was Death, yet he seemed to fit the part better than I did. "What can I do you for?"

He didn't turn around, but crossed his legs and bounced his thigh. "Is Petre alive?"

"Yes, he is alive." Strolling to my desk, I answered with truth.

Veric hissed, "Shite, real fucking wanker he is. Don't go after him."

"Is that an official order?" I lit the oil lamp on my desk. Soft light bathed the completely dark room. Sulfur released into the air, quickly overpowered by the kerosene. I eased into my chair. How long had Cain and I been in bed?

Red rims swelled around Veric's crimson eyes. "No. I know why you want the sodden bastard, no offense, but he's a bit of a pain in the arse." He winked. "And not in a good way."

"He called her Korri didn't he?" I leaned back in my chair. "Cain was just filling me in before you arrived. She's the baby, right?"

Veric nodded and shielded his mouth with his palm. "Bloody hell this whole façade reads like a bad science fiction novel." His fist closed and trembled. "I need to bring my brother down. Petre complicates that."

The least I could have done was hear the man out before making up my mind. But I didn't understand the connection. Cain, fully dressed, leaned against the doorframe, and I assumed he wanted to understand what had happened all those years ago. My fingers tapped over the desk.

When an explanation hadn't come, Cain said, "It's true, then? Mother died...Boric killed her, but Angel looks—"

"Almost the same?" Veric twisted around. "I know...she's still in there, and sometimes, our Angelica pops out, recalling everything."

Cain dragged a chair from Belle's desk and sat next to me.

Veric faced us; sparks alight in his eyes. One departed, and the tiny speck hovered beside his head. He blew on the flicker, and it raced toward the hearth, alighting the logs in a crackling glory. Veric sighed, shoulders slouching. "Yes, Angelica Garland and Korrigan Garland are one in the same."

My brows scrunched together. "How?"

"Magic," Cain replied, and shrugged. "You asked how I escaped, but you never asked why Veric helped me."

Lying by omission was still lying, but I'd meant the spark trick. But as I opened my mouth to correct him, Veric spoke.

"Luna was their mother, and she cast the spell removing Angelica's soul. Even Tomas doesn't know, though, I'm certain the bloke figured it out already."

"You said their mother?" I reached for my pen.

"Our mother sacrificed her life to save Angelica's. Boric sentenced Angelica to the brothels, but she chose death rather than service."

Something was off the way Cain spoke of Boric, but I couldn't figure out what. My brows rose. "You can do that with magic?" Both men nodded, but I shook my head. "Cain, I admit…it's all a little crazy." Wiches and warlocks weren't my domain, so even before the Sundering, I rarely dealt with them. Give me a vampire any day.

"I promised to save her remaining children," Veric said to Cain, "Lily wasn't with Jules when I left Angel. Should've seen his deceit then. Maybe she hadn't arrived, or he hid her away, but I saw nothing off."

My temples throbbed, and I rubbed small circles over my flesh. *Do I want to know? Now, there was a question.*

I lifted my hand and butted in. "Let me get this straight." I motioned to Cain. "You have two sisters, one died but had her soul removed, and another who went missing among the brothels." I pointed at Veric. "You're married to Angelica aka Korrigan, but the actual woman died and arose as a vampire?" And I thought my family had problems.

Both men chuckled, but it was the truth.

I knew extraction and bloodsuckers, not crazy family drama and magic. "And how the hell does Petre fit into all of this again?"

Through gritted teeth, Veric said, "He bought Korrigan from Jules on her eighteenth birthday."

"Did they marry?" Legally purchasing her, though a bit tasteless, wasn't enough.

"No, mate, they never exchanged vows."

"You're certain?"

"Of course, I'm bloody certain. She's been my wife for over three hundred and fifty years."

"But you left her with another man?" I replied.

"Like I had a choice?" He slammed his palm onto my desk, and Cain jumped. "My brother would've killed them both and then me. She slowed us down, and I trusted the fucking tosser to keep her safe until I could return." His face softened as he eyed Cain. "I had planned to retrieve her after you were secure. Botched it all up when he caught up to us."

"He holds no claim then," Cain whispered, "according to the laws unless...he turned her." Cain's eyes glistened. "I don't blame you. Never did."

I squeezed Cain's hand, and he tucked my fingers into his before bringing my knuckles to his lips.

"So, Death, eh?" Veric forged a crooked smile, the light reflecting off his scar that cut deep and jagged into his jawline. "Well, you're certainly an improvement over—"

Cain coughed. "Yes, he is, but back to business. Why is Petre such a problem? I never met him, but Tomas spoke highly of him."

Veric cracked his neck and stretched. "Petre, from what I've gathered, is squeaky clean. He's good and so are his intentions." He leaned forward and rested his elbows on my desk. His amber gaze widened. "Thing is mate, Angelica loves him, and her love for him is fierce. When she thought him dead, I thought, finally, my chance to win her back. But no...never seen a woman pine so much over a scraggly bloke."

Yeah, Petre had changed her all right. But I believe she truly loves Petre, just as I love her brother.

"The problem is bigger than that I'm afraid." I leaned back in my chair and wrapped my arm around Cain, drawing his head to my shoulder.

A distant look had appeared in his eyes that hadn't been there before he'd stopped Veric. Did he not want me to know the man's name? Watching both men for clues was like watching paint dry. Neither gave the slightest hint. Were they speaking privately?

"Petre and Nicolai both pose a huge problem until they've been marked again by me or Conquest."

I allowed my words to sink in over the gentle hissing fire. Fauna and Markos had both met Nicolai, but he needed no temptation. He was mine. My fingers gripped around a pen. Petre was another story, and few knew his tales. He'd kept his past hidden, but I had known the truth. Before Petre Von Baron had died, he'd been a lowly vicar. In his family and time, it was common for the second son to join the priesthood. Understanding him, I doubted he'd knowingly broken any law. I scribbled the newfound connection between Korrigan and Petre and Veric into my notes.

Veric offered, "Adulterer?" My boss wore the truth on his face, lacing his gruff tone in hate.

"Not technically." I stopped writing. "You were married under God's laws, but only Korrigan's soul survived, and Petre then laid his claim under the new laws."

"Arcadia doesn't recognize slave ownership." Veric crossed his arms over his chest and stuck his nose into the air.

"True." My lips pursed, reaching for the pen again. "He used vampire law, but now, if he's human, that claim no longer applies…" The slippery slope slickened. My breath blew out. Veric appeared incapable of judgment for those crimes or anything revolving around her. I didn't blame him. Hell, I would fight tooth, nail, and blood for Cain. My pen tapped against my dry lips, clicking.

If the body died, did the marriage absolve? Father didn't have rules or laws for magic, which meant no matter what, Angelica willingly participated. Otherwise, I didn't understand how else a spell, such as soul swapping, wouldn't be evil.

"I need to speak with her alone," Cain responded to my unspoken questions.

Veric objected, but I raised my hand, waving at him to shut up. "If Petre is in the wrong, he will be dealt with according to the laws of Arcadia, and then judged by Conquest and myself. But, if he's in the right or at no-fault, I will send for him, because frankly, we need all the fucking help we can find to overthrow your arsemonkey, whorebag, wanker of a brother and still manage a quick getaway."

"I think you missed a few adjectives," Cain muttered under his breath.

Veric grinned and barked a laugh. "Oh please, don't hold back on my account. The fucking bastard can rot in Hell for all I care."

Cain excused himself, disappearing into the downstairs bathroom. I lifted my pen and shuffled papers around.

"Dorian," Veric whispered, so low I had to strain over my desk to hear him. "Cain once belonged to Boric."

The pen in my hand snapped. Black ink poured over my hands. Images of the monster, I'd once called Brother, flashed through my mind, and I glanced to the bathroom door.

"It was a long time ago," Veric said. "But I figured you of all people should know my brother only gave him up, because the Arch demons said he must. Even then, he never let go and tossed 'em around. In his twisted mind, I do believe he loves Cain.'

"Why are you telling me this?" my whisper hissed through my tightened jaw. The back of my mind nagged, piecing bits together.

"Of all the lovers my brother took," he nodded toward the bathroom, "he coveted him the most." The toilet flushed followed by running water. "And Cain, although a child himself and easily influenced... I think he loved him before...maybe still. We don't need anything jeopardizing the mission. You share a common weakness with Boric."

"What are you suggesting I do?" I rubbed the ink over my jeans. My heart ached more for Cain, and though I should've been pissed, rage didn't rise.

"Put him in a safe house, Sanctuary. Don't let him near my brother."

The bathroom door creaked, and Cain strolled back to his seat. "Don't act like y'all weren't talking about me." He shoved my shoulder. "I can read the guilt on your face."

"Nonsense. We were just figuring out who should go where." Veric shifted in his chair. "I offered Dorian use of a safe house for you, while we're in the field."

Cain's wide amber eyes glowed. "No. Screw that. I'm not staying behind, while y'all go out gallivanting. I'd rather go back to living my life."

"Cain, Dorian and I are trained agents." He extended his hand toward me.

Cain stomped his foot. "I have magic, and I can use a gun. Damn it, Veric, you taught me."

I rested my hand on his thigh, rubbing over the rough denim. "I'd rather you not rely on magic or discharge a weapon, babe."

He only stuck his bottom lip out, turned his body and looked away. Shite. He was adorable, but Veric had a point. Sanctuary would protect him better than I could.

"C'mon, just listen." I squeezed his shoulder, but he tossed off my hand. "Besides, I don't have time—"

Cain's chair slid into the wall and his feet pounded over the stairs as his cute ass retreated from my office.

I glared at Veric, his warning still weighing on my mind. "Can he shoot?"

"Yes." He offered a half-shrug. "He's not the greatest shot, missed Boric." He dragged a finger along his scar. "Gave me this instead."

I tore a hand through my hair and rested my chin on my fist. If anything happened to him, I'd never forgive myself. But would he forgive me if I left him behind? We had finally broken through some of our trust barriers.

"Fuck it. He's coming with me." A groan slipped through my lips. At least with me, I could still keep him protected and safe. Besides, we wouldn't be alone once we ventured south. "I've gotta smooth shit over with him. Can you call everyone back?" Bounding the steps two at a time, I called, "Babe."

Cain sulked on the sofa, his scowling face rested on his hands, and he stared at the fire. "What? Come to order me around?"

A smile flitted my lips at the twang his accent created whenever he was upset. "C'mon that's not fair. Babe, I need you safe, but if you really think you can help..." I knelt in front of him and tore his hands away from his face.

"What did he say about me?" Slowly, he turned his attention toward me.

"Please, can we not fight? There's enough bad shit in this world without having you hate me, too."

He chewed his bottom lip and studied the fire. "Everyone is treating me like I'm that sixteen year old boy." His mouth opened, as if he was about to say more.

From downstairs, Veric shouted, "Dorian, Cain."

Cain and I rushed to see what Veric was carrying on about, but we found him yelling into the phone and pacing the length of the hearth. Our gazes connected for a minute as he shook his head.

"I want more men," Veric demanded into the clunky receiver. "At least a dozen." He tore at his hair. "Not Gabriel, I don't need a slaughter on our hands."

Gabe was ferocious, dependable, but also a loose cannon. I liked him.

Cain rearranged the furniture, the chairs making echoes reminiscent of squeaky chalk on a blackboard. "I don't like everyone standing," he explained, and proceeded to shiver, gooseflesh erupting over his forearms.

Veric's fire had died. I strolled to the fireplace and added a log to the embers. I lit a match, hoping the key was to add more fire, though I seldom built them. The front door let in a cool breeze and blew out my flame. Heavy footsteps and murmurs entered the house.

Markos' boots dripped water onto my tinder pile. He asked, "Have you decided?"

I shook my head as his grimace set into a deep scowl.

"Then why have you called us, Brother?"

"He wants to know if I'm Angelica." Her amber gaze narrowed and skated to Veric. His ginger hair fell into his face but didn't hide the blush settling in his cheeks. "You came back? How could you invade their privacy like that, over something so trivial?"

"Luv, I didn't invade." Veric, no longer on the phone, tossed his hands into the air.

Was she always this worked up over small stuff? Korrigan slapped his shoulder, and I waited for steam to leave her ears. Cain nodded his head and cleared his throat. Quite comical for a vampire, I had yet to meet one this new who couldn't dampen their emotions.

I interrupted their argument before it escalated. "He didn't... bother us. If you don't mind, Korrigan, I'd like to ask a few questions?"

Her gaze flittered over Cain, who was sitting by my desk again, ignoring me. "You. You stole Boric's keys," she accused. Dainty legs clipped over the wooden floor and stopped in front of him. Even with Cain sitting, he was taller than she was. She stabbed a finger in his chest.

Lady or not, I grasped her hand and stepped in-between them. "No one touches him."

"Excuse me," she yanked her hand free, "Cain had the keys."

"Keys? What the hell are you going on about?" I stepped aside and stared at him.

His fingers drummed on his thigh. Cain had alluded to more secrets, but this was larger than a surreptitiously hiding his past with Boric—that I didn't blame Cain for—the keys, though...I didn't know what to say. "Babe?"

His butterscotch eyes closed, neither denying nor admitting, but the suspicions were there. It made sense, more than his blood or some passing fancy, why Boric would enter Arcadia for him...why he would punish the whole bloodline. I sighed, palming my neck.

"The rumors are true, then," Markos said, and crossed his arms over his chest. "The Garlands mean to open the gates and destroy the families."

I held my hands up and the room silenced. Why did I have them all come and not just Korrigan?

Markos asked, "Did Boric preserve the keys?"

"Preserve?" Cain rose and turned toward the windows, growing more than silent, broody almost.

"Did he take them? Sorry, I'll refrain from big words."

Something weighed on Cain's mind. Those broad shoulders slouched, and he stroked his chin, his gaze meeting mine in the reflection. He flinched, as I reached for him, and I froze with my hand hovering in the air.

"Preserve isn't a big word, or the right word. Yes, he *had been* collecting the keys." Cain said, "They are safe."

"How do you know?" Hallo asked, as I opened my mouth.

"I hid them, and only I can retrieve them. Fauna and you called me the Keeper." Cain opened his hands, which I had known to be empty moments before. Purple fire pulsed into his palms. He muttered Latin words, and the fire disappeared, but in his palm rested a handful of skeleton keys.

Korrigan reached into her bodice and withdrew another, and my brow rose.

Cain scratched his nose and said, "Two are still unaccounted for."

Why is he still lying?

"Boric must have those. It's why he enslaved the six families," Korrigan whispered, rubbing behind her ear.

So she had recalled her previous life, and she was a liar, much like her brother. I wanted to judge her, truly, but deception enabled them to survive. Still, they needed to trust me with their endless secrets.

"This one is the Garland key." Her heels clicked over the wood, as she stepped to her brother again, and placed the key in his palm. A wide smile crept over her lips, and she flung her arms around Cain.

"I've made my decision." With only two keys, Boric wasn't a real threat, not to mention I held the eighth and final key. "We do not strike. Not without a plan to mark and save those who are innocent."

Markos rolled his eyes.

"Furthermore, we do not attack without the full support of the ABDA and the councils, because we will need their help. Veric and Markos, I would like you to lead up the military end. Fauna may assist you if you can drag her from the Wilderness."

Both siblings and the Elioud nodded.

Korrigan's eyes pled. "And Petre?"

My breath blew out in a steady stream, her amber eyes welled. Von Baron, wherever he might be, was a genius. While I personally had little use for another vampire, the ABDA engineering department would have use of him—we needed a way into the south that didn't involve magic and that could transport an army.

Hallo stepped forward and squeezed her shoulder. "I will escort you to Petre."

"No, Sister, I need you to rally the support of the councils. They don't respond to me." No one liked Death, except the other rebels. "They'll listen to you."

"We got a wee problem, bloke." Veric scratched his head. "Angel drinks only demon blood. You going to let her feed on Cain?"

I glanced between the siblings, and both shook their heads.

"Right, thought so. Guess I'll be tagging along, then."

"Tomas, Nicolai?" I asked since neither man had spoken more than a polite hello.

"My connections will help in the government. I have contacts in Delphia and Garland. Nicolai should accompany you."

We didn't have much of a choice. Red tape stood between the south and us, and the French bastard certainly did have acquaintances. But a tiny leak could unravel our plans. Could we trust them? Did we have a choice?

Great, we headed into the frozen tundra with a caravan.

"I could stay with Tomas," Cain offered.

I snorted, knowing he didn't want to, and said, "Like hell you will. You're staying by my side." Forever, if I had my way.

Chapter Twelve

Cain

For years, I hadn't believed my mother's spell had worked. Hell, I could barely believe my eyes saw Veric in the flesh or the tiny woman, who resembled my sister. Mother had sacrificed her life and told me her plan; I still blinked at the amber-eyed woman before me. Korrigan Garland was Angelica Marie Westcott in appearance, if not at heart. And by appearance, I meant facial features, because Angel hadn't been nearly as short or frail. She had changed or not developed, and that much I could not ignore.

Dorian excused everyone and himself, but she hovered behind, fidgeting near the doorway to his office. Veric stepped outside with the others, and their lumbering voices carried. Few seemed pleased with Dorian's new orders, but I stood behind his decisions.

I approached her. "How did you meet Petre?"

Angel slid into a chair and cracked her neck. Long, dark hair sat on top of her head; the mass looked more painful than fashionable. Same for her dated clothing and lace and leather corset vest. Another theater raid? Her skirt swept the floor.

"He bought me from Jules six months ago." Angel narrowed her gaze and wagged her finger. "I like my clothes by the by, and they hide my weapons rather nicely." To demonstrate, she hefted her leg onto Dorian's desk and inched up her skirt, revealing her leg, guns, and knives.

"Some things never change," I said.

"What do you mean?" she asked, blinking her large, amber eyes.

The front door slammed, rattling the windowpanes, and my gaze widened. As Veric's heavy boots stomped over the floorboards, Angel didn't flinch. The air shifted. Her spine straightened and chin lifted higher. My gaze darted between the two who, once upon a time, had been crazy for one another.

"Cain," he started, and rubbed his cheek.

A long scar ran from the edge of his jaw and jutted to his neck, but it wasn't there before I shot him. It hadn't been the first time I'd fired a gun, but I hadn't shot another since.

"It's been a little crazy. I'm sorry we haven't had a chance to catch up. But thank God you're well, mate."

The chair skidded back. I leapt up and engulfed my brother-in-law in a hug. I hadn't done so before partly from shock, and partly because I feared, he might disappear on me. "What the hell happened?" I asked. "Thought you were dead. Thought…I'd killed you."

Veric halted, shaking his head, and slid away. Dorian entered, gaze burning and composure rigid. His mind reeled between jealousy and relief, but my concern wasn't his reaction.

The worry read clear in Veric's eyes. I didn't envy either of them. I saw firsthand the love they had once shared. Was it truly gone?

Dorian strolled over to the desk and glanced between the three of us. His gaze flickered to the steps while he nibbled his bottom lip. "We'll rest tonight."

"I don't sleep," Angel whispered, and flexed her pale fingers.

"Some of us do require rest. Keep watch for all I care." Without another word, he stormed the stairs and shook the house.

My brow rose, but I couldn't decipher his thoughts. *What is he hiding?*

"Is he always a mardy arse?"

I chuckled, staring at stairwell, but honestly didn't know. In time, hopefully distinguishing Dorian's moods would come easier for me.

Veric added, "Sorry I didn't come back for you. When the ABDA found me, I was close to death."

Sounded like Boric's doing. I scoffed at the thought. Use and leave was his motto, whether it was sex or violence. Too early for sleep but I didn't feel like dredging through the past, either. We all knew what kind of demon his brother was.

"Let me show you around." A quick tour of the upstairs ended in a non-verbal argument. Blocking them was impossible, but I kept my mouth shut. Torn between my sister and the man that saved me from death, there wasn't a side for me to take. But I wanted to fix them, I wanted Angelica back, but I wasn't certain she was really in there. Maybe Dorian would know, or he could help me figure this out. My gaze drifted to the wall separating the rooms. "I'm sure Dorian wants an early start."

I closed their door and sat on the sofa by the fireplace in the upstairs living room, instead of bothering him. Dorian had his own problems without adding my crazy family into the mix. Embers burned in the fireplace. My sister was miserable, free, but not free, in an odd sense, as I was before meeting Dorian. But Veric held on, waiting for his Angelica. How much of her was even there, and how much had become Petre's Korrigan?

Hugs felt empty, and her ambitions had changed. Angelica wouldn't have put another person before tearing down Boric from his lofty throne. My fists clenched at the thought of the bastard King. None of her situation had made any sense. Mother might have saved her soul, but she wasn't the sister I once knew and loved. As if her rebirth washed the slate clean but allowed her to retain old memories.

The door creaked, and Dorian whispered, "Come in here."

I shook my head and stared into the cinders. Until this whole debacle connected within my mind, I was not moving. My head rested on my fist, and he eased down next to me.

"It'll be fine, babe." His burly arms encompassed me and dragged me against him.

I sighed, allowing Dorian to hold me. When was the last time anyone had cared enough to coddle me? Never unless I had counted my mother or sisters' attentions. "She's not the same."

Angelica and Veric were not trying to be subtle about their argument. Furniture squeaked and rattled from the spare bedroom. Muffled voices followed, but I couldn't make out exact words. I didn't want to either and clutched onto Dorian instead.

"I know, and that's why we're going after Petre." Dorian's lips kissed the top of my head. "Do you mind if she feeds from you?"

I shook my head, wiping my stinging eyes on his t-shirt, and breathed in his fresh soap. My fingers twined into the fabric and tugged, revealing the dark hairs of his furry chest. Mindlessly, I stroked the silky hairs.

He said, "Not sure I like the idea, but Hallo needs Veric more than we do."

I snorted at his sister's name, but she held a lot more pull with the demons, so I agreed. She had come to me under false pretense and had led me to Dorian, but the former turned the acid in my stomach. Fauna had tried the same, forcing me to grovel at his feet, as if they were all privy to a grand plan.

"I'm glad you did," Dorian whispered, twisting the ring his sister had gifted me. "Look at all we talked about."

I shifted, gazing into green eyes. "Yeah a bit of talking had been thrown in there." I grinned.

Dorian hooked my chin and rubbed his thumb over the stubble. Slow circular strokes like a hundred caresses against my tender skin. Inky eyelashes fluttered. My hand slid around his neck, cupping the back of his head and drawing him closer. Staring into his captivating eyes, both my wishes and hopes collided. Would I always be enough for him? As they whispered in my ear, I couldn't quiet my inner demons.

"Looks like your family's as crazy as mine," he whispered.

Crazy wasn't a strong enough word to describe the Horsemen. In their own ways, they were all a bit twisted, but one had to be to survive this hellish world. It didn't say much for Dorian and me.

The fire popped; our tender moment fizzled. Easing against his chest, I willed the flames to grow, chanting and channeling my energy into the spell. Dorian gasped at the dancing spirit burning purple in the hearth.

"You don't use your magic often."

I shrugged. Magic was a gift from God but easily abused. That made us different in some circles and viewed weaker in others.

"I like that," he added, and snuggled closer.

His hands roamed over my chest and snuck beneath my t-shirt. My body arched; he collected me within his arms, cradling me.

Nodding his head, he said, "It's going to be all right, Cain."

"We haven't spoken about the keys." Curiosity killed the cat, but I always wanted to know what they unlocked.

Dorian stared into the fireplace and gulped. "Are you with me because of them?"

"No," I said, and meant it.

"Didn't think so, babe, and that's all that matters, right?" He flashed a smile, dismissing the topic a little too quickly for my tastes, but I let it go.

Floorboards squeaked. Angelica paced in the guest room. Veric's mind had shut down, and Dorian's plan unfolded within his. I wasn't sure how he knew my brother-in-law was asleep, though. A sneaky plan and it involved ditching Veric while he slumbered. It bothered me, but I couldn't figure out why my sister would toss Veric aside without accepting the truth. Unless Korrigan wasn't my sister, but the woman inside that room was Korrigan. How could two souls occupy one body? Still made no sense.

His grip tightened. "Your sister's soul is within her body, but that's not Angelica, babe. Not truly."

Dorian had said similar words before, but I didn't want to believe him. Soul magic was tricky and dangerous, but I'd understood Mother's wishes. The slaves saw what Boric had done to her body, but our mother couldn't perform the spell until the end.

A tear slid down my cheek, and Dorian swiped the wet streak.

"Bedtime, babe." He groaned, lifting me from the couch. "We have a long road ahead of us."

Thoughts between the future and why I cried bounced in his head. Dorian showed me his darkness, his deepest secrets, but I grasped onto mine, stroking them as a reminder never to give up this fight. Shadows over his heart led me to lie; life in the south had led me to flee. Did he suspect the closeness I'd once shared with his enemy? Would he understand how a boy fell in love with a monster? My body trembled, fighting control and warring within. Would Dorian sympathize or condemn me? He had no notion of slavery, even if he had lived through pain. What could Death know of living life without choice or the inability to deny one's masters? I couldn't release those secrets, for my choices had cast me in shame, shame that I hadn't realized myself until Dorian's love touched me.

He laid me on the bed, removing my boots. I rolled onto my stomach, watching as he retrieved two sets of sweats from his dresser. Dorian tossed me a pair, and I changed, allowing my façade to fall before sitting up again. My shaky fingers grasped the hem of my shirt. I removed it, baring all, seeing no use in hiding the riveted flesh and wasting energy.

A gasp left his rough lips before kissing my shoulder. "Do they hurt?"

I croaked, "No," and glided the faded, soft ABDA shirt over my head. Scars—burned into the depths of my soul, each one was a memory Boric had carved into me.

I slid beneath the covers, and Dorian did the same. Our fingers folded, connecting and forming one. My other hand cupped his coarse cheek. We rested, side-by-side, holding each other and embracing each other's dimming light, as if the radiance were air needed to survive.

The Four Horsemen hadn't needed the power of the government. A snap or simple blink and they could've undone the world. That left one option and the thought coated my mouth in bitterness. Dorian was holding something back, though; I didn't have the right to judge him for it. For two people in love, we couldn't let go of our secrets. All roads pointed toward trust. I smoothed my thumb over his lips. "Why are the keys important?"

Dorian made a noise half between a grumble and words. "I dunno." His leg curled over my thigh, and he scooted closer. "The others seem to think it's a great evil we cannot contain." The Bible had referred to the gates of Hell, or purgatory, but Dorian guarded Sheol. "I have the final key."

But the Bible also spoke of every step in sevens: seven days, seven signs, seven seals, seven Archangels, seven princes, and sevens keys.

My brow scrunched as my head tossed on the pillow. Dorian would have made eight, and more than seven Archangels existed. Were there truly eight steps, or another connection?

"Stop worrying and get some rest. We'll be trekking through the Arcadian backwoods, and you need your strength."

As he pressed his lips to my forehead, I closed my eyes. Dorian didn't move, cuddling me through the evening and into the twilight hours. But I couldn't quiet my mind. Once his light snores vibrated against me, I slipped from the bed.

Low light flooded in from beneath the bedroom door. I cracked it open. Heat washed over me, and a lump formed in my throat. A fire roared in the hearth. Angelica stood at the mantle, staring into the swaying flames. Behind me, I closed the door and approached my sister, careful to keep noise to a minimum.

"I'm not her," she whispered. "But doesn't mean I can't care and love you. What you did for her, few would have endured, Cain What you do now, continuing her work…"

The lump in my throat tightened. "She endured more."

Angel nodded but didn't glance at me.

"I'm trying to understand, to grasp what happened to my sister, where Mother's spell went wrong."

"That's not why I refuse him. Jules is dead." Angel might as well have spoken about the weather. "I killed him…ripped his heart out and squeezed the life from his worthless body. My only regret is I didn't do it sooner."

But there were hundreds more, like Jules, out there in the broken world. No peace would come until they all fell.

Angelica eyed me. "Peace is a state of mind. It cannot be achieved across the boundaries."

I leaned against the wall. "Why bother trying? What are the boundaries?"

The fire popped and her lips curved into a gruesome, devilish smile. "Because I cannot sit idly and watch as the world falls again." Her hair fell into her eyes. "Their actions must stop, even if we are all damned and forgotten by God. We are still his children."

She sounded more like Angelica—or Tomas—her emotions bled into her tightened jaw and fists.

"The spell failed. It couldn't fully cross the boundaries of time and space...I don't know what that means, but it's in my head."

I shifted gears and asked, "What are the keys for? Angelica had to know—her memories are yours, are they not?"

Korrigan spun and pinned me against the wall. She wrapped her tiny hand around my neck, and she squeezed, wielding the might of a hundred men. I gasped, struggling for air, and clawed at her hand. My heart thundered. Pristine fangs extended in her mouth, clicking louder than the popping fire, and my gaze widened. No words escaped; I would die. Fuzzy lines formed around my vision, flickering in and out. Harder, she compressed my windpipe.

My back slid up the wall, my legs dangled, kicking the wood, and I prayed Dorian woke from the ruckus.

"Stop," she hissed to herself, and dropped me.

I slid to the floor, landing hard enough the house tremored and windows rattled. Rubbing my neck, I caught my breath. Dorian's door banged, and as he swooped into the living room, the hairs rose on my neck. Green eyes blazed, and he grasped Angel, tossing her to the other side of the room, crashing into the kitchen table. Wood fractured. She sprung to her feet, crouching toward the ground. Lightning splintered the air outside, and a hazy, swirling vortex filled the space.

I blinked, still unable to speak. Death held his scythe against Angelica's neck. The guest room's door creaked.

"Don't," Veric said, rushing to her side. "Angel, bloody hell, I can't leave you alone." He palmed his red hair and shook his head. Veric glanced toward me. "What'd you say to her?"

My cheeks warmed, and my gaze dropped to the floor. Didn't I have the right to know what I'd put my life on the line for? Veric scowled but ignored my thoughts.

Dorian dropped the blade and removed his hood. He hadn't transformed, evident from his skin-covered hand and dark head of hair. I hugged my knees into my chest and shivered. He knelt by my side, brushing his hand through my hair. His fingers hooked my chin and forced my attention. I flinched, expecting anger, when concern flickered in his emerald eyes.

"Babe? Did she hurt you?" He stroked my face.

Yes and no. I nipped my inner cheek. Tears welled, threatening to drown me from the inside. My sister was dead. Soul or not, the woman across the room wasn't my sweet Angelica. She had truly died when Boric slit her throat and forced me to watch. Would he have taken my life instead if I had given him the location?

"He would've of murdered you both, mate." Veric sighed. "You especially, Cain."

Dorian released me, and my head bowed toward my chest. I had belonged to Boric. When he'd shared me, the bastard never let me forget that. Stealing the keys had been a slap in the face, but by me swiping them, it had been like hitting Boric with a bat in the back of the head.

"What aren't you telling me?"

My mouth dropped, but Angel shook her head and placed a finger to her lips. Large, amber eyes appeared as lost as I felt inside. He deserved to know the truth, to know why Boric hunted the Morning Stars, but it meant admitting part of me would always love the monster who'd betrayed me.

"Cain?"

I rasped, "What?" and cringed at the state of my voice. Starring into his eyes, I knew part of the lie would release from my shaking lips. "The keys…have them all now." I closed my eyes and rested my head against the wall. "She gave them to me, and I hid them before his hunters found me."

"That's not it."

Again, yes and no. Dorian knew about the keys, but I hadn't given him the real ones. Sometimes magic reflected smoke and mirrors.

Gesturing toward my pocket, my head nodded, and Dorian retrieved the skeleton key Angelica had slipped me. To the untrained eye, the key seemed like nothing important, just an old brass skeleton key. The metal never dulled and shined in the darkness. Dorian removed his chain and slid the key next to his iron one. Angel said nothing of my act, but her fiery gaze spoke enough.

"We'll retrieve the rest later," he whispered, and brushed his lips over my wrinkled forehead. "Angel," Dorian said, and faced my sister still crouching to the floor. "Next time, I won't hesitate if you threaten my boyfriend."

Boyfriend? Guess he'd upgraded me from lover, and I smiled at the thought. But my stomach ached at my continued betrayal: smoke and mirrors had prevailed once again.

In the whirlwind, he came in on, Death departed, and a barefoot Dorian stood in his place, rocking on his heels. He extended his hand and hefted me up, brushing non-existent dirt from my body. "You really are the Keeper." Dorian's mind wandered over the past, an old scroll, but the image quickly faded. "They are safest with you, for now."

I nodded and refused to glance at Korrigan. No longer could I call her Angelica. Whether she had foamed at the mouth, scowled, or hadn't cared at his threat, I didn't want to find out.

"Well, it changes a few things, but nothing immediate." He added, "But, babe, it doesn't change the fact that I love you."

Will the truth of me being Boric's lover change his mind?

Veric asked, "What's that awful smell?"

The scent of decay had belonged to Dorian, but the aroma wasn't offensive to me. Like fallen leaves and overturned earth, the fragrance brought comfort to my being.

A smirk curved over Dorian's lips. "Guess I better shower."

Veric snorted. "Death smells like death?"

Dorian ignored his jab and stormed into his bedroom.

The three of us stood there in silence, in the living room. Pipes groaned. I broke through first. "I had to tell him the truth."

Korrigan nodded. "You love him. There shouldn't be secrets."

But secrets existed. Dorian knew I was a former sex slave. My father might have sold me, but the first hundred or so years, I had been content, happy even. Boric hadn't always been a monster, not at first. One day my luster had disappeared, and he'd lost what remained of his mind.

"No, he wasn't always like this. You made him better, Cain. He talked of change, but then the Arch demons rose from the cracks of Hell."

I shot Veric a glance and clutched my stomach.

"Doesn't make what he did to you—to anyone—right, but it is the truth." Veric curled his fists, but he, too, gave a slight nod. "You were always too good for him, mate, but I understand. Dorian will understand."

"I met them. The beatings started afterward," I whispered, wincing at the words leaving my lips. "They didn't command him to hurt me, just the others, but the control became a drug. If he didn't have it, he took it by force." Memories strangled my breath. I might have been sixteen my first time with Boric, but he didn't force himself on me.

Everything had slowly started to change around the end of the American Civil War when the Arch demons emerged. Little by little, they'd transformed Boric, eating away at his mind, and an altered man rose in power, taking but never giving a damn. At first, I'd asked God to forgive me and blamed myself for the differences in him. One day, I'd opened my eyes to the truth.

Thoughts tremored through my body, and my head shook them aside. Villains were not born evil, and the same rule applied to Boric Garland.

I excused myself and slipped into Dorian's bathroom. My clothing joined his, and I slid open the door. Water poured over his muscles, and I bit my lip to keep from panting like a crazed dog. "Sweets," I said.

Dorian spun around.

A huge grin plastered onto his face and he reached for me, dragging me into the steamy spray. My mouth opened, but before I had a chance to say anything, his lips consumed me. Boyfriend, yes, we could do this, and I deserved happiness too. Grasping control, my hands curled into his thick, wet hair, and a moan released into Dorian's mouth. I pressed his ass against the tile.

Chapter Thirteen

Dorian

A late evening sky blanketed Nova Scotia. I drew my palm over my rough face. Everyone except Korrigan and I slept. Vampires didn't sleep, but they were capable of falling asleep. The petite pixie of a woman stood guard downstairs, by the front window. Trains whistled and chugged their forced tunes. Wooden boards squeaked beneath my feet. I joined her silent watch.

"Death doesn't sleep much?" She didn't turn around.

"I do, but the night comforts me. Do you drink?" I halted by my desk.

She shook her head, but I reached for the decanter anyway. Cain didn't drink either, and he hated whenever I smoked.

"Don't blame you. This stuff could peel paint." No laughter or signs of amusement played on her pale, reflected face. "Are you nervous?"

"Yes."

I poured the whiskey into two glasses, stepped beside her, and handed one to Korrigan.

Her lips sipped the amber surface, but she offered no reaction to the smoky burn. "I have a problem, Dorian…I can call you that, right?"

I nodded at the usual question. Calling me death seemed morbid for many.

"There are two sides warring inside of me for control." She lifted her hand. "Over here is Korrigan the slave," she shifted the glass and raised her other hand, "but over here is Angelica. Both want different goals."

Hearing her speak of herself in such a way baffled me. Some humans had suffered from a split personality disorder, but I had yet to see a demon with a mental condition. Then again, as an Elioud, Korrigan had human blood. "Do you share any common ground?"

"Freedom." Angelica savored another sip. "Killing Jules was another, but we accomplished that. He tortured so many for so long."

A smile played at her lips, and I chuckled, shaking my head. She barely came past my waist, yet she attacked and killed Nephilim and joked about the fact. The feat was a daring and difficult maneuver.

I eyed the empty street below us. "Who is in control now? What do you fight over?"

"Korrigan is stronger. That's why Veric calls me Angelica, I think. As if the name itself will invoke power and force me to love him. I like him. Don't want to hurt him…but." Her smile disappeared with a sigh. "All I have are her memories, but I am and forever will be Korri, no matter what. He refuses to accept the fate of the spell, or that I love Petre."

Was it the spell, or her upbringing, that caused the multiple personalities? I jotted a mental note, but I wasn't a doctor. Raphael might shed some light on it, though.

"Defeating Jules unlocked pieces of my mind, parts and memories I hadn't known about. My heart, however, belongs to Petre. You say he lives, and I believe you, but I've built walls around myself in case you're wrong, Dorian."

"And Veric?" Unfortunately, for the Elioud, her answer alleviated Petre's crimes in my eyes. I pushed them aside. My decision was final. This beautiful creature wasn't to blame and neither was Petre. They hadn't known her true past. Although, she recalled life as Angelica, she saw herself as Korrigan and wanted to live as her. Who was I to force her to change?

"He will love again, but you may call me Angel or Korri. Don't use that dreadful slave name."

I asked, "And Cain? Lily?"

A few moments passed, but I couldn't tell if she pondered my question, or her thoughts drifted elsewhere. I lit a cigarette and inhaled a long drag, relishing in the smoldering taste of tobacco and whatever byproduct they had laced into the cancer stick. The habit calmed my nerves. My gaze glanced overhead. I had refrained since Cain disapproved. Anytime I lit up in his presence, he knocked the cigarette from my hand or scowled.

She turned and leaned against the windowpane, crossing her bare arms over a flat chest. Chopsticks stuck out from her hair, but she wore no make-up and needed none. If it were not for Veric, Markos would have tried to hit on her.

Her brow rose. "Doubtful. He's smitten with Belle."

I chuckled at her words. Markos didn't do smitten until Belle.

"Neither did you. You love my brother." Korrigan swiped the cigarette from my hand, stared at the smoke rising, and handed it back.

"True."

"I want to help." The glass rattled, and the ground rumbled. Korri gripped the ledge, and her large eyes enlarged. "Is it happening again?"

"The tremors are Markos, or the trains." At least I had hoped but didn't know the true cause of the continuous quakes, which had ranged from earth-shaking to a dull, rolling thunder. If the tremors were not his doing or an approaching train, than it meant our time grew shorter each day. But it had nothing to do with the keys, and I still couldn't fathom their importance. What did matter was my family. The Horsemen had failed to secure the quarter of the world, and God's plan sped into action. The question remains unanswered: are we already too late?

Korri touched my hand. The faintest sensation itched across my skin.

"Dorian, have faith. The final end is not as near as it seems."

How had she and Cain survived? If she were human, Korri wouldn't have become one of mine, despite her pride.

"Until reuniting with Veric, I actually thought there were humans left." She giggled and shook her head. "I'll forgive your judgments, but I am not innocent."

I winked. "Are any of us?" I sighed. "Whatever you did, whatever you will do, you realize Father is loving and forgiving?"

She dragged down her hair, and dark brown waves cascaded over her corset. "I'm not a woman of faith."

Korrigan created her own fashion by blending her past constrictions with the present. More and more women had adopted the new-old southern style and added modern flair. She retreated upstairs.

In the covert stillness, I vowed what once was would rise again. Our world needed change, innovation, and to rebuild, but none of it would happen as long as oppression ruled, and our greatest innovator was lost in the snow.

Demons scarred the sacred Earth, but that didn't mean we had to destroy the harmony. Not all demons were evil: holding the simple thought, I edged into the frosty night and crossed the street. Shortly thereafter, footsteps echoed mine, and I spun around. Cain smirked, and his broad shoulders shrugged.

"Took you long enough." Mind reading had posed a problem to our hushed plan to sneak away from the others. His fingers folded into mine, and together we headed into the train station.

Cain inhaled and scowled. "You stink."

"Old habits die hard, babe." I winked.

After purchasing our tickets, the two o'clock chugged in, and we found our car suite. Lights flickered and power rushed through the line. Whistles blew. By morning, weather permitting, we would arrive near enough to the crash site where Tomas had buried Petre.

Cain plopped onto the bench seat asked, "Do you think she will follow?"

I shot him a side-glance and nodded. The train jostled, and something clattered against the roof. A smile crept over my face. "Oh, I think we'll see her sooner than later."

From the outside, Korrigan opened the door to our compartment and squeezed inside.

"I didn't think you had it in you." I fished out her ticket and handed it over.

The problem all along wasn't her, but Veric. As for her dietary needs, well, plenty of demons were onboard for her to feed on, and if not, we would figure something out.

Korrigan plopped across from us and shivered. "What if you're wrong? I waited over a week, and he never woke-up." She cringed, and tears pooled in her eyes. Tiny fists were balled at her sides, and an unneeded breath whooshed from her lips. "I should've waited longer. Why did I listen to Tomas?"

Long hair, worn wild and loose, hid her bowed head. I believed she would've waited there for as long as it took to awaken Fetre, if not for Tomas's interference. Before Cain, I hadn't witnessed a love rooted into the depths of the soul, and what I had thought about love was not truth. We had love; Korri had love, and I wanted everyone to see and feel the sensations. Fluttering hearts, breathless sighs, unfettered need, and caring rushed through my veins when it came to Cain. He squeezed my hand and kissed my cheek.

Perfection wasn't our goal, and no one should ever seek the notion, but love, love would always be enough.

"There were times I questioned how Petre could have loved me." She lifted her head and wiped her eyes. "He sought me out," she chuckled, "and stalked me for years." Korri touched a hand to her neck where a chain rested. An amber pendant hung between her breasts. "After my recapture, everything changed. I became a vampire and confessed my love."

I never did ask her why, or how, she'd become a vampire, and Cain's twisted brows appeared equally curious.

"Jules' fault. He raped and tortured me within inches of life. Petre had given me blood before fighting with him." She brushed a stray wisp behind her ears and dipped her head again. "Jules snapped my neck and fled." She shrugged her shoulders. "When I awoke, I was a vampire."

Lights dimmed. Our car swayed; the train chugged along its icy track. Cain's attention remained on his sister, and his fingers drummed over his thigh.

"Let it go," I whispered, even though Korri would hear. I rested my hand over his, silently willing him to still.

"My sister is raped and murdered, but let it go, he says." He brushed my hand away. His jaw tightened, and his teeth ground out his words. "Mother would roll in her grave."

"Dorian is right. You need to let it go." Korrigan straightened her shoulders and rose from her bench. She knelt at his feet and grasped Cain's hands in hers. "Look at me."

He shook his head and stared out the darkened window.

"Babe," I whispered, and wrapped my arm around his shoulders. "C'mon, remember what we talked about."

Cain's bottom lip quivered, but he nodded. "She wants to help, and we're helping her in return." His tone lacked enthusiasm.

"Please do this for me," I thought, hoping he chose to listen.

He tilted his head and faced her, but his body had remained stiffer than a sheet of ice. Without dismissing Korrigan, his fidgety composure was as relaxed as he would be. I couldn't force Cain to come to terms, but time wasn't a luxury. The pain in his eyes stayed and left a bitter taste in my mouth. Lights dimmed again, and both their gazes shot upward to the bulbs. I glanced out the fogged windows and wished for the ability to reverse all the demons had done to his family.

Korrigan broke through my thoughts. "I forgave Veric and believe he didn't know. Jules Garland is now dead, and he'll never hurt another soul. Petre taught me not to live in the past, and you cannot either, Cain. Or you, Dorian." She turned to Cain. "I see Mother, and the love she held for us. Let's not let her sacrifice be in vain and finish the dream she envisioned."

"Veric still loves you," Cain shook his head, "you can't push your husband aside. Don't you remember how much you loved him?"

Korri chewed her lip and stared at the floor.

He pled, "You're hurting him, and I can't hate the man who saved my life."

"I'm not asking you to hate him, Cain—I don't hate him. In some ways, he saved me, too, reaching out to me through dreams and giving me strength to hold on, but my heart doesn't belong to him."

My brows twisted. Veric had saved him on more than one occasion, and until recently, no one else had known the extent of Cain's abuse. He shifted, and Korri returned to her seat.

I still allowed him to keep secrets. My arm slid around his shoulders. Forcing him to relive nightmares wouldn't bring us closer. On the contrary, it would tear us apart.

"Dad sold us, but you and Veric didn't learn about it right away," he said, light bleeding from his eyes. "We lived fine for the first hundred years."

I winced. *He lived fine?* Cain stared out the window, but our gazes locked in the reflection.

He whispered, "I was his lover, willing at first. One of many actually." A nervous chuckle left his lips, but he raked his nails over his denim-clad thighs. "The war started among the humans, and our war began. His new council crawled from the cracks of Hell." Cain gulped; his lips trembled. "You and Veric returned from England."

Korri said, "And everything had changed. Boric obsessed over the keys, demanded ours, or else. But Father didn't have it, I did. Mother had sent it to me in England before Boric collected—she thought it would be safest with me."

"Boric kept me chained, like a dog, in his room after that." He bit his lip but couldn't hide the tremble or watery eyes peering back at him from the train window.

My brows lifted wondering how my father could create such an evil creature, but the answer didn't lie in our creator. People—Elioud—were not born evil. Maybe the others weren't either. Father had created us to serve him, but the two hundred fallen angels, countless ones who had followed, had all chosen their fates. Some of them were not evil beyond their choice.

"After Boric was through with me, he tossed me into circulation, failing to tell his guards I wasn't straight. They thought I was just being difficult. At first, they forced me to service women and would beat me when I couldn't finish. Within a week, Garland's men had beaten me within inches of death. After I healed, they sent me back, but the results were the same."

I asked, "What changed?" and regretted the question. I clenched my fists.

"One of the men raped me, and the other noted my arousal, despite being forced. I didn't want it, and I sure as fuck didn't enjoy it, but my body reacted to the prostrate stimulation."

"Bastards." I coughed into my hand.

"I spent years chained for the guards' personal use. Boric still visited me during the time. I escaped a few times, too, but his guards dragged me back. You don't know how many times I prayed for death, but the healers always brought me back."

"Your family didn't know?" I narrowed my gaze at Korrigan.

Korrigan stretched her fingertips, curling and cracking the knuckles. Her back was ridged, like steel, the sway of the train un-wavering her muscles. "How do you think he escaped?" she said. "Veric and I both put our necks on the line, but—"

Cain slid his hand over mine and squeezed. "Dorian, I was too weak and defenseless to navigate the desert. I didn't make it that far, not often."

"From Angel's memories, it appears she didn't want to leave Mother or Lily behind. There weren't enough people to get them all out, and Cain was too injured and scrawny," she whispered, tears pricking her red eyes. "Boric knew someone on the inside was helping, and naturally, Angelica was his first suspicion. Boric accused her because she was free—married, not sold into the Garland family."

I nodded, squeezing Cain closer, and chewed my lip. Why didn't he tell me sooner? Parts of me had loved the men who'd turned on me. It happened among the humans all the time when they were still alive. How many women or men stayed in abusive situations out of love? Maybe beneath the surface we, too, were like humans. I brushed my lips against his temple, and Cain turned, burying his face in my neck.

"It's all right, babe."

"Your assumptions are wrong, Dorian. Yours too, Cain. While Angelica loved Veric, the marriage had been arranged. She was a prisoner, lucky enough to find an ally in her husband. He treated her fairly, as his equal, and Veric still fights for her, for me, until the end—yet despite all of this, it is simply too late for me to love him as more than a friend."

Silence settled over the car. Bitterness surrounded me, not because Korrigan or Veric failed, but because they were in the position to begin with. Why hadn't we intervened? We all knew about the slave trade, maybe not the extent of Boric's underground system, but we did know. Long before the Sundering, before Boric gained the power, we—the ABDA and Horsemen—could've squashed him like a bug.

"Angel brought the keys, shortly after Veric freed me, and told me to hide them."

I stroked his back, offering what little support I could muster.

"Two weeks later, Boric captured, tortured, and executed Angelica, while I watched, helpless to save her life. He must know I have them," he whispered. "Jules moved Lily and himself north. Veric, me, and Korrigan ran for eight years, dodging Garland's men as we ventured from beyond the Mexico border, crossing into Texas by boat, and using public transportation and foot to cover our tracks. When Korrigan turned eight, Veric had brought her to Jules in Philadelphia, knowing we couldn't run any longer. Jules must've had Lily hidden." He shook, and closed his eyes. "But Boric caught up to us."

"But you have no recollection of this?" I asked her.

"Fuzzy details. I vaguely recall Veric leaving me with Jules and telling me to be a good girl."

I shut my eyes, clutching hold of a sobbing Cain. The world had shattered that same year, and the humans disappeared, ascending or descending, to their rightful places. Two continents had survived. Father spared Canada for a reason—most of the Archangels were already living there. Sure, many had migrated north or south, but why had Philadelphia survived the destruction encircling the city? My head tilted, lashes fluttered as I eyed the Elioud vampire. Father had wanted her to survive. Her red eyes trained on me, and I nodded. Everything in life happened for a reason.

"It's hard to imagine the world before." Cain sniffled. "I wish I'd known you then."

Me too but would I have been prepared to love him?

"Did Lily know?" she asked.

Cain responded with a curt, "No."

For the majority of the trip, we kept to small talk. Eventually, Cain fell asleep, and I laid his head on my lap, stroking my fingers through his wavy hair. My thoughts wandered to what Korri had said about Petre earlier at the house, shedding a different light on the vampire I'd met only a few times through Tomas. Love, forgiveness, and revenge all held a place in this hell-forsaken world.

Slivers of color peaked on the horizon, churning the sky into fiery reds, oranges, and shades of blue. My fingers stroked Cain's jaw and I smiled at the natural beauty outside the window. Our era didn't need to become Hell on Earth. We had time to fix the wrongs, even if time had to move forward. No one but Father could change the past, and that wasn't in his grand design.

Korri's breath sucked in, announcing her appreciation of the world flying by. "Petre taught me to see the beauty in the darkest places." A grin widened over her petite features and wrinkled the edges of her eyes. "I do hope you're right."

"I'm always right." I chuckled.

Some might have asked what role Petre could have played and why he was important. Another might have argued he had money and power, but it was neither of those reasons. Petre Von

Baron had wealth all right, a wealth of knowledge. In a few years' time, he had most of Arcadia and parts of Delphia on alternative energy. His teams had developed biofuel, and rumor had it, he dabbled in airplanes. Delphia and Garland already used crude, unreliable versions, but Petre's company didn't cut corners. Many inside the ABDA aligned their opinions of Petre with Korrigan. For all his glory and accomplishments, though, he was humble.

Smoke from chimneys and factories rolled into view. Our train slowed. Cain stirred from where he'd fallen asleep in my lap, blinking his brown eyes. A five o'clock shadow fell over his handsome face and hid the dimples. In the entire world, I wanted to see no other man.

"Good morning," he muttered, stretching.

Hot breath blew over my groin, through my cargo pants, and I bit the inside of my cheek. Having an erection pinned under his head all night didn't make for a good morning at all.

Korri mumbled her morning and left us, assumedly, to fetch breakfast.

The door had barely closed before Cain pinned me to the bench seat, his lips feathering over mine. His tongue slid into my mouth and I moaned. My hands dipped into his jeans pockets and kneaded perfect cheeks. Though there would always be someone to save, when this crazy mission ended and his sister was safe and we had all the time in the world to be together, I wanted the world to know how much I loved Cain.

His kiss deepened with my trailing thoughts, and I grounded myself in his fiery flavor and fragrance. The past weeks had been nothing but Hell and lust fueled moments with sprinklings of tender love. Cain deserved better. A home, a devout lover, and no worry to crease his brow ever again. No pain or heartache, either, yet I didn't dare promise what I couldn't keep. Love, though, I promised him love and forever.

The train rumbled and hissed. As we approached Montreal Station, our alone time ended.

My hands pressed Cain against my aching cock, reminding him how much he drove me wild. If I could have stolen a few more minutes, I would have bent him over the bench. Cain drew away, and I caught the glint in his wide eyes.

"Your thoughts," his head shook and a grin spread over his lips, "sweets, think pure thoughts." He grabbed his bag and changed his clothes. Bit by bit, his beautiful chest disappeared under the cotton, and coolness crept where our skin had touched.

Within, I cursed our mission, and the world we lived in, because fewer chances would arise in the future for us to be alone. A sigh tickled my chest, and Cain cupped my cheek. I mimicked the action, running my thumb over his rough skin. At a glance, he appeared a bit older, but still not old enough to reflect the wisdom in his muddy eyes.

"If we survive this crap, babe, I want you to move in with me. For real."

Cain kissed my nose and rolled from my lap. I reached for him, and he paused, staring at our joined hands. A lump formed in my throat, and his brows scrunched, trying to follow my thoughts. I slid from the bench and rested a knee on the vibrating floor. Blush rose in his cheeks, and he glanced behind him before looking at me once more.

"Marry me."

Cain said nothing but spun toward me.

"I know I'm not perfect, and you deserve better."

He blinked.

"Neither of us knows how anything will play out in the future," I shrugged, "I love you and don't care who knows the truth. You stormed into my life, kicked the shite out of me, and little did I realize my heart had chosen you then, Cain. When you left me, I was lost, and I can't continue without you. So…marry me, please."

"Will you do the dishes?" he asked, and cracked a smile.

I nodded.

"Take out the trash?"

Again, I nodded, and he knelt to the floor, joining me. The train car swayed.

"Will you quit smoking?"

My brow rose, and I slanted my head.

"Just kidding sorta, but I'd rather have you stinky than not at all."

My lips brushed against his, and I gasped. He still astounded me with nothing but contact. "Will you?" I held my breath

His lazy grin rolled over his face. "Yeah, sweets, when all this shit is done, I'll marry you."

He barely said it before my arms crushed him against my chest.

Cain strained his words. "Does Death have a last name?"

"No, but Dorian does."

His gaze lowered to the floor.

"Why?"

The train squealed to a complete stop, and a sighing hiss released into the air.

Korri opened the compartment door and yelped. Wide eyes greeted us.

Cain turned as the blush deepened.

She said, "Sorry, I'll come back."

"No, we were… testing out the floor," I said.

Amusement sparked in her amber eyes as the heat burned my neck.

"We should grab some food to go in the central court and head on out."

Korrigan revolved on her heels and departed.

As I stood, Cain stopped me and said, "I love you."

Hearing the words caused my heart to race.

He glanced to the window, and the wrinkles sunk into his brow. "I thought I loved *him*…I'm sorry."

"Babe, there's nothing to be sorry about." My finger tilted his chin, and a smile spread over my face. "Love is strange and wonderful, and we can't always help who we love, or where it takes us. When love dies, it's like the person died too. We mourn the loss from our lives, even if he is a sadistic bastard."

An audible breath blew from his parted lips. Boric might not have been a sadist to him at first. I hated thinking it, but I was glad he did end up that way. If not, we never would've met. A life without Cain didn't seem worth living…without his charming smile or his silent strength…so many pieces of him reminded me of the little things. No more could I have pinpointed why I loved him any more than why we needed air to breathe.

"There's a spell I can cast…I won't if you don't want me to." Cain shook his head and rambled, rubbing a palm over his jeans.

"Babe? What does the spell do?" I grasped his face and forced his gaze on me.

"Oh." A sheepish smirk gave him a youthful glow, despite the wisdom of his golden eyes. "Allows you to hear my thoughts."

"Tempting," I thought, but my stomach did not agree. "Do you want me to hear your thoughts?"

He whispered, "Yes."

People exited their cars and more noise made it harder to hear. I jumped up and glided the door across its track until it closed. Muffled sounds inside and out still reached me, but this equally satisfied me; I would hear Cain easier without the distraction. His freckled nose wrinkled at the black smoke billowing past our window.

"Then, yes, I want you to cast the spell."

His palms flipped upward, and kneeling again, I caught the glistening perspiration. Why was he nervous? I cocked a brow.

"Kiss me," he said.

"Kiss you?" I blinked, grasping his arms, and lifted him from the floor.

"Yeah, you have to kiss me while I cast the spell."

I mouthed an "oh" and wound my fingers into his hair. Glowing purple hands cupped my face, and my heart rate increased. I trusted him not to harm me, but for the most part, magic wasn't something I saw on the day-to-day.

"Don't pull away until I let you, or the spell won't hold," he stroked a purple finger over my skin, "it won't hurt."

Soft lips brushed against mine, and my eyes closed. A warming sensation washed over my brain. As if a thousand fingers massaged me from the inside out, his magic caressed my skin. The sensation built within me. My cock twitched. He slid his thigh between my legs, and a groan ripped from my lips.

"Don't pull away, sweets."

I had no thoughts regarding pulling from his embrace. Instead, I had wanted to crawl deeper until we had fully connected. My body trembled, fighting the desire to grind against his thigh. From head to toe, the sensation further attacked me. Floating with my head under water. Each second passed and his voice grew clearer, thoughts and spoken words filtering in and out. How did he function with hundreds of voices at once?

"Don't fight the feeling. Go with it," he said.

Cain opened for me, massaging his tongue against mine. His breath caught, and I rocked my groin over his thigh. Surging heat boiled over and burned along my skin. My belly tightened, churning with tingling awareness.

I dropped my sweaty hand to his jeans and freed his hard cock. His tip sprung into my hand, wet with his excitement. Developing a rhythm with each thrust of my hands and hips, I stroked Cain. His breathing deepened in time with mine. I drew his tongue into my mouth and suckled. Each nerve within my body fired in a rushing volley and left me gasping.

Fighting against his body and mind, Cain's body vibrated and struggled.

"Let go, babe."

His shout died in my mouth. With the initial twitch of his cock, my cods erupted and we released together, gasping and struggling to hold on against the light blinding our eyes.

We coupled and we saw as one: no beginning and no end to our union of mind, body, and soul. I released his tongue, but didn't end our kiss. Together, we shuddered, together, we had orgasmic bliss, and in some ways, we would never break apart. I loved him more for that last fact, for Cain alone had held the power to complete me.

"You can pull away if you want."

"But I don't want to." I grasped his t-shirt and tugged him closer. How easily he made me forget the world.

Cain stumbled backward "Sweets, Angel is waiting for us."

"So, let her wait a little longer." I moved with him.

He rubbed his palm over the wet spot on my pants. "You're a mess."

"Your fault." The front of my jeans had soaked up our evidence.

A knock sounded at our door and it slid open. "Excuse me, gentlemen, but all passengers must depart the train at once," the elderly ticket master said.

Shielding his body, I tucked Cain away and re-zipped his jeans.

Our cheeks heated, and I forced my gaze straight ahead, instead of at the disarray we had made. My body sill tingled, but I doubted the cause was the after effects of his spell.

Cain winked. "I look good on you."

We departed the train in Montreal, stopped in the station restrooms to tidy ourselves, grabbed food-like substance, and caught up with Korrigan.

She waited by the main entrance fountain. Old coins and tokens lined the bottom from before the Sundering, but nobody wished anymore. Yet there she stood, staring down at her reflection in the clear ice with a coin dancing between her slender fingers. The metal clinked against the frozen surface as she dropped the money and faced us. The smirk on her face spoke a thousand words, her gaze pausing on the wet spot of my jeans.

"Wouldn't take you as the wishing type," I said, and eyed her little balled fists. "Did you eat?"

Korrigan shook her head.

Cain offered his wrist, but she glanced at the fountain. What did she wish for?

He answered, "Petre."

Cain's mind stayed quiet with a few slipped thoughts here and there about our future and Lily. I wasn't certain if this is how all minds worked, or if he was controlling it for my sake. I know only my own mind and the hundreds of thoughts that raced through my head were hard enough for me to follow. However, his didn't seem to dwell on any singular thought.

We pushed through the crowded station and hit the blistery cold outdoors. Vendors lined the street and hawked their wares. I palmed my jacket for a cigarette. Pure habit, but I hadn't worn my trench coat.

"I threw them out anyway."

Korri asked, "Threw what out?"

"My smokes," I muttered, stopping at a map vendor.

Cain fished out his wallet and paid a ridiculous sum for the paper map, but none of us knew where to head. All Korrigan recalled was they'd passed through Montreal, after a short layover to restock the train. Both distracted themselves by eyeing up various souvenirs, and I bought another pack of smokes, removing one and slipping the cigarettes into my jeans pocket.

I watched them smile and laugh at the various products, most leftover from the Sundering. Before Cain and Korri, tales of the Morning Star's kin reached my ears. They weren't like other demons, although, their father seemed to fit the bill. I lit a cigarette, and Cain's nose curled at the smoke tendrils.

"Mother was a Morning Star," he said aloud. "Most of the original families try to lead better lives than those who fell."

Korri said, "That's part of why I fell in love with Veric. He wanted a better life for all demons and their offspring. Boric didn't agree."

Chapter Fourteen

Cain

Following the train tracks, Dorian, Korrigan, and I headed into the Arcadian wilds, past the outskirts of Montreal. Leaving the half-ruined city in our wake, we hiked into the thick forests and through knee-high snow banks. Strange how the snow didn't pile any higher.

I hadn't slept in three days, or complained, but even so, I had grown grumpier with each passing night. Half-frozen, every muscle ached, and on my feet, my blisters had blisters. White-painted evergreens and dormant oaks surrounded us. Un-showered male stench and acrid cigarette smoke wasn't pleasant, either. Dorian would not give up his habit making each kiss taste like a stale ashtray.

"What's that?" I asked, pointing to what appeared to be red bricks poking through the treetops. *Finally something new.*

Dorian smacked his cigarette pack against his palm and cocked his brow. "Looks like a house."

Our feet tore through the snow toward the first sign of life.

Korrigan arrived first. "It's empty."

"We should stay the night," Dorian said.

"But we're close," Korrigan whined. "I can feel it."

The two bickered while I explored the outside. No tracks or pathways in the snow. A well, likely frozen, sat in front of the red brick farmhouse. A weathered barn rested a few hundred yards away, and the barren fields collected snow.

I peered in through the backdoor, but saw nothing. Snow crunched; Dorian paced behind me. My sister didn't weigh enough to break the thick ice on the banks.

I removed my glove and touched the chilly knob. It opened, and I sneaked inside, leaving them to their petty dispute. Unlike them, my body required food, shelter, and rest.

"Hello?" I called into the dark house. Only my soft footsteps replied. The open kitchen housed a large hearth. Dried wood was stacked near the fireplace. Pots hung from a rack. With any luck, I'd have a hot meal to warm me from the inside out. Shivering, I knelt and prepared the kindling before willing my magic forth. Sparks jumped from my fingertips, igniting the wood.

Standing, I dusted my hands, not actually feeling them. I strolled to the pots and retrieved two large ones as Dorian framed the open door, smelling of burning ash.

"Need a hand?" he asked.

I handed him one the pots. "Where'd she go?"

"Exploring the perimeter to make sure it's safe. What am I doing with this?" He held up the pot, smirking.

"Snow collection."

We boiled the snow we'd gathered into steamy hot water for broth and collected more for bathing.

Upon further snooping in the barn, I found an old-fashioned wooden tub, but little else remained. Cobwebs littered its rounded corners, and I cleared them out, along with a thick layer of dust.

Whoever had lived there were likely human. They'd left belongings and valuables behind, but the elements had taken their toll on the structures and the unattended animals. Bones of horses and livestock rested in the deserted stalls. I sighed and whispered a silent prayer, though their souls were free. Slave life hadn't been much different. Caged and starved, few survived it.

Smoke burned my nose. Dorian eyed me from the barn door, resting against its weathered frame, smoking another cigarette.

"I'll quit when this shit is over, and you are safe." He puffed and exhaled.

It hadn't dawned on me before that his concerns were for me alone.

"I do care for the others, don't get me wrong, babe. But—you come first." He tossed his cigarette on the ground and snuffed it out with his boot. "I'm going to explore inside. Don't stay out too long."

I shrugged and bent back to my work. Time passed, but I wasn't sure how much. I scrubbed and scrubbed, the motion warming my muscles and causing me to sweat.

Footsteps shuffled along the dried hay and dirt floor. A glance spared over my shoulder revealed Dorian had changed into a button-down flannel and baggy jeans, almost fitting the part of a farmer. Grinning, I closed my eyes and imagined him walking behind a plow. A sexy farmer whose eyes alone exhilarated my heart rate into unchartered tempos, but a farmer nonetheless.

Palming his chest, Dorian's thoughts flittered to the keys, but he'd still refused an explanation of their purpose. The nagging question rested on my tongue. Why eight keys, and why was Boric willing to torture and kill for them?

He didn't answer, and I didn't ask aloud. I stared at the tub and tossed a rag onto the dirt floor with a long sigh. The tub was as clean as it would be.

"Let me get that," he offered.

Together we lugged the tub inside. More so him than me. It was too heavy for my half-breed self to carry alone. Pot by pot, we filled the sucker, stripped down, and slid beneath the water's surface.

"Found a dried bar of soap by the kitchen sink," he said, and handed me a tiny sliver, keeping one for himself.

I worked the bar into a lather and motioned for him to stand. "You've been quiet, more so than usual, sweets."

He grasped the side of the tub and stood.

My soapy hands slid over his thighs, but Dorian didn't answer in words. He didn't think I wanted to hear his reply. I rose, working the suds over his body.

"Yeah, I do." I grasped his arm and squeezed the thick bicep, staring deep into emerald eyes, but the words didn't roll from his tongue. "No secrets," I reminded.

"Lift your arms," he said, rubbing the soap over my chest, back, and arms. "I have no secrets."

I snorted and crossed my arms. "How do you have a key?" I pointed to Dorian's chest where the two keys rested against his skin. "There are seven keys, yet you have an eighth."

He sank into the tub, dunking his head beneath the dirty water. "All anyone ever cares about is my key. The others are meaning-less without mine. Even my own blood refuses to listen and now Cain. Everyone thinks the keys unlock some great evil or give the owner power. Is this all Cain wants? Have I read him all wrong?"

I jumped from the tub, water splashing and sloshing to the floor and soap bubbles sliding along my body. I braced my arms on the mantle over the hearth. It wasn't about the damned keys. Every secret I had, except one, I'd uncovered and shared with Dorian, thinking we could make this work.

Crud-covered photographs and knick-knacks lined the ledge in a neat row. Humanity had its perks, I grunted; at least they were all dead. Lifting a frame, I studied the photograph of a smiling, happy couple and their children. Their eyes reflected all I'd ever wanted as a child: love, joy, and acceptance. I glanced to Dorian. He eyed me from the tub's edge, rolling his gaze along my exposed bits. His actions sickened me, and my hand rubbed over my stomach. My other hand shook, and I placed the picture frame back on the mantle. "You can shove the keys up your ass for all I care."

My dirty clothes were soaked. I bounded upstairs and retrieved clothing from the closets. Musty from years of storage, but they were free of moth holes. A few days of perspiring and they would reek of man sweat anyhow. I pulled on the jeans, Henley-style T-shirt, and a flannel.

I stood before the mirror, and it reflected an image I didn't recognize. A few days growth covered my winter-pale skin, and

I rubbed the scruff, wishing the lighter colored facial hair away. Hell, I would've wish my life away, but death wasn't the answer, either. I loved Dorian, though. My eyes closed and a tear fell free, before they blinked open.

He stood, leaning against the doorway. Water pooled at his feet, and lazy drops dripped from his nude body. Wet hair framed his face, and thick pink lips parted.

Or was death the answer? Maybe God had made a mistake when I'd prayed. My hand itched to caress the fuller beard growing over Dorian's angelic face. He stepped over the threshold and slammed the door. Windows rattled, and my throat dried. I inched backward, the hardwood floor protesting beneath my feet. A wall blocked my progress, and his hands thudded on either side of my head, pinning me in place.

"I told you not to run."

My brows rose, and I shook my head. What was he talking about? "I got dressed. How is that running?"

Dorian's fingers caressed my cheek and trailed own my neck. Gooseflesh erupted in shivers from his touch. Each button of my flannel popped free.

"Now, you're getting undressed."

"Distract me, huh? Can't face the truth?" As I'd done so many times before.

My clothes fell and piled onto the floor, and Dorian kicked them away. He grasped my hands and restrained them overhead.

"Don't do this." My heart hammered hard enough its beat echoed in my ears. Wincing, I turned my head away and closed my eyes. Please God, I silently prayed, no.

He leaned in close to my ear as green eyes blazed to life. Face-hardened, he groaned. "Cerberus guards the Golem, and the keys control the creature. My key unlocks his prison. The keys won't unleash Lucifer."

"I don't understand." What harm or power could a Golem have?

"I have lied to my family, and anyone who has ever asked, including past lovers, but I will not lie to you, Cain." He evaded the question. "Nor will I ever hurt you." He shifted my wrists into one hand.

My forearms ached from flexing and shoving against him. Try as I might, he was too strong. "You accused me of only being with you for the keys." I stared at the ugly floral wallpaper. No action or word could erase his thoughts of me in the tub. "I might lie, I might use my body as a distraction, but I don't use people, Dorian. That's why I wanted you off the fucking case."

"It's your continuous lies that put the doubt in my head in the first place." He slammed his open palm against the wall. "The sex, the stalling, all of it…Damn it. Make me understand." Dorian released me and stepped backward, hovering by the double-sized bed.

"Sweets." I rubbed my wrists and shivered in the icy room. "Knowing what you know now, can you blame me for trying to protect myself from you? You, who swore off loving another, who lived only for his own pleasure? Your mind, which practically shouts, reminded me daily of how you could never love me. So yeah, I fucking lied to you, but it didn't seem to matter." And it wouldn't. Even if he managed to love me, I was still stuck with the nightmares of my past. At first, I had wondered if I would always be enough for him, but would he always be enough for me to forget? "You can't blame me for protecting my heart."

"I was protecting the planet until you showed up." With that, he turned before storming from the bedroom. Thoughts ran through his mind: *I am right, but so is he. What is more important? The world or Cain?*

"The world." I sighed and glanced between the empty doorway and the bed. After three days on the road from Montreal, the dusty covers invited me more than continuing an argument. "Just once, I want to be someone's world."

Light peeked through the window the following morning, and I squinted at the brightness. A good night's sleep was what I'd needed, and I stretched, releasing a long yawn. Dorian stood before the window, holding the curtain aside, and stared out at the farm.

"Morning," I said, cracking my neck. My muscles protested the movement, and cold seeped into my already stiff joints.

"Korrigan says we're close. She found the wreckage last night." He spun around. "I told her you needed another day to recuperate, but she insists we leave as soon as you're up," his gaze trailed down my waist, "sure look up to me."

"My sore muscles have sore muscles," I half-joked, not playing into his innuendo. After last night, I wasn't sure what to believe or expect.

"Flip," he said, rubbing his hands together, but I didn't move. "What you've never had someone massage you before?"

My tone bordered on cautious. "Nope."

"Really?" Dorian grabbed lotion from the bedside table and opened the container. "It's a bit separated and cold, but it'll do." He bit his lip and shook the bottle. "Waiting on you, babe."

Had he forgotten about last night? Was this his way of apologizing? I slowly turned onto my belly, not wanting to leave the warm cocoon of blankets, but intrigued by his version of a massage. My muscles did ache, after all. Icy air kissed my skin. "Holy shit, put that back on."

Warmth replaced the chill. Dorian melded against my backside. He whispered, "Babe, how am I supposed to massage you with a blanket covering you up? It's bad enough that you're wearing clothes."

I could've casted a spell, but it seemed like a waste of precious resources. "Screw the massage. Need heat..." My ass wiggled against his hard cock poking my cheeks.

"Naked? Horny?"

I chuckled into the pillow. He was always horny.

"Well, horny's easy, babe. I only have to think of you." He kissed the back of my head.

Our conversation twisted into an interesting turn. "You mean you think of me naked?"

"Nope. Just the idea of you."

Dorian's hot breath sent shivers across my skin.

"Your eyes, smile, or that cute little laugh are enough to drive me crazy. I can't imagine a day without seeing or hearing you, don't want to spend another night apart."

I twisted around, dislodging him from my back. "We had that week apart."

Dorian leaned on one arm. "Let's not talk about that." His gaze flickered to my face, and he reached for me. "Ever."

"I tried to jump off a ferry on my way to Meat Cove," I whispered. "Figured if Death didn't want me, then who else would."

His mouth opened and closed. Did he know his sister was up there? Dorian nodded at the thoughts I'd allowed to slip through.

"I didn't leave my bed," he said, and buried his face in the pillow.

I slid across the small mattress and kissed his shoulder, trailing a path to his red-tipped ears. "We work better together than apart."

He grunted but still hid his face. *"And that's what scares the shite out of me."*

"I'm not without protection, Dorian. Your sister gave me a gift—"

"Cain? Dorian?" Korrigan called from downstairs. "You're burning daylight. Let's go lover boys." She paused, but her feet thudded on the stairs. She must've done it on purpose. "Don't make me stand here, or come in there."

I groaned and Dorian echoed me. We jumped from the bed and redressed, borrowing warmer clothes suited for the area from the closet. Unlike Korrigan and him, the elements would harm me if I weren't careful.

A hanger rattled in the closet before falling and clattering against the floor. He withdrew a navy down coat and held it up to me. "This should fit over your wool one."

"Sweets, I'm not sure I'll be able to walk with all this bulk." Hell, I'd look more like a dark blue marshmallow man.

He folded his arms, brows touching. "What's a marshmallow man?"

"How did you live for centuries and not see Ghostbusters?" But Dorian's brows only rose higher. "Never mind. It'll make me look fat, and I won't be able to walk right."

"Humor me. I'd rather have you fat and slow than blue with frostbite."

I rolled my eyes and put the heavy coat on over my peacoat, but as I strutted around trying to prove my point, I found moving in the bulky layers easier than expected.

By the time we finished upstairs, Korrigan wasn't downstairs. Quite reminiscent of an impatient Angelica. We searched for gloves, hats, and scarves. Dorian didn't need any of them, but he insisted I wear them.

I kept thinking about the house and barn. The abandoned house was a shame. All it had required was a little care and some new paint. The barn needed more attention, but an empty farm was a total waste. With some hard work, it could be transformed into something more, something to give back to the world.

"I'll see who owns it," Dorian said, wrapping a scarf around my neck. He leaned in and kissed my cheek before whispering, "Consider it an engagement present."

"My home is Halifax." I shrugged and rolled my gaze over the hand-carved staircase. "The waste of good land is a shame." Besides, I liked his home, and the location was convenient for work.

"Don't know what you do," he said, sliding into a chair at the kitchen table. Dorian shook his head, as if trying to clear his ear of water. "Will I get used to hearing your voice in my head?"

"Maybe. After a while it becomes white noise." My hands gripped one of the dining room chairs. "I tend the farms. Grunt work." I opened my mouth to say more on the subject but found nothing else to add. The farm paid the bills, but it wasn't what I'd dreamed of doing with my life. "Before the Apocalypse, what'd you do for a living?"

Korrigan yelled, "No more dallying." She didn't come inside, though.

"Don't get your knickers in a bunch," Dorian said. "We'll catch up, go ahead without us."

He strolled out the backdoor, and I followed, but he only swooped down and grabbed a handful of snow before almost running into me.

"We're not leaving yet."

Inside again, he knelt and dropped the snow into a pot by the hearth. The coals hadn't gone out yet. "I moved around a lot, throughout the dawn of man, my job and much of my life required it. That meant no home, not unless I count Sheol, no friends, or much of anything. All I had was my purpose, marking souls, and my family."

All I had owned was inside my little apartment and all of that I'd received after the Sundering. "Can I ask you another question?"

He nodded and motioned for me to continue.

"You can't wipe the demons out can you? I mean, I know you're powerful and have the key, but I keep asking myself why y'all haven't intervened. Is it because we aren't worth it?"

He twisted around. "No. You are more than worth it, Cain. It sickens me to think you've even considered it."

"Markos doesn't think much of my kind." I removed a few layers of clothing and hung them on the back of the dining room chair.

"Your kind?"

"Demons. I wonder if he feels that way about all them."

"You're not a demon in my eyes, but an Angel." Dorian walked to the sink and poured steaming water into a washbowl. He dipped his hands and shook his head. The water splashed. "I can fight them, kill them, and send their souls to purgatory, but it's not as simple as my brother makes it. Demons are not human—never were. They require different methods to execute. Methods that work on a small scale, but nothing large, and weapons that I don't have access to." He held the bowl above his head. Slowly, he tilted the container.

As he poured it over his head, I cringed. Steam engulfed him. "Dorian, what the hell are you doing?"

"Washing my hair." He spun around, eyes blazing and skin beet red.

I grabbed a towel, flicked my wrist to release the dust, and wiped his face. "Don't do that again without warning me."

"There's someone who can." He stepped closer, dripping water over the grimy floor.

My brow rose and I dabbed his face. "Someone who can warn me?"

"No," he splattered me with water, "Father created one to hold the power, or so it's been prophesized." Dorian snatched the towel from me and grinned. "It's cute that you care."

Whispers and rumors always circulated among the brothels about a chosen one, but nobody found any proof to back the claims. I chewed my lip and glanced to the door. All this time his thoughts had held crumbs and hid true intentions. We needed Petre not for his brains or money. The world needed a true king. I whispered, "You think he's the King of Babylon," and fell into a chair. My chin sank to my hands, and I thought of all I knew about the strange, cursed vampire. Did Korrigan think the same about Petre? Her loyalty was nothing more than a ruse.

Dorian ran a hand through his wet hair and sat next to me at the quaint table. He grasped my hands and shook me out of my thoughts. "Do you love me? Do you trust me?"

"Yes." My eyes burned beneath his intense glare. "I'm not the enemy, never was, and if you love me like you claim to, then you have to trust me too, Dorian."

He sighed and kissed the top of my head. "It's not the king." He laughed to himself. "The Bible scholars tended to get the facts wrong. We need the queen to gather her people and free the slaves."

My mouth gaped, and he tickled my chin. *No.* Dorian nodded. "Angel?"

He shook his head no.

"Not Lily."

"Korri, babe. That little pixie will save what's left of the world. Hallo says..."

A tear slid down my cheek and into my hands. I buried my face. Holding onto Korrigan as if she were still Angelica made me foolish. That made Veric a fool also, but she was *my* sister. She acted like her, though. Coughing, I turned away from him and wiped my face. "We should get going."

"I know you wanted to save your sister, but Angel is gone." Dorian stretched his hand across the table and patted my arm. "Hey." Dorian grabbed my hand and tugged me, almost yanking my body across the table. "I would bring her back if I could, but her soul isn't in Sheol. Maybe it's buried in there."

My chair skidded against the floor. Standing, I stared at him over my shoulder. My brows scrunched, digesting his words. Bring a soul back from purgatory? His phone rang before I'd the chance to ask for an explanation.

He released me and fished his SAT phone from his flannel pocket. "Fox speaking," he covered the receiver, "give me a second." He pecked my cheek. "No, not you, James. Yeah, go on...What? Bloody fucking piece of leeching shite."

The ABDA, from the sounds of it, cursed him out on the other line. Not being one to eavesdrop, I slipped back into my layers before venturing outside and allowing him privacy.

Crisp air shocked my lungs, but the scenery stole my breath. Beams reflected off the snow and ice crystals creating a rainbow prism of dancing colors. Icicles hung from the barren trees, and I reached on my tiptoes to touch a delicate formation. As a kid, I hadn't witnessed such beauty in the world. We had lived in Texas and Central America for over three hundred years, but the Westcott bloodline spread across the globe, dating back to Lucifer's fall.

The Garlands had originated in England, though, and neither brother had lost their accent. Seven families all descended from one of the Princes of Hell. I laughed. Garland had supposedly changed their name to fit in, as did the rest of us, but from what I didn't know, let alone care.

My boots crunched through the snow, leaving a trail behind me. I halted beneath a large maple tree. I liked Dorian's accent, even though his British words slipped out from time to time. I spent the last twelve years trying to lose my southern one. Granted, I tried fitting in and blended with those who lived in Arcadia. But running from my past didn't work.

"Her." I leaned my back against the ice-encrusted tree, my mouth dropping.

Man had translated some Bible passages wrong. Mistakes happened all the time. Who could've said if they'd done so on purpose? So the King of Babylon was a woman. I rubbed my chin and slowly smiled.

Demons had walked the Earth, but the churches also left out missing books of the Bible, simply because they weren't canon. The Book of Enoch had been one of those, but even I understood why the Catholic Church had ignored the texts. Hard to explain to the world God had allowed us to live, and his mighty flood had failed to eradicate us from the Earth. Our ancestors had fled into the depths of Hell and escaped his wrath. After Noah and his family repopulated the world, they, too, had returned and bred new Nephilim. Eventually, the Elioud blinked into existence. But it also claimed Revelation had already occurred, and even I admitted the author was wrong about it. We'd lived it, survived it, and we would continue to do so.

Korrigan's face popped into my mind. "She assassinated an Arch demon and a Nephilim," I whispered. Jules had been a Nephilim, but what I hadn't corrected was that Jules wasn't Veric's father. No. He was Boric's son. Veric wasn't Veric, either. Loyalty to him kept me from revealing his secret.

Snow crunched in the distance, growing closer. I tilted my head. Dorian stumbled through the snow.

"Ready to find our queen?" Dorian kissed me and folded his hand in mine.

"Who called?"

"Veric tattled. I may be Death, but I still work for that blimey bastard." He glanced over his shoulder. "They arrived at the Summit, and the ABDA agreed to back a rescue mission. They've already spoken, thanks to Tomas, with Delphia officials and are amassing a treaty as we speak. Still need the council's approval, though they're basically the same as the ABDA." He pointed to tiny divots in the snow. "She left us a trail. We can follow these."

I didn't know what the Summit was and didn't ask. We trailed the pint-sized footprints, trudging our own path through the snowy banks.

"Have you heard the story of the Golem?" Dorian asked after a period of silence.

I shook my head, but pictured the stone creature from old games I had watched the masters play prior to the Sundering. They let us have a turn sometimes—depended how good and obedient we were. "Mindless creatures made of earthen stone and a man often controlled them. Some games created them from metal, or a mixture of metal and stone," I relayed my experiences.

"Close enough. The legend says man created the Golem, and God locked the creature away. He thought the creature proved to be a bigger threat than your ancestor, or any other manmade creation, including nuclear weapons." Dorian stumbled into knee-deep snow, and I fell on top of him, laughing. No laughter left his lips. "I lost my boot."

"Calacha," I whispered, and his missing boot flew into my hand.

Wide, green eyes stared.

"Sorry."

Dorian cupped my cheek. "Don't be. It's who you are. If you can accept me, I can accept you."

A timid smile forced itself over my lips, and I swallowed hard. Busying myself, I brushed the snow from his sock and fixed his boot.

Dorian tipped my chin and stroked his thumb over the furry growth. "You know I mean that, right? Don't fight who you are."

Without answering him, I arose from the ground and dusted the snow from my clothing.

He warned, "Cain."

But I ignored him and withdrew the map from inside my coat pocket, checking our location against Angel's footprints. Dorian held a bag of trail mix out and shook it in my face. As tempting as it was, I had a feeling he'd found it in the farmhouse. He shook it in my face.

I snapped, "Do you mind?"

"Yeah, I do. What the hell is your problem?" His hands fell to his hips.

I mumbled, "Don't expect you to understand." My gaze rolled over the landscape. We had reached the end of the property where the fields ended.

"Try me," Dorian said.

I sighed and glanced at the map. "Not having this conversation." I used my end of discussion tone and veered back on course, careful to follow the footprints into the woods.

He didn't trail me at first, but after a few minutes passed, his steps crunched behind mine. The argument was stupid. My father was a warlock, not the first of our long line to be both Elioud and magical. Men preferred the oath breaker term of warlock over witch, and I never understood why. My breath hissed through my teeth, puffing into the air. I hated using the power, even though God himself had created us. Friends and family fell into greed and sloth like existences. I refused to be like them.

The forest spun around me, Dorian knocked the air from my lungs, and I plummeted into the icy snow.

"Damn it, Cain, stop ignoring me."

A barking cough rose from my lungs, and I fought for precious breath. *"Asshole."*

"Takes one to know one."

I snorted and attempted to rise, but Dorian had my legs and arms pinned.

"Not letting you up until you talk to me like an adult."

The ice nipped at my skin, and a shiver rolled into my bones. He shifted, keeping me trapped. His hard outline pressed into my ass, and his warm lips grazed my neck. A lump formed in my throat.

"Now, what's the problem, babe?"

After all his profound love, Dorian could not accept me for whom and what I was. No, that was a lie. I couldn't accept myself. The reason we became enslaved, captured, and sold. Hell, even Mother had arranged Angelica's marriage. But my sister had loved

Veric, regardless of the contractual marriage. For three hundred years, my family suffered at the hands of the Garlands because of my power to see, steal, and hold the keys.

I coughed again, squirming beneath Dorian. Long before Boric, hatred had run through my veins. Pride kept me from showing it. Satan's ilk, Hallowed was right. Did that make me as bad as the fallen angels? Maybe in their eyes, but the Garland family wanted to rule us all. How could I accept the part of me that brought this pain? Without it, Garland never would have targeted us to begin with and…a sob ripped through my chest. I hated magic—all of it. How could Dorian accept that vile part of me?

"You think you're cursed because Lucifer is your ancestor?" Amusement touched his tone. "There's not an evil bone in your body, Cain. God created me to mark evil, and you know what, babe? I would never mark your soul, not even if it meant we could spend eternity together. Hell, if it weren't for knowing we need the Queen of Babylon, I'd have pegged you as the king." Thick hands kneaded into the tight muscles spanning my back. "Forgive yourself and let the anger go."

I thrusted my shoulder backward, attempting to throw him off. "I'm not angry, more disappointed." In myself, but I was sure he caught my self-pity broody bit.

"Should I carry the scythe more often and kick some demon ass?" Dorian laughed, and the sound vibrated against my skin.

"I forgot you're the Angel of Death."

He laughed again, missing my sarcasm, and rolled from my back.

"Glad to amuse you," I muttered, and rocked to my knees.

"Oh ye of little faith." Dorian yanked my arm, and I crashed into his chest as his arms squeezed the air from my lungs. His warm but rough hands combed through my hair. As my head lay there, listening to Dorian's pounding heart, a peace rested in our stillness. I clung to his flannel shirt, as if he would blink out of existence.

"You lit the fire under my ass I needed to right the world and fix the ABDA." Dorian tilted my chin and forced my gaze. "But

that's the excuse. The truth?" His brows rose. "I'm doing this because I love you and will do whatever it takes to make you happy.
Finding Lily will make you happy, right?"

A lump reformed in my throat, and I swallowed hard. "We
should find Korrigan."

"I mean it, Cain."

Maybe I lacked faith that we'd ever find Lily, or take down
Boric, but it wasn't a lack of faith in him. Among us all, the weak
link was me.

Snow buried the ruins of the train wreck, but we navigated
with keener senses. An empty grave greeted us, but no sign of
Petre remained there, except for bloodied snow.

"This must be where she buried him." Dorian pointed to
the ground.

"Thanks, Captain Obvious."

Dorian's brow crinkled.

I sighed. "Never mind."

We spent the next few hours searching for fresh tracks, but
found none. No signs of a struggle, or even crimson-tinged snow,
littered the snowy landscape indicating a recent fight. Dorian
and I shared a confused glance, but weeks had passed since his
death. Layers of snow could have covered old evidence, and heavy
winds could've explained why Korrigan's footprints disappeared.
My gaze lifted to the trees. Or she'd looked to higher roads. Yet
the trees and their boney branches appeared undisturbed from
their eternal winter.

"Did you ever consider joining the ABDA?" he asked, sifting
the top layer of snow away with his boot. "You have an impeccable
eye and fast logic, babe."

Petre could've awoken minutes or days after my sister and
cousin had departed the area. Either way with the sun setting
and the nearest town hours away, we would have to rough it for
the night and renew our efforts come morning.

"Your thoughts right there. Perfect example," he said, brushing the snow from his hands. "See you still think, like an Elioud, whereas I wouldn't have considered the time."

"Please tell me that you've considered the evidence clearly pointing toward a vampire in the vicinity?" I kicked an empty blood bag. Too many could be's were piling up, though.

Dorian stuck out his tongue. "Actually, I think Petre is the vampire." He tossed an armful of snow at my feet. "When this shit is done, if you want, you should at least consider it."

"What am I considering again? Becoming a vampire?" I scoffed at the idea.

"Becoming a detective," he replied, squinting. "I'm already short-staffed in Halifax. Think about it, babe, okay?"

"Okay," I said, and started hefting armfuls of snow.

"Nope, let me do that." He knocked the snow from my hands and proceeded to bend down and wiggle his ass at me. "I know. I'm hopeless." He unearthed a door a few minutes later and flung it in my direction. "Sit on that and look pretty."

"Pretty?" I placed my hands on my hips and cocked a brow.

"Oh please, you're bloody gorgeous. Don't you know that?"

At his compliment, my face burned, despite the chilly wind cutting through me.

He pressed his lips into a slight smile, but it faded quickly. "You really don't know, do you?"

I rubbed my arms. A time ago, I would have believed him, but not after the scars.

Dorian shucked his flannel off and tossed it at me. He added, "Put that below your sexy arse."

Obeying, I balled up the shirt and sat on it. His thoughts scattered, leaping back and forth between Korrigan and Petre and taking down Boric. Fast at work, Dorian discovered more wreckage, so at least we didn't have to sleep in the open wilderness.

"What do you think caused all this?" he asked, pointing to the crushed bits of metal and strewn luggage.

"Explosion of some sort."

"Most people wouldn't jump to that conclusion." He scratched his head. "The official report said it was a derailment. Why do you say otherwise?"

With a groan, my stiff muscles unraveled, and I leapt to my feet. Joining him, I pointed to the metal. "This is melted, and the train cars are iron. The heat required to do this kind of damage means this was the impact, or point of explosion."

Dorian grabbed my face and pressed his lips to mine. "Fuck me. Smart and sexy." His hands dropped to my waist before sliding below the layers of clothing. "You know I want to toss you in there and bend you over, right?"

Black birds flew into the air behind us, and I watched their ascent. "I'll stop distracting you, then." Snow glittered along the path toward the ledge. My gaze stuck to the horizon, spanning over the cliff. Ocean waves crashed where New York had once stood.

Painting the sky a vibrant hue of purple and fiery reds, the sun descended on another day. I sighed at the dismal beauty and glanced back to Dorian, building a fire near our hollowed out shelter. Green eyes blinked beneath his mink lashes, and my hand rubbed my heart. A long road awaited us. An even longer, windier road unfolded before me.

"Hey babe, I'm just about finished."

I heard him, but stared out into the watery ripples, waiting for my purpose to leap from the waves with a flashing sign. How did I let go of the past? Was it as simple as looking to the future? Dorian's boots crunched behind me. His arms slid and squeezed me from behind, and his chin rested on my shoulder.

"Puts everything into perspective doesn't it?" He pointed toward the crashing whitecaps. "How something so beautiful can destroy. Letting go isn't about forgiveness, not by itself, Cain. It's about accepting that we're not responsible for another person's deeds—good or bad."

"You're wiser than anyone gives you credit for." I leaned my head against him. "I've blamed myself for a long time, but Boric and the masters did those things to me, not because I deserved them. They were...are sick."

"They'll still rot for what they did." Dorian stepped toward the makeshift shelter, but I stayed. "I promise you, Cain, and I don't make promises I can't keep. They'll pay." Dorian turned around and scooped me up. "Please let me be the knight in shining armor you deserve. I'm not perfect, and I don't shine, but let me avenge you."

"You've already saved me more than you know." I fastened my arms around his neck. "You've restored my faith too."

He ducked us into the fireside shelter, laid us down, and buried makeshift blankets he'd found in luggage around us. Elioud felt the biting chill; I felt warmth where Mother Nature had assaulted me with her wintery temper. Neither of us spoke. Words seemed more and more meaningless once I had allowed his love and he mine.

Trains chugged along the tracks every few hours, releasing their hissy steam in the distance, but those were the only signs of life. The long trek had worn even his bones; although, Dorian hadn't verbally complained. I saw his winces and the relief following each stretch or popping bone in the firelight. We found sleep quickly in each other's arms and awoke to cracking tree branches.

I shot from my sleepy eyed reverie and bounded toward the noises, but halted a few steps from the crude campsite. Already awake, Dorian dragged himself from the fire, craning his neck toward the sounds. The echo…I hung my head and shook.

"Babe," he started, but there were no words.

"Why aren't you investigating?"

"For one, you needed rest. Two, I wasn't about to leave you here alone. Three, I have no fucking idea where the noises are coming from because of the echo." Dorian melted snow over the embers. The steam rose as the water boiled. Two canteens sat near the fire. "Plus, you have to drink."

But I'd survived on air and sand.

He added, "Found these. They'll sustain you better than hot water."

Dated pre-collapse, two MREs rested in his large palms. Dorian prepared them both and forced me to eat the strange roasted chicken. Certain the food would rear its head later; I buried some when he turned his head. Long gone were the days of Mother's home cooked meals that stuck to the ribs. I closed my eyes and breathed in the salty air.

"We'll find her, and now, I don't have to worry about you toppling over from exhaustion or starvation."

His chapped lips brushed my temple, and I turned into his embrace. Who would have thought seven months ago my life would have altered forever. Dorian interrupted my trudging existence, and faster than a gunshot, I fell not from grace, but toward the beauty of God's creations. Laughter shook me. God gifted me the one notion I understood: death.

"I love that sound," Dorian whispered into my hair. "The world's gone to shite, but your laughter wipes the ache away."

My chin lifted from his chest. My thumb skimmed his dry lips, hidden beneath the bushy whiskers. "You'd make Al jealous."

Dorian's barked laughter shook the trees. "Who is Al?"

I shook my head. "From Home Improvement? Al Borland?"

Dorian blinked emerald eyes and smirked.

"You need to get out more, sweets. C'mon."

Before the Sundering, most demons had lived normal lives. Those of us beneath the masters had to earn the freedoms. For the free, my kind had blended into society and few humans suspected their neighbors, friends, and lovers were anything but ordinary humans. Magic helped when we didn't age past thirty, or for some demons, there was possession. Those demons weren't Elioud, though, but from Hell itself.

I insisted on helping with camp clean up, and Dorian grumbled.

"Getting alpha on me?"

He snorted and tossed a cushion at my head.

"Should I pack it into the car, in case we're here another night." I motioned toward the half of a train car we'd used for shelter.

The back of his glossy head nodded, and a chopping sound echoed off the trees again. He froze, cocking his head. Birds flung themselves into the air, and I eyed their ascension.

We dropped everything and in unison, we called, "Korrigan?" My heart pounded and my legs lunged toward where the birds had flown.

Dorian yelled, "Over here."

And I followed the sound of his thick, resounding voice off the ledge of a small cliff and landed near another pile of charred wreckage. The snow there also bled deep crimson and tapered into splatters of light pink. On closer inspection, more of the empty, plastic blood-tinged bags scattered the broken surface.

"Bagged blood," he said, stating the obvious. "All Petre's trains carry it for vampires."

I scratched my chin. But had Petre caused the bloody scene or had Angel? Dorian pointed at the ground. All I saw before me was disaster, but he saw a crime scene.

"Fresh footsteps over here, but they're tiny. I think they're Korrigan's, but…"

Cracking returned. Birds, in a new location, fled toward the skies. I grasped his hand, tugging him in the direction of the racket, and followed the trail. My legs protested climbing the hill. I found a second set of footprints and pointed to them. Dorian's hand dropped to his gun. We dove into the tree line, insane laughter replacing the crackling of wood.

Male laughter, deep and throaty, reached our ears, and my brow arched.

"What the hell?"

Shoulder length hair blew in the slight breeze, and the ebony locks glistened in the morning sun.

I whispered, "Is that Petre?" Not much taller than a kid and waif-like. His quick and jagged movements were a blur to my squinting eyes. Pale skin appeared sallow and sunken in around his cold, gray eyes, creating a stark contrast between the man I'd never met and the one I'd pictured in my mind.

Dorian said, "Yeah."

Petre stood near a makeshift cabin; well, the ruins of one. Half of the structure remained intact, but soot and snow covered it. He wore denim jeans and a formfitting t-shirt. No demon could've withstood these elements without protection, except a vampire or Archangel. Understanding their connection to

Dorian made me realize why God created such a powerful race to assist him.

"That's the gist of it," he replied to my thoughts.

Approaching the estranged vampire, our steps slowed, each crunch overpowering my breathless lungs and hammering heart. Tools clattered against one another, and Petre spun around. A blink of the eye and he bowed before us, crossing the distance before my brain could've processed the information. I scrambled backward, but Dorian clenched my hand tighter and inched in front of me. What had he sensed?

Petre knelt at his feet. "Death, you have come for me at last." His thick accent and slow words blended into a rich and formal tone.

Brow raised, I slid from behind Dorian's wide shoulders. We were roughly the same height and build, and I doubted the action had fooled Petre into forgetting there were two of us. His uncanny alpha behavior tickled my heart, but I held my own power.

Dorian glanced to me and shook his head, before he asked, "Petre Von Baron, where is Angelica?"

"I know no one by that name." His slender chin lifted into the air and revealed a strange, faint scar below his right cheekbone shaped almost like part of a horseshoe.

"Korrigan?" I offered. "Angel? Korri?"

Petre shook his head.

"A woman, no larger," I held my hand to Dorian's waist, "than a child passed this way. Long, brown hair? Big amber eyes?"

He chewed his lip, glanced away, and then shook his head again.

"She's a vampire and has peculiar eyes like mine." Skin tingled and warmed, and I dropped my façade.

"The devil's eyes?" As he enunciated the word devil, his gaze sparked.

My breath blew out in a steady stream. *This is leading us nowhere.* Petre Von Baron stood before us, but he should have recalled the one who sired him, let alone the woman he loved.

A strange grin lit his angular face. "I tied the witch to a tree and am cutting the driest lumber, but there isn't much with all the snow."

I snapped, "For what?" I tensed my jaw

Dorian's hand draped my shoulder and shoved me back again. "Petre," he said. "Who am I?"

Korrigan's strangled cries reached our ears, and Petre glanced over his shoulder. At least we had her location, although she was still hidden from our view.

"You are Death, God's Angel of Vengeance."

Wrong. I snorted.

"Have we met before?" Dorian shielded his eyes from the rays of morning light poking through the barren landscape.

Petre chewed his lip. Luminosity reflected from his extended fangs. "No."

I nudged Dorian. Something wasn't right, and a sinking, falling, sensation nagged at my gut. Dorian's fingers grasped and squeezed my hand. *"Let me try,"* I said to him, before turning my attention to Petre. "Tell me, what year is it?"

"1845."

"Fucking-A." I palmed my face. No wonder he hadn't a clue who any of us were.

Dorian added, "And what country are you in?"

"My beloved Romania," Petre said with a wide toothy grin, extending his hand and swinging his axe.

Either he played us, or the change backfired. Neither thought eased the ache growing in my stomach. I covered my lips and muttered, "Then, why are we speaking English?"

Dorian coughed and turned wide but amused eyes on me. My brows rose, and I bit my smile.

I asked Petre, "Do you recall Tomas?"

"No, the name is not familiar."

Out of ideas, my shoulders shrugged, and my brain attempted to process the strange event. Something had gone wrong, evident by the peculiar behavior of a man who'd lived for well over three hundred and fifty years as a cursed vampire. His brother's mind wasn't altered, either, although he acted strange too. I chewed my lip. Then again, his curse was to live as a horse, and he was living as a human in an apocalyptic world.

"Let me help," I offered my hand, "take me to her."

Petre jumped back and screamed, "Do not touch me, witch." The axe sliced through the air.

I knocked his weapon to the ground.

"You run with the devil's brood, Death. Kill him." Petre lunged for me.

My hands sparked purple fire.

Dorian slid between us, placing a palm to each of our chests to push us apart, before waving his hands in the air. Emerald eyes pled with me to stop. Dorian thought, "Put out the damned fire, babe. I got this. Keep your mouth shut."

I knelt to the ground, maintaining eye contact with Petre. He wouldn't take the upper hand from me. I dipped my hands into the snow and extinguished the fireballs.

Dorian reached down, grasped the axe, and flung it into the trunk of a tree. A smirk played at those kissable lips as he brushed his hands. "Show me your witch, and leave Cain be." Dorian placed his hand on Petre's shoulder. "Witch or not, he's mine. Understand?"

Petre didn't flinch, but his slanted gray eyes bore into me. "He stays." He spat at my feet and wiped his arm on his black shirt.

Dorian nodded, his brows pinched together. We had wandered into a real predicament, and I read his face clearly. How the hell would we get out of this mess, and the more intriguing question, how the hell did this happen?

Vampires and their problems were the least of my worries. Korrigan's well-being weighed on my mind, and I connected the dots. Petre meant to burn her body, as they once had in the eighteen hundreds. Burnt alive seemed like a horrendous death, and only a lunatic would torture a soul, innocent or damned.

Dorian faced me; I cupped his rough face and risked a quick kiss.

"She'll be fine," he whispered, and rubbed his nose against mine. "Don't make any sudden movements and stay put. He can kill you."

I nodded, rubbing my arms before wrapping them around my chest, as Dorian's boots crunched a path toward a house.

"All right, Petre, show me your witch."

Chapter Fifteen

Dorian

Cain scowled, holding himself. I stepped backward toward Petre. My palm ran over my face. What the bloody hell had we walked into?

"She is out back," Petre said.

Clearing my throat, I spun around. My boot caught in the snow. "Shite," I muttered, and reached for it, but it wasn't there. At least I didn't feel the bitter ice biting through my sock, but where had it gone? My brow rose, and my gaze flickered to Cain, who shook his head and released a cloud of condensation into the air.

Petre tapped my shoulder. "You should be more careful," he whispered, and handed me my boot.

Careful of what? My hand slid to the holster, hidden underneath my flannel and palmed the butt of my revolver. I brought weapons; even Death liked guns. Quicker to draw than my scythe, but they wouldn't kill Petre. However, I could slow him down, though. More likely, a gunshot wound or two would only piss him off.

I slipped my foot into the boot one-handed. Cain didn't move, and mentally, I repeated my earlier instructions.

"Think you're reading too much into it, sweets."

Korrigan whimpered from wherever he was keeping her. One could never be too safe, so I relinquished my position, trusting

Cain would have my back, and tied the boot. Once done and standing, Petre gestured for me to go first, but I shook my head, insisting he lead the way.

Vampires didn't frighten me. What alarmed me was I had crossed paths multiple times with Petre over his 300-year life, yet he had no memory of me, or his best friend and business partner, Tomas. If that wasn't bad enough, the loony bloodsucker thought we were in a different age and place.

The tiny cottage was half-burned, but the damage wasn't new. I glanced to Cain and flashed a reassuring smile. I turned left at the burnt end of the house, sparing a minimal scan of the blackened surface and interior. Except for Korrigan, he was alone. A small broken path existed ahead of us, but my feet were larger than Petre's. Knee-deep snow crunched beneath our feet conquering the small hike to the rear of the house.

Bound with knives to an erected cross, fastened from felled logs, Korri struggled. Spacious amber eyes released all her emotions. Brown-red snow collected the blood gushing from her wounds.

Words flooded my mind, and my fingers rubbed my temples.

"Somethings wrong. He doesn't know who anyone is. He…"

Everything she communicated, I already knew. Petre had lost more than his memory—he'd lost his damn mind.

"This is your witch?" My voice lowered.

"She spoke of demons and kiss…kissed me." He pointed toward her. "Me, a vicar. Look, look at the unholy, devil's eyes." Petre spat again.

I released a long breath. Drumming my fingers against my thigh, I reached for anything to right his mind, even if that something was a lie. "But you are a demon, Petre."

His head cocked and neck cracked.

"You are a vampire, Petre."

Pale fingers stroked his mouth and hooked his lips. Fangs jutted out where his canines used to be.

"Korrigan," I extended my hand, "she is a vampire and your maker."

Cain interrupted me, "Stop pushing him."

As if we had never met, I studied the man halting before me. A slight snarl curled his thin lips, and his posture stood stiffer than a board. But his gray eyes reflected confusion, glancing between Korrigan and me. Petre tugged the strands of his black hair, slicking his locks back. A torn man. I didn't know their history, but I did know Korrigan had to live to save my broken world, and he had to survive because I didn't think she could do it without him. I stepped forward.

"Stay back," he yelled.

Footsteps followed his outburst. I hoped Cain approached.

"Shite." My head shook, but my attention remained on Petre. My hand fell to the butt of my gun. I would maim Petre, if forced. "He means you no harm. This is her brother, Cain." A tickle caught my throat. "And my lover." Warmth filled my insides at the truth released. "He's mine. Remember? My boyfriend."

"What is a boyfriend?"

What the hell was the Romanian word for soul mate? Fuck it. "Cain is my soul mate." Our fingertips touched, and I folded my hand in his. "Take my hand and see the truth you have forgotten."

Petre eyed us; his stare settled on our hands. He shook his head.

"Transform," Cain whispered. "Show him skeletor."

I smirked. With his fragile state, I wasn't certain he needed to see my skeletor persona—whatever that was.

"He needs to see the world and understand. Like you showed me, sweets."

Swallowing, I glanced to Korrigan.

"Show...him." More tears streamed along her angelic face, and her eyes held pain no one should possess. Tattered clothes hung from her body. What had Petre done to her? Why allow him?

"Show me what?" Petre crossed his arms over his chest and tilted his chin. Narrowed gray slits rolled over me. "What could Death have to do with...with...*iele?*" *White ones or a woman who bewitched men.*

"What if she could prove it?" Cain probed, smiling at Petre.

Petre's brows rose and fell, contemplating his words.

"Can you prove it, Korri?" Cain asked without removing his gaze from Petre.

"Your brother...Nicolai...raped...servant," she stuttered through her agony.

Petre spun around. "Many of my people know this accusation." His muscles relaxed a bit.

Korrigan's eyes closed, her lips parted, but words didn't release.

"You watched from the loft in the barn. A game, you told her, at least that's what you thought," Cain relayed.

"No." Petre's hands rubbed his temples, turning his white skin pink. "No, no, no," he repeated in a hushed whisper so low the breeze carried it away. Long, inky strands flittered in the wind, his head violently shaking. "Enough, witch!"

Cain nudged me and motioned to Petre, who withdrew matches, striking and tossing them on the piled wood at the feet of the stake. My mouth dropped—dumbfounded.

Flames ignited at Korrigan's feet, and her eyes flung open. Finding a second wind, she said, "Your family made you tell lies," her shrilled voice climbed higher, "forced others to tell them. You hated yourself. Hated what Hestin transformed you into," she cried, smoky liquid streaming along her face, and inched her tiny legs away from the flames.

Petre clutched his head, his body shaking, and screamed, "Shut up."

"He haunts you still, Petre. Please, please, don't do this to us."

Petre's knees crashed to the ground, and Cain used the distraction to kick snow onto the flickering flames. My breath held. Purple fire emitted from his fingers and doused the fire. *Fighting fire with fire?*

"Mine won't burn," he said, and the lavender essence spread over her body.

Knives slid free from her flesh and she screamed. But her wounds closed, healing rapidly.

I knelt to Petre. Sobs filled the air and rocked his thin body. I didn't have a clue. Crazy wasn't in the ABDA rulebook, not like this.

"Petre," she whispered, voice hoarse but calm. "Please God…"

Cain held her back, his knuckles turned white, and his jaw tightened.

Petre glanced at me. "How could she know? Only Nicolai and my family knew. I was so naïve, so indebted to my family. I broke my vows to save a disgusting murderer."

My hand hovered above his bent back. "Because you told her and maybe," I glanced to Korrigan, "you cared enough to tell the truth and she loved you, despite it."

I love Cain enough to trust him with my secrets. Why can't he do the same?

Petre sniffled and ran a hand through his inky locks. Slowly, he glanced at her. The rest of us remained silent while he considered Korrigan. Wind whipped through her long hair, and fresh tears blinked from her amber eyes. Petre's head tilted.

"Show me." He grasped my hand without averting his gaze.

The wind gusted again, whooshing, and I glanced toward the clouded sky. "Shite."

"Bloody hell you will, mate." Veric dropped to the ground and folded his black wings.

Black? Only the fallen had black wings. Ten more agents descended—all with white wings.

"You dare turn on me, luv? Think I didn't know?" he whisper shouted at Korrigan. Red eyes pled in both directions and the two squared off.

"I had to find him, and you know it, Veric." Korrigan's chin jutted into the air.

Cain shoved her behind him. Purple sparks emitted from his palms, and his eyes alit in a storm. "Leave my sister alone."

The thunder of his temper rumbled from my feet, rocking my steady legs. Fuck me; he was beautiful in the glow of purple fire and sparks in his eyes.

"Arrest him." Veric pointed at Petre.

"On what grounds?" My gaze stayed on Cain.

"Adultery," Veric spat.

Korrigan pushed Cain aside and ran after Petre, but Veric's snatched her up and held her back. She screamed, "No. He's innocent."

Obeying his order, the ten guards leaped and shackled him, pressing his face into the snow. But Petre didn't fight back. A vampire could've taken everyone present down, except for Korrigan and me. Had a memory returned? Maybe he didn't realize he could kill them.

I glanced to Cain and rubbed my neck. Veric refused to see the truth. Cain dampened the fire before tapping his head. Right, he could hear my thoughts, not that I cared what the bastard thought about me.

"How dare you do this," she hissed. Korrigan spun in his arms and whacked him across the face. Blood splattered from his tightened jaw, misting a crimson cloud into the air.

He wiped his face and held her tighter, but she kicked and screamed bloody fucking murder. Men were stubborn.

"Veric," I warned. The ABDA detective may have technically been my boss, but I wasn't about to sit back and let him arrest Petre. My booted feet stormed through the snow, and I tore his hands from Korrigan.

"Don't let her get away," Veric ordered.

The Elioud advanced on her without drawing weapons. His eyes blinked at the tiny pixie sending his men flying into the trees, breaking one in two, and blood dribbled where she bit one. However, she didn't kill any of our agents.

"She isn't Angelica." He scratched his red head and stared, mouth agape.

I drew my gun and cocked the pin, aiming it at Veric. What the hell was he? "I don't believe she is."

"No shit Sherlock, welcome to reality." Cain coughed, covering his chuckle at his unspoken statement.

It was one thing for her brother to see her as Angelica. But how obsessed was Veric to insist and demand Korri to love him? "You're all fucking crazy," I said, but perhaps we could move forward.

"Crazy in love." Cain pushed my arm down. "Can we put the gun away?"

"You get a pass, babe. The rest of you need straightjackets."

I re-holstered my gun, Cain un-cuffed Petre with the wave of his hand and handed them to me. I threw the shackles at Veric's head, but they sank soundlessly into the snow. Too bad I missed.

We hauled ass toward the farmhouse, but only made it to the wreckage before sundown; Veric and his men followed. Petre said nothing during the journey, but he did cast looks, long curious glances, at his maker.

Korrigan had spoken to him, but her gaze remained down, and her voice shook. "I need blood." She stood near the broken train car. "But I don't want to ask Veric."

"I would, but I'm too weak." Cain plopped onto the door positioned near a small, burning fire. Dry wood was scarce, seeing as Petre used most in his attempt to kill Korrigan, so Cain used his magic to keep it from going out.

"You can try me," I offered. I still didn't understand why she had to have demon blood.

"Petre's never tasted right to me. Elioud blood satisfies me more." She inched over to Veric, who piled kindling onto the fire. Korrigan cleared her throat. "I wouldn't ask..."

"Of course, ducky." Veric lifted his sleeve.

Her small hands wrapped around his forearm, and she bit into his flesh, slurping deeply. Crimson dripped over a black tattoo, a mark I hadn't seen for eons outside of the Council of Seven—the Seven Archangels the ABDA reported to. An eye, but instead of an iris, it had a cross at its center. Yet no Grigori had ever bore the name Veric. No one else noticed the mark on Veric's forearm. He wasn't Elioud at all. He wasn't Nephilim, either. I stepped backward and cocked my head. Did the ABDA know a damned fallen angel was leading their extraction division? There were others, but I knew them. They didn't hide their identities or use fake names. *Who are you?* I held the question in my mind.

Veric's gaze lifted from Korrigan and landed on me. *"You're mistaken,"* he said, before returning his attention to her. "Good now? Don't be afraid to ask. I'm not the heartless monster you've painted me as."

She stared up at him, craning her neck. "I know you aren't, Veric. I know you think you love me, but you only love the idea of me being her."

His detectives sprawled around the fire, unearthing anything to rest on that wasn't snow. A few shared their rations with Cain. Although, he refused at first, he eventually caved. Aside from an occasional wild animal calling into the night, quietness settled over our little group.

Cain and I excused ourselves, taking leave in our shelter. Without the need for sleep, Korrigan and Petre guarded the campsite. The remainder of us rested for the long journey ahead. But my mind refused to still, flashing to the tattoo on the inside of Veric's forearm and the image of his mark churned my stomach.

The following morning, we renewed our trek through the Arcadian wilds, passing lofty pines and old maples. The sun peaked on the horizon and painted the sky in shades of fire. Beauty didn't alleviate the weight, and a somberness spread over those in tow. Most of all, Veric seemed affected by the truth of his situation, not from my seeing his mark, and tore his shoulders down and deepened his scowl.

Cain attempted conversation with him, but after grunts and gruff no's, he left Veric alone. My brow rose, Cain's grasped my hand. I questioned why he would bother.

"He saved my life. You should be grateful."

And I was more grateful than words could ever do justice. But who was the fallen angel parading as Veric Garland? My lips brushed Cain's temple as his pink cheeks lifted into a smile. I raised his cold knuckles and kissed each one. "Where are your gloves?"

"I must've left them at the crash site."

"Everyone hold up," I shouted over the group. "Anyone have a spare set of gloves?"

Heads shook and murmured answers repeated the same. Cain said, "I'll just shove them in my pockets."

"Nope, we're turning around. Unless you can conjure a pair or something with magic." I stepped backward. "You guys go on, and we'll catch up." I waved on the rest.

"I'm still drained," he said, spinning around. "None of the Elioud are warlocks, and Korrigan wouldn't know how to conjure."

I bit my lip and nodded; the others in our group followed. "Can you fly?"

"I can walk, but even if I had the strength to summon my wings, I wouldn't have the strength to fly." He yawned.

Silently, I cursed myself for not allowing that extra day of rest. His sunken eyes, lined with heavy bags, spoke more of my negligence. I knelt in the snow. "Get on my back."

"What? No, you're not carrying me."

"Piggyback or I'll throw you over my shoulder."

"What's the hold up?" Veric asked.

Cain's pale face turned a bright red.

"Bloody hell, I'll do it."

"No," Cain and I said in unison, followed by Cain stumbling behind me and lowering himself on my shoulders. I grasped his legs; grunting, I hoisted us from the ground.

Courtesy of backtracking, we spent three more days on the road. His gloves weren't at the campsite. No. We found Cain's missing gloves at the burned cabin, but we wound up having to camp-out again. Despite his protests, I'd continued to carry him. While he'd rested, Cain couldn't sleep and hold onto me at the same time.

Though our trek was uneventful, we finally arrived at the farmhouse; I quickly realized there'd be no hanky-panky with a house full of ABDA agents.

Cain slid down and landed on the stoop. "You really didn't need to carry me all the way, but I do appreciate it."

"Go get yourself cleaned up and rest." I shrugged and bent over to grab the large pots we'd used for gathering snow.

He reached for another pail. "I'll be fine. Let me give you a hand. At least I won't feel like dead weight."

Knowing better than to argue, my teeth dug into my lip and I lugged in buckets of snow to melt by the fireplace. Agent Veric knelt in front of the hearth, his magical essence pouring into the cold stone. His agents sprawled themselves on the tattered sofas.

Cain placed his pail next to mine. "Couldn't we use magic to power the house?"

"We could," Veric replied without turning from his task. "But this takes less energy. Too bad they didn't have a generator with some bloody fuel." A deep dimple formed as he cracked a half-smile. "You should rest and let my men do some heavy lifting."

Cain glanced to me before nodding. He strode toward the stairs.

"Right. You lot get off your lazy bums and collect snow. Then we take turns bathing."

One by one, the agents fetched snow, cleaned themselves, and changed into appropriate clothing left behind by the former occupants. I settled into the kitchen, not wanting to disturb Cain.

"No bath for you?" one of the agents asked.

Dark had fallen outside and the only light arrived from the roaring fire. Chatter and splashing reached my ears, but I paid no attention to it. I merely shook my head, wondering why Cain so easily accepted orders from Veric, the same ones I'd given. I stared at the pots hanging overhead.

As the door opened and closed, a chilly breeze rushed into the warm space. I leaned back in my chair as icy hands clamped and shook my shoulders. "Rest well?"

Cain replied with a groan before sitting beside me. "Warmer in here."

He's been outside? Without a coat?

"Did a little exploring and found canned goods in the root cellar. Moving kept me warm, so stop fretting." He stretched and cracked his neck. "Did we check the cupboards? This place is remote. It's possible no one's been here aside from us."

Petre sat at the table, too, but I rose and strolled toward the first set of cupboards near the sink. Dusty glasses filled the shelves. I searched the others, finding plates and more cookware.

Veric meandered over and opened a door adjacent to the fridge. "Jackpot, I believe. We could eat for weeks without touching our rations."

Cain leaped to his feet and joined him. They brought out armfuls of dry goods and placed them on the table. Did they plan to eat expired goods? Wouldn't it make Cain ill?

"I'll check them," he replied to my thoughts. "The cold would've slowed spoiling of the oils used during processing, but it stinks when rancid." Cain dumped another armload on the table before kissing my forehead.

All I cared about was his wellbeing. I brushed his hand, but didn't grab it. He glanced at me, caramel eyes alight in a playful glee.

"You can start going through them. I'll grab the rest," Veric said.

Cain slipped into his chair, his knee knocking against mine. His contagious smile caught on, and my lips spread wider. Veric rustled around before delivering another load to the table.

"What is all this?" Petre asked, holding up a package of dry soup mix. "Such wondrous inventions. This... this is food in the future?"

Cain chuckled. "Not really. It's all derived from food, but mankind made it in a lab, and then mass-produced it. Humans paid good money to eat products of little nutritional value in the name of convenience."

"I do not understand. How did they survive if it isn't nutritious?"

"Many didn't." Veric sat next to Cain and withdrew another box of soup mix. "They died slow deaths without even knowing it. Their arteries clogged, they became lazier and lazier and fatter and fatter. That's one thing you never bloody see anymore."

"What's that?" I asked.

"Fat Archangels," he said. "They don't need to eat, and anymore, food is so scarce that no one can overeat. They're either busy not freezing to death up here, or trying not to sweat to death in the south." He sighed. "So how about some onion and herb soup?" Veric asked his men.

Cain started to rise, but I stopped him. "I can make it. You keep resting." I eyed Veric. "Don't let him lift another finger."

Thirty minutes later and everyone had had his fill of soup. With more than enough to go around, one of Veric's men made a second batch, and it was simmering on the hearth. Small talk continued, and all seemed well. Petre and Veric even carried out a normal conversation, mostly about the food changes and health related topics.

But after their conversation had pattered out, my boss paced the length of the hearth. I zoned out his constant shuffling, staring at everything and nothing, and wished to be home again with Cain.

Creaking noise drew my attention. Korrigan eased down the steps, playfully kicking the hem of her checkered dress and laughing at the cowgirl boots peeking from beneath the frilly number. On anyone else, the costume might have hit the knees, but on Korrigan's petite frame, the lace edge swept against the hardwood floor. Leather holsters dangled from her tiny waist and drooped from the weight of the revolvers. All she lacked was a shepherd crook to complete the Little Bo Peep meets Annie Oakley ensemble—according to Cain's thoughts. The bonnet framed her cherub face and shone false innocence over her ruddy cheeks.

"Such light inside." Petre grimaced. "To think I meant to snuff her out." He excused himself. The kitchen entrance clicked and served as an indication of his departure.

Before she made the landing, her head shot upright, and her pink lips scowled. Cain halted mid-slurp of his herb-flavored soup. Her amber gaze scanned the kitchen and attached dining room. I inclined my head toward the back door, and her wind gusted past my face.

"That your plan, mate?"

I cleared my throat. "Is what my plan?"

"Reuniting Romeo and Juliet." Snickers sounded around the room. "Or you plan on doing your job and leaving mine to me?"

The fire crackled and hissed. I hadn't thought that far ahead, or expected a memory-less Petre. Time ran shorter with each day we dawdled, and we were still another three away from Montreal Station. Veric must've called me from there, or on the road, but how had he found us? Cain shrugged at my thought and offered no insight.

"I knew your plan." Veric palmed his neck. The veins throbbed and pulsed beneath his tanned skin as muscles pushed off the hearth. Heavy boots stomped on the floorboards. "You're good at your job, but I'm better. Satellite phones have trackers in them."

"And I can see the soul of a person where you see your past," I whispered, and met his narrowed gaze. "You can see me as an asshole, a grunt, but our father blessed me with a unique ability."

Wrinkles creased deep lines into his forehead. "I sent dream messages to her."

But as he spoke the words, I sensed his hidden truth. Veric hadn't said anything when I'd said our father. Only an Angel wouldn't have objected. My fingers tapped along the tabletop, now devoid of food. Who could he have been? I knew all of my brothers-in-arms, fallen or not.

Cain said, "But she didn't know who you were. No one is arguing that Angel's soul didn't survive Mother's spell. The girl's mind comes and goes. She has Angel's memories, but not all of them. Even then, she's made a new life for herself. Who's to say she'd be the same Angelica we remember. Am I the same man you knew?"

The men murmured about the room, and Veric commanded them to bed and strolled to the table. White-knuckled, he braced his hands against an empty kitchen chair. "How," he whispered, and shut his eyes. His lips opened and closed.

"You found her. You found me. Let's find Lily, and then see where the cards fall," Cain offered, and the towering, redheaded Grigori nodded.

I asked, "How do we find her? She is still my top priority. Fauna hasn't checked in, and she should've found her by now." The other missing souls were a priority, too, but I wanted to reunite his shattered family as much as I wanted to rip Boric's limbs from his body.

The door opened, and a snow covered Korrigan and Petre slipped inside. The vampires retook their seats, Korri slipping into the chair Veric leaned on.

Her swift hands removed the bonnet. "Petre, Tomas, and I were on our way to the summit." Her chestnut hair shook and melted snow splattered onto the table. "He meant to design a ship," she pointed up, "for the air."

"Korrigan informed me of what I've accomplished, but I have no memory or knowledge of such advancements," Petre said, tapping his fingers on the surface. "It doesn't mean she's wrong, and I am inclined to believe her…" He drew his long, black hair to the side. Only a few days had passed, and his speech was improving; though, his heavy accent still tainted his words. At least he spoke faster, and used more contractions.

"Jules," Veric mumbled, and covered his mouth with his hand. "Thought we were done with that sod."

"What do you mean?" she asked.

Veric rose and extended his palms. "Can I see? Won't hurt you."

Petre glanced to me, and I nodded.

"Aha just what I thought. Sneaky wanker." Veric shook his head. "Nephilim shape shift. Bloody fucker." He muttered something else, but I didn't catch it.

Not news to me and I waved him on.

"Jules came to you," he motioned to Petre, "shortly after the crash, but before you tried changing him over is my best guess."

Petre shrugged.

"You probably shared his blood or saliva. He could've altered your memory."

Korrigan said, "But I killed him."

"Saw it with my own eyes," Veric said.

"You weren't there yet," she countered. "Tomas was."

"Wouldn't having killed him break his spell?" I asked, easing my chair back, teetering on two legs, and followed their conversation. I accepted Cain and his magic. Since they were witches and warlocks, perhaps I never would understand how it worked. Still, the idea of it intrigued me.

Cain answered, "Not always. Minor spells, yes, but a curse has to run its course. That's what happened to you and your brother, Petre. There is always an out, and according to Korrigan, it's how you defeated Hestin's spell."

Korrigan clutched her stomach and pinched her eyes. *Is that her problem too?*

"Bloody hell, you might be on to something, Dorian." Veric gasped. "Luv, what if that's why you're split?"

Cain cleared his throat, and I blinked.

"Nephilim don't hold that much power," Cain thought. "Do they?"

"No." I leaned my elbows on the table. "I think that's how Jules controlled those in his brothels. If anyone got out of line, he could manage them, make them forget a little here and there, but you and I know what you're suggesting was beyond his reach." It had to be. *What I wouldn't give to have Fauna or Mark here.*

Cain rose from the table and added, "Petre had three hundred years, give or take a decade, removed."

Maybe Korrigan had new memories implanted, because she lived a new life. Jules erased the first few years and covered up Veric. At the time, it was probably for her own safety, in case anyone from Garland showed their faces. That I could've seen, but locking away the soul? My fingers tapped against the kitchen table.

Cain tended the fire and removed the buckets, sloshing water into a basin by the sink. "Petre needs to remember," he said, and rolled up the sleeves of his shirt. "No one else is close with airships, are they?"

"Not even close," she said. "That's what he told me."

Veric nodded in agreement.

"Babe, what are you suggesting?"

Color flushed Cain's rough cheeks. A sigh rattled forth and his shoulders rounded over the sink. "I can reverse the spell, but Mother's books are in Halifax. Jan, too, I need her help, since we don't have Tomas, and Korrigan forgot." Cain rambled off a list of ingredients.

"Don't you just say words?" My fingers wiggled in the air, and Veric barked a laugh. Heat rose into my cheeks.

"No, this is ritual magic, and I might need Fauna as well."

The word ritual twisted my gut, and acid reared up my throat. "Is it dangerous?"

"Very." Cain twisted the metal ring on his finger as the snake head wiggled on his neck. The audible gulp spoke more than his tone and words, but it was his decision to make.

"Do you know which books you need," Veric asked, and yanked out his phone.

I slid a mini notebook and worn pencil nub from my flannel pocket and laid them on the table.

Cain dried his hands on a dusty towel. "I wish I had all of my mother's books. It'll be a long shot. A hope and prayer that I even have the spell." He stared at the floor.

"I can have Jan relocated and all your possessions sent to the Summit," I added, and Cain glanced to me. The headquarters of the ABDA was located in former Anchorage, Alaska. Over five thousand kilometers, or three thousand miles, of land lay between us. The train ride would take up to fifteen days without using magic or portal abilities. Fifteen more days without my lover's touch sounded like purgatory.

Veric raised his eyebrow. "You know we can hear you, right?"

I shrugged and stared into the caramel eyes capturing my heart. A slow, hissing breath released from Cain's full lips, and the world around me ceased to exist. Veric spoke again, but the words trailed into the fogginess of my mind. Sex was natural, and my primal appetite bordered on insane, but I didn't care if others knew the truth.

I crave the touch of Cain like my vampires crave blood. Pain radiated across my face and blood tainted my mouth. Veric drew his fist back. My chair skidded across the dining room floor, slamming into the wall. I jumped on him, ignoring the shouts and gasps sounding around me. My hands grasped his neck, and I squeezed. Cold metal touched my temple, and a click of the revolver echoed in my ear.

Veric's eyes bulged.

"First of all, your gun is about worthless." I shoved him. "Second, hitting the man who can end your pathetic life is about the dumbest shite you can pull."

Cain's hand landed on my shoulder, but I shucked him off. "Sweets," he whispered. "Let 'em go."

"Son of bitch punched me." Not to mention all the other trouble the Garland brother caused on the trip. Plus, the tattoo marked him as Grigori. All he cared about was Korrigan. All I cared about was Cain and that meant saving Lily. My fingers released, and the dark red welts on his skin healed. "Don't pull that shite again," I muttered, my racing heart pounding against my ribcage. Beneath my sleeves, my bones were exposed. "I need a smoke."

I stormed past Cain and out the backdoor. Rattling windows added to my twitching nerves. All these people, demons, bah whatever, were driving me crazy. They stood in my way with their rules and laws. I drew a cigarette from the pack and frowned; it was the last one.

"Let it go, sweets." Cain closed the door.

I snorted. His breath blew out in steamy puffs, and his rough hands rubbed together. Cold seeped into his bones through the borrowed down coat, and somehow, his shivers, as if they were mine, prickled my skin. Elements blinked from his eyelids, snowflakes melting on his darkening, beard-covered cheeks. The energy of his body worked harder against the plunging artic temperatures.

Cain motioned toward the barn and trudged through the short path. I glanced around, but we were alone in the darkness. My insides stirred to life. *Alone.* One foot moved, and then another of its own accord. The barn door sat ajar, and I slipped through the opening, closing and latching the weatherworn wooden panel behind me. *Alone at last.*

My eyes adjusted to the dim, lavender light coming from the ceiling. Purple balls danced, hovering midair, and illuminated my surroundings. Warmth pulsed from their crystalline centers and heated the barn.

"Whoa," I whispered at the beauty of his magic. Never before had the unexplained become a wondrous obsession.

"In the wrong hands it can be a destructive weapon," Cain said from the loft. "C'mon up."

He turned and disappeared from my sight. A wry smile spread over my lips. I pocketed the unlit cigarette and strolled to the ladder. The rickety heap of wood had seen better days, but I shrugged and placed my boot on the first rung. When it held, I tried the next, and the next. Never ending, each wrung groaned beneath my feet. Reaching the top, Cain came into view. Old hay bales lined the walls, creating a makeshift bed, and he flicked a crisp sheet over the tops. Muscles moved and perspiration glistened on his forehead. Magic was beautiful, but Cain was beyond words.

"Don't get any ideas." A smirk tilted his lips and transformed into a wide smile. "I want you to be comfortable with my magic." Cain's shoulders fell and his thick arms hugged his body. "Maybe that will help me."

After all, he had accepted of me…I shook my head and hefted myself from the ladder. Four strides and my arms encompassed him, pressing his head to my shoulder.

"What's bothering you, babe?"

"The closer we get, the farther away it seems." Cain said, "I've spent years searching. What happens after we rescue her?"

Wind rattled the barn, and my gaze darted around the structure. My eyes closed, and my face rested on his head. Deep, fiery aroma surrounded me, and I'd forgotten how comforting Cain was to my nerves. "We all live happily ever after," I whispered. "Or we keep fighting, but either way, we don't give-up. I'm never giving you up, babe."

Cain's head lifted from my shoulder, and a small smile touched his lips, but profound pain reflected within his welling eyes, deeper than I recalled ever seeing. If only a kiss would solve his conflictions and the agony of losing so much of his life. A sigh tickled my throat, a sound to wash over our imperfect lives and make us whole again.

"Dorian, am I…enough," he swallowed hard, "for you?"

My hands cupped his rough jaw. Noses hovered and caressed. Eyelashes kissed, like fluttering butterfly wings. "More than I ever deserved."

"There's more than sex between us, right?"

"Yes," I replied without hesitation, even though parts of me didn't understand what existed beyond complete love and devotion. For Cain, I would give my life…anything in my life I would give for his happiness. My lips brushed his, and electricity sparked over my skin, igniting beneath my false layers. He alone penetrated into the dark depths of my bones. But when, not if, but when this world ended, I still had Sheol to rule and protect. A day, a month, years, or centuries, whatever time we had, I wanted to spend it with him.

Love—I'd thought it wasn't part of Father's plan, for me, but I'd met Cain, and then I'd met him again. Without him, my life had little purpose…without him though; I still feared my grief would end this world.

Heavy lidded eyes peeked at me. "What drives you, Special Agent Dorian Fox?"

"You." A touch, a kiss, making love, being with him drove me to become a better person and take responsibility for the world Father had entrusted to me. "I don't know if anyone still does this."

"Does what?" Brows rose and fell.

I grinned at my sweaty palms and racing pulse. "Let me finish."

Cain's arms skimmed around my neck. We danced to the tinkering sounds of falling snow and howling, angry wind. Giggles erupted from his chest; we spun and twirled. Like a rollercoaster, my belly flip-flopped, and the butterflies came to life at his giddiness. Bright grins and light chuckles mixed with breathless fun. Granted, we were two gay men with no clue about dancing, but neither of us cared. Cain's happiness was the key to mine.

After a badly executed spin, we collapsed to the ground.

"What were you going to say before?" he asked, catching his breath.

His butterscotch eyes blinked. A spark ignited and shone through the darkness of our lives. Well before that moment, Cain was it for me, the one and only. I had said the words and hinted at wanting him in my life forever.

"I was serious on the train," I started, rubbing my hair from my face.

A strange sound released from his lips, not quite a sigh. "Oh."

"Would you, Cain Morning Star, do me the favor of becoming my..." Wife sounded odd, but husband did too. My brows scrunched. I sought the word, any word. But true love cannot be expressed in words. From sonnets to prose, no words would ever define our spark, and any who would seek one had never felt the true draw of a loving heart.

He whispered, "Partner, lover..."

My hand slid down his side.

Cain's lips shot into a goofy half-grin. "Didn't I say yes already?"

I kissed his nose and my heart pounded. He'd said yes before, but something drove me to ask again. "Yeah, babe, my partner for life. Marry me?"

Chapter Sixteen

Cain

My nose tingled where he'd kissed me, but my mouth dropped. A marriage proposal I hadn't expected, not again. After spending countless hours preparing the barn, I had meant to give him the keys, head to the Summit, perform the spell, and say adios. We wouldn't work. Bonds born in lust weren't enough, and I didn't believe love would've been any stronger. Our lives were too different. The risk of us being together was too high—if we broke up, the world would end, and I certainly wasn't worth it.

Dorian's warm fingers caressed my cheek, and he awaited my answer. Lights hummed and flooded the ratty barn in romantic radiance; his words stemmed from his heart and soul. But I couldn't bring myself to say yes again. The pounding in my chest settled.

"It's okay to say no." Dorian rolled onto his back and closed his eyes. It wasn't okay, not to him.

"I'm not going anywhere. I'm just…" Just what? A pussy. I raked my hand through my hair. Marriage and commitment didn't scare me. I was torn.

"What changed?" he whispered, the hurt evident in his tone.

I sighed. Hell, I'd only learned his full name a few days ago, yet we'd already memorized every inch of each other's bodies. I wanted Dorian, and I loved Dorian. More than the idea of him, too. But he didn't know my middle name or my favorite color. I didn't know his, either. *How can we love one another and know nothing?* My shoulders slumped forward and legs crossed. How had I loved a monster, who beat, starved, and raped me? Wasn't that proof enough? My judgment was as altered as my mind.

I sucked in a deep breath and held the air in my lungs. None of "us" was in my original plan. My fingers drummed over the dirty wood. *Save my sisters and then die.* That had always been my plan. Dorian never factored into the equation. Somewhere along the line, I lost control and sight of it. Burning eyes closed. Another secret smoldered in my dry mouth.

Wood boards groaned; he shifted. A lifeline: his hand grasped mine.

"C'mere." Dorian tugged and dragged my body against the gritty floor. "As long as you love me nothing else matters." He squeezed me. "You still love me, right?"

My hands held his face. Dorian was not a liar, not like Boric or me. "Yes."

I stared into his green eyes as a low hum vibrated the barn. *Chop, chop, chop…* a sound all too familiar assaulted my ears. Shivers ran through me, paralyzing me, and the sound steadied into a constant, roaring decibel.

Dorian's brows pinched, and he yanked my arm. His mouth dropped, words spewing, but the airships drowned out his voice.

Korrigan and Veric sounded in my head together, and they screamed, *"Run."*

Their warning arrived too late. The barn door rattled, squeaked. Voices filtered into the barn, along with diesel and cold air. "Oh yeah, the source is inside."

"Don't move," Dorian thought.

Piecing it all together, my eyes widened. If they found us by sensing the magic, one of them had to be a witch or warlock. They could read our minds. I had no weapon and doubted Dorian had his guns. The men from before were simple demons. I tapped my head and ran a finger across my throat. He nodded. A chuckle choked inside my throat, and he shot me a quizzed look.

Dorian would finally get to play the alpha. Appearing from thin air, his jeweled scythe flew into his hand. Dorian and I jumped to our feet.

Someone asked, "You hear that?"

"The loft, you go check."

Dorian pointed to the hay bales and pressed his hand down. We scurried behind the obstruction. The ladder creaked, and I held my breath. My heart pounded, but I didn't dare utter as much as a prayer. Voices continued whispering downstairs, but their minds remained shut. I searched for my sister and Veric. Finding them seemed pointless, since I couldn't communicate with them, but at least I would know they were safe.

Wings beat. Air buffeted my face. Engines roared, sputtering, and fumes puttered through the cramped space. Rotten hatred and burning loathing crept along my nostrils. Had to be Boric.

Diesel clung to my throat. The ground and structure groaned. Broken windows rattled. My gaze darted, never staying on one noise for too long, and sweat dribbled, trailing a drop over the bridge of my nose. Tickling my skin, it clung to the edge.

"Oi, must've been the wind."

"Since when does wind create light? Are you daft?"

Skin smacked skin. "Oi, wha' you do that for?"

I shut down the whole of my body and mind, but the tremble within refused departure. My teeth chattered. Tears cascaded over hot cheeks and my hands clutched the hay bales for support.

Stars dabbled and dotted my vision. Blood rushed from my head to my toes and the room spiraled around me. My foot slipped, and I landed on a wooden beam, cracking and splintering the dry-rotted board. Stench-filled ice whipped around my face, and my heart leaped into my throat. Stale, moldy hay entered my mouth and fluttered to the ground. Aches splintered through my body as it had done little to ease my fall.

"Ha, knew it wasn't the wind."

Blinking, I stared upward at the ragged hole in the floor. Sharp teeth and red eyes blocked my view, his amused face looming over my body. His black tail slithered around my neck and tightened. Gasps sounded from my chest while the whip-like tail constricted my airwaves. Massive black wings jutted from his back, and the power rolled from him in waves, crashing against my burning skin. Two Arch demons, Elioud, and a lone Nephilim surrounded me. I knew them all, hating each one equally.

Armoni Cross sneered and said, "Now, now fellows looksie what I found. We caught us a rat. Master will be pleased." Boric's personal guard strode over the threshold and halted.

I grunted, still unable to shake the fall.

He knelt and drew his weapon. A thud sounded behind me. Cold metal pressed into my temple as Cross glanced over my twisted body and smiled. "Think you can hit me, before I pull the trigger, Dorian Fox? Or do you prefer Death?"

"Wanker," Dorian cursed. "Let him go, Armoni."

I should've been surprised they knew one another by name. How many times had their paths crossed?

"Where's the fun in that?" Cross's feet shuffled.

Pairs of boots blinked into view. They had us surrounded, but their minds raced and waited for Death to make his move. The men wanted me alive, needed me alive. With Cross here, Boric had to be behind it. Ugly puke green uniforms solidified the fact.

For years, I'd outmaneuvered Boric Garland. For years, I alone had hid the keys. No. *This is personal.* "Sweets, you have to let them take me." My stomach lurched at the thought.

Dorian's mind tore into two. *"It's like my worst nightmare coming true,"* his mind replied.

My eyes burned, and heavy gulps kept the tears at bay. I held faith; Dorian would find me again. Metal clanked and clasped about my wrists. Cross hefted me up and shoved me toward another demon. Gravity spun a web of blurring objects. A gun found its way back to my temple.

"I love you." Our minds spoke in unison.

Green eyes glowed, Dorian's gaze ping-ponged from demon to demon. Another demon cocked his gun, and then another until all barrels touched my head. Would they pull the trigger?

Stars littered my vision and an odd whooshing sound, like a dull engine roar, filled my ears. But a voice blended, soft and feminine, and heightened over the noise. "Brother," Korrigan said. "Stay strong. I'm safe."

Stay strong, I repeated in my mind. For Dorian and for her, I would endure anything, even if it meant losing myself again.

A bag obscured my vision, but Dorian relayed his thoughts and observances: *Cross and his posse dragged me backward. For every step they took, Dorian advanced, but his twitching fingers and cold stare didn't affect the men.*

Powerless—all of us knew it. My dry, shaking lips parted, but what else could I say?

"How sweet," Cross whispered. "Drop the harnesses," he yelled, his tone rattling in my ear.

Dorian's mind relayed our surroundings, the airship, and Garland emblems, still forced to do nothing, but I understood there was nothing he could do short of ending the world. They would take me or kill me, even though they probably would execute me anyway. Eventually.

Seconds dragged on like hours. A harness hooked around my waist. Wind cut through me.

Demons connected themselves to me. One thrust a rope into my trembling hands and my thoughts ceased. Repeating the truth of my shitty situation wouldn't change it. Wind whipped the rope from my hands.

"Hold it or die," Cross snapped, and shoved the rough material at me. "You're pathetic and not worth the resources. Do us all a favor and fight back."

I wouldn't, though; his offer was tempting. Dorian deserved better than to watch me die.

Ground disappeared beneath my feet, my stomach tingling and grip tightening its hold. We swayed, but their guns didn't falter. Garland had caught up with me at last. And for what? A bitter smile pulled at my hidden lips.

One time, Boric had shown me the plans, a giant ship made for the sea, but its blades chopped the air, not the surf. The same type I had seen in the skies weeks ago.

Engines and propellers roared louder, drowning the voices, but Dorian's mind shouted, "I love you, babe. I won't be far behind."

I chuckled and shook my head. My existence meant nothing in the grand plan, but my life meant something to Dorian. The future I wanted was Dorian but I'd kept telling myself I hadn't deserved him.

Tighter my fingers curled around the rope. Diesel fumes intensified and swirled their exhaust into my face. I coughed. Vomit burned in my throat.

"You hurl, and I'll shoot you." Cross lifted me onto a hard surface replacing the air beneath my feet. His hands shoved me.

Laughter, sinister and conniving by its squealed tone, reached my ears.

"Ello, what we 'ave here then? You know, mate."

I blinked at the voice embedded into my mind. The voice held more madness and evil than the history of the Morning Star himself.

"They say if you want a job right, you 'ave to do it yourself." He yanked the scratchy hood from my face and tossed it on the deck.

I stared into menacing eyes I'd never wanted to see again. "Boric," I whispered. His calloused fingers wrapped around my neck, and I spat in his face.

"Where are my bloody keys, you cackpipe cosmonaut?" he snarled, and wiped the spittle from his mouth. Boric's cold, lifeless blue eyes narrowed as we came nose-to-nose.

His hand fell to my ass and squeezed. My skin crawled. Once upon a time, I'd craved his attention, his touch. Bile scorched my throat and churned holes into my stomach. So blind before…

"Cat catch your tongue? No worries, we'll loosen you right up." He addressed Cross, "Toss the crafty butcher in the brig." Boric stepped left and turned his back to me. "If he gives you any trouble, toss 'em around a bit, yeah. Cain loves it rough."

The deck beneath my feet swayed. His airship propelled through the star-littered, cloudless sky, its engines puttering and releasing thick plumes of exhaust. Blood rushed from my face. From behind, strange, rough hands steadied me. I stumbled, despite their attempts, dry heaving from the strange vertigo.

Boric spun around, stroking his chin. "On second thought, lads, put him in my quarters."

Blood dashed through my veins, leaving a sheen along my skin, and my mouth slackened. Smart move for him, seeing as anyone attempting a rescue would expect me downstairs. But Dorian wasn't anyone—we had a connection stronger than any bond I had once shared with Boric.

Cross and his men shoved and pulled me upright. My heart raced faster with every stumbled step. I shook my head, but they forced me through the slender, dark doorway. My feet dragged against the wooden floor, and my nails dug into my captors arms.

"Shackle 'em to the bed," Boric said, and motioned to a double bed. A desk sat in the corner by the window with a single lantern on top illuminating the cramped quarters.

Please God, no. Cross pressed his knee into my back and his men extended my arms, one at a time, followed by my legs. The thick chains rattled. Cross attached each one to the hooks in the wall and the other two to the foot of the bed.

"Arse up." Boric stepped into my view, winked, and blew me a kiss. Tooth by tooth, he slid down his zipper.

Vomit rose into my mouth, coating my tongue in bitterness. I gagged at the room spinning around me. Cross snickered. As the edges of Boric's lips spread into a sinister smile, I prayed.

Pain served as an enduring reminder of days passing in the air, marked solely by comings and goings. Boric, the menacing twin of Veric, proved himself as disastrous as acid. My eyes closed and I willed my empty stomach to calm. However, the jostle of the ship and sharp odor of exhaust didn't cause the lurching sensation within my body.

Lashes marred my skin. Each miniscule movement burned. His venom invaded me, scorching scars engraved into my bones. My lip ached from biting it. Cries and tears brought harsher punishment, and my silent prayers wrought on a wrath more ominous than my namesake's legacy.

With a shiver, I shook the imagery away.

Dorian hadn't come for me; Korrigan hadn't arrived with Veric and a sea of agents. I still loved them, but each visit from Boric and his men wore my spirit down and ground me into nothingness. Soon, they'd tire of my body, but death, no; he wouldn't grant me death.

Not until I gave up the keys.

The door swung open, smacking against the wall, and heavy boots stomped into the Captain's Quarters. A slight stagger meant the visitor drank—At least I hoped. My exposed body meant nothing to him. I held my breath and crawled into myself, thinking maybe, if I were small enough, than he wouldn't see me.

He stumbled and rummaged through drawers. "Sodden wanker, where's the bleedin' uniforms?"

Uniforms? Why was anyone looking for a uniform? Shuddering, I craned my neck, but still couldn't see who my mysterious visitor was.

Where the Soul Never Dies played through my mind. Smiling, green eyes haunted me for the millionth time. But instead of warmth, realization smacked me in the face. Dorian had accepted my broken body once before, but could he do it again? The thought paralyzed me and my chest ached.

The visitor slammed the door, and I breathed, thanking God for the reprieve.

Measuring time was difficult. While my scenery had altered from Boric's personal quarters to a storage room, his visits continued unabated. Salty sweat and excrement coated my skin. Funny, but I'd give anything to spend another week or so on the road with Dorian, sans the bathing.

Cross stuffed a bag over my head, obscuring my vision, but the exhaust and loud engines told me we were still flying. Overnight, the air had seemingly warmed, too, the heat penetrating the hood. Years had passed since I last saw the summery, dry lands of Garland, Texas.

Chains shifted, rattling. My screaming muscles gave out, and I fell onto the mattress. Stars littered behind my clenched eyelids.

"Get up," Cross commanded.

My limbs wouldn't obey, but a groan slipped free from my parched lips. Opening and closing my mouth, words refused to release. His rough hands grasped my shoulders and lifted me halfway before another set of hands, their owner unknown, grabbed my legs.

"Set him upright. No special treatment." Softness touched Cross's tone.

Unlike many of the others, he never visited me. It didn't mean he hadn't beaten me, humiliated me, or tried to stop his master, but he'd never defiled me. I should've been thankful for the small miracle, yet I wasn't.

"C'mon," Cross said, kicking my leg.

Chains rattling, I stumbled down a staircase, and the scent changed from stuffy, dusty room to sweaty men to moist air tainted with exhaust and perfume. Soft, feminine whispers halted midsentence.

We stopped. Guards—I assumed—stripped and tore the ratted clothing from my body. They ripped the hood from my head, and strong arms lifted me. Boric grinned, his eyes raking over my filthy form. Cross grabbed my hands and raised them into the air before he fastened the chains, hanging me by my wrists from the rafters.

My gaze wandered, blinking in the strange luminance of the large space. Black iron bars lined and cordoned off cells. Women, children, and men filled them, but they didn't speak. I wondered if they were the lost souls Dorian had spoken about.

Shackles cut into my tender skin. Ulcers had erupted from the forced position on the bed and burned into my knees, elbows, and thighs. But I gulped and trained my attention on small, hexagon windows lining the space. Blue sky and white clouds surrounded us, yet freedom wasn't mine. "Hold on," Korrigan had said. But each day another piece of me died. Would there be any part of me left for Dorian to love?

"I'm tired of your games," Boric grumbled in my ear, his hand stroking me in front of the crowd.

My face heated, but my body rejected his touch.

"You'll end up like your sister if you don't tell me where the bloody keys are," he thought, directing it to me.

Cross grasped my feet and tugged while my shoulders stretched upward. A cry rippled through my gritted teeth.

"Again," Boric yelled. "More weight. This is what happens when you steal from me."

"You call this punishment? You call this pain?" I forced a smile, clenching my teeth. After what he'd done to an innocent boy's spirit and heart, the makeshift rack was nothing.

The guards grumbled; some offered sympathetic looks. I glanced left and right. Colored blurs stained my vision.

I felt *her*. And then, I saw *her*. Dark curls framed her delicate, freckled features. *Sweet Lilith, I've found you at last.* My gaze snapped upward, and her mouth dropped, color draining her cheeks. Folded around the iron bars were her pale, thin hands. My head shook, but my grin spread, widening over my lips. *Boric doesn't know. I must hold on and not give in to his humiliating stunts.*

All grown-up, Lily was no longer a little girl, but her light illuminated all the shadows of my cruel world. Like a beacon of hope flashing and guiding me.

Cross attached more weight to my legs, stretching my muscles to their limits. Skin and muscles burned, tremored, and convulsed. Tears filled my eyes.

"More," Boric commanded.

Cross hesitated and glanced from Boric to me.

"It'll be you up there next, you bastard."

Cross added another weight, and I swore he whispered, "Sorry, kid."

Another scream ripped through another until the pain had guided my weary soul into the darkness. No flashing, golden light carried my blackened soul home. Minutes, hours, or days passed, throbbing agony suspended me in limbo. My mind tumbled through the nightmare of my life.

A tender voice called to me, beckoning me awake.

"Psst. Cain."

Refocusing, my eyes blinked. Lavender light encircled my skin, and a blue and coppery essence joined it. Warmth and tingles spread over my body; their magic eased my injuries. But the prisoners and I were alone, and I still hung from the ceiling, tethered by my ankles.

"Thank you," I whispered in a hoarse tone, and my gaze focused on a woman who could've been my sister. Hair, inky and dark, fell loose around her shoulders. Unlike the others, she wore tight pants. Why I noticed this detail was beyond me, but I zeroed in on her and the blue magic shooting from her fingertips, combining with Lilith's lavender and copper, and spreading over my body.

The ship puttered and rocked. Prisoners murmured while their gazes darted, and my heart raced. Were we under attack?

"We're landing," Lily replied.

Ah, so she had manifested powers after all.

The waiting game remained in place. But could I hold out? Because no way in hell Boric's torture was ending on this ship.

No, the torture had only just begun, but I had hope. I had my sister. But above all, Dorian loved me, scarred and broken, and I loved him, shattered heart and skeletor persona. The latter thought rose a chuckle from within, and my hands clutched its warmth.

Chapter Seventeen

Dorian

Korrigan, Veric, Petre, and his goons dropped from their hiding spots among the treetops. I stared, mouth gaping, at the departing airship. Where the hell were they? We could have stood a chance with Petre and Korrigan's speed. My nails bit into my palms and drew slick crimson blood.

"Boric's onboard," Veric said, the airship disappearing from view.

Already, I had broken my promise, but waltzing into Delphia or Garland without a plan was suicide for Cain. My eyes closed and a tear slipped down my cheek. A tiny voice said maybe it was for the best, but I shook the thought aside. Cain loved me, and I loved him.

"What's the plan, mate?" Veric stepped in front of me.

My fist slammed into his chest. Now? Now, he wants to put me in charge!

Colored lights flashed as Fauna, Markos, and Hallo appeared in a rainbow soiree of red, gold, and lavender. "Take out the ship," Markos said, his gaze scanning the stars. "Let's be done with it."

I pivoted and lifted my fist, but my brother caught my hand. My teeth ground, and a growl ripped free. "Are you insane? Cain's on there."

Markos shoved me aside, and I stumbled, landing on my ass.

Korrigan stepped forward. Child-sized, she clenched her hands and pounded on his chest, sending him flying into the barn door. Metal rattled. "Innocents are on board, you idiot."

Fauna said, "Collateral damage."

Korri lunged for my sister, clawing at her. No one stopped her and she tore at them.

"You're a feisty one." Markos laughed.

Korrigan didn't relent, gouging deep gashes into Fauna before jumping on him, fangs audibly sinking into his neck. I cringed as she tore a hunk of his flesh and spat it out. He shouted, his wound turning black before lightening to his natural olive tone.

Petre and Veric watched in staggered stages of horror and amusement. Veric jogged over, head shaking, and ripped her free. "You can't kill the Archangels of War and Pestilence, luv."

She hissed, scratching at him to get back to her prey.

"You will not kill my brother." I shook my head, my eyes blinking. "He won't kill yours. No one is blowing up anything... yet." I sighed at the twinkling stars shining through the lingering exhaust plumes. "Fauna, retrieve Belle and Tomas."

She nodded, disappearing before I had a chance to remark on her lack of clothing. Hallo placed a hand on my shoulder, but I glanced at Petre.

"Veric." I snapped my fingers, but my attention remained on the vampire staring after the steamship, as if its presence were igniting a memory. "Fetch Jan and whatever she needs. Petre," his gray eyes shifted to me, "needs his memory righted, now. We depart for Montreal as soon as Fauna arrives."

In the large abandoned farmhouse, I slept alone and hated it. Unshed tears assaulted me in waves while my mind replayed the evening's events, searching for a way I could've prevented Cain's kidnapping. From taking a shot to calling my siblings...Why hadn't we listened to the warning and fled? Would it have made a difference? One more day on the road and maybe we would have missed them. If only we hadn't turned around...

I palmed my face. "If only I had let you go." My hand slid down my neck and settled on my key. If only I'd had the cods to end the world.

The bedroom door creaked and a soft glow entered. Hallo said, "I sense your despair."

"Can't you blink on board and take him back?"

"It's moving... if I knew the layout." Blonde hair tumbled into her face, head shaking. "What happens if I blink into an engine or a wall?" Warm fingers stroked my hair, and her calm settled into my soul.

Bile scorched my throat and my fingers curled into my palms. "I won't forgive... if Garland touches him, I will kill him."

"That's not your destiny." She stroked my brow.

I snorted. "Fuck destiny."

"Cain is strong. About that, I have no doubts, but the secret he keeps threatens us all. Rest, Brother. Father will protect your love. With any luck he will aid us."

"The Archangels—"

"Don't you dare. Sleep, we'll talk come morning."

My eyes closed; I tossed my arm across them. No dreams came and we didn't convene that night. Cain's smiling face greeted me until the morning rays peeked through the curtains and revealed the nightmare of my existence. He wasn't there.

Fauna hadn't arrived, but we hit the road anyway. Elioud leaped into the skies, white wings replacing clouds, except for Veric's inky stain. Korrigan didn't have wings and neither did Petre—he wouldn't have them as a former human. As the four Horsemen, we had mounts, and although seldom summoned, our three-day trek was narrowed down to one by horseback. I closed my eyes and reached for the tethered connection to my horse, mentally tugging its reigns.

Green, red, and white: one by one, the three horses crunched through the snow, their snorts creating giant puffs of frozen breath.

They rested before us and Korrigan gasped.

Mark grasped the red horse's reigns, Hallo reached for the white horse, and I nuzzled my pale horse. Petre's eyes lit and he tilted his head before petting my horse.

"Do you ride?" I asked him.

He bowed his head. "Yes, I think I owned horses." Petre glanced to Korrigan, who nodded.

Korrigan rode with me, clasping her tiny hands to my sides. Her arms were too short to encompass my waist. Vampires required no sleep, so there was no fear of a fall. Even if she had, she would have healed. Petre rode with Hallo and held a pinched face.

We stormed east into the morning sun, tackling the frozen, Arcadian tundra, stopping only when the Eliouds' wings could carry them no farther.

"Sorry, mate, but there's not enough horses." Veric and his men perched on an oak tree.

I nodded and reassured him, understanding their limitations. We still hadn't spoken about his tattoo, but it didn't change the fact his men were Elioud. At least Eliouds required less sleep than humans, and in the Witches Hour, we bounded out again.

Urging my mount faster, farther along the sightless trail, I saw nothing, cared for nothing, except Cain, and tasted zilch, but the bitter defeat of our situation and my guilt at failing him. He always laughed about my alpha tendencies and over protectiveness, but… my eyes shut; my head shook and a branch scratched my face. My sweaty hands gripped the leather controls, snapping them against the pale horse and driving him.

Feelings and guilt could wait. Revenge was nigh.

Metal clanked and steam rose on the fiery horizon. Steam engines whistled. I reared my horse, rounding as the others caught up.

Korrigan's nails bit into my hips, her hold tightening. Montreal loomed before us in iron frames and sun-glaring glass jutting into the sky. The first rays of light glittered from the east. An empty beauty without Cain to share the scene with.

Korrigan patted my side. "You love him."

Not a question, but I answered, "Yes."

"Even though he kept secrets?"

Her final word twisted me in the saddle. "We aired our secrets."

Korrigan eyed the ground.

I whispered, "Cain promised." But I'd already assumed he was still keeping secrets.

The others trotted behind, and wings beat overhead. Landing, Veric said, "He promised her too. Cain promised Angelica first."

Korrigan slid from the saddle before I could stop her, settling without a sound. Powdery snow kicked into my face. My eyes blinked at her form sprinting toward the city. Veric yelled and raced after her.

"What the fuck was that about?" My putrid horse neighed, and I steadied him.

"Dorian?" Mark's fingers snapped in my face.

But I ignored my brother, instead observing a sulking Korrigan, and a scowling Veric shoving her from behind, bounding toward me. No Elioud could have caught up to a vampire.

All attention trained on her before shifting to me. She halted at my feet, but studied the ground. I dismounted, placing hands to hips, and loomed over her. "You will explain," I grumbled. "You too," I added, pointing to Veric. "I know what you are."

Her skinny arms crossed over her frilly Bo Peep dress, and her chin lifted.

"Damn it, woman, swallow your pride, and tell me the bloody truth! What's Cain still hiding from me?"

"Cain still has the keys," she whispered.

I didn't understand. "No. I know that."

Amber eyes didn't falter. My palm rubbed over my face while I glanced to Hallo and Markos. Jaws slack, both shook their heads.

"Shite." I never removed them from his possession, and Boric had them because he had Cain. My hand lifted and Korrigan flinched, but I simply wiped the snow from my eyes. Did she think I would hit her?

Crunching sounded behind us. Markos guided his red horse closer. In a gentler voice, he asked, "How many keys does the Keeper have?"

Hallo followed suit and stopped to my right. I lifted one, two, three, and my fourth finger. Cain had them all, but the ones around my neck.

Korrigan giggled and shook her wind-tangled hair. "He still has them all, Dorian." Korrigan fluttered her lashes. "I wouldn't be surprised if he has yours."

I palmed my neck and withdrew my chain. No, my key was still there, but the one Cain had given me was gone.

"He didn't give you a real one."

"Boric," Veric said. "That's why... he knew Cain had the keys... how?"

Hallo leaned back in her saddle and asked, "Who knew he had them?"

"Has," I whispered, shrugging. Did Tomas know? "He has them." Bitter bile filled me, and my burning eyes closed. As if the depths of Hell knew my nightmares, they came alive, swirling at my feet. My stomach lurched, expelling the tainted substance churning in my gut.

"Oi, Dorian, get yourself together."

"Gross," Korrigan said.

"You alright, mate?"

Their voices rattled in my shaking head.

"He wanted to tell you," Korrigan muttered. "To give them back to you. Cain tried the night they stole him."

I winced recalling his reluctance. Had he been trying to say goodbye?

"He planned on giving them to you. All of them, Dorian. He... Once he knew Lily was safe, he—"

"He's the Keeper." The red horse snorted at Mark's gruff tone. "He's supposed to keep the damned keys."

I spun my horse around and urged the steed west of Montreal. Weaknesses exposed and tears caught in my beard. Betrayal surrounded me, and I trusted nothing but my own heart. Once again, Cain had lied, but I forgave him. Boric stole him. Cain nicked my heart. He held all the damned keys. Boric knew. How did he know? Cain held the final piece, the knowledge of my key around. Boric would torture him until he had cracked, splintering him, and only shards would remain before he set his sights on me.

Screw Petre and his memories.

I had to save Cain, but first to find a way into Garland. Faster than possible for a normal horse, the pale beast galloped. My skin turned to ash and swept across the pristine snow. Clothes tattered and the silver robe shimmered to life. Bone and scythe emerged and Death rose. Laughter echoed from my hollowed soul.

Killing Cain wasn't an option. Boric needed the keys. I held that fact close to my blackened heart.

"'Ăḇaddōn," in Hebrew, I commanded the vortex forever following me to manifest. Shades swirled and screamed as Sheol appeared before me, taking shape of an ominous graveyard. Black-iron gates opened before me and swallowed us whole.

I entered the first level of Purgatory. Darkness didn't exist. Fire and magma spun and spurted. Balls of mist floated. Distraught faces battled and faced their sins. Pale horse's hooves clobbered over the hardened lava stones as we ascended.

Purgatory housed seven levels, and each level brought more ear piercing shrieks. I closed my eyes and allowed their pain to radiate against my bones, but I hadn't condemned them to this torture. No, Father had only selected me as their judge and protector, but they had chosen their own sinful lives.

I sighed and departed the final level. My heart ached, but I entered the realm of infants. Children's laughter and babies' coos reached my ears. Balls of light fluttered, bounced, and flew about the glittering cavern. The lost ethereals played. Aborted and those young, unbaptized souls rested in my domain, but they didn't suffer. Knowing neither hunger nor pain, Father's light reached them there.

A grim smile pressed my lips, but I surged onward toward the next set of waiting gates.

Tartarus.

Quakes vibrated through me.

His power rolled like a sonic boom. "Hallo Death," he said.

I halted my pale horse, inclining my head at the Archangel's royal blue aura surrounding the highest level of Sheol.

"What brings you? Do you need me again?"

I shook my head. "Michael, I need to see Lucifer."

"Why?" His aura shrank, and I shielded my eyes until the Archangel Michael re-formed on the stone floor in his golden armor. He ran fingers through his cropped golden curls. His sword swung with his pacing steps.

I didn't glance away and fixated on my brother-in-arms. Breath escaped my clenched teeth. I didn't have time for explanations. He was always difficult.

"You can't just—"

All roads led to the Morning Star's line. "He has answers." I dismounted, my feet clacking and echoing from the marble walls. "His line on Earth will soon see eradication if we don't intervene."

Without flinching at my skeletor form, Michael spat, "What do you care of demons and their spawn?"

"I love them." My bones clicked against stone, my scythe scratching along the ground behind me. Michael towered over me, but I was Death, 'Ăḇaddōn, and ruler of Sheol and my swarm of vampires. His domain merely rested within mine. I pointed my bony fingertip at his chest, my shoulders and skeletal wings pinned back.

He brushed my hand away and curled his lip in disgust. "They're creatures that even Father cannot tolerate, yet you love them?" Michael flexed his full, white seraphim wings. "Death cannot love, Dorian Fox. Angels cannot love."

But we had. I cocked my brow. At one time or another, each of the Horsemen had loved another, and the bitterness Michael spouted said he, too, had loved before. But having loved or not mattered little. I had to see Lucifer. My arms crossed over my chest, hugging the scythe to my robe.

Michael sighed and stepped aside. "Father won't like this. Tread carefully. I'd hate to see you in there one day."

Yet the Elioud ascended there when they died. I didn't collect their souls, though, nor the demons. Father created my kind for marking humans. I eased through the iron gate, but Michael's warm hand stopped me.

"Dorian, I mean it."

For a moment, I stared into his icy eyes.

"Love isn't worth the sacrifice of Heaven and eternal glory."

The memory of Cain's laughter filled my ears. Flashes of his smiling eyes danced before me. Bone-radiating warmth, quickened breath, and fluttering heart. The hardness of his flesh and the flavor of his fire were worth the threat of Tartarus. Eternal pain and memories, albeit short, without him were purgatory. If I damned myself, the promise of forever… my bony hand patted Michael's shoulder. Fear of unending prison or torture was worth saving Cain… the price of love knew no bounds.

"We all have to do our part. I am failing Father in controlling the demons. The Horsemen have failed, brother."

He dragged our foreheads together. "Then, do not enter the gates, ask for my assistance. You've done so a hundred times before, my brother. What halts you now?"

Weakness, failure, Hallo, and so many other excuses popped into my mind, but it was my pride. The ABDA thought me the best extractor, but all this time I had enlisted the aid of other Archangels in rescuing the unreachable demons in the south.

My brethren didn't know the lengths I had gone to in order to save the others. Vanity blinded me, but I had to free them… the death, the destruction… my blackened soul didn't deserve ascension, and rescuing others was all I could do to wash the horrors away. Pride turned the tables.

My fingers curled into Michael's collar, and I collapsed against his chest. His arms righted me and held my bony face within his hands.

"He's my lover. I'm in love... with him."

"Bloody hell, Dorian, what else?"

"And he holds the keys. He's the Keeper."

Michael's eyes brightened. "How could you be so foolish," he said through clenched teeth. "Does he have them all?"

"I don't know, yes... He doesn't have mine."

"Change back at once. You know I hate seeing the bones, and you stink." Michael waved his hand, releasing his blue magic. Clothing manifested in his palm. He handed me the fresh garments, but spoke little. Turning away from me, his magic engulfed his body. Essence clearing, he wore normal clothes, but a sword still hung from his belt. Two guns protruded from his waistband. Knives graced his thighs, hidden in holsters.

"Arm up," he muttered, tossing me two Colt .45's, and I slipped them into a holster he supplied. "Where are they?"

"Airship." I glanced around the main foyer. He'd set it up as a home away from home, complete with a sofa, table, and various chairs. Either he was meeting with others here, or he was letting someone out when I wasn't around. I didn't visit as often as I should have.

"Shite." Blond brows creased with concern. "I can't transport us onto a moving object." Michael rubbed his forehead. "Too risky. We could end up in a wall or in the bleedin' engine, and that's if we're lucky."

"Hallo said the same." The lump swelling in my throat stopped me from swallowing and I nodded. Prison walls spun, and my aching body dissolved into the sofa. My shoulders rolled forward. Cain: I spoke to him, prayed for him, and hoped he held the strength to hold on until we reached him. "How long?"

"It's not the fact you love him that qualms me, Dorian..."

Ignoring him, I stared at my trembling hands. Wincing, I felt Cain... his pain seared through me. It had to be him, and the thought of Boric inflicting the damage curled my fists. Silent tears fell, gurgled, and choked. My heart hammered and puttered.

"You've thought of the alternative?"

"Trust me... I do want to go home... not like that. Not... yet." What I didn't say was the actual truth. If I had Cain for eternity, why would I want to go home? He encompassed everything once associated with Heaven. My body curled, shivered, and trembled.

Michael sat next to me. "I do understand more than others believe. You were right, you know. I loved before, still love her madly, but Father forbade us from pursuing our relationship." Soft words flowed from the seraph's lips, though the meanings were tainted.

Bitter laughter ripped through my throat, and blue eyes blinked, as if I had gone mad.

"Dorian, Dorian, you better not be where I think you are." Hallo's shrilled voice screamed in my head.

Her pleas fell short. Whatever past Hallo and Michael had was none of my business, but this predicament affected us all.

"We need your help," my dry lips whispered. "Do the others share your opinion?" I leaned up and ran a hand over my scruffy beard. If the other Archangels, Father had assigned to Earth, wanted the world to remain ours, we could band together, drive the south back, and have our little slice of life for eternity. But we had to join forces; the ABDA was not enough. Korrigan wasn't enough. I needed the Council of Seven at my disposal as well.

"Most," Michael said. "Rag won't like this. Certainly not Metatron."

Raguel was the self-appointed leader of the Seven Archangels on Earth and had deemed them as the new Watchers, replacing the original Grigori. Metatron was their actual leader, but he'd stayed in Heaven. Instead of watching over the humans, they watched over the choirs of Angels living among the demons, witches, warlocks, vampires, and the ABDA. I never thought to ask why, but doubted it was a punishment. What other choice would Rag have, but to side with me?

Hallowed's voice reverberated again, hissing her displeasure. Bright, white illumination flashed, and her tall, delicate form winked into view. "I told you not to do this," she said, shaking her finger in my face.

"It wasn't your decision to make," Michael replied, standing. He was right since I led the Horsemen of the Apocalypse. "Nice to see you too, Hal."

Hallo shoved her nose into the air and crossed her arms over her chest. "Well, I'm here to talk some sense into my brother." Red and green light followed her words, announcing the arrival of Fauna and Markos.

I hung my head and shook it. "They cannot be here. Sheol is not a fucking country club. Leave now," I spat. They were not alone, my fists clenched.

Multiple sets of eyes blinked at me. Arguments erupted, and I covered my ears. Everyone but Cain stood in my domain. I sat back on the couch.

"A human?" Michael rose and stood before Nicolai.

Wide eyes turned toward me, and I shrugged. We didn't have time for this debacle ... distraction. They should not be in my abode ... the walls of the damned ... Sheol was for the dead and its protectors.

Michael's brows twisted, and his mouth dropped as he stared at the last man in all of humanity. "Fascinating... I must—"

"Tell no one," I said. "He's mine," I pointed to the mark on his neck, "see for yourself."

Michael nodded as Nicolai's body trembled under our combined scrutiny. The bastard could die for all I cared, but the Archangels would do God knew what with him. Angels were always fascinated with humanity. Korrigan's brow rose; Veric stared, stunned into silence, while Tomas jabbered, pointing to the beveled iron gates behind me. Had Hallowed, Fauna, and Markos forgotten the tour? The entrance of Tartarus was the least fascinating part of Sheol.

Circling, like a vulture, Michael held his chin. Nicolai straightened his shoulders, his dark hair pulled away from his reddening face. Petre eased forward and slipped in front of his brother. Rolling my eyes, I leaned against the sofa, laughing. Everyone was there, except Cain, from Veric's agents to my siblings. So much for Father's rules.

Tomas strolled the perimeter of the large room, muttering to himself. Veric's agents did what most agents do best: nadda. Fauna and Mark spoke in low tones and stole glances at Hallo and Michael. Had I missed something? Probably, though, the question should've been, did I care? Not really.

Shifting my legs, I levered myself from the couch, and long, lazy strides brought me before the identical twins—save for their scars, builds, and eye color. My arms crossed and my brow rose, waiting for one of them to speak.

Silence won over their attentions, and all gazes turned to the wiry Petre and beefier Nicolai Von Baron. Their choices in life reflected more—one a pompous lord and the other a man of the cloth. Petre faced his brother. Blue and gray eyes blinked at one another before the twins settled into a glaring contest. Black brows twisted, as if Petre was recalling something, but of course, I couldn't read his mind.

As his lips parted, my breath held.

"You... this is your fault." Petre patted his chest, his heart. "You cursed us... You murderer..." A low growl rumbled from within him, and furor sparked in his eyes. "Korri! Where is she?" He spun around, his gaze scanning the room.

Korrigan eased from behind Veric, but eyed the marble floor. Wetness shimmered and reflected on her pale cheeks, illuminated by the sconces lining the walls.

"Korri," he yelled, spinning and searching the crowd once more. "Angel—my Angel. What have you done with her?"

The demanding shrill in his voice sent shivers along my skin. She trembled and stared at her hands. Michael whispered, but I didn't catch his words. The scene before me transfixed my attention. Love conquered and hope bloomed inside of me. Slowly, my breath released.

Petre shouted her name again. Korrigan blinked. His breath caught, their gazes connecting. Along his cheeks, wet streaks glistened into the valley of his scars.

Thomas strolled to her side and nudged her. Pain etched over Veric's twisted face, and his hands rose, hiding the evidence. In a way, my heart broke for him.

"What's happening," Michael whispered.

I waved him off. "Love, this is love, Brother."

Petre broke the spell without anyone's help. Two for two? I didn't know how, nor did I care. Emptiness encompassed me. Again, I held my breath; my hand habitually seeking for Cain, but my empty grip reminded me where he was, and a tear slid free.

Korrigan managed a small step forward. Petre grinned wide, bearing his fangy smile.

"Angel." Petre cupped her face

My hand rubbed my heart, and I spun around, retreating to the couch.

Nicolai's chin jutted into the air. "Always the naïve one," he snorted, "look at you now. Love sick and broken by a whore."

"Big words," Michael said, and chuckled, "for the only human in a room of God's deadly assassins. Tell me, Nicolai. Are your cods as large? Made of brass?"

My head hung, supported by my hands. His amusing truth didn't tickle my bones. I clenched my eyes shut; fists closed tightly, drawing warm blood from my palms. Petre kissed Korrigan's head. Veric bit his lip, but nodded his acceptance. Two agents shadowed him, watching and waiting for his orders, but none came. A single tear slid down his cheek. *No dry eyes in the place.*

"He is mine."

I blinked; the words hadn't left my lips. My empty hand squeezed the air again, wishing for Cain's presence to fill the gap.

The three Horsemen stepped forward, joining Michael and me. Tomas muttered about the bare room and snapped his fingers.

Chairs appeared, and he took his seat, motioning for the others to sit. He leaned on his cane. A smirk flashed across his goggled face, but my jaw only clenched.

Concern and curiosity crossed my sibling's faces. I scanned the small crowd searching for Belle. She too deserved a spot next to me. Her lithe form eased from behind the ABDA guards, and I motioned her forward.

Introductions proved tricky since the Archangels often sneered at the Elioud. Belle's high-heeled steps echoed in the room, and rising from the couch, I stole a side-glance at the Michael.

A different tension entered the marbled room, one I knew all too well. A smirk played on Markos' lips as Belle halted. Large, red eyes lifted. Michael reached for her hand and brought it to his lips. Markos' smirk melted into a tight scowl.

"You didn't tell me how beautiful your junior was."

Crimson blush filled her cheeks.

"Absolutely breathtaking." Michael released her hand, but Belle froze.

I swallowed my laughter, chuckling under my breath.

"Sorry, poppet, didn't mean to embarrass you. Always a pleasure to meet one of Lucifer's children."

Markos grumbled.

Belle swallowed, opened her mouth, but she shook her head. "Thank you," she managed to whisper.

Archangels held a beauty to them in appearance and voice, but our power was humbling in an awestruck way few truly understood. The Horsemen were Archangels, too, and like our brothers and sisters-in-arms, we all served a purpose.

I motioned for Belle to sit. "Moving on to business... We, the Four Horsemen of the Apocalypse are officially asking the Seven Watchers to intervene and form an alliance with the Arcadian government. Veric." I motioned to him, and he stepped forward. "Represents the Arcadian Bureau of Demonic Affairs. Tomas stands as the Witches and Warlock council. Petre will lead my vampires."

Michael whispered, "And the Light Bringer?"

Korrigan whirled around.

"I'm getting there… Korrigan… I propose will lead us all."

Dark hair shook around her cherub face and her lips parted. She didn't believe in herself, but I expected the reaction and nodded. Petre kissed her temple, but Korrigan's temper flared into white knuckled fists and a stony stature.

Michael said, "Rag won't go for that without seeing her." Pointing at her, his finger curled and summoned her forward. Korrigan didn't budge. "She needs work… so much defiance and spark. Are they all this way?"

I chuckled. Yeah, every last one of them. Like a spitfire waiting to explode. Cain was the same way. I glanced to Belle, then to Tomas. They all held Westcott blood… Lucifer's blood.

Michael shrugged. "Father made us choose the strongest and the most benevolent to fall. Is it any wonder his children are the strongest willed?" The smile in his voice twisted my spine. Our gazes met. "No, I think not. Wait here while I summon the others."

Michael's blue aura flashed, and we shielded our eyes. The others muttered quietly among themselves, but Tomas, Veric, and Hallowed chatted with vivid and hardened expressions. Their whispers reached all ears, including mine. Petre and Korrigan sat in the corner, intertwined, staring into each other's eyes and ignoring everyone else; their lips moved.

Keeping time with every beat, my finger tapped. "None of this would've happened if I let him go."

"You don't know that." Belle touched my thigh and squeezed.

Markos leaned over us. "She's right, Dorian. You made the only decision you could."

I glanced away, hugging myself tight. "I let them take him anyway." Laughter shook my shoulders. Figuring people out was my forte, but for the life of me, I couldn't figure a way to get Cain away from them. Past extraction missions weren't as hands on. Sometimes, I knocked out a guard or two, but there'd been too many at the farmhouse, and the others had hid in the trees, like cowards.

"We'll get him back, boss. Right, Mark?"

Mark? My brother gulped. He hated anyone shortening his name, hence why I did it.

"Right." His hand slid behind Belle and patted my shoulder.

Maybe I was a shitty extraction agent, but I could still read a room or situation. I saw no way to safely rescue Cain from the Garland. Even with an alliance, we weren't ready to take Garland down by force. But I couldn't push Cain to the back burner and ignore the swollen ache rising inside of me. I grasped Michael's sword. My fingers curled around the silver hilt. My feet tapped against the marble. Tears threatened to drown me from the inside out if we didn't move soon.

Patience is not my virtue.

My eyes closed, and my mind reached for a memory. The first time I saw Cain when he'd strode through the door. My breath had caught, heat surging and coursing through my body, electrifying me from within. The rise of my belly had etched into my brain. His butterscotch eyes had captured me. Emotions I couldn't have handled had reflected and overwhelmed my entire being. Love at first sight: the humans had called it, and I never believed until Cain reappeared and everything rushed over me.

Belle brushed my arm and brought reality crashing back. Bloodshot eyes cried. Silence trickled across the waiting room. All gazes switched their focus on me. There it was. My weakness, my heart all laid out, and I bowed my head, burying my face into my hands. Without Cain, I was nothing more than a pussy-whipped asshole.

"No," Korrigan shouted; her words reverberated from the walls. "Tears are no weakness."

Remiel's voice thundered. "The Light Bringer is correct." His black hair fluffed in the breeze as he entered my abode, dressed in black from head to toe. Service weapons and his shiny, silver badge hung from his muscled body. Many of the Archangels also worked for the ABDA, heading or teaching the various departments. His hands hid behind his back.

Remy surveyed us; his icy gaze settled on Korrigan. "You," he said, and pointed to her. "You." Belle next, followed by Tomas. "And you." Remy ushered them aside. "You are pride." He claimed Petre as sloth, Veric as envy, to which he rolled his eyes, and his cronies became greed. That left Nicolai, who had said nothing since his jibe. "You are a disgrace… but if I must… lust suits you." Remy turned to me and grinned. "Dorian, did you enjoy my game?"

I glared at him and assumed my siblings did the same. "Did Michael speak with you?"

He nodded, clasping his hands to his front.

"And?"

"Of course, he's in," Saraqael said, her red fire scorching the floor. As usual, she wore a pantsuit. Unlike the others, her position in the ABDA was a technical role—she handled logistics and tech. Deadly in the field, she preferred computers, phones, and gadgets to guns. Still, her cheery smile was always a welcome sight. "As am I, though, I'm probably already up to speed." Her boyfriend was my liaison.

"And I'm always up for killing some bloody fucking scum," Gabriel stated, storming into the room. His angular features solidified, as if becoming stone, and his bi-colored, blue and gray, eyes pierced me. Also dressed in the standard ABDA uniform, Gabe stood by Sara, arms crossed over his broad chest.

He had a story, as did most of us, but it wasn't mine to tell. However, few liked him, and even fewer understood the broody and brash Archangel who had once been Father's faithful messenger to humanity. Perhaps I sympathized with him best. Like him, my purpose had altered the moment the humans had died.

One by one, the Seven Archangels arrived. The last two were Michael and Raguel. His opinion and blessing mattered, and his gaze immediately jumped to Korrigan. "Interesting…"

"Hallo, Fauna, and Mark, can you take everyone elsewhere?"

"Not everyone," Rag said, flicking dust from his shirt. "Take the filthy human away. The agents can debrief as well. Headquarters should do."

My siblings removed Nicolai and the ABDA agents to safety.

Tomas clasped his hands together. "This won't do." His magic swirled at the room's center, and the seating he'd summoned before blinked from the space. In its place, a large table and leather, executive chairs manifested.

Rag cleared his throat and glared at him.

I had one chance to win Rag over and by the frozen sneer painted on his delicate features; it wasn't an easy task. My stomach churned. Everyone else grabbed a chair, but I remained standing. Drumming my fingers against the wooden table, I searched for the words, pushing thoughts of Cain aside. My lips parted.

Rag said, "No."

"No?" I blinked.

"She's not ready, Dorian."

Petre smacked the table and said, "I'll make her ready."

Rag smirked. "You can't train her, vampire." He pointed to Veric. "But he can." His tone said he knew exactly who Veric truly was.

"Whatever's necessary," Veric said, "but ducky might feel more comfortable with another bloke."

Tomas's brows rose, and he whispered, "Rag wants an Elioud to train her?"

"He's not an Elioud," I said, staring at Veric. "None of the Garland family are Elioud, are they?"

Murmurs spread around the table. I didn't doubt the discovery, but I had one question. Why hide? From the moment I met Veric... he wielded power too great for an Elioud. The tattoo cemented my belief. Almost too great for Nephilim, but he wasn't evil.

Veric's head bowed, and his shoulders rolled forward. "Millennia we remained hidden," he whispered, and tilted his ginger head. "I'd like to point out that Boric and I rarely saw eye-to-eye, then or now..." Veric turned to Petre. "Remember when I asked you about Asmodeus back in Delphia?"

I froze at the name we seldom used for Boric anymore. Prince of Lechery—one of the original watchers and the first to spread his seed among the humans—ruled over sexual desires. No man or woman could resist him, but that didn't mean him charming. Boric took what he wanted; he stole my Cain.

Petre's black brows creased. "In Delphia, yes."

"That is Boric's real name." Veric rose and met Rag's curious stare. "You know who I am, my brothers and sisters."

"Azazel." His tone seethed. "Although, Raphael will need to explain how it is you are among us and not in Hell." Rag's attention drifted. The Archangel leaned on his staff; black hair framed his pale face.

"I tied him, but freed him after Remy had a vision," Raphael said, motioning to Remiel. "He's been undercover with us ever since. I sent a memo."

Rag's eyes narrowed on Veric. "You should be locked away, burning for eternity, like Father sentenced you." Azazel had given humans weaponry, magic, and taught them war. Father hadn't wanted this for his humans; it led to sin. "Tartarus is too good for you, but I have half the mind to march you into a cell this moment."

Veric gulped and nodded. But I disagreed with Rag and opened my mouth.

"I take full responsibility," Remy stood, "but my visions are never wrong, and Azazel has been a powerful asset, both before and after. Like most of the fallen, he is misunderstood, but his heart belongs to our father."

Politics... All talk and no action... I shook my head. We needed to save Cain, not mosey down memory lane. Would there be any good news at this gathering? So far, they'd remembered Boric was a damned fallen angel—a damned Prince of fucking Hell. Vital information that would've been nice to have.

"Who was Jules?" Korrigan asked. "He couldn't have been your father."

Veric whispered, "Jules was Boric's son. Asmodeus is bisexual with a stronger attraction toward men, toward one man in particular, your brother."

"Shite." I tore a hand through my hair. "Anyone else have a bomb to drop, or can we get my boyfriend back now?" I kicked my chair and it skidded backward. I gripped the tabletop. As the seat smashed against the marble, a crash resonated and echoed from the walls.

Rag thudded the table with his hand and said, "Grow up, Dorian."

Heaving for breath, I scowled at him. Heat creeped along my neck. "I will not grow up. I don't give a shit about politics." I clawed at my neck, ripping the key free, and tossed it on the table. It clattered before resting. "Either we shut the hell up and rescue Cain, or I will destroy us all."

"Michael and Raphael will accompany you. The rest of us will head to Anchorage."

Gabriel glowered, muttering to himself.

"Fine, take the watchdog too, but keep a leash on him, Dorian. We don't need to wipe out any innocents, yeah?" The remaining Archangels each grasped a hand, and white light flooded the small space.

A flash of copper light shimmered before Gabriel manifested in front of me. "Sorry, Dorian but you know how Rag gets. We had to do this by the book. But chin up. We're a go, yeah?" His tone bordered between cheery and excited.

"You wasted time... time that Cain doesn't have." My knees slumped to the floor, and my head followed.

Gabe's hands grasped me and hefted me up.

Michael said, "You can't fall apart on us now. Let's go, my brother."

"Where? How? You said you can't blink on a ship."

Michael and Gabe shared a strange glance.

"What aren't you telling me?" My hardening bones pressed against my skin.

"Calm down... It's..."

Gabe interjected, "Time moves differently outside of Sheol. Garland should've landed by now... in Texas..."

"What do you mean by now? How long has it been?"

"Weeks," Michael whispered. "Give or take."

"As minutes ticked into hours inside of Sheol, those hours had ticked into days on Earth," Gabe added. "No one argues that time wasn't wasted, but let's not squander anymore. Time to armor up."

Chapter Eighteen

Cain

The airship had halted, engines died. Guards, dressed in green, entered the makeshift prison. Hinges groaned their sorrowful tunes. An unknown guard barked, "Move it."

They emptied each cell of its precious cargo. Meaty paws gripped and shoved my sister, Lily, and her friend. I bit my tongue. Their magic eased my pain for a bit, but it didn't heal the gaping wounds covering my body. Gaze averted, she whispered my name. But the butt of a rifle flung into her back, and Lily slammed against the wooden floor, landing on her hands and knees.

A guard cracked a whip against my flesh. No strength remained and shouting proved no good.

"Slaves stick together. Thought you fancied the harder variety." I rolled my eyes.

"Boss said you like it rough... well boys, let's show 'em once we've had our fill of tender, wanton screams." The guard behind me chuckled.

Gritting my teeth and swaying my body, chains rattled overhead. "Don't touch her." No use.

His buddies laughed, but I knew the truth. The young and beautiful would go to the brothels. Others would see work camps or death. But where would they take me?

Lily stared at the floor. So docile and obedient. Jules had trained her well.

One of the guards reached down and hefted her to her feet. "Tell me, would you prefer a real man or your friend?"

"A real man."

He leaned in and licked her face. Lily didn't move.

"Hear that? She doesn't want the likes of you, but she'll answer for her," his gaze traveled the length of her body, "crimes…"

Once the ship's cells were emptied, the guards returned. Two men lifted my battered body while a third removed the chains from the hook. They didn't say a word, and I didn't either. The man who'd touched my sister grabbed my head and pressed my face against the grimy wall. He kicked my legs apart.

I accepted my fate… every thrust, grunt, kick, and blow with a shit-eating grin. They could break my body… my secrets, heart, and soul belonged to me.

"Oi!" Cross stormed in.

I lay on the floor, bleeding. His sharp breath said I looked worse for wear.

"What the fuck are you doing? Get off him." He yanked one of the guards aside, sending him flying across the room. "No one gave you rejects permission to touch him. You two, take him to medical, and then to Boric's chambers."

The larger of the two guards scooped me up, scowling; the second one tagged along.

Sunlight blinded me. He carried me outside. The stench of their fluids sickened my stomach. Clattering noises and voices carried, but I made nothing out, not that it would have mattered. Hotness swept over me, and the stink baked deeper into my skin. Branded, like a pig, and displayed, like a common whore: they marched me through the busy streets of Garland, Texas.

My head swung; people appeared upside down, and the images churned my stomach even more. Desperately, I searched for Dorian's face in the crowds, heart sinking when he wasn't there. Would he bother? Would I? The thought swelled in my throat, and wetness burned my nose. A cough lodged in my chest, but I lacked the strength to release it.

A door jingled and my guard stepped over a threshold and into a building. "Another one, doc."

"He's in bad shape…" Cold metal brushed my skin, his brown, bare feet shuffled over the dirt floor. Odd for a doctor to walk around without shoes, but stranger events had occurred in the south. "Place him in the basin."

He deposited me into a tub. "Orders are to treat and—"

Glass crashed. "He's my patient, and you will do as I say." Fingers snapped, his maybe, and a strong odor burned my nostrils. "He's too close. If Boric wants him dead, then by all means take him away." As the doctor shouted at the men, I gasped for breath. Ammonia filled and assaulted my senses. Pointing his finger, he snapped again, shooing them away. "I'm sorry," he whispered, after they had left, and knelt. "They did a real number on you." His lips pursed while gentle fingers smoothed over my skin.

"Thanks," I mouthed, and leaned my head back. The long tub had no water inside of it.

"Syringe," he said, and footsteps followed, but I saw not who made the sound. Metal scraped against metal. "For the pain," the doctor said. The needle's pinch didn't compare, nor did the medicine's burn, to torture and rape.

Relief rolled over in varying waves as I fought the gentle pull of heavy eyelids. I lost the battle quickly.

A cool, moist cloth rested on my head, and warm water soothed my stinging cuts and bruises. Alcohol filled my nostrils.

"He's coming to." A feminine voice spoke in a hushed whisper. The cloth fell from my face.

My eyes refused to open; brightness bled through the thin lids.

"Doc'll fix ya up real good."

No. Not feminine, but the voice was childlike. My lips parted, licking the dried surface.

"What's ya name?"

"Cain Westcott," I said, tilting my head at the softness and whispered pitch of my tone. Daggers followed, stabbing up and down my throat.

"Westcott you say... Boyo get me the aloe." A chair creaked, and someone sighed. "No wonder you look run over."

"Why's that?" I blinked and tried to focus.

"Boric has laws against consorting with the Westcott family, and you fling the name around, as if it means nothing."

It didn't in the North, and I shrugged.

"Name like that'll get ya killed 'round here." The doctor mumbled something about time. "This might sting a little. But it's better than the alternative."

Nothing the doctor did could've hurt as much as Boric's acid touch.

Shivers wracked my body, and my eyes flew open. White sheets were draped over my body, stained with dried blood and urine. Scratch, scratch, scratch: a brown-skinned man hovered over me, scowling and scribbling away on his notepad. He must've been the doctor.

"Sleep," he commanded me.

Shaking my head, I fought the compulsion to shut my heavy eyelids. My mouth opened and sticky dryness greeted me.

"You must to survive. He's coming for you."

For a moment, my heart leaped, thinking he meant Dorian. Boric's voice boomed, and I shut my eyes, willing my breath and heart to steady. Sleeping patients didn't have panic attacks. A needle pinched my arm, and euphoria followed if only in my mind. The doctor's words made sense. He was keeping me under to keep me safe; Boric wanted me conscious. Bless this man, God. Another needle punctured my skin, and darkness enveloped me in a warm cocoon of endless dreams.

Dorian greeted me, arms wide and inviting. My lips parted, we connected, and my hands fisted into his hair. He drew away and whispered, *Hold on, babe. I'm coming.*

On the sixth day in Garland Hell, I awoke and ate a light broth.
The doctor said, "I can't hold off Boric forever."

I asked, "Have you seen Lily? My Sister?"

"No." He glanced at his papers. "It'd help if you knew the name
they gave her. Don't anybody keep their names."

I kept mine. Boric liked it. "Thank you for taking care of me.
But why?"

"He is my master, but I don't condone his actions. You seem
like a good kid. Before the collapse, doctors held an oath, and I
take mine seriously." Doc sighed and rubbed a hand over his black
brows. His mind was a blank slate, but his compassion lit hope,
like a wildfire. "I'll see what I can find out."

Fourteen days after my arrival—the doctor kept me apprised to
the days—Cross hand-delivered my healed, naked body to Boric's
chambers. I recognized the room, and it wasn't my first dance in
the den of the true devil. Stale blood tainted the air. Mine would
join it soon, but remnants of me already existed within the old
outpost walls.

"Remember the drill, or do I need to give you a refresher?"
Cross asked.

As instructed, I stood in the middle of Boric's bedroom floor,
gaze obediently aimed at the wooden slats, and bowed my head.

"Good lad." Footsteps carried away from me. Drawers opened
and closed. "You know how I feel about all this." He stopped in
front of me, leather shackles in his hands. "Hands behind your
back and don't try any magic. We have the crystals up, so you'll
only be hurting yourself."

After years of freedom, I didn't think I'd ever wear them again. He
grabbed each wrist, though gentle, and wrapped the cuff until it clicked.

"Do I need to do your legs?"

"No, Master," I replied beneath a shield of heated flesh. My
arms were useless behind my back. I closed my eyes and faced the

demons of my past. Me then had changed some, but I had been scrawnier, weaker, and without much willpower.

Long before the keys, I had become a plaything for the King of Garland. For all his talk and names, he never entertained women in these walls. He despised them, raped them, yes, but even his Queen visited only when necessary to produce an heir.

The door creaked and slammed, rattling the old fort floors and glass windows. Garland had stood as an Army base before the Sundering, and its military strengths were perfect for the rising south. Footsteps stomped, as if to intimidate me; I counted three sets.

"Pillow biter," Boric said, and rubbed his hand over my naked back, sliding down to my exposed cheeks. His nose dripped sweat on my neck. "Undo those binds and fasten them in the front."

Cross obeyed.

"Push him to his knees."

Cross's hands applied pressure to my shoulders and my knees bent toward the floor. Aches speared through me in anticipation for Boric's assault. Teeth gritting, I gulped and fought the sweltering edge of tears. My forehead scraped against the sandy floorboards. Dirt and a citrusy oil coated my tongue.

"You are nothing more than a dog." A black, leather boot kicked forth.

Lights blinded my vision. My rib bones cracked. Mouth open, nothing but a strangled hiss released. Another sickening snap sounded, along with a huff. My teeth mashed together, and I lost my balance, toppling onto my side. Burning for breath refusing to fill them, my lungs ached. He thrusted his boot again. My hands rose to protect my face, but he didn't stop kicking.

I screamed, but no vocal sounds announced, only a gasping hiss.

"Worthless, can't even bloody-well-stay-righted. Fix this wanker, Cross."

"Yes, Master," he replied in a solemn tone.

Blood filled my mouth and poured from my nose. Metallic flavor lingered on my tongue. Cross lifted me from the ground and placed me on my knees again. But Boric's fingers gripped me hard, and his nails sliced into my shoulders. His boot swung backward and propelled forward again. Nothing existed beyond the pain, sweat, blood, and tears seeping into the walls and floors holding me captive.

I had become their prisoner, and the walls laughed.

Once more, I awoke in the good doctor's care. I didn't catch his name, but the young boy called him Doc. Bandages covered my middle. Air filled my lungs, yet each intake caused me to wince. Balls of light procured my vision, but the quaint, whitewashed cinderblocks and putrid ammonia overwhelmed my senses.

Boric roared unintelligible words. I pinched my eyes shut, despite him arguing behind a closed, sound-muffling door.

"Doc a good man… no more pain for ya," the childlike voice whispered. "He keep Cain safe till help arrives."

Help? No one was coming for me. No one loved me. I turned my head away, wondering how many days had passed without word from Dorian. Only in my hallucinations did I see him. My eyelids fluttered to a close.

A door groaned, followed by footsteps. "Let him rest. Now get on out of here," Doc shot back, laying into Boric.

"You dare tell me how to treat my own prisoners?" Boric's voice drove nails into my spine as my whole body stiffened.

Either he valued the good doctor, or he would end up in chains sooner than later. I prayed for the former rather than the latter because he was a respectable man, and those were hard to find since the Sundering. Chills swept over me, but I dared not move a muscle, or so much as twitch. He didn't need to lose his head over me. Heavy boots scuffed; someone snorted, and a door slammed shut.

The child said, "He's gone."

Slowly, I opened my eyes to the flickering lamplights flooding the room.

"What did you do to him?" the doctor asked, scratching his balding head. "You weren't gone half a day before Cross toted your bruised and bloodied ass back to me." He glanced to the door. "Cross said I'd do well to put ya down."

A slow smile spread over my lips. Defiance radiated and willed me to survive, and I clung to the notion that I'd bested Boric Garland once again.

"Don't be so smug, kid. I won't always be here to piece you back together. Even Humpty Dumpty had his great fall."

Tears sprung in my eyes; laughter rumbled. Damn that hurt, and I would've killed for magic, just enough to erase the pain. But I couldn't draw on my birthright, not even a tiny spark emitted from my bruised fingertips.

"All royals are bound before the ship docks."

I asked, "Warlock or Elioud?"

"Neither," he said, smiling.

Ah, that explained much and I nodded. His ebony skin darkened to blue-black. Two small horns jutted from his head; he transformed into a creature spawned in Hell. I tossed my head.

The doctor scolded, "No moving."

Why did he care for me? His smile revealed sharp, yellowed teeth, and I swallowed hard. Maybe he wanted to eat me. Wait, but he spoke of an oath before. Hell born demons didn't come until after...

"The medicine is strong. Native American's called it Peyote."

"For?" Dry lips cracked as I spoke.

"Pain, but you may see, or hear, some vivid things."

"Not working very well, Doc." I grimaced, holding my ribs. "For the pain... you look like a beast."

"Sorry, it's all I have left... have to keep... lock..." His voice rose and fell, cut in and out. He jabbed a needle into my arm. "Give a bit more, but you may see things or people who are not here. Do... can... to keep."

I nodded to sleep, falling into a dream as explosions rocked the ground, and the acrid smoke filled my lungs. Great instead of a beautiful memory of Dorian, I found myself tossed into some hellish nightmare. Coughing seemed impossible, and a damp cloth covered my face. In the distance, my name… people shouted for me, but one voice rang over the others.

"Dorian," I whispered, unable to scream, and played along, hoping it ended. All I wanted to see: a pair of green eyes and his handsome face smiling.

"Cain!"

God if you are listening to my heathen ass … if I could do it all again, I would have told him everything that first day. He might've rejected me and tossed my sorry ass on the street, but my heart said otherwise. Such a fool not to trust him. Dorian deserved a better man. A man who was honest and forthcoming with his secrets, but he found me instead.

Metal clashed against metal. Gunshots blasted. Women screamed. I fought, tearing the cloth from my face. Children cried. Voices yelled, but they came from the hospital wing, not the streets. My body turned and teeth ground against the sharp stabs movement brought on. My eyes opened.

Doc sat in his chair, run through on Boric's cutlass. The devil loomed over the man, smiling. His dark head tilted. "Looks like a party, mate, but I guess you're not invited."

Doc still breathed. His eyes twitched, motioning toward the tray sitting by my bed. Syringes, filled with God knew what, rested on the surface. Peyote maybe, but I didn't know.

Boric stepped closer, away from the doctor, but his attention trained on the events unfolding outside. With his last breath, the good doctor nodded, and my fingers slipped around two of them. His decapitated head thudded against the floor, and I paused wondering how much of this was a dream. Not that the needles would do me much good, since I couldn't exactly run away, but if I died today, hell, I would go down in a trip-faced glory of peyote.

"How did you manage to skewer Dorian Fox?" Boric rubbed his chin, his image smearing.

I blinked at his question. Was he jealous of Dorian? If it were not for his sword and voice, I wouldn't think it was him asking such a bizarre question.

"No bother, he'll never find you. Too bad I can't kill the sodden bastard, I can kill you."

My name boomed through my ears. Dorian's voice rattled and throbbed inside my head. I inhaled a deep breath, as deep as I could manage, and shouted, "Dorian." But my mouth issued a cross between a wheeze and a whisper.

Boric laughed at my feeble attempts, but Dorian truly came for me. Boric wouldn't have killed the doctor; he wouldn't guard me personally, waiting for the doors to fling open. Preparing to fight.

"If anyone can hear me… find Dorian … Tell him, Cain is in the hospital. Boric is with me."

"You think they'd approach the madman setting their town on fire? You're a loon, like your old man."

"Takes one to know one." But he didn't hear my muttered words.

"I cared for you once, loved you more than the others too." Boric's tone softened. "As I recall, you loved me as well."

A snort pinched my chest. "They call it Stockholm syndrome."

"Then you stole from me." His knuckles cracked.

"Angelica swiped the keys, not me."

"You are the Keeper." Wild eyes reflected in the glass.

I glanced away.

"Think I didn't know? I've always known, Cain. No one knows you better than I do, not even Dorian Fox or your dear mother. Your own father didn't know. I set him up, let him gamble with the high rollers until he was so deep, he would do anything to pay."

"You didn't tell me." I tossed my legs over the side of the bed. Boric distracted himself with the window again, fire and gray smoke blurring the scene.

"Why would I? We never discussed business. It wasn't your place in my world."

"What was my place? You didn't exactly make it clear." Had to keep him talking… I stared at my hand, dripping with sweat and still clenching the syringes. My legs wobbled from lack of use, and short breaths followed.

"You were a consort. I never wanted to give you up, but you were my weakness, they exploited it. I was given a choice, and I did what was best." He sighed. "They said I must, or they would kill you. I couldn't imagine the latter, so I let you go, keeping you close."

"Because I am the Keeper?" Did he expect me to believe any of that?

"Partly, yes." He didn't turn around.

"And the other part?" My bare feet shuffled along the red dirt floor. I stood close enough to taste his sweat and fear, and my hand rose, hovering centimeters from his neck.

"I love you," he said.

My strength depleted. Stars attacked my vision, and the spiraled colors swirled into a whirlwind whipping against my face. "Never... loved..."

Haunting laughter cackled. I hit the dirt and rolled; wincing, his boot stamped and crushed my ribs, pinning me to the ground.

I managed thoughts. *"Never... find... them."*

Boric shrugged. "You're unbreakable for a pillow biter." His leg lifted, hovering. Shrilled voices called for him. "Playtime's over, luv, but we'll meet again soon enough in Tartarus. Ta-Ta."

Fire ignited from his hands, and he tossed the balls across the room. Bottles crashed, spilling their sickening aromas. Heat blistered, and I eyed the seductive dance of flame spreading among the doctor's medicines.

Boric glanced to me, lip curling. But his eyes glistened, reflecting pain I'd only witnessed within survivors. He turned, drew his shoulders straight, and marched from the room. He left me to die. Never... never about the keys. Boric used them as his excuse to find me, to own me again.

Death: I welcomed its warm, clean, soap-scented embrace. Death wrapped around, lifted my body, and bathed me in a bright, purging light.

"Stay with me, babe... don't you die on me."

Dorian's voice comforted me in those final moments, soothing me toward the other side. Peyote side effect, I was certain, but I wasn't complaining. "No regrets," I whispered. "Love you always."

"Open your eyes... Put that fire out, Raph... Cain, you aren't allowed to die on me... I'll bloody murder him." The words shouted, as if he spoke directly into my eardrum. My slanted eyes burned from the smoke but saw enough to catch the blazing green haze illuminating his scruffy face.

I coughed at the acrid air filled my aching lungs. "Dori—OW"

Strong arms crushed me against his chest. "Shite, did I hurt you?"

I shook my head and blinked the tears away.

"Liar." Rough hands cupped my face. "I'm putting you where he'll never find you."

"We've got to go, Dorian." A man ducked his head around a bend, but I couldn't focus on him. "Boric's army amasses, and we're not ready for that."

"Lilith," I said, clutching Dorian's collar.

"Sorry, babe, we got her first... I'm going to carry you. Gabe flew her to safety."

I nodded and winced, biting into my cheek; his arms lifted me from the ground.

"Michael, tell Raph to be ready."

Michael shouted, "Bloody move your arses," as another explosion ripped through the chaos. Thick, black smoke covered us, and breathing in the tarred fumes dizzied my head. Babies wailed in mother's arms. Slaves scurried through the streets. They froze in our path, like rabbits, but Dorian ushered the innocents past us and kept marching, ducking, or heaving his shoulder into coming guards. Each movement like a knife through my center, as the drugs wore off, but I ground my teeth and buried the pain. Life would end soon enough. Death saved me in more ways than I thought possible.

We hunkered behind a stack of crates. My head lobbed against his neck, my lips tasting the rolling sweat, tainted with oily grime: petroleum. They were blowing up their fuel source, and the thought churned bile within my stomach. Innocents needed fuel to survive, but I shoved the thought aside. What had Markos preached about casualties?

Black smudges smeared over his cheeks and crimson gashes oozed with the black marks. I whispered, "You should see the other guy, huh sweets?"

"Just a scratch." Dorian smirked, but his eyes concentrated. He pointed to the two men, who'd flanked us, hunkering behind oak barrels. "That's Gabriel and Raphael. Long story. You've met Michael." He nodded behind him to the blond...

Laughter gurgled in my throat. I eyed the angelic cowboys. Dorian spoke again, but gunfire deafened my ears, his words drawing in and out over the pops and bangs. Both men produced pistols, scurried across the dirt side street, and re-flanked Dorian on either side. The source surprised me.

Warm metal lined my mouth; pressure built around my nose. So much, I had wanted to say to Dorian, to show him, but the shadows of my soul blinked the world out before I had the chance.

Nothingness engulfed me. No bright light or eternal fire greeted me. Air didn't fill my lungs; my heart didn't beat. Voices didn't sing and no shrieking, screaming agony of the damned.

"Still no regrets?" a voice thundered, and interrupted my observance. "Open your eyes."

I blinked at soft yellow light filling the small room. An iron gate loomed before where I stood. Quickly, I spun around and saw the voice. My knees dropped to the ground, and I bowed before Hallowed, Markos, and Fauna.

"Keeper," Markos said, rolling his eyes. "Rise."

A flash blinded me for a moment, but it retreated. Dorian and his angels returned. Two of the three men held a body, but only one didn't move. The battered form, beaten and bruised, had survived for as long as possible. I couldn't tell where one bruise started or another ended. Blood seeped from my mouth, nose, and ears. My spirit, I, drifted to his side. From the hallway, footsteps echoed off the shimmering marble.

"We waited too long." Dorian stared at the blond Archangel framing the doorway. "Damn it, Michael."

My fingers stroked Dorian's face; his lips kissed my dead body. "I… love… you."

I said, "I love you, sweets." Even with all the secrets and lies that part was always true. I turned to the three Horsemen. "What now? How can you see me and he can't?"

The trio exchanged timid smiles. Hallowed motioned for me. I glanced to Dorian while he caressed my body, whispering words I didn't understand in another language. Latin maybe or something similar, but he drew me with his tongue as the phrase repeated. The mantra struck a beat, a chord within me. Tingles spread across my limbs, and warmth pulsated from my center.

Dorian's head flung back, shouting, "Revertor. Reverti. Reversus." Green eyes bore into me, as if he saw the spirit and not the body. Dorian pled, "Babe, come back to me. Please… if you can hear me… come back."

Tears poured from my eyes. "How? Oh God, tell me how to go back."

Hands grasped my spectral shoulders from behind and tugged me away. I kicked and screamed, "No. I'm not ready. I don't want to go. I want to live, damn it. Don't take me away from him."

But the iron gate creaked, and their forlorn faces remained quiet as they tossed me through the opening. The metal lock clicked.

Fauna said, "See you soon, Keeper."

Chapter Nineteen

Dorian

Three days later…

Near a tree, I stood in front of the abandoned farmhouse. Neither held symbolic feeling for him or me, but I hadn't traveled home yet. Flakes glittered and descended from the moody clouds, reflecting the blackness of my heart and soul… mirroring the color of his skin. Bruised, battered, and gone. Three images I had faced as my punishment. "I killed you the moment I fell in love… the moment you'd lied to me and sheltered secrets. And I let you do it."

Pacing, my footsteps crunched through fresh snow. The barn and empty farmhouse were nothing more than skeletons standing in the wind.

"This wasn't your home. Happy memories we would've made don't fill the walls. But this is where I lost you… where I failed as a man and an Archangel." I wiped my cheeks. "No one else knew what to do." So I had Gabriel bring me to the house. My toes dug through the snow. "I wanted to buy it for you."

My eyes squinted against the rising sun glaring across the whitewashed landscape. A shiver washed over me. Odd. I didn't have those reactions to the weather. I shoved my hands into my denim pockets, and I stared at the crude, gray headstone I'd carved. No flesh lay below it.

Bitterness boiled inside of me every minute that passed, and Boric Garland continued breathing. I leaned on the tree. My eyes blazed at the time I had wasted before contacting the Council of Seven, and then again, for not leaving Cain be, for not taking him to Sanctuary and insisting he stay. Instead, I'd insisted, for my own selfish reasons, he stay by my side. Perhaps I didn't alter from my old ways.

"No one blames me." I sighed. "Except for me." I knelt. "Lily is safe. You died knowing your sisters are free. That should make me feel better about your passing, but it doesn't. I was selfish there too…We moved her to Anchorage, and she's staying with Gabriel. Not sure how you would feel about that." Gabe seemed a bit more than smitten, and I grinned at the thought. "Korrigan's training with Veric for the war. Belle and Mark are following up a lead on the leak in Nova Scotia." I didn't know what else to say.

A branch snapped nearby. Footsteps halted behind me, but my body didn't turn. A compulsion yanked at my seams, but my mind played the dirtiest tricks on me. My hairs stood on edge. Invisible eyes watched me. Sometimes, his voice called to me, or he whistled a long forgotten tune.

But unlike before, thoughts of destroying the world didn't hinder me. Becoming the better man that Cain drove me to be consumed my other thoughts. Books and doctors say never to change for another. Maybe they were right, but I'd only transformed back into the man I had once been.

"Why?" Tears fell for… oh, I had lost count. Lost pieces of my heart and soul. My eyes closed, and I saw his grinning face and golden eyes brimming with love and mischief. "Fauna, Hallo, and Markos all hoped I would find closure. I told them our love has no beginning, no middle, and certainly no end." I sniffled. "I'll never love again… never thought I could love until you stormed into my life and kicked my ass." Running fingers through my locks, I trembled, and my face twisted as I fought against the crashing tide. "Cain you altered all my views from life to love. Keeper, revertor, reverti, reversus."

"Wow. That was some speech."

My eyes flung open at that voice.

"Who died?"

"Cain," I whispered, and spun around. "But how?"

"You look like you've seen a ghost, sweets." Cain smirked, but his eyes were as red as mine felt. Colored lights flashed behind him. "Your crazy family is how." He held up his hand and twisted the ring. "It's made from St. Michael's chain and allows me to escape death. Pretty nifty, huh?" He motioned over his shoulder.

Brows scrunching, I still didn't follow.

Cain turned toward me again. "Dorian, you said it yourself. I'm the Keeper."

I cupped his smooth cheek and gasped when his image didn't waver. My trembling hands drew his smirking mouth closer. "You're real, bloody fucking hell, you're really here." My forehead rested against his, but my heart pounded faster, aching.

"I'm real," Cain whispered, his nose nudging mine. "I'm not going anywhere. You're stuck with me, Dorian Fox."

My hands skimmed his sides, brushing against two holsters hanging from the standard issue ABDA uniform.

"You going to play with my guns?"

I shook my head and my siblings laughed. In time, I'd learn the roles they played in Cain's survival, and they would answer for keeping the truth from me. Their lights flashed again leaving us alone at the farm. My grip tightened, hands shaking.

Cain's lips hovered, his breath caressing me in heat. "Or are you going to kiss me already—"

I lifted him from the ground and spun us. His words found silence in my mouth.

"I love you," we said together, and have continued our love all days since.

A Sneak Peek at Lilith and Gabriel in

Captivated

Beyond the Brothel Walls #3

Prologue

Enoch the Metatron

The Voice of God

Metatron paced in the observatory, clouds covering his view of Earth from Heaven. He lowered his dark head and shook it. Father wouldn't release him until he discovered the truth and solved the mystery of betrayal. A single question lingered on his tongue:

"Who opened the gates of Hell?"

His narrowed eyes glared at his magical cube, sitting on the ledge overlooking the cosmos. Mocking him, the artifact offered no imagery in reply. Inside the metallic wonder, he'd stored the history of the universe from the creation to a nanosecond ago. Always, it was recording, and yet his cube refused to show him the truth.

"Enoch," Father summoned him.

But a sliver of golden radiance peeked from a tiny crack in its smooth surface. Metatron halted and cocked his baldhead, his brown hand reaching forward.

"Enoch, I need you." Father's essence manifested into the observatory, wavering, but not taking a solidified form.

Metatron bit his sigh and swallowed it. He glanced at the cube. Every trace of light had dissipated.

"Yes, Father."

"Michael has discovered a young woman, another child of Lucifer's—"

Rattling sounded behind him, and he spun around. His cube refracted beams, scattering its coppery luminance throughout the white-walled observatory.

"Gabriel…" Father spoke, but the artifact burst into a cloud and imageries reflected from its vapor surface.

Year 3167, Fort Garland, Garland—12 years post-apocalypse

Lilith Westcott focused on the "G" embroidered into the guard's uniform, while he pinned her against the wall and squeezed her throat. The world distorted, but she couldn't travel away. Not that time.

Ceiling bits rained on her. Fort Garland's fortified-brick walls rumbled behind her bare back. But the guard's wide eyes offered no comfort. He loomed before her, thrusting harder. Another blast vibrated through her backside, tearing her into reality and further distorting the safe place her mind had retreated during the rapes and beatings.

Former Earth flickered into her mind before tearing asunder; it had so done twelve years ago. Iron bars slammed around her, swirling with magical energy, and a coppery haze tinted the air. Grunting, the guard pulled himself free, scowling at the cracking ceiling and thundering boots battering over the floors.

At least he hadn't finished, and she cradled the thought against her exposed breasts.

"Getting too close," he said. "Guess I best go investigate, huh, Roxie?"

Lilith didn't respond to her slave name. She didn't move. Inside, she was already dead. Motionless like those in the surrounding cells, but her heart was still beating, lungs breathing. But their bodies were lifeless because of her.

"You're on your own, Rox." He yanked up his uniform pants.

Her legs and back slithered along the wall to the ground. The guard ran his tongue over his teeth, and she swallowed the rising bile.

"Oh, I'll be back to finish, sweet thang." He hooked her chin and forced her gaze. "Such a perty mouth."

Gray smoke snaked through the iron bars, chasing the copper away, and Lily crawled toward her cot, scraping her kneecaps on the dirt and hiding her aching, filthy, and bruised face behind a curtain of matted curls.

Her guard opened the entrance to her cell, closing and locking it behind him. His footsteps carried, and she stole a glance; his fat ass disappeared into the stairwell.

Chains binding her wrists rattled but didn't reach underneath the only measure of safety in her cell. Grasping the iron, she yanked, as if it would give more slack or break free from the rusted base.

"C'mon." She gritted her teeth and heaved again, wishing for a flaw in the chain mirroring the weakness of her body.

Instead of cowering beneath the cot, Lilith curled into a tiny ball, tucking her knees and chin against herself. On the streets above, a woman screamed and children cried, quickly overpowered by the popping gunfire, tremoring earth, and crackling blazes. Dust and debris trickled from the ceiling with each quake.

"Please, God, just kill me," Lilith prayed. Plaster covered her face, mixing with the humid sweat coating her skin. "Let the nightmare end. Forgive me, Father, forgive me." Another explosion rattled her bones. She shuddered and yipped. "I didn't know they'd find us... I didn't mean it... It was an accident."

Lily had prayed the same every night before bed and every morning on waking. Sometimes, she prayed for a time machine to erase the last three hundred years she'd spent as a Garland slave, to erase the magic she'd unleashed in Nova Scotia that lead to her recapture and the murder of her friends. If she had such a machine, she would've erased her ancestor and his mighty fall from grace.

Heavy boots thumped along the stairs, and she held her breath, forcing her gaze away. *Maybe they will ignore me... If only I could make myself disappear.*

Hiding her head, she continued praying, begging God to forgive her sins, for allowing the men to use her, for whatever she did that made them covet her. Lily prayed for the strength to refuse them, to rid herself of the chains binding her to the masters.

His reply arrived in more explosions and a voice. "Gabriel, I found a live one. Last cell."

Lily peeked through her tangle of dark curls at the two men, clad in all black save for their massive wings. Seraphim, she was certain.

"Archangels. Behind you," she said, but not loud enough. The guard returned and drew a strange three-pointed weapon. Pointing, her finger trembled, and she mouthed the words. "Guard."

Gabriel shouted over the blasts, "Are you Lilith? Lilith Westcott?" before raising and firing his silver gun into the guard's chest.

Covering her ears, she blinked at him. *How did he hit him without looking?* But as more explosions rumbled beneath her bare feet, she cowered in the corner of her jail cell again.

He withdrew a photo from his black cargo pants and glanced to the tintype, smirking. "It's her. Get those bloody keys, Michael." His gray wings flexed, shimmering like a jewel, and he cracked his neck. "Listen, luv, I'm here to help you. Your brother sent me."

Cain, yes, they had arrived in Garland together on the same airship. Her mouth opened and closed. Michael tossed him the keys.

Archangels... Michael... Gabriel... God finally answers my prayers.

"I'm coming in for you, and I'm not going to hurt you," Gabriel said, holding his hands in the air. Guns littered his body, strapped here and there, and he carried more than the Garland guards did.

Lily drew herself into a tighter ball, peeking at the coppery haze surrounding his aura; the same color always brought her comfort in her special place. Even though she was sure, she had to ask, "Who... are... you?"

"I'm Gabe," he said, his two-toned gaze locking onto hers, one azure blue and the other a steely gray. He nodded to the blond-haired angel. "That's Michael."

However, Lilith couldn't look away, and her heart raced. Inside, she fluttered, as if flying. *Gabriel, God's Messenger.*

He inserted the skeleton key into the lock and turned it. The door creaked and groaned on its hinges, banging when it hit the end. Gabriel's feet shuffled over the dirt floor, and he knelt at her side. "And you are?"

"Lily," she whispered, grasping at her scorching throat. Fire exploded in the hallway. Gunshots echoed in her head, pulsed in time with her heart, but her name screamed louder within the confines of her mind. No one had called her Lily in over three hundred years. Only another Westcott or Jules himself would've recalled her name.

"S'alright now, luv. I'm going to take you away from all of this, but I need to see your hands." He jingled the keys.

Lily still couldn't look away from his eyes. So cold and dark, yet drawing her in and captivating her curiosity, but not like the masters' eyes. Where hatred and malice would've shone, Gabe reflected a different emotion, one she couldn't name.

He fiddled with the keys, glancing down and breaking eye contact. Bits of plaster littered his midnight hair, and her fingers itched to run through the curly mass. Her nails dug deeper into the dirt while he released her shackles.

"Michael, do we have clothes for the Lady Lilith?" he asked over his shoulder, before piercing her with his gaze again. "Rag was right about Lucifer's children. You are beyond the words of beauty."

At beauty, she inclined her head.

Michael replied, "Bed sheets?" and tossed one through the open cell door.

"Inside and out." Gabriel wrapped the sheet around her and scooped her into his arms. "Mind the wings, yeah?"

She clung to him, trembling from head to toe; the smoldering world whizzed by her head. Plastic and metal jutted into her bony frame from his uniform. His voice trailed into the ricocheting pings and booms, and she settled her chin on his shoulder, breathing in his earthen cologne. Shifting in his arms, her fingertips brushed the downy soft, high ridge of his wings, and he quivered from the touch.

"Your prayers brought me to you..."

They eased into the blazing night, farther from the Arch demon's device binding her power, and his thoughts flowed into her mind.

"I've heard her for so long, but couldn't find her."

Was she a disappointment to him? He halted, sliding into an alley. Guards in green Garland uniforms jogged past them toward a fire. Beneath his shirt, his heart pounded as hard as hers did.

"Father, forgive me."

Gabriel deposited her on the ground and pressed a finger to his lips. Withdrawing a Colt Peacemaker, he gave a nod, followed by a peek around the corner. His free hand tapped on his thigh.

Metal clacked against metal. Smoke burned her eyes. Shots rang and she shrieked. He raised his weapon, stepped away from the brick wall, and returned fire. She couldn't see; she didn't want to see and shut her eyes.

"Lily?" a stranger's voice said her name. *"Gabriel's going to take you away from here. He's going to take you to Sheol."*

"Sheol?" she questioned, but the flying bullets and crackling blazes drowned out her voice.

Opening her eyes, she gaped at a colossal, talking skeleton, robed in silver and holding a jeweled scythe. Lilith's fingernails scraped at the orange clay, scurrying away, until her back hit the garrison wall. Gabriel, Michael, and the skeleton man discharged more rounds, pausing and taking cover to reload, and her hands flew to her ears.

"Dorian, over there," Gabriel said, while Garland's men returned fire.

They spoke with their hands, pointing and shaking their heads.

Dorian, the skeleton, shouted, "Aim for the barrels. At least they won't be able to follow in their flying contraption."

Michael nodded toward her and said, "Gabe, you need to get her to safety."

"If anyone can hear me. Tell Dorian, Cain's in the hospital." her brother's draw filtered through the noise.

"Dorian?" she asked, voice pitching.

The skeleton man spun around and tilted his head.

"My brother…Cain…the hospital…" A vortex surrounded the skeleton, and she shielded her eyes from the sand. "Boric's holding him there," she added, dropping her hand from her face.

"He said that?" Dorian asked, no longer a skeleton, but an olive-skinned man with a strong jaw and glowing, green eyes the shade of emeralds.

"I can see him," she said, unsure how to explain her gift. She didn't spot Cain in the flesh, but his fading lavender aura streamed through the town. Gabe's emitted coppery hue, and Michael's revealed a shade shy of midnight blue. Dorian's was black. "I can see all of them."

"Who do you see?" Michael asked, kneeling in front of her. His white wings extended beyond his broad shoulders. He reached for her, and she flinched. "I'm not going to hurt you. Gabriel—"

"Leave her be. I'm taking her home."

Home? She had no home. "What about the others?"

"I'm here for you, Lily, just you." Unspoken, he thought, *"And Dorian's here for Cain."* He sat beside her on his knees and stretched his arms toward her.

Shivering, her mind replayed the events, the deaths of her cellmates. Her hands covered her ears. "No, no, no it's all my fault," she cried. "I've killed them."

Michael angled his head, but she couldn't read his mind. Gabe's thoughts flashed through images, the empty cells in the prison where Garland's men had held her hostage. The guards had emptied them of life, but the bodies had remained.

Eternal silence had followed their screams. Lily would've been next, if not for Gabriel and Michael who both slowly nodded, as if following her thoughts. Mentally she reinforced her safeguards. Another thought flittered through her head. *A secret.* They'd saved her baby, too, the one growing in her womb.

Gabriel holstered his weapons before lifting her from the ground, slipping her hands around his neck. "Hold on and don't let go no matter what, petal."

Petal? Copper haze flared to life, and she buried her face in his chest. Gunpowder, the ocean, and earthy, masculine sweat calmed her and tightened her belly. The reaction was unlike any she'd experienced before.

Light faded. Darkness encircled her, and wind whipped her hair. Warmth bled into cold; her teeth chattered. Whooshing filled her ears from Gabriel's wings working harder. But he focused on Lily, and his mind said what his mouth did not. *"I finally found her, Father. I told you she was worth falling for. Worth the curse you placed upon my head."*

Whom had he found, what type of curse could've plagued an Archangel?

Acknowledgements

Many people helped bring this story to life. Writing is only one aspect of creating a book.

I'd like to thank my alpha reader, Aimee LaValle. My beta readers, you ladies all rock, and I would be lost without your guidance. My designer, Zack at Raven Tree Design, who helped shape the cover and develop the theme for this saga.

Book bloggers and readers for taking a chance on an unknown author, I thank you too.

If you enjoyed *Altered*, please leave a review or send me a message. I love to hear feedback from fans—good or bad.

Love, Rae Z. Ryans

Coming Soon

Captivated (Beyond the Brothel Walls #3) 2016

Sign up at www.raezryans.com for news about upcoming titles.

About the Author

Rae Z. Ryans is a member of the RWA and RWA Fantasy, Futuristic, and Paranormal chapter. She currently resides in Alabama with her family. Published since the age of fourteen, Rae enjoys writing romantic, erotic, fantasy/paranormal stories and poetry. Her name pays homage to her brothers: Specialist Ryan D. Rexon and Zachary L. Berthot.

She is currently working on Beyond the Brothel Walls #2: Altered. This post-apocalyptic paranormal romance is emotionally driven, dark fantasy.

Also available on Amazon and other major retailers,

Chivalry and Malevolence: Alfheim Book One

www.raezryans.com
www.facebook.com/raezryans